INTRODUCTION

Doctor St. Nick by Jeanie Smith Cash
Annie Benson, widowed and seven months pregnant with twins, is convinced God doesn't waste time on unimportant people like her. She's working as a waitress in a little California town when she receives word she's inherited a small ranch in Wyoming. Excited and relieved, Annie wants to spend Christmas in her new home. As she exits the bus, a very handsome man offers her a hand. He is both the local doctor and her new neighbor, Gabriel St. Nick. While stuck in a snowstorm and in labor, can Gabe convince Annie that God loves her and so does he?

Rescuing Christmas by Linda Lyle
Christmas "Chris" Jennings was hoping for a birthday getaway in Yellowstone National Park, but what she gets is snowed in with her ex-fiancé, Paul Rogers. When Chris is separated from her group while snowmobiling, a sudden snowstorm leaves her stranded, and it is up to park ranger Paul Rogers to rescue her. Will being trapped in a remote cabin for Christmas bring them together, or will their anger extinguish the last sparks of their love?

Jolly Holiday by Jeri Odell
Kloie Olson has found the perfect man for her and her mom—problem is her mom, Holly, doesn't seem interested. However, nine-year-old Kloie isn't easily deterred, and she arranges a few accidental, surprise rendezvous between her mom and the firefighter, Luke Jolly. Will Kloie's persistence pay off, or will her mom remain stubborn to the end?

Jack Santa by Tammy Shuttlesworth
Firefighter Jack Trenton looks forward to playing Santa in order to fill some empty weekend hours. Then he meets Stacy Waters, and his act of kindness becomes more than brightening a widow and her young son's Christmas holiday. Though flattered by Jack's attention, Stacy remains guarded. She believes if she falls in love again, her young son risks forgetting all about his biological father. Jack is determined to prove Stacy wrong, but can he succeed?

Wyoming
CHRISTMAS
HEROES

LOVE COMES TO THE RESCUE
IN FOUR SEASONAL NOVELLAS

LINDA LYLE • JERI ODELL
JEANIE SMITH CASH •
TAMMY SHUTTLESWORTH

BARBOUR
PUBLISHING

Published by Barbour Publishing, Inc., P.O. Box 719, Uhrichsville, OH 44683, www.barbourbooks.com

Our mission is to publish and distribute inspirational products offering exceptional value and biblical encouragement to the masses.

ecpa Member of the
Evangelical Christian
Publishers Association

Printed in the United States of America

Doctor St. Nick

by Jeanie Smith Cash

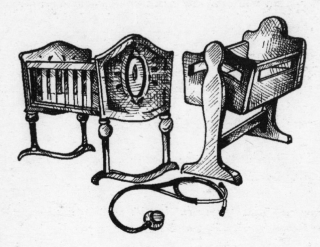

"For I know the plans I have for you," declares the LORD,
"plans to prosper you and not to harm you,
plans to give you hope and a future."

JEREMIAH 29:11 NIV

Chapter 1

Annie Benson rushed to the park across the street from the restaurant where she worked in Isleton, California. The benches filled up quickly at lunchtime; if she didn't hurry, she wouldn't find a place to sit. She slid into the last available seat and struggled to catch her breath.

Tears filled her eyes as she glanced around the beautiful park where she and Alex used to meet and have lunch. He had always told her worrying didn't accomplish anything, and she knew it couldn't be good for the babies, but what was the answer? She couldn't continue to work eight hours a day standing on her feet. At seven and a half months pregnant with twins, her ankles were already swelling. What would it be like in another month? Somehow she had to pay the rent on her tiny trailer and buy food. Alex had died so suddenly, and they hadn't had a chance to start a savings account.

When they'd turned eighteen and had to leave the orphanage, they decided to get married. They weren't in love, but they were best friends. Alex had been in a wheelchair and needed her to take care of him, and she had no family and nowhere to go.

She knew if he were here, he'd tell her to pray about the situation she found herself in, but what kind of a God would allow her to get pregnant and then take her husband? One who obviously didn't care about her, so what good would it do to pray? None. Somehow, she'd have to manage on her own. She glanced at her watch. *Lunch break's over.* She sighed. *Better get back to work.*

That evening, Annie stopped by the post office on her way home. As soon as she unlocked the door to her tiny one-room trailer, she went to change into something more comfortable. At this point in her pregnancy, there wasn't much of anything that made her comfortable.

Annie grabbed a bottle of water from the tiny apartment-sized refrigerator and sat in the gold chair that had come with the gold and green plaid sofa and scarred oak coffee table when she'd rented the trailer. It wasn't much, but it was all she could afford and it was within walking distance of the restaurant where she worked. She certainly couldn't afford a car, so she had to live close to her job.

As she shuffled through her mail, one item caught her attention. She turned the envelope over and read the name at the top left-hand corner. GATTLER, STALKS & WHITMIRE, ATTORNEYS-AT-LAW. Why would she be getting a letter from an attorney? It must have something to do with Alex.

She slid the folded paper out of the envelope, and her eyes widened as she read the letter. Her great-aunt had left property to Annie? Why would a great-aunt she didn't even know she had leave her a small ranch in Wyoming? Annie's first reaction was a combination of hurt and anger. Obviously, since she'd received the letter, this aunt had known Annie existed. Why hadn't she contacted Annie before now, instead of leaving her to be raised in an orphanage believing she had no family? Because she hadn't wanted her, just like no one else had ever wanted Annie—except Alex. He was the only one who had ever wanted her, and he was gone now.

After thinking about this development, her feelings started to change, and she began to get excited. A home of her very own in a brand-new place. But how would she get to Wyoming? She slipped her shoes back on and walked to the corner to use the pay phone. After looking up the number, she called Greyhound to get the rates from the Sacramento NE station to Rexburg, Idaho, the closest bus depot to Yellowstone City, Wyoming, her new home.

With tomorrow's paycheck, Annie would have enough money to buy a bus ticket, and according to the letter, her great-aunt had left her a small bank account. If she was very careful, she could live on it until after the babies were born and she got back on her feet. Then she'd have to find someone reliable to watch the twins while she worked a job to support them. It would be hard by herself, but she'd manage. Nineteen hours on a bus was a long time in her condition, but she could do it. She smiled for the first time since she'd lost Alex. Annie called the Greyhound station back and made a reservation for a seat on the bus the following afternoon.

Next, she called her boss and her landlord to let them know she'd be moving. She explained about her inheritance and apologized for the short notice. They were both very understanding and wished her well. The last call she made was to Miss Caroline at the orphanage. She'd raised Annie. They'd always kept in touch, and Annie would really miss her; Miss Caroline was like a mother to her.

Annie spent the evening packing her few belongings into a duffel bag that would be easier to carry than a suitcase. The next morning, Annie bade her coworkers good-bye, and at three thirty, her neighbor dropped her off at the bus station in Sacramento on her way to work. At four ten, she boarded the bus. Nineteen hours and fifty minutes later, she arrived in Rexburg, Idaho. Excitement filled her at the thought of what might lie before her as she lifted her duffel bag and walked to the door of the bus. She only had ten dollars to her name, but somehow she'd find a way to get from here to Yellowstone City.

❄

Gabriel St. Nick noticed the bus pull up as he finished loading the new saddle into the back of his truck. A young woman with auburn hair stepped up to the doorway, catching his attention. From her appearance, he'd guess she was about eight months pregnant. The ground was still quite icy from their last snowstorm; it certainly wouldn't do for her to fall. Since she appeared to be alone, he rushed over to assist her.

"Good morning. May I help you down?" Gabe offered her his hand. "The ground is still pretty icy." She smiled and placed her small hand in his much larger one. He balanced her until she stood safely on the pavement; he enjoyed the feel of her soft hand in his. She was lovely, small in stature, with smooth creamy skin, and eyes a brilliant green. The color reminded him of fresh new leaves budding in the spring.

"Thank you. I appreciate your help."

"You're welcome. I'm Dr. Gabriel St. Nick. Do you live in Rexburg, or are you just here for a visit?"

"This is my first time here. I'm Annie Benson; my great-aunt left me a small ranch in Wyoming, and I'm here to claim it. Could you tell me how I might find transportation from here to Yellowstone City?"

Gabe wondered at the pleasure he experienced at her statement. He was attracted to her even in her condition. She didn't mention a husband or boyfriend, and he couldn't say he was sorry about that. He'd like to get to know her. Katie walked up, and he introduced them. "Annie Benson, this is my sister, Katie St. Nick; she and I are about to head back to Yellowstone City right now. I'm the local doctor there, and Katie teaches kindergarten. You're welcome to ride with us if you'd like." Gabe noticed her hesitation. "We're perfectly safe, I promise."

"It's nice to meet you, Annie," Katie said. "Come on. Gabe will carry your bag; we can chat on the way back and get acquainted. It'll be nice to have some female companionship for a change, not that I don't enjoy your company, Gabe." She grinned.

✳

Annie liked Katie immediately and hoped they could become friends. Her brother seemed gentle and kind, as well. He certainly didn't look like any doctor she'd ever seen. His tall, muscular frame didn't sport an ounce of fat, and he had gorgeous blue eyes and dark brown hair that barely brushed his collar. An instant attraction seemed to flare between them, but surely it was her imagination. No one would be attracted to her in her condition.

But that was okay; she'd make it just fine on her own. She'd promised herself when she lost Alex she wouldn't let anyone that close again, because it hurt too much to lose them, and she didn't ever want to go through that kind of pain again.

Katie slid into the middle of the front seat, and Annie climbed in the big Ford crew cab pickup after her. She admired the soft leather upholstery, its color a shade lighter than the metallic tan on the outside. "Nice truck."

"Thanks, I had it delivered last week," Nick said. "I decided it was time for a new one."

"To my relief! I don't have to ride all this way in his farm truck." Katie grinned.

"And when did you ever ride here in my farm truck?" Gabe glanced at her.

"Well, I didn't, but I just knew there was going to come a time when Mom needed hers and I was going to have to ride in that thing for sure," Katie teased. "Actually, to be totally honest, he used Mom's truck. Once in a great while I get to ride in his Corvette; now that's a treat."

"Okay, now if you're being *totally* honest"—Gabe raised his eyebrows as he glanced over at her—"how many times have I taken you for a ride in my 'Vette?"

"Several," Katie admitted, laughing.

Annie enjoyed their bantering. It put her at ease and helped her relax.

"Where in Yellowstone City are you going, Annie?" Katie changed the subject.

"I'm not sure; my great-aunt left me a small ranch. I need to stop by the lawyer's office—Gattler, Stalks, and Whitmire—to pick up the keys and sign some papers, if it isn't too much trouble."

"That's no problem. It's on our way," Gabe assured her.

"Mr. Gattler sent me this letter." She pulled it from her purse. "It says the property is located at Route 3, Box 500 B. Do you know where that is?"

Gabe glanced at her and then returned his eyes to the road. "You're Molly Cromwell's niece?"

"Molly Cromwell was my great-aunt's name."

"She and our mother were best friends," Katie said.

Annie had to swallow against the lump that formed in her throat at Katie's words. They knew her aunt.

"Your place is right next to mine." Gabe interrupted her thoughts. "Workers have been out there painting, and the roofers just finished putting on new shingles. They laid new carpets and floors a few days ago. It should be ready for you to move in."

"I never even met my aunt." Annie glanced at Gabe and then Katie. "Why would she do all of this for me? My parents died in an accident when I was seven. She let me be raised in an orphanage. It's obvious she knew where I was. Why didn't she send for me?" Annie wiped at the tears that managed to escape even though she tried hard to control her emotions in front of these strangers.

"Molly was a warm and loving person, Annie, but she was crippled from childhood by polio, so I presume that's why. It was a very slow process for her to even make it up the stairs at night and back down in the morning. A lady came in twice a week to help her and clean house. I'm sure she felt you'd be better off with someone who could take care of you," Gabe explained.

"I just figured it was because she didn't want me."

"I would never believe that." Gabe glanced at her. "Knowing your great-aunt, she would have taken you in in a minute if she'd been able to."

"Gabe was her doctor and he's right, Molly was very sweet." Katie smiled and patted Annie's hand gently.

Gabe parked in front of the lawyer's office. When they went inside, Annie walked up to the young woman at the front desk.

"How can I help you?" she asked.

"I'm Annie Benson, and I'm here to see Mr. Gattler." Annie handed her the letter she had received in the mail.

The receptionist opened and read the letter. "Please have a seat and I'll be right back."

She disappeared down the hall and in just a few minutes was back.

"Mrs. Benson, would you follow me please?"

❄

"Did you hear what she said?" Katie asked. "I wonder where her husband is and why she hasn't mentioned having one?"

"I was just thinking the same thing." Gabe ran a hand through his hair as he sat back in the chair, crossing his ankle over his opposite knee. "I suppose she'll tell us in due time."

Chapter 2

Annie returned a few minutes later, and they left the lawyer's office.

"Well, it's official now; the ranch belongs to me." She grinned as Gabe pulled out of the parking lot. "I can't wait to see it."

He smiled at the excitement dancing in her pretty green eyes. She was beautiful, and he had to remind himself that she was also pregnant and married. How could he be so attracted to her when she was off-limits? *Lord, I could use some help here.*

"It won't take long to get there." Gabe smiled. "It's about five miles out of town, but before we go we should stop by the utility companies to make sure you have electricity and a phone. You might also want to get a few groceries. It looks like snow, so it may be a few days before you can get back into town."

Gabe drove the few blocks and parked. Annie went in the door of the building that housed the electric company on one side and the phone company on the other, very convenient. She was only gone a few minutes. "The electricity is still on at the ranch, but since this is Friday, I won't have a telephone until Monday."

"Well, I'm relieved to know you'll have power at least." Gabe drove to the grocery store and found a parking place by the door. When Annie came out, she only had one small bag with a can of hot chocolate and a gallon of milk. "Annie, there isn't any food at the ranch."

"That's okay. I brought a few things with me. I'll be fine."

All she had was a duffel bag, and there couldn't be much in it to eat. He wondered if she was short on funds, but he didn't feel it was his place to ask, so he headed out to the ranch.

Fifteen minutes later, they turned off onto a gravel driveway lined with snow-covered pine trees. Annie gasped, and a wide smile crossed her face when she saw her new home for the first time. The two-story Victorian-style house was painted yellow with dark green shutters. A wide porch with white railing stretched across the front of the house, and there were matching rails along the six steps leading to the front door.

"Oh my, I love it! It's perfect." She grinned at Gabe and Katie. "I can't believe it's mine. I've never had anything so grand." She nearly fell out of the truck in her haste to see the inside.

"Whoa, hold on; you don't want to fall and hurt yourself." Gabe helped her down. "Hold the rail and be careful; it's still a little icy." He grabbed her duffel bag, and Katie carried the grocery sack. Annie unlocked the front door, and Gabe and Katie smiled at the awe on her face as they stepped inside.

"Where do you want me to put your bag?" Gabe asked.

"You can set it right there." She indicated a wooden high-backed chair with a dark green cushion across the foyer from the stairway that led to the second floor. To the left was a large dining room and kitchen with a laundry room and bath off of it. To the right a living room with a big fireplace faced the dining room. On each side of the fireplace were wood bookcases. The doors and window frames were dark mahogany, matching the bookcases and furniture in the dining and living rooms. A gorgeous grandfather clock stood in the entryway.

"It's beautiful. I've never seen such lovely things. Is this actually real?"

Annie looked at Gabe, half expecting someone to burst in at any minute and tell her this was all a dream.

"Yes, hon, it's all yours and no one can take it away from you." Katie set the milk in the refrigerator and handed the hot chocolate to Annie.

"Let's get you off of your feet, Annie. You need some rest."

Annie sat in a forest green recliner, and he flipped the handle to put her feet up. Once she was settled, Gabe brought in some wood. While he started a fire, Katie sat down on the floral sofa across from Annie.

"I noticed the receptionist called you Mrs. Benson, Annie. If it isn't too forward of me to ask, where's your husband?"

"Katie!" Gabe said as if he couldn't believe she had just asked that.

"No, really, it's all right. I know you must wonder," Annie said. "I'm a widow; my husband died from pneumonia six months ago."

"Oh, I'm so sorry," Katie said.

"Yes, I'm very sorry, too, for your loss, Annie," Gabe said. "If there is anything you need, please don't hesitate to ask."

"Thank you so much for taking me by the lawyer's office and for bringing me home."

"You're welcome. If there's anything else we can do, let us know."

He stacked the woodbox full. "That should last you until tomorrow. Get some rest. We'll let ourselves out and lock the door."

Gabe decided he'd come back and check on her later that evening. It looked as if it might snow again anytime, and he wasn't comfortable leaving her alone without a phone. He climbed in and started the truck.

"Gabe, it concerns me that Annie didn't buy any groceries. Do you think she's low on money? She couldn't have much in that duffel bag in the way of food."

"I don't know. I wondered the same thing, Katie. It concerns me, too, but that's not something you can just come out and ask. I'll mention it to Mom when I take you home."

"Good idea; she'll know what to do. Annie's very pretty— nice, too." Katie grinned. "I noticed you admiring her."

"She's pregnant, Katie." Gabe backed up and headed down the driveway to the road. "She'll be my patient soon. I'm just concerned about her health."

"Right." Katie looked at him. "She's not married as we thought, so there's nothing wrong with you being attracted to her."

"Katie, I told you she's a patient."

"I know what you told me, but I have eyes, Gabe. I can see your interest in her is more than as a patient. I've seen you with Rachelle, and this is different."

What could he say? She was right, and he'd be less than honest if he said that he wasn't attracted to Annie Benson. But he wasn't going to admit that to his twenty-two-year-old sister.

"Mother always says you'll feel different when the right one comes along. Who knows, Gabe. That may be the reason the Lord brought Annie here. She may be your chosen mate. Believe me, she'd be an improvement over Rachelle."

"Thank you, but I don't need you to be a matchmaker, Katie. We have enough of that with Mother and Grandma Larraine. Besides, we just met Annie, and she's still mourning her husband," Gabe reminded her.

"I'm not matchmaking. I'm just stating the facts the way I see them." She grinned.

Later that evening it began to snow. By the time Gabe arrived at Annie's there was at least four inches on the ground and it was coming down steadily. He parked in front of the house, and as he climbed the steps, he found Annie sitting in the swing.

"What are you doing out on the porch? It's twenty-eight degrees!" He couldn't believe she was sitting out here in the cold.

"This is my first time to be in the snow. I wanted to be out here so I could see it up close."

"You aren't used to this weather, so you don't realize how quickly you could get frostbite. You have to think of your health and the baby's."

"I didn't realize it would be dangerous. I would never do anything to jeopardize my babies."

"Let's get you inside." Gabe softened his voice, realizing that out of concern he'd been a little sharp.

Annie started toward the front door, clearly upset by his comment, but her feet slipped and she cried out as she started to fall. Gabe barely caught her before she hit the ground. The clean fragrance of her soft hair as it brushed across his cheek stirred his senses. "Are you all right?"

❄

Annie saw the concern in his eyes as he held her until her feet were steady.

"Yes, I'm fine. Thank you." She allowed him to hold on to her until they got into the house.

"I'm going to have some hot chocolate; would you like a cup?" she asked, hoping to get her mind off the fall she'd nearly taken on the porch. She had to be more careful; the babies were the most important things in her life. She'd be devastated if anything happened to them. She hoped Gabe liked hot chocolate. It was her favorite, but besides buying it and milk, she couldn't afford anything else. She'd brought a jar of peanut butter and a box of crackers with her in her duffel bag; they would keep her from starving until the bank opened on Monday.

"Hot chocolate sounds good. Can I help?"

"The cups are in the first cabinet on the bottom shelf." Annie indicated a cabinet right across from where Gabe stood.

They took their hot chocolate into the living room and sat on the floral sofa in front of the fire. "Annie, did I hear you say 'babies' out on the porch, as in more than one?"

"Yes, I'm having twins." Annie lovingly rubbed her hand over her protruding belly.

"When is your actual due date?"

"December twentieth." Annie took a sip of her hot chocolate.

"You're only seven and a half months. I'd guessed about eight, but since you're having twins that would explain why I thought you to be further along. When was your last appointment?"

"I've only been once, when I was three months." Annie waited for his reaction. Disbelief clearly showed on his face.

"You've only been to a doctor once, and you're over seven months along with twins? Why, Annie?"

She glanced over at the fireplace for a minute, watching the flames leap and dance around the logs. "I couldn't afford to go. I felt good, and I've been taking my prenatal vitamins faithfully." She looked back at him.

"There are clinics you can go to, Annie."

"Not when you live in a small town and can't afford a car. I worked at a restaurant and lived in a small trailer within walking distance. I had no way to get to a clinic. I didn't have the money to pay for more than one visit to the doctor. My neighbor was a prenatal nurse, and when I was five months along she listened for the baby's heartbeat and told me I was having twins." Annie set her cup on the end table. "I love my babies, Gabe. The doctor wouldn't see me unless I paid up front when I went in. I barely made enough to pay rent, buy food, and get my vitamins; I did the best I could."

"I'm sure you did. It just sickens me that a doctor wouldn't see a pregnant woman because she couldn't afford his office fees. I couldn't have turned you away. I became a doctor to help people." Gabe glanced at his watch. "I'd better go; it's getting late, and you need to be in bed."

He handed her his card and pulled a cell phone from his pocket. "I wrote my cell phone number on the back, and this is Katie's phone, in case you need anything. I'll pick you up at noon on Monday. My office is in town at the emergency care, I want to make sure everything is okay with you and your babies." Gabe went into the kitchen and put his cup in the dishwasher before he slipped his coat back on.

"I really appreciate that, but my situation hasn't changed much, even if you take me. I still can't afford to pay for an office visit."

"Don't worry about that; the most important thing is that you and the babies are cared for properly."

"Okay, but under one condition—when I get a job you'll let me pay you a little at a time until I get it all paid off."

"We'll work something out that will be acceptable to you."

"Then I'll be ready. Please tell Katie thank you for letting me use her cell phone." She walked him to the door.

"Sure, and if you need anything, call, okay?"

"If I do, I will, but I'm sure I'll be fine." His intense blue eyes scanned her face for a moment.

"Good night." He closed and locked the door as he left.

Annie checked the windows to be sure they were locked and thought about Gabe as she went upstairs to look around. She loved her babies; it upset her that he would even think she would neglect doing what was best for them. She would have gone for regular appointments before if she could have.

Chapter 3

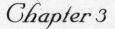

Annie was amazed as she reached the second floor; it was just as lovely as the downstairs. There were three bedrooms upstairs besides the master bedroom. They were all decorated beautifully. One in yellow and white gingham, one in pink paisley, the third, which was across from the master bedroom, was done in red and white gingham with a Raggedy Ann and Andy motif. It was perfect for a nursery, whether the babies were boys or girls, and there were two white cribs with matching crib sets. How had her great-aunt known Annie was having twins?

She stood there for a moment, thinking. Alex would have loved this room. She missed him so much. Sadness threatened to engulf her, but she forced the memories out of her mind and walked across the hall. She couldn't dwell on Alex or depression would get the better of her, and if it did, she wouldn't be able to take care of her babies. They were her first priority, her whole world; they were what kept her going each day.

Annie gasped as she stepped through the doorway to the master bedroom. A beautiful wedding ring quilt in shades of mauve and forest green on a cream background draped a gorgeous king-size four-poster bed made from dark cherry wood. It stood on a cream carpet; a stool with two steps was fastened to one side, allowing access to the high mattress. A matching set of nightstands flanked the bed, and an armoire, dresser, and chest of drawers were neatly placed around the room. Priscilla curtains in the same quilted pattern covered the large window. Several different-shaped pillows in a cream-colored eyelet lay against the shams at the head of the bed. Double doors opened into a master bathroom with a matching decor.

A large Jacuzzi tub sat in the corner. She could just imagine how it would feel to soak in it. But it would have to wait until after the babies were born. If she got in, she chuckled, she'd probably never get back out; the shower would have to do for now.

She couldn't believe this. Everything seemed to be decorated in exactly the colors she would have chosen had she done each room herself. How could her aunt have known what Annie liked? For a moment, she was overwhelmed with sadness that she had missed out on knowing her aunt Molly. She must have loved Annie to leave her all of this. How sad they had both lived their lives basically alone, without any family.

She decided to sleep in the pink bedroom until after the babies were born. There was no way she could climb in and out of that big bed.

The next morning Annie had just showered, dressed, and poured a cup of hot chocolate when the doorbell rang. She opened it and found Katie on the porch along with four other women.

"Hi, Annie." Katie smiled.

"Please come in; it's cold out." She smiled and closed the

door once they were inside.

"Annie, this is my mother, and my grandmother, Ruth and Larraine St. Nick. This is Karen Vincent and Charlene Welch. Ladies, this is Annie Benson." Katie smiled. "We brought you some food to welcome you to town, and we'd like to invite you to church on Sunday."

"It's so nice to meet you. Thank you for the food. It was very thoughtful."

Annie led them into the kitchen, thankful she wouldn't have to eat peanut butter and crackers all weekend after all.

"Oh, honey, you're welcome. We're just so glad you're here," Ruth said and smiled.

"I'm glad to be here, Mrs. St. Nick. I understand you and my great-aunt Molly were good friends."

"Honey, you can call me Ruth, and yes, we were the best of friends. Soon we'll have to sit down and talk. I'll tell you all about her; she was a special lady."

"I'd love that."

Annie and Katie served everyone hot chocolate then took a seat by the fire.

"Annie, we're getting ready for the Christmas pageant. It's always a big event at our small country church. Everyone in town will be there. The ladies make refreshments. After the program, we gather in the fellowship hall to eat. We want you to be a part of it." Ruth smiled.

Annie didn't know what to say. It was obvious they just assumed she'd be going to church. She was rescued from having to comment when Katie said, "I don't suppose you play the piano, Annie?"

"Well, yes, I do. But I haven't played since I left the orphanage over a year ago." Annie glanced at Katie then changed the subject. "Would anyone like more hot chocolate?"

She refilled their cups, and they went on to discuss the upcoming pageant.

"Our pianist recently got married and moved away," Katie explained. "We don't have anyone who can play for church now, or for the pageant. Annie, won't you consider playing for us?" Katie pleaded.

"Katie, I'm really rusty. Surely you can find someone else who would play better than me."

"There is no one else; you'd be doing us a big favor. The pageant just won't be the same without music. We've been praying the Lord would send us a pianist. I just know you're the answer to our prayers."

Annie doubted that seriously. She'd never been an answer to anyone's prayers. But she had to admit she was excited by the possibility of having access to a piano again. She loved to play.

It looked as if everyone in this small town attended Sunday services. Since this was to be her home, she guessed she'd have to start going. She certainly didn't want to offend anyone. Besides, they needed her to play the piano, and there hadn't been many times in her life that she'd felt needed. It felt good to be able to do something to help someone else.

"Okay, if someone can give me a ride. But if you want me to play for service in the morning, I'll need to be there a little early, so I can run through the music at least once."

"We'll pick you up." Katie gave her a big hug. "You're a life-saver, Annie."

"We appreciate it, honey. Last week we sang without any music, and it just wasn't the same." Ruth gently patted her on the shoulder. "Well, I guess we had better head for home. Thank you, Annie, for the wonderful visit and refreshments. The house looks great. Molly loved it here, and I'm sure you will, too."

"I already love it. It's beautiful." Annie glanced around and then accepted hugs from all the women before they left, promising to see them in the morning.

She went in, put the dishes in the dishwasher, and then decided the recliner looked awfully inviting there by the fire. The next thing she knew, she awoke to the sound of someone knocking. She glanced at the grandfather clock and went to answer the door; she'd been asleep for three hours.

She opened it and was surprised to find Gabe on the porch. "Would you like to come in out of the cold?"

He stepped inside. "I can't stay long. I just came by to see if you needed anything."

"I'm fine, thanks, but that was nice. Your mother, grand-mother, Katie, and two ladies from the church came by this morning. They brought me several dishes of food; I won't have to cook for a while. I really appreciated that, and I enjoyed meeting them."

"Mother mentioned they were coming over. I'm glad you had a nice visit. I guess I'd better go. I've still got to feed, and it's going to be dark soon."

"Feed? You have animals?"

"Yes, two horses, two spoiled barn cats, a German shepherd, twelve hens, and fifty head of cattle."

"Oh my, it must be fun to have all of those animals. I've

always wanted a small dog, but I couldn't have a pet at the orphanage."

"When you get settled, maybe you can get one."

"I might just do that."

"Katie and I will be here to take you to Sunday school and church at eight forty-five tomorrow morning. She said that will give you a little time to go over the music on the piano."

"Thank you, I need the practice."

"I'll see you tomorrow, then. Good night."

Chapter 4

Annie was ready the next morning when Gabe knocked and she went to answer the door. She stood there for a moment before she could find her voice. She'd thought him handsome in blue jeans, but he was breathtaking in his navy blue suit, white shirt, and navy tie. She swallowed and said, "Hi, I'm ready. I just need to get my jacket."

"Do you have some gloves? It's cold out there." Gabe held her coat while she slipped it on.

"No, I need to get a pair."

"Is this the warmest coat you have?"

"Yes. It didn't get this cold where I lived in California."

"I have some blankets in the truck. You'll freeze in that lightweight thing; you're going to need a heavier coat here."

Annie didn't object when he took hold of her arm as they walked out to the truck. There must have been at least a foot of snow on the ground. She appreciated Gabe's support as she waded through the drifts, but she moved away from him as soon as he opened the door.

"Good morning, Katie." Annie climbed in next to her. "My

goodness, it's cold out here. Talk about a winter wonderland! This is definitely it. It's so beautiful with all of the pine trees covered in snow."

"Yes, it is. I love it here. I wouldn't want to be anywhere else."

Gabe pulled a blanket from the back and draped it across their laps. "That, along with the heater, should keep you ladies warm."

"Thank you." Annie smiled. "The heat feels good."

"Annie, you mentioned it'd been a long time since you'd played the piano." Katie adjusted the blanket so it covered their feet. "Didn't you and your husband have one?"

"We couldn't afford one." Annie was thankful Katie let it drop, because she wasn't ready to talk about Alex. It hurt too much.

A little while later, Annie was thrilled to be sitting in front of a baby grand piano. She'd never even seen one up close, much less had the opportunity to play one. It was gorgeous, and she couldn't wait to get started, so she opened the songbook to the first hymn and began to play.

Gabe had heard a lot of pianists, but Annie was exceptional.

"If she's rusty now, I can't imagine what she'll be like when she's practiced," Ruth said beside him. "Molly would be so proud of her."

"Yes, she would, Mom. It's a shame she didn't have a chance to get to know her."

"Yes, it is. She seems to be such a sweet girl, but I know Molly felt she was doing what was best for her."

Gabe listened to Annie play for a few more minutes, and when she was through, he helped her down from the podium.

"Annie, you worried for nothing. I've never heard anyone play more beautifully."

"Thank you. I'm glad it sounded all right. It's been quite a while."

Gabe led Annie toward the Sunday school rooms. He'd noticed from the time he'd picked her up this morning that she'd been a little distant.

Was she still upset over their conversation last night?

Brother Chris was standing just inside the double doors. He greeted them, interrupting Gabe's thoughts.

"Good morning. This must be Annie?"

"Annie, this is Brother Christian Grayson, our pastor. Brother Chris, Annie Benson."

"I was enjoying your music. We're so grateful to have you here and playing for us. Welcome to Trinity Fellowship."

"Thank you. It's nice to meet you and to be here. Everyone has made me feel so welcome. You have a beautiful piano." Annie smiled and shook the minister's hand.

"One of our members donated the piano to the church; it was her grandmother's. Gabe, I'm sure you can show Annie to class and introduce her around."

"I will, and we'd better head that way." Gabe placed his hand beneath her elbow and guided her to class. They found two seats next to Katie and sat down.

The lesson was about a man named Jonah, who was swallowed

by a whale. He didn't want to do what God asked of him and ignored God's request. Could that really happen today? Annie certainly hoped not, and she didn't want to find out.

Annie enjoyed the message, but she didn't know anything about the Bible. She was thankful Gabe knew where to find the place the pastor was reading from and shared it with her; otherwise, she would have been lost. As they left the Sunday school class, an attractive woman approached them.

"Hello, Gabriel." She smiled.

From the way she looked at Gabe, it was obvious to Annie that she was more than a friend.

"Rachelle, how are you this morning?"

"Very well, thank you. Mother asked me to extend an invitation to you for lunch today."

"Rachelle, this is Annie Benson. She just moved here."

The young woman glanced at Annie's abdomen, raising her eyebrows. For a moment, Annie didn't think Rachelle was going to acknowledge her.

"It's a pleasure, I'm sure." She dismissed Annie as if she were of no consequence.

"Rachelle, I'm sorry, I can't make it today. Please extend my regrets to your mother and thank her for the invitation."

"That's a shame. Call me and maybe we can do something one evening this week." She smiled up at Gabe.

"It was nice to meet you, Rachelle," Annie said as they walked out the door. Rachelle blatantly ignored her, and Annie felt her face heat in embarrassment. She knew she wasn't anyone important, but Rachelle didn't need to be rude.

"Gabe, I hope you didn't turn down the invitation on account of me. I could have found another way home."

"No, if I could have made it, I would have taken you home and gone back. I have another commitment this afternoon."

"I take it she's a girlfriend. Oh—forget I said that. It isn't any of my business." Annie's cheeks heated again. She couldn't believe she'd blurted that out.

Gabe smiled. "Rachelle and I have dated a few times."

It wasn't the fact that Gabe was involved with Rachelle that bothered Annie. She didn't want a relationship with him or anyone else. What upset Annie was the way that Rachelle had treated her. She couldn't believe that anyone could be so rude.

On the way home, Annie commented, "I can't even imagine how awful it would feel to be swallowed by a whale."

Gabe chuckled. "I doubt that it was very pleasant."

"That's amazing. I'd never heard that story. I've only been to church twice before today."

"I hope you enjoyed it and you'll come again." Gabe glanced at her.

"I enjoyed the message, and Brother Chris didn't yell at us. When I went with Alex, the minister yelled and pounded his fist on the pulpit. I only went twice, and that was enough. From then on, Alex went without me."

"Annie, the Lord loves you. He doesn't want you to be uncomfortable in His house."

"Why would He love me?" Annie looked at him. "I've never given Him any reason to."

"You don't have to give Him a reason, Annie. He loves you anyway."

Gabe had to be mistaken. God couldn't love her; if He did,

he wouldn't have let her get pregnant and then taken Alex away from her and the babies. But she wasn't ready to discuss that, so she changed the subject as they reached the ranch. "Will it get colder than it is today?"

"I'm afraid so. It'll drop below zero as the sun goes down. Please don't be out on the porch."

"I won't. I'll stay inside. I don't want to take a chance on falling. Thank you for the ride."

"I'll pick you up at noon tomorrow, but if you need anything before then, call me."

"Thank you, but I'm sure I'll be fine." Annie went inside then closed and locked the door.

She hung her coat in the closet and went up to change clothes. On the way back down, her feet slipped and she slid down the last two steps. She sat there too shaken to move. After a few minutes she slowly stood. She didn't seem to hurt anywhere, but she still felt a little shaky, so she carefully made her way to the rocking chair and sat down.

Should she call Gabe and tell him she'd fallen? No, she seemed to be all right. If she had any problems, she'd call. She wouldn't do anything to jeopardize her babies. She spent the rest of the afternoon reading by the fire.

The next morning, Annie held on to the rail as she went down the stairs. After the scare she'd had the night before, she wasn't taking any chances.

Gabe knocked just as the grandfather clock chimed twelve times. She liked that he was prompt, but she wouldn't have expected anything else. He struck her as the kind of person who would be very efficient in everything he did.

Annie opened the door. "Hi, come on in."

"What happened? Are you all right?" Gabe lifted her chin so he could see the bruise on the side of her jaw.

"I'm okay. I slid down the last couple of steps yesterday evening as I came down the stairs, and I hit my chin on the railing."

"Why didn't you call me?" Concern clearly showed in Gabe's face.

"I would have if I'd had any problems afterward. Fortunately, I didn't hit very hard. I grabbed the rail and broke my fall; that's how I hit my chin."

"Annie, you have to be careful on the stairs. You could have really hurt yourself. It's good that we're going into the office so I can check you today."

They walked down the steps through several inches of snow and out to the truck. She noticed Gabe's leather gloves as he turned the key in the ignition. Warm gloves and a heavier coat were two things she needed, but they would both have to wait awhile. She'd make do with the coat she had and put her hands in her pockets to keep them warm. The money her aunt had left her would have to see her through until after the babies were born and she could get a job. She had to have a few things for them, so she wouldn't be spending any on herself.

Chapter 5

The roads were icy, but they made it safely to Gabe's office at the emergency care facility in town. As they walked inside, Gabe introduced Annie to Suzie, his receptionist, and Grace, his nurse. Annie filled out the necessary paperwork, and Grace took her into one of the examining rooms. She handed Annie a gown and showed her where she could change. Once she was settled on the examining table, Grace returned.

"Okay, honey, let's get your blood pressure. The doctor will be in shortly."

Gabe came in with her chart in his hand. "Annie, since I don't have any medical records on you, I want to do a blood workup." The nurse handed him a rubber tourniquet. He wrapped it around Annie's arm and tied it just above her elbow.

"Try to relax. I'm not going to hurt you. You'll feel a little stick, but that's all."

Annie jumped when the needle pierced her arm, but it was more from fear than anything else. She barely felt the needle.

"Easy now, the worst is over," Gabe said.

Annie was glad she was lying down. The sight of blood

always made her faint, and it was worse when it was her own. "I—I don't feel very good."

✻

Gabe glanced at her. She was pale as a sheet. "Gracie, we need a wet cloth here quickly, please."

"Here, honey." Grace placed the wet, cool cloth on Annie's forehead and patted her shoulder.

"Better?" Gabe asked as he finished with the vials of blood he'd collected and placed them in a container. He pushed an intercom on the wall and asked Suzie to take them to the lab.

"Yes, thank you. I'm sorry. I've never been very good with the sight of blood."

"There's no need to apologize." Gabe finished the exam and listened to the babies' heartbeats. "I'd like to do an ultrasound, Annie."

"What's an ultrasound?" She raised up. "Are the babies okay?"

"Their heartbeats are strong. They seem to be fine. It's routine, Annie. I always do an ultrasound on my expectant mothers at twenty weeks. Since you're well past that at thirty-four weeks, I'd like to do one now." Gabe moved the ultrasound equipment next to her.

"This is the machine we use. See this? The end of this resembles the end of a stethoscope." Gabe held up a hose that was attached to the side. "I'm going to put some of this jellylike substance on the end here and turn on the machine. When I move it around on your abdomen, we'll be able to see the babies on the screen here." He indicated a monitor that resembled a computer.

"I'll be able to see my babies?" she asked.

Gabe smiled at the excitement on her face. "Yes, and if you decide you want to know, I'll be able to tell you their genders."

"Really?"

"Yes, so you think about it and let me know what you decide."

Gabe smiled again at the expression of amazement that came over her face when the babies appeared on the screen.

"See there's four tiny feet, and there are their hands. See their little hearts beating?" Gabe pointed them out on the screen.

"Oh, my!" Tears filled her eyes, and Gabe handed her a tissue.

"It's pretty incredible, isn't it?" He'd done many ultrasounds, and yet he was always moved by the awesomeness of God's creation.

"Yes, it is, and a little scary. I've never been around babies; I know I have a lot to learn."

"I have no doubt you'll do just fine, Annie. What did you decide? Do you want to know what gender the babies are, or wait until they're born?" Gabe handed her a towel to wipe the jelly off of her skin while he moved the machine back across the room.

"I want to know." She grinned.

"You're going to have two little girls." He smiled.

"They're girls?" Her green eyes lit up, and the wide smile that crossed her pretty face caused Gabe's heart rate to shoot up a notch or two. The attraction he'd experienced previously increased by twofold.

"I take it you're happy about that?"

"I'd be happy no matter what, but two little girls will be so much fun." She glanced up at him, alarm visible in her eyes.

"They're okay, aren't they? There's nothing wrong, is there?"

"They're just fine, Annie. As far as I can see, everything looks good. I'll let you know the results of the blood tests. You can get dressed, and when you're ready, Gracie will show you to my office."

Gabe left Annie with Gracie and went to see his last patient. He was closing early today, since it was his mother's birthday. He and Katie were fixing dinner for her, and he planned to ask Annie to join them.

Gabe walked into his office a few minutes later and found Annie sitting in one of the light blue chairs in front of his oak desk, reading a book. "You like to read, huh?"

"I love to read. I keep a book in my purse. You never know when you might want one." She grinned.

"That's true." He sat down and opened her chart. "What do you like to read?"

"Romantic suspense is my favorite."

Gabe nodded as he filled out all of the information in Annie's folder. "That's what Katie reads. You two should have a lot in common."

"I like Katie. She's very nice." Annie closed her book and put it in her purse.

"We're having a small birthday party for Mother this evening with just a few friends. Katie and I are cooking dinner, and we'd like for you to join us if you can."

"I don't want to intrude on your mother's birthday. She just met me, and I hardly even got a chance to talk to her."

"Believe me, she's heard all about you." He chuckled. "Katie has talked nonstop about you since we dropped you off at your house Friday. Mother can't wait to spend some time with you. She loved your aunt like a sister. The invitation came from her as well as Katie and me."

"Okay, then I'd love to come."

"Good. I'm through for the day, so let's go. Do you need to go home first?"

"No. But could we stop at the bank, and somewhere to get a birthday card on the way?"

"Sure. The drugstore carries cards, if that's okay."

"That's fine, thank you." Annie grabbed her purse, and they went out to the truck.

After stopping at the bank and then the pharmacy, Gabe drove out to his parents' ranch. He went through the gate and headed up the long road.

❄

"Oh, my! This is beautiful." Annie had never seen a house quite like it. The outside was made of logs and had dark green shutters. It sat on a knoll and had a large porch with five steps leading up to the front door. A three-car garage was attached at one end. Just enough pine trees had been removed for the house and a grass-covered front yard, but a few still resided there. Annie glanced out across the property and saw a pond in the distance. The setting was so peaceful; it made her feel good just looking at it.

"My mother and dad designed the house and then had it built. My property joins theirs on this side and yours on the other side."

"Is your house made of logs, too?"

"Yes, in fact it's real similar to this one." Gabe walked Annie up to the door and knocked. It was only a moment until his mother and dad answered. "Come on in." Ruth smiled.

"Mother, you met Annie the other morning."

"Yes. Hello, Annie." Ruth gave Annie a hug.

"Happy birthday, Ruth. It's nice of you to include me." Annie smiled.

"Dad, this is Annie Benson, Molly's niece," Gabe said.

"Hello, Annie, it's good to meet you. Make yourself comfortable."

"Thank you, Mr. St. Nick; it's nice to meet you, too." Annie sat in a large wooden rocking chair, its rust and navy plaid cushions matched the sectional across from a huge rock fireplace on the far wall.

"Just call me Nick, Annie. Everyone does." He smiled.

Annie returned his smile. She could see the kitchen's large center island from her chair.

She had barely gotten comfortable when the doorbell rang and Nick went to answer it. Rachelle and an older couple walked in.

Great! Just what she wanted: to spend the evening with Rachelle being rude to her.

Chapter 6

Annie, Gabe said you met Rachelle at church yesterday. These are Rachelle's parents, Charles and Marjorie Hanson."

"Hello, Rachelle. And it's nice to meet you, Mr. and Mrs. Hanson."

"Oh, honey, it's good to meet you, but please call us Charlie and Marj. We're so grateful to you for playing the piano; church just wasn't the same without music."

"I'm glad I could help. I love to play."

Rachelle put her hand on Gabe's shoulder and smiled. He returned her smile and reached up to pat her hand.

"Mother, why don't you sit down while Katie and I fix dinner? It's your birthday. We want you to relax and enjoy the evening. You and Marj can keep Annie company, and it will give you a chance to get to know each other better." Once Ruth sat in the chair next to Annie and Marj, Gabe and Katie went to work preparing dinner. Rachelle glanced at Annie and grinned then turned her attention back to Gabe as she sat on a stool next to him while he fixed the salad.

Annie turned her attention to Ruth and Marj and tried to ignore the fact that Rachelle continued to fawn over Gabe—and that he obviously enjoyed her attention.

"Annie, it's so good to have you here. It's like having a part of Molly still with us." Ruth patted Annie's hand, effectively interrupting her thoughts.

"Gabe and Katie told me about Aunt Molly having polio and how hard it was for her to get around. I wish she had sent for me so I could have known her."

"Believe me, honey, she desperately wanted to. When she received the letter about your parents' accident, she was beside herself. It was a very difficult decision for her to leave you in the orphanage. But she felt you'd have a more normal life than you'd have with her."

"I would have helped her. Even though I was only seven at the time, there were a lot of things I could have done to make her life easier."

"Yes, probably so, but she didn't want that for you. She called and talked to Miss Caroline. She was so kind and caring, and Molly felt you were in good hands and that she would give you the love you needed as you grew up. You wouldn't be saddled with a crippled aunt to take care of. She wanted better than that for you."

"I guess I can understand her reasoning. Miss Caroline was very good to me, and I love her, but it wasn't the same as being part of a real family—someone who was truly related to me. I would have gladly taken care of Aunt Molly if she had only given me the chance." Annie sighed.

"Now that I've met you I can see that, and you would have

been so good for Molly, but she was thinking of you. She really had your best interest at heart, honey."

"Is that why she left me the ranch?" Annie shifted to try to get more comfortable.

"Yes, she wanted you to have a place of your own. She has the land rented out; two of our neighbors take care of it and bale the hay. They'll pay you the rent now, if you want to continue with them."

"Yes, I do. That's great. The house is decorated exactly the way I would have done it, Ruth. How did she know what I'd like?"

"She kept in close touch with Miss Caroline, who sent Molly pictures of you regularly. When she realized she was dying, she was determined to have the house renovated. The wiring and the plumbing were redone, and everything was redecorated. When it came to decorating the inside, she called Miss Caroline and asked her your favorite colors and what you would like in decorating the nursery."

Annie looked at Ruth. "Now I know why Miss Caroline asked me so many questions during the last few months."

"I'm sorry you never had a chance to get to know her. Molly was a wonderful lady—you would have loved her. I tried to convince her to send for you when she got the results of her tests from Gabe, but she said she wouldn't do that to you. She didn't want you to get to know her just in time to lose her. She refused to put you through that. She loved you, Annie, even though she never saw you in person."

"I'm sorry, too, Ruth, for your loss of a good friend."

Annie suddenly felt an overwhelming sadness. Gabe and Katie soon called them to the table for dinner, which took her mind off their conversation. Time spent at the table with Gabe's family lifted her spirits. The only damper to the whole evening was Rachelle.

"Annie, when are your babies due?" Rachelle asked.

"The twentieth of December."

"Oh, my goodness!" she gasped. "I thought you'd be due sooner, as big as you are."

Annie felt her cheeks heat in embarrassment, which she was sure had been Rachelle's goal.

"Annie's having twins, Rachelle," Katie said. It was obvious she didn't appreciate Rachelle's comment.

Nick said the blessing, and the food started around the table.

"Gabe, have you tried out that new saddle you bought?" Nick asked as he dipped spaghetti onto his plate.

"Yeah, I saddled Sandman and took him out for a ride Saturday, Dad. It's great. It was worth the trip to Rexburg."

"You got a new saddle?" Rachelle wiped her mouth with her napkin. "I'd love to go riding, Gabe."

"We'd better wait awhile, Rachelle; it's too cold, and you'd freeze. I just took Sandman out for a short time to try out the saddle."

"All right, but as soon as it's warm enough you'll have to take me out." She glanced over at Annie and smiled. "Do you ride, Annie?"

"No, I've never had the chance to learn."

"Well, you certainly won't have the time with *two* babies to take care of."

Annie could see right now this was going to be a long evening. Rachelle seemed intent on embarrassing her. Annie wished she'd known Rachelle was coming. After the way she had treated her at church yesterday, she would have declined the invitation and gone home.

"Annie." Katie interrupted her thoughts. "I almost forgot, Karen Shepherd asked me to tell you how much she appreciated you playing for the pageant. The kids did so much better on their singing parts since they had music."

"That was nice of her." Annie smiled, grateful to Katie for changing the subject. "I really enjoyed playing for them and hearing the children do their parts."

"You play well, Annie. You're a real asset to the church in more ways than one." Gabe smiled.

"Thank you. And you two are good cooks." Annie glanced at Gabe and Katie. "The dinner was delicious."

"I'm glad you enjoyed it." Gabe stood to help Katie clear the dishes from the table. Annie started to stand up to help, but Gabe said, "We'll do it, Annie. You're our guest. Sit still and enjoy the time you have to relax."

Annie noticed Rachelle didn't follow Gabe into the kitchen this time, nor did she offer to help with the dishes.

By the time they had cake and Ruth had opened her gifts, it was getting late, so Rachelle and her parents said good night and left.

Annie had a wonderful time in spite of Rachelle's pointed comments. Gabe and Katie had a very loving family, and they made her feel a part of it, which she so appreciated since she'd never had one of her own.

Annie said good night to Nick and hugged Ruth and Katie as she and Gabe left.

Once they were on the road, Annie said, "Thank you, Gabe. I had a very nice time tonight."

"You're welcome. I'm glad you enjoyed it. I'm just sorry for the way Rachelle acted. Sometimes I don't know what gets into her."

Annie knew Rachelle was jealous. She didn't realize that Annie wasn't a threat to her. Gabe was Annie's doctor, and if it hadn't been obvious before tonight, it certainly was now that her and the babies' well-being was his only interest in her. He only invited her tonight as a neighbor, to make her feel welcome.

"Annie." Gabe caught her attention. "Grandma Larraine is cooking Thanksgiving dinner. Why don't you join us for the day?"

"I don't know. It's nice of you to ask, but that's a day for families. I don't want to impose."

"You won't be; we want you to come. You can't spend Thanksgiving by yourself." Gabe pulled up in front of her house and walked her to the door.

Annie searched his face for a moment, and then asked, "Will Rachelle be there?"

"No, just family," he assured her.

"Then, I guess it would be okay."

"Good, then it's all settled. We always have a relaxing day and lots of good food." He grinned.

She groaned. "Food doesn't even sound good right now, I'm so full, but I'm sure it will by then."

He chuckled. "Yes, I think so."

"Where were your grandparents tonight?"

"They both have the flu."

"Oh, no. I hope they feel better soon. Would you like to come in?"

"I better not. I can see how tired you are, and you need to get some rest. I'll take a rain check for another night." Gabe reached up and slipped her hair behind her ear. She was so lovely it nearly took his breath away. When he cupped her chin and ran his thumb across her soft cheek, he felt her stiffen slightly and pull away. He knew she still mourned her late husband and he should go, but somehow he couldn't bring himself to say good night just yet. How could he be so attracted to her? They'd only known each other for a short time, and she wasn't a believer. And as long as she wasn't a child of God, he could never have a relationship with her. *Lord, I know You must have a plan here, I just pray You'll use me to lead Annie to You.*

"You have dark circles under your eyes. I'd better go. Sleep well and be careful on the stairs."

"I will."

"Good night. Call if you need anything."

"Okay. Be careful going home."

Gabe waited until he heard the lock click before he headed to his truck.

Chapter 7

Annie went upstairs to get ready for bed, but as tired as she was, she couldn't sleep. She was kidding herself when she tried to deny her attraction to Gabe. She had thought for a minute tonight that he was going to kiss her. She should've refused Gabe's invitation for Thanksgiving and just decided to stay away from him except for her appointments, but she couldn't bring herself to do that. She enjoyed his company, and because of that she worried she was being disloyal to Alex.

Annie, forevermore you're worrying for nothing. It was just your imagination. He's in love with Rachelle. Get a grip; the attraction is one-sided. Just look in a mirror and you'll know that his only interest in you is his concern as your doctor. Your only concern right now has to be getting these babies here and then finding a way to support them.

Gabe came by every evening the next two weeks and brought in firewood for Annie. She really appreciated his help. She probably could have managed to bring in a few logs at a time, but it would have taken several trips each day in the ice and snow to have enough to keep a fire going. Independence had its merits, but she knew her limitations, and she wouldn't put her babies at risk.

Even though Annie knew Gabe was seeing Rachelle, she enjoyed his company and was looking forward to him coming by this evening to take her to the store. She planned to get a few things for the babies plus the ingredients to make two pumpkin pies for Thanksgiving at his grandmother's. It didn't seem possible it could be just two days away.

Gabe and Katie would also be by tomorrow evening to take her to the practice for the Christmas pageant. The only downfall to that was that Rachelle would be there. But in spite of that, Annie was looking forward to it. She loved to play the piano.

Some of her fondest memories of her mother were at the piano while she patiently taught Annie to play. Fortunately, there had been an old upright piano at the orphanage, and Miss Caroline had continued to teach Annie over the years she was there. After she and Alex married, she hadn't been able to play. They couldn't afford a piano, and they were too far away for her to go to the orphanage.

A knock on the door interrupted Annie's thoughts. She went to answer it and found Gabe on her front porch holding a large box in his hands.

"Oh, my, come in. What's in the box?" Annie asked excitedly.

Gabe grinned and set it on the floor. Annie squealed when the cutest little black ball of fur jumped up on the side of the box and yelped. She reached in to pick it up, and the puppy snuggled under her chin and licked her.

"Oh, Gabe, it's adorable!" She giggled, and her eyes sparkled with excitement. "Where did you get it?"

Gabe loved the way her face lit up when she was excited about something. "My best friend raises them; she's a toy Scottish terrier. I told him last week I wanted her when she was old enough to wean. She just turned six weeks."

"She's so cute. What are you going to name her?" She held the puppy close and hugged her.

"What are *you* going to name her? She's yours."

"What?" Her green eyes widened in surprise.

"I got her for you. You said you'd always wanted a puppy; now you have one." He grinned.

"B—but I can't take this puppy. She had to have been very expensive." Her beautiful eyes clouded in worry.

"No, she wasn't. She had to have a hernia repaired. They couldn't sell her for full price. She was the last of the litter and the runt besides, so I got her for a song. And all her puppy shots are included, so you don't have to worry about that expense."

Her face brightened. "You sure you don't want to keep her?"

"No, I want you to have her. I have a dog already. What are you going to name her? I don't think she'll be very big."

Gabe was glad he'd made the decision to buy the puppy for her. He had debated on whether it would be the right thing to do, but now, watching her with the tiny puppy, he had no doubt that it was.

"I think I'll name her Zoë." She smiled. "Thank you, Gabe. This is the best present I've ever received. I love her already."

"You're welcome. She needed a good home, and you needed a puppy, so it's a win-win situation."

"You've been so good to help me ever since I arrived in Rexburg on the bus, Gabe. I would have had a hard time managing by myself. I don't know how I'll ever be able to repay you for all you've done."

"You don't owe me anything. That's what friends do; they help each other." Gabe wanted to kiss her, but he resisted. Even though he'd only known her for a few weeks, he'd fallen in love with her. But they had one major obstacle: she still didn't know the Lord.

He enjoyed watching her with the puppy. "Oh, by the way, your blood tests came back and everything looked good."

"Oh, that's great. I'm relieved to know that my not going to the doctor regularly didn't cause the babies any problems."

"You're fortunate, Annie."

"I know, and I would have done it differently if I'd had a choice."

"Speaking of the babies, I guess we'd better get Zoë settled in her box so we can go shopping for the things you need. We can get some puppy chow while we're there."

"Okay." Annie put the tiny puppy back in the box with a soft towel to lie on. "I'm going to put a clock next to her so she won't feel alone. Oh, look, Gabe. She's so cute."

"Yes, she is. She suits you very well." Zoë had curled up contentedly and gone to sleep.

They locked the door and went out to his truck. Once Annie was settled, Gabe turned the key in the ignition. "All set?" He glanced at her.

"Yes, I'm all buckled in. Oh, look, it's snowing." Annie glanced over at him with a smile that lit her pretty face. "Isn't it beautiful? I love to watch it snow."

"Yes, it is." Gabe pulled away from the house and started down the driveway to the road. The truck slid as they hit the pavement, and Annie gasped. "Are we going to make it?"

"It's okay. I'm used to driving in this weather. We don't want to stay too long though. It'll accumulate on the roads fairly quick with it coming down this heavy."

"I'll hurry; I just want to get a few groceries and some clothes for the babies. I'll feel so much better knowing I have something to put on them when I bring them home."

"You don't have any clothes for the babies?" Gabe asked. He guessed he shouldn't be surprised. She'd said she'd barely made ends meet.

Her face turned bright red, and he realized he'd embarrassed her. He certainly never meant to do that.

"No, I didn't have the money to buy anything extra. Aunt Molly left me some money, and I thought I'd use just a little of it to buy a few things. I don't plan to spend very much. I know I'll need it to live on until after the babies are born and I can get a job to support us."

"I'm sorry, Annie. I shouldn't have said that. I didn't mean to embarrass you."

"No, no, that's okay. I'm sure you'd wonder why I'm not more prepared."

They arrived at the department store in town, and Gabe helped

Annie down from the truck. "Be careful, it's slick."

They went inside, she bought the things she needed while Gabe grabbed a bag of puppy chow, and then they went to check out.

He offered to pay the whole bill, but she wouldn't let him. "I'll get the puppy chow. I brought you the puppy, and I intend to provide the first bag of food for her, and that's not negotiable."

Gabe carried the grocery sack in one hand and held on to Annie with the other as they went out and got into the truck. It had started snowing hard again, and the ground was getting slicker by the minute.

"Are we going to make it home?"

"We should be okay. We'll take it slow."

They had almost made it back to Annie's when they hit an icy spot in the road. But Gabe quickly got the truck back under control.

"I'm sorry, Gabe. I shouldn't have asked you to come out in this weather. Your excellent driving was all that kept us from having an accident."

"Annie, there are times we have to be out in it; we just have to be extremely careful."

Annie slipped twice on the icy steps and would have fallen if it hadn't been for Gabe's quick reflexes. "I'll give you a cup of hot chocolate to warm you up, if you don't think staying will make it unsafe for you to drive home," Annie offered as they reached her front door.

"I'll come in for a little while. I can drive across the pasture.

That way I can kick in my four-wheel drive and it'll get me there."

Annie went into the kitchen to check on the puppy. She was still snuggled up fast asleep. Gabe came up behind her.

"She seems perfectly content. Where do you want me to put the puppy chow?"

"Here in the laundry room will be fine for now." Annie opened the door so Gabe could carry the food in and set it down.

"I'll stir up the coals and start a fire so you can warm up," Gabe said.

"Okay. I'll fix the hot chocolate while you do that. How about some popcorn to go with it?"

"Sounds good to me. I like popcorn." He grinned.

Chapter 8

A few minutes later, Annie came in with two hot choco-
lates and a big bowl of popcorn on a tray.

"Here, let me get that for you." Gabe put the tray
on the coffee table and then sat beside Annie on the sofa.

He took the mug of chocolate from Annie and grabbed a
handful of popcorn to go with it. She handed him a napkin and
took some for herself. "Oh, that fire feels so good."

"Yes, it does. Annie, would you mind telling me a little about
yourself and your husband? If it's too painful and you don't want
to talk about it, I'll understand."

"It's okay. What do you want to know?"

"How you met, if you had a happy marriage...I'd just like to
know a little about you and your life before you moved here."

"Actually, we grew up together. Alex was the first person
to befriend me when I arrived at the orphanage." Annie set
the hot chocolate on the table. "I was so scared, and he came
over and sat next to me. He said his name was Alex and he was
seven and a half. He asked my name, told me not to be afraid,
and said he'd be my friend." She smiled at the memory. "I had

just turned seven, and from that day forward we did everything together." Annie watched the fire leap against the logs for a minute as tears welled in her eyes.

"When we were seventeen, we signed up to go on a skiing trip. I came down with the flu the evening before we were supposed to leave, so I didn't get to go." She swallowed hard before continuing, pulled one of the throw pillows into her lap, and wrapped her arms around it.

"That evening, Miss Caroline came into my room, and I knew by the expression on her face that something was very wrong." She sighed dejectedly. "She told me that Alex had had an accident learning to ski, and he was going to be paralyzed from the waist down for the rest of his life." She blinked, and a tear rolled down her cheek. Gabe reached up and wiped it away, his touch so gentle her heart nearly skipped a beat.

"I'm sorry, Annie. I can't even imagine what you were feeling that night."

"Alex was so active, Gabe. I was devastated for him. I just couldn't believe this could happen to him. I had to go to the hospital. I wanted to be with him when he woke up and they told him the news. Fortunately, I was feeling better, so Miss Caroline took me to see him. Alex dealt with it better than I thought he would. He told me he had accepted Jesus two weeks before the accident at a revival meeting, and he said the Lord had a purpose for all things that happen."

"He was right, Annie. Sometimes it's hard for us to understand, but the Lord has a plan for all of our lives."

Annie wasn't sure how she felt about that, so she didn't comment and instead continued on with her story. "The one thing Alex wanted more than anything else in the world was to get married and have a child. It was his lifelong dream, but he was convinced that he would never be able to see it happen. I'd never seen him so sad and depressed. He told me he knew no one would want to marry a cripple who was unable to have children."

Gabe took hold of her hand, and she glanced up at him for a moment and then continued. "When we turned eighteen and were about to be released from the orphanage, I had no family and nowhere to go, so I told Alex I would marry him and give him a child. I didn't love him as a mate, but I did love him as a friend and felt I could do this for him. We checked with Alex's doctor since we couldn't get pregnant in the normal way, and he suggested artificial insemination. As I'm sure you know, it's expensive, so I went to work as a waitress to try to help save the money we needed."

Annie got up from the sofa and walked over to the window. It was still snowing.

"We finally made it. It was amazing how thorough they were in matching us as close as possible with coloring and back-ground so the child would have as much of Alex's personality traits and coloring as possible. Alex was ecstatic when we found out I was pregnant. I'd never seen him so happy." Tears ran down her face, and Annie wiped them away. "When I was six weeks along, Alex contracted pneumonia. The doctors did everything they could, but his body just couldn't fight it off and we lost him. He was my best friend, Gabe, and I miss him so much."

"I'm so very sorry, Annie." He came up behind her and placed his hands on her shoulders.

"Alex wanted these babies so bad, Gabe, and he'll never

get to see them. If God is so loving, why would He let me get pregnant and then take Alex before he even had a chance to be the father he so desperately wanted to be? I just don't understand."

Gabe turned her to face him and wiped her tears with his handkerchief. "God didn't do this, sweetheart. Yes, He allows things to happen that we don't understand, but He has a plan for each of our lives. We don't know what that plan is, or what factors play into His plan. It's hard for us, without being able to see the whole picture, to accept some of the things that happen throughout our lives. But I assure you, God is with us through every aspect of it."

"Alex used to tell me to pray when I was upset about something. He said life is like a puzzle and God holds the pieces. Every piece has a place, and when all the pieces are in His puzzle, He will return again for His children."

"He's absolutely right, Annie. I've never heard it explained quite like that, but it puts it into perspective where you can understand it."

Annie heard Zoë start to cry, so she went into the kitchen to pick her up. When she came back into the living room, Gabe grabbed his coat. "I'd better go so you can go to bed; it's getting late. Thank you for the hot chocolate and popcorn." He bent down, kissed her on the cheek, and ruffled the puppy's fur. "And thank you for sharing this with me. I know it's been hard for you. Will you be all right?"

"Yes, I'm fine."

"I'm glad you're here now, Annie. And if you need anything, I'm close by. Just call me and I'll be here."

"I will, and thank you for taking me shopping and especially for the puppy, Gabe. I'll take good care of her."

"I have no doubt of that." He smiled. "Before I forget, Grandma Larraine said dinner will be at two o'clock on Thursday. I'm glad you're going to join us for the day."

"I'm looking forward to it." She stroked the puppy affectionately.

"Good. Try to get some rest, and I'll call you in the morning."

"Okay, good night."

Gabe waited on the porch until he heard the lock turn then went out and climbed into his truck. He sat there for a moment and thought about what Annie had shared with him. Their marriage wasn't a love match. He knew she missed her friend, but it wasn't the same as mourning a mate. He wanted to share his feelings with her now that he knew they were two friends who had married to accomplish a goal, rather than because they were in love.

Lord, You know how I feel about Annie. If she is the mate for me, I pray You'll present Yourself to her and she'll accept You into her life.

It was still snowing, so he cut across the pasture, engaging his four-wheel drive. As he came to the fence that separated his property from Annie's, he stopped to open the gate. By the time he climbed back into the truck, he was covered in snow and soaked to the bone. The weatherman said the wind chill would be down to about four degrees tonight, and Gabe was sure it had made it. He drove through, closed the gate, and made it back to his ranch in record time. Once inside the house, he built a fire and took a shower. He had just climbed into bed when the phone rang.

"Hello?"

"Hi, Gabe. I haven't seen you in a while. I miss our time together."

"Rachelle, I explained to you the other night at dinner that we were just friends and you needed to look for someone who wanted a more permanent relationship."

"I don't see why we can't still go out as friends at least."

"I don't want to hurt you, Rachelle, but I don't think so."

"I suppose all of your time now is spent with Miss Annie Benson."

"I've been helping her, yes; she can't do everything right now."

"Well, can you at least pick me up for pageant practice tomorrow night? My SUV is in the shop."

Gabe sighed. The last thing he wanted to do was expose Annie to Rachelle, but he couldn't refuse to give her a ride. "I'll come by for you about a quarter to six."

"Thank you. I'll see you then. Good night."

"Good night, Rachelle."

Gabe thought about Annie. He looked forward to seeing her again the next day, and he wouldn't put up with Rachelle insulting her.

❄

The following evening, Gabe came to pick Annie up, and she was waiting anxiously for him to arrive. She couldn't wait to get to the church. She enjoyed playing the piano for them, but watching the little children practice their parts for the pageant would be the highlight of her day. When he knocked, she opened the door with her coat on and stepped out onto the porch.

"I see you're ready. You aren't anxious, are you?" He chuckled.

"Yes, I am." She laughed. "I've been waiting all day for this. I just love to watch the little ones' faces. They get so excited, and they're so cute."

"Yes, I have to admit I enjoy it, too. That's why I volunteer to help every year." He grinned.

"Annie, Rachelle is in the truck. She called me for a ride since her SUV is in the shop."

Annie smiled up at him when she really wanted to cry. But she knew he had a relationship with Rachelle. She didn't have a right to be upset, but she was. "That's fine, Gabe. She needed a ride."

When they got into the truck, Rachelle moved to the middle, next to Gabe. Annie climbed in next to the window.

"Hello, Rachelle. How are you?"

"I'm just fine, thank you."

Annie rode in silence as Rachelle talked nonstop to Gabe, leaving her completely out of the conversation.

When they arrived, Annie went up to the piano and played for the children to sing their parts. The reminder that Rachelle was Gabe's girlfriend put a damper on Annie's excitement. She didn't enjoy the evening nearly as much as she had anticipated. It took about two hours to go through the program twice. When they were through, Gabe turned off the lights and helped Annie and Rachelle out to the truck. He took Rachelle home first and walked her up to the door. Annie shouldn't have been watching, but when Rachelle wrapped her arms around his neck and they kissed good night, her heart cracked a little. *Annie, you knew he was with Rachelle. You shouldn't have allowed your feelings to get involved, but you did and now you're hurt.*

Gabe came back to the truck, and they headed to Annie's. "Thank you for taking me tonight." She unlocked the door. "Do you want to come in?"

"As much as I'd like to, I'd better head on home. It's getting late. But before I go, I wanted to tell you I'm sorry about Rachelle."

"I appreciated the ride, Gabe. There's no reason for you to apologize. Rachelle is your girlfriend, and I didn't have anything to say anyway, so it doesn't matter."

"Okay, we need to get something straight. Rachelle is not my girlfriend. We've dated a few times, that's all. I made that clear to her, also. She wants a permanent relationship, and that's not going to happen with me. She's never been more than a friend."

"Well, it sure looked like more than that to me when you walked her to the door. Not that it's any of my business."

"She kissed me, Annie, and I guarantee you it won't happen again."

Gabe smiled at her and cupped her chin in his palm. "Now, I'd like to see the return of the smile I saw earlier. I'll pick you up about noon tomorrow to go to Grandma Larraine's."

The relief Annie experienced at his words brought back not only her desire to smile, she also wanted to do a little dance— but she'd better not try it under the circumstances. She grinned at the thought. "I'll be ready; I'm looking forward to it."

"That's better." Gabe kissed her cheek. "I'll see you tomorrow, then."

"Okay, good night." Annie stepped in and closed the door, quickly sliding the lock into place, knowing Gabe wouldn't leave until he heard it click, and it was too cold for him to be standing out there. When she heard his truck start and pull away, she went to get Zoë. She took her upstairs with her since the tiny puppy loved to sleep at the foot of Annie's bed. Annie felt sorry for Rachelle, but she couldn't help that she was glad Gabe and Rachelle were no longer an item.

Chapter 9

Bright and early the next morning, Annie was up in the kitchen baking pumpkin pies. She was excited about going to Gabe's grandmother's for Thanksgiving. She had never spent the holiday with an actual family before. Annie slid the pies in the oven, and while they baked, she went upstairs to get ready. She took a shower and got dressed in a pair of teal cord pants and a rust and teal maternity top that said "Babies are Beautiful" on the front. It had shiny little silver hearts in a circle around the lettering. Miss Caroline had bought it for Annie for her birthday in September.

She had just lifted the pies out of the oven when she heard a knock at the door. Annie glanced up at the clock. It had to be Gabe; it was time to go. She went to let him in and glanced in the mirror above the mantel on the way. She wanted to look nice and wanted everything to be perfect today for Gabe's family.

"Hi, come on in. I'm almost ready. These pies are still hot. Will they be okay on the floor of your truck if I set them on pot holders?"

"Sure, they'll be fine. Let me carry them out for you." Gabe went into the kitchen then took the pies out to the truck. Annie picked up her purse and waited until he came back in to help her. She didn't dare try to walk across her icy front porch and down the steps by herself. The last thing she needed now was to fall.

When Gabe helped her into her coat, her soft hair brushed against his cheek. She looked so pretty and smelled so good. He paused and looked down at her, and his breath caught in his throat. He wanted to kiss her, but now wasn't the time. He took hold of her arm, helped her out to the truck, and made sure her seat belt was fastened before he went around to the driver's side.

They arrived at his grandmother's just as Katie and his parents were walking in the door.

He took Annie inside, kissed his mother and grandmother, and hugged his dad and grandfather. They greeted Annie, the ladies giving her a hug then introducing her to Jonathan, Gabe's grandfather.

"Come on into the living room; dinner's about ready," Larraine said.

Annie sat in the rocker by the fire, and Gabe went out to get the pies. After he took them into the kitchen, he sat in a chair next to Annie.

"This is a lovely house, Larraine. It's so warm and cozy. I love it." Annie smiled.

"Thank you, dear. We're happy here. We've lived in this house for fifty-four years, ever since Jonathan and I married. There are a lot of memories here."

"Good memories, too, I might add." Jonathan wrapped his arm around his wife and gave her a hug.

She smiled at him affectionately. "I'd better go finish dinner."

"Can I help you with anything, Larraine?" Annie asked.

"Oh no, dear, you stay there, off of your feet. We'll take care of everything."

Larraine, Ruth, and Katie went into the kitchen to finish the last-minute preparations for dinner.

"Did you ever get your old truck running, Grandpa?"

"No, Gabriel, I didn't. I worked on that old thing nigh on four hours yesterday, and I finally just gave up on it. I guess I'll have to take it in to Tom's shop on Monday and see if he can get it running."

"I looked at it when I came out to bring the turkey, and my guess is that the water pump is shot."

"I think you're probably right, son. I kind of figured that's what it was."

"Dinner's ready. Let's gather around the table," Larraine said.

After they were seated, Gabe's grandfather said grace and they started serving the meal.

❅

Annie had never seen so much food on one table. At the orphanage, there was enough for everyone to have a plate, but nothing extra. She guessed that here there was enough for seconds, and there would still be food left over.

Gabe held the turkey platter while she served her plate

and then passed the platter on. It smelled so good her mouth watered. She didn't realize how hungry she was until now. She listened as Gabe teased Katie about her new boyfriend at church.

"He isn't my boyfriend, Gabe. We've only gone out once." Katie made a face at him, and everyone laughed.

She enjoyed the different conversations throughout dinner. It was great to see how a real family interacted with one another at the table. This was the best Thanksgiving she had ever celebrated. She was so very thankful that these wonderful people had included her in their family gathering. She would love to be a part of a family like this.

Later that evening, as Annie was getting ready for bed, she noticed her throat was a little scratchy. It hurt to swallow. She hoped she wasn't coming down with something. She was cold, so she took Zoë and climbed under the covers to try to get warm.

It was almost noon the next day before Annie dragged herself out of bed and down the stairs, wrapped in a blanket. She felt terrible. Her head hurt, she could hardly swallow, and she was freezing. She had just started into the kitchen when someone knocked at the door. She went to answer and it was Gabe.

"Good morning." He smiled.

"Hi, you're welcome to come in, but I hope I don't have something contagious. I don't feel very good."

Gabe stepped in and closed the door. His demeanor changed immediately to doctor mode. Concern was clearly written on his handsome face as he reached over and gently laid his hand on her cheek.

"Annie, you're burning up. Sit down here and let me take a look at you."

Annie sat on the sofa and rested her head against the cushions.

"Stay right there. I'm going to get my medical bag."

Gabe returned quickly and stuck a thermometer in her mouth before she could say anything else.

He checked the thermometer. "Your temp is 103, Annie. Where do you hurt?"

"My throat. I can hardly swallow, and I have a headache."

Gabe helped her to lie down on the sofa. He placed a cushion under her head and covered her with the blanket she had brought from upstairs.

He used a tongue depressor and looked at her throat, then swabbed it. After listening to her chest and checking her ears, he said, "I'd guess you have strep throat, Annie, but this will tell us for sure." He placed the swab stick into a container and put it in his bag. "I'll take it into my lab and run a culture."

Gabe pulled the blanket up to her chin, tucked it around her, and gave her two Tylenol to take her fever down. "I'll start a fire. It'll be warmer in here in just a few minutes. I'm going to take this to the lab. I won't be gone long. Where are your keys so you don't have to get up to let me back in?"

❋

"They're in my purse over there on the chair." She indicated the rocker across from the sofa.

Gabe was only gone an hour. He put a rush on the test and then went to the store and the pharmacy. He bought some soup and Sprite, went by to check the test results, and then headed back to Annie's.

She was sleeping when he let himself in, so he took the groceries and her prescription into the kitchen then came back to check on her. He gently laid his hand on her cheek. It still felt warm, but cooler than earlier. Her temp had come down some, and for that he was grateful. *Father, please lay Your healing hand upon Annie, and don't let this affect the babies.*

Gabe's cell phone rang, and he pulled it out of his pocket. "Hello, Dr. St. Nick."

Chuck Grayson, the sheriff, was on the phone. "Gabe, there's been an accident in town. Shane Jackson was involved. He's been taken to the emergency care."

"I'm on my way, Chuck."

"What happened?" Annie asked. "Is everything all right?"

"I have to go into the emergency care. A friend of mine has been involved in an accident." He slipped into his jacket, but before he left, he went into the kitchen and returned with her meds and a glass of water. He helped her to sit up so she could take the capsules.

"Annie, the test showed just as I suspected—that you have strep throat. You need to stay down and rest. I'll be back as soon as I can. If you need anything, call my cell phone."

Gabe had only been gone for a little bit when Annie heard a key in the door. She thought he had forgotten something, but it was Katie who walked in.

"Hi. Gabe stopped by and told me you were sick. I'm to stay

out of your face but take care of you." She grinned.

"Oh, Katie, I would've been okay. You didn't have to come over here."

"Yes, I did. You don't need to be up, and someone needs to take care of the puppy while you're this sick. Gabe said he bought some soup when he went to fill your prescription, and he wanted me to fix you a bowl. And at four o'clock, if he isn't back, I'm to give you another dose of the meds."

"That was nice; he must have done that while he was in town."

Katie fixed them both a bowl of soup then said, "Get some rest, Annie. I'll sit here and read while you sleep."

✳

Gabe knocked on Annie's door and Katie let him in. "How's Shane?"

"He has a broken arm and a mild concussion, but otherwise he'll be okay. He was very fortunate it wasn't worse. A man just passing through hit some ice and ran a red light. He hit Shane broadside."

"I'm so thankful your friend didn't get hurt seriously, Gabe. Did the other man get hurt?" Annie asked.

"Just some cuts and bruises—nothing serious, thankfully."

Gabe went into the kitchen and came back with a glass of water and another dose of meds for Annie to take. When she woke up three hours later, Gabe checked her temperature and it was down some.

"We'd better go. It's getting late." Gabe slipped into his jacket.

"I hope you feel better, Annie," Katie said.

"Don't try to get up. We'll let ourselves out. If you need me in the night, call."

"I will, and thank you for everything."

About an hour later, Annie decided to get up from the sofa and go to bed. She was feeling a little better. Her fever was down and her headache was gone. Gabe had given her strict orders before he and Katie left: to stay in bed, take her meds, and drink lots of fluids. She went into the kitchen, took another dose of her medicine, picked up Zoë, and headed upstairs to bed.

The next morning she had just come downstairs when her phone rang.

"Hello?"

"How are you feeling, Annie?"

"A little better this morning, Gabe. My throat isn't quite as sore, and my headache seems to be gone."

"That's good, but you need to rest today and keep taking your meds. Even if you feel better, I want you to take all of them. Strep is stubborn, and it'll come back if you don't completely get rid of it."

"I'll take every last one, I promise." She smiled at his concern.

"I have a patient due in about five minutes. I'd better go. I just wanted to check on you before I got busy. Call if you need anything."

"I will, and thank you for taking care of me yesterday."

"You're welcome; now take it easy and rest. I'll talk to you later today."

Annie went into the kitchen after she hung up. She made a bowl of oatmeal, as it would be easy to swallow, and she took it over by the fire. Zoë sat at her feet and promptly went to sleep.

For the next several days, all Annie did was sleep, read, and relax in her rocker by the fire where it was warm.

It took her a week and two days to completely get over the strep throat and before Gabe would agree she was totally well. She had missed church the Sunday after Thanksgiving and pageant practice that same afternoon. Gabe flat refused to allow her out of the house. Plus, she didn't want to take a chance on giving it to any of the children, so they'd practiced without music, but she was looking forward to going tomorrow. Annie was looking through her closet to find something to wear when the phone rang. She went across the room to answer it.

"Hello?"

"How are you doing today, Annie?"

"I'm fine, Gabe, other than being as big as a house."

He chuckled. "Would you like to get out for a little while, since you've been cooped up all week?"

"I'd love to. Where are we going?"

"Mom, Dad, Grandma, Grandpa, Katie, and I are going on our traditional trip to cut our Christmas trees. I thought you might like to go along and get one for your house."

"Oh, I would love to go. I've never had a real tree, much less had a chance to go cut one," she said excitedly.

"Dress warm, and I'll be there to get you in about twenty minutes."

"Okay, I'll be ready."

Chapter 10

Gabe came in and handed her one of his heavy coats. It swallowed her, but he rolled up the sleeves, and it was much warmer than hers.

Annie was very excited as they climbed out of the truck at the back of Gabe's grandparents' property to find each one of them a Christmas tree. She'd never seen so many all in one place. No one would miss the few they were going to cut. She drew in a big breath. "Oh, it's beautiful and it smells so good out here."

"Hi, Annie." Ruth hugged her. "It does smell good, doesn't it? I'm glad to see you're feeling better."

"Thank you. Me, too. Strep throat is no fun." She made a face and they all laughed.

"Don't get chilled out here now. We don't want you to have a relapse." Grandma Larraine walked up next to them.

"That's why she's wearing one of my coats, so she'll be good and warm. I'm not taking any chances that she'll get chilled. That thin little excuse for a coat that she wears isn't nearly warm enough." Gabe frowned.

Annie smiled at him. She appreciated his concern, and

he was right. Her coat wasn't warm enough, but they were expensive and she couldn't afford a better one right now.

They walked through the trees and looked around until they each found the one they wanted, and then the men started up the chain saws. In just a few minutes, they were loading the trees. Half the trees went into the back of Gabe's truck and the other half went into the back of his dad's. They unloaded a tree at each house and then Gabe and Annie took her tree to her house.

"I don't have any lights or decorations, Gabe. I don't know what I was thinking."

"We used to bring Molly a tree every year when we went to cut ours," Gabe said. "I'm sure there must be some decorations up in the attic. There's probably a stand, too. Come on; we'll go look."

Annie climbed the stairs to the attic with Gabe following behind her. He opened the door and reached up to turn on the light.

Annie gasped. "Oh my, there are all kinds of things up here. I wonder what's in all of these boxes."

"I have no idea. Keepsakes, I'd guess. Look over there." Gabe pointed to several boxes across the room.

"They're all marked 'Christmas decorations'!" Annie exclaimed and hurried across to open them. "Look, Gabe, you were right. There are lots of decorations in here, lights and bulbs. . ." She grinned.

Gabe had to chuckle, she was so cute. Excitement sparkled in her green eyes as she looked over at him.

"I can't believe all of these; look at all of the wooden ornaments. Each one has a year marked on it." She read the date on each one as she unwrapped a few of them. "I think we should take them downstairs before I unwrap any more. It will be easier to carry them all together, don't you think?"

"Yes, I agree. Here, let me get them for you and you can follow me down. Be careful. I don't want to take a chance on you falling."

They took the ornaments out, and Gabe helped Annie decorate her tree. He had never seen anyone so excited over a Christmas tree. Of course, everyone he knew had a tree every year and almost anything else they wanted. Annie was so appreciative of everything she received. She'd never had very much, and he figured that made the difference. He was glad he had invited her to go with them to cut the tree. He'd never enjoyed tree-cutting day, as his mother called it, or decorating one as much as he had today. Annie's excitement was contagious.

They sat by the fire with a cup of hot chocolate and enjoyed the lights as they twinkled on the tree.

"Oh, Gabe, my first Christmas tree. Isn't it beautiful? Thank you so much for making it possible for me to have one, and for helping me find the decorations and trim the tree." Annie kissed his cheek, intending it to be a gesture of gratitude, he was sure, but Gabe couldn't resist. He lifted her chin, covered her soft lips with his, and wrapped her in his arms. She kissed him back but then, as if she realized what she was doing, she stiffened and pulled away from him.

"Annie, what's wrong? Have I misread your feelings or done something to offend you?"

"No, you haven't done anything, Gabe," she sighed.

"Talk to me, Annie. What's going on?"

"I'm just a little scared, Gabe." Annie glanced up at him. "When I lost Alex, I told myself I wouldn't ever let anyone that close to me again because it hurt so much when I lost him."

"Annie." Gabe gently cupped her chin with his hand. "There are no guarantees in life, sweetheart. But if you don't allow yourself to get close to people, it will be a very bleak future. Isn't it better to love someone and have the time you're allotted together than to be alone for the rest of your life?"

"I—I don't know, Gabe."

"Annie, I don't believe the Lord wants you to be afraid nor does He want you to raise these babies alone. I believe He has a plan for your life and that's why He brought you here, but you have to come to the point where you're willing to put your fear behind you and trust Him."

Gabe stood up and put his coat on. "It's getting late. I better go. I'm glad you're enjoying the tree. I was happy to help." He grabbed his medical bag from the table. "Get some rest, and I'll pick you up tomorrow for church."

After Gabe left, Annie couldn't get that kiss or his words out of her mind. She cared so much for him, but she was scared. Was he the person that he felt the Lord had for her? She was afraid to hope that was what he meant. But would he have kissed her the way he did if he didn't care for her that way? And if he did, could she put her fear behind her and admit that she loved him?

The next morning Annie was tired; she hadn't slept well. But in spite of that, she was looking forward to the day ahead.

They had church service that morning, and in the evening, the Christmas pageant. It didn't seem possible it was only one week until Christmas. She had found some yarn in one of the boxes from the basement, and she was crocheting a pair of slippers for each of Gabe's family members. Along with Gabe's pair, she also planned to crochet him a scarf. She had noticed he never wore a scarf and hoped it was because he didn't have one, not because he didn't like them.

On the way home from church a couple of hours later, Annie thought about what Brother Chris had said in his sermon. His message had been on the birth of Jesus. He said that Jesus had come to this earth to save us from our sins, and that He had lived on this earth and died on an old rugged cross in our place. Jesus loved us and would forgive us, no matter what we had done in our lives. He offered salvation as a free gift; all we had to do was accept it. Annie had never heard of anyone giving away anything for free.

They pulled up in front of her house, and Gabe came around to help her to the door.

"Can you come in?" Annie found the key so she could unlock the door.

"I'd love to, but I promised Dad I'd help him this afternoon. He has a mare that's about to foal, and he wants to move her into the birthing stall. We need to move some things around in the barn and get some straw put down in there before he can move her."

"Oh, how exciting. Can I see it when it's born? I've never seen a baby horse."

Gabe chuckled. "Yes, I'll make sure you get to see this one.

Take it easy this afternoon, and I'll pick you up about five thirty."

That evening when Gabe came to pick Annie up for the pageant, her back had been hurting all afternoon. She couldn't imagine what she'd done to strain it. She didn't say anything to Gabe as he helped her into his truck, because she was afraid he'd insist she stay home from the pageant, and the kids were counting on her to play for them.

Annie barely made it up onto the podium and over to the piano. Gabe must have noticed her grimace as she sat down on the bench.

"Annie, are you all right?" He came up next to her.

"Yes, I'm okay. My back's hurting from all this extra weight I'm carrying around. If I get much bigger, I don't know if I'll be able to walk." She frowned.

Gabe smiled sympathetically. "It shouldn't be too much longer; the babies will be here soon."

Their conversation was interrupted when the children came up onto the stage. Gabe took a seat in the front, and Annie began to play the first song. She enjoyed seeing the children in their costumes. Mary, with a baby doll Jesus wrapped in a blanket, was seated at the back of the stage inside the stable. Joseph was next to Mary, and an angel stood watching over them. Animals were sitting around just outside the stable, and the three wise men arrived with their gifts. They knelt in front of the manger, and the children began to sing.

Annie was very touched by the story and how attentive all of the children were to it. Not one of them made a noise or disrupted the program.

Everyone went into the fellowship hall for refreshments after the pageant. Annie was sitting between Gabe and Katie. Her back was hurting so she could hardly sit still. No matter how she moved, she just couldn't get comfortable.

"Annie, is your back still hurting?" Gabe handed her a cup of punch and sat down beside her.

"Yes, and it doesn't seem to matter what I do; it doesn't relieve it any."

"Do you have pain anywhere else?" he asked, concern evident in his eyes.

"I didn't have until just a few minutes ago, but it's different now than it was earlier. Now it feels like it's coming from my back around into my lower stomach. I can't imagine what I would have done to cause it, Gabe. I've been so careful."

"Earlier? How long has your back been hurting?"

"It started early this afternoon."

"Does it feel like stomach cramps that come and go, or is it constant?"

"Yes, that's exactly what it feels like, and it comes and goes. Like right now it's stopped. My back still hurts, but the cramps have stopped."

"Sweetheart, you didn't do anything to cause it; you're in labor. We need to go right now."

"She's in labor?" Katie grabbed their purses and coats. "I'll tell Mom and Dad."

Gabe helped Annie out to the truck, and Katie climbed in next to her.

"Mom and Dad said if you needed them to call, and they'll be praying."

"Oh!" Annie doubled over and grabbed her belly. It was really beginning to hurt.

"Annie, take quick little breaths like you were panting. It'll help some."

Annie tried to relax as the contraction subsided, but it wasn't long before another one started.

"Oh!" She doubled over again.

"Already? Katie, how long has it been since the last one?"

"Only two minutes, Gabe. We need to get her to emergency care."

"Her contractions are too close, Katie, we can't make it all the way to town. I'll have to deliver her at home. It's a lot closer; we don't have any choice." Gabe turned the wheel on the truck as it started to slide.

"Are we going to make it?" Annie looked up at him as her contraction began to subside.

"It'll be all right. Try to relax and rest as much as you can in between contractions." *Please, Lord, take us to Annie's, help me as I deliver her, and don't let her or the babies have any complications.*

Chapter 11

Two minutes later Annie had another contraction. Katie looked at him, and he could see the concern in her blue eyes.

"It'll be okay. We're almost there." Every time Annie whimpered in pain, Gabe tensed. He hated to see her hurting, and he knew it was going to get a lot worse before it was over. He didn't have access to the meds he usually gave to help with the pain; she'd have to have the twins by natural birth. He wasn't thrilled about that. The roads were getting worse; they were slick and dangerous. The wipers were having trouble keeping the snow cleared from the windshield, and it was difficult to see.

Gabe jerked the truck to the right, the tires sliding over the ice-coated road. He fought the steering wheel, trying to avoid a collision as a car slid through the stop sign from a side road. Annie and Katie both screamed as the truck went over the edge of the road and slammed into the ditch. They were jerked forward as the air bags went off.

"Annie—Annie! Are you all right?"

She felt his hand against her cheek. "My head hurts." She touched her forehead and felt blood on her fingers.

"Katie, are you okay?" he asked as he examined Annie's forehead and placed a napkin against the small cut.

"I'm okay, but what can I do for Annie? And are you all right?"

"I'm fine."

"Oh, Gabe, it hurts!" Annie cried as another contraction gripped her.

"I know, sweetheart. I wish I could make it easier." He held her hand until it was over.

"Katie, hold this against the cut on her forehead while I try to get us out of this ditch." Gabe jumped out of the truck.

"Katie, what are we going to do if Gabe can't get us out?" he heard her say as he returned.

"The Lord will take care of us, Annie. He always does."

"Oh, Katie, these really hurt!" Annie doubled over again with another contraction.

"Oh, no! I think my water just broke!" Annie cried as Gabe climbed into the truck.

"I have some towels here behind the seat." He handed them to Katie, and she helped Annie dry herself off the best she could.

Lord, please, we need some help here, Gabe prayed.

"We're stuck, aren't we?" Annie handed Gabe the wet towels.

"Yes, but we'll be all right. I called Dad on my cell phone;

he'll be here soon. I'm going to move you into the backseat; I need to check you." Gabe got her settled just as another contraction started.

"Oh, Gabe, it hurts and I'm so scared!" Annie cried.

"I know, sweetheart, I'm sorry. Pant as you breathe and try to relax as much as you can. There's nothing to be afraid of. I'm going to take good care of you and the babies." Gabe pulled on a pair of rubber gloves from his medical bag. "I need to check you to see how close you are to delivering."

"Gabe, what can I do to help?" Katie asked. She leaned over the seat and took hold of Annie's hand until the contraction subsided.

"Help her focus on taking short, quick breaths. It won't be much longer. The first baby's head is crowning." Gabe realized that unless the Lord provided a miracle he was going to have to deliver her in the truck. It would be awkward, but he could do it.

"We can do this," he said. Gabe pulled his handkerchief from his pocket and wiped the tears from Annie's cheeks. He wished he could give her something to make it easier. "It'll be over soon."

"Gabe, I see lights. I pray that's Dad coming down the road," Katie said from the front seat.

Gabe jumped out and flagged the truck down. It was his dad and mother.

"I'm sure glad you made it. Annie is about to deliver."

Gabe lifted Annie from the backseat and carried her to his dad's extended cab pickup. They drove the few miles to her house, and his dad pulled up as close as he could to Annie's steps.

"How're you doing there, little girl?" Nick asked Annie as Gabe lifted her into his arms and carried her up the steps.

"Gabe says I'm doing okay, Nick. But I'm ready for it to be over with." She groaned as another contraction hit.

Katie retrieved Annie's keys from her purse and opened the door for Gabe.

"I better get back to your mother. Call if you need us. Annie, we'll be praying."

Katie helped Annie change into a nightgown as Gabe went upstairs and brought some blankets and a sheet down. He laid them on the floor by the fire and helped Annie to lie down on the soft pallet. He pulled on another clean pair of gloves and checked her. "Okay, let's get these babies delivered."

Katie held Annie's hand as she pushed and labored to deliver the twins. Gabe thought he felt her every pain as he prayed and worked to safely deliver the two tiny little girls. He handed each one to Annie after cutting the umbilical cords and wrapping them in one of the receiving blankets she had purchased. He finished taking care of her, bandaged the place on her forehead, then tucked a nice warm blanket around her.

Gabe sat down beside Annie and took hold of her hand. He loved her and both of these little ones. He wanted all three to be his very own.

"Aren't they beautiful?" Annie smiled up at him and Katie. Love shone brightly on her pretty face for the two tiny babies she held in her arms.

"Yes, they are," Gabe answered, Katie nodding in agreement from where she sat beside him, emotion shimmering in her eyes.

A few minutes later, Gabe took the babies, handing one to Katie. Exhaustion had claimed Annie, and she'd gone to sleep.

"They're beautiful, Gabe." Katie smiled as she admired the babies. "They look just like Annie."

"Yes, they do." He looked at them and felt an overwhelming love and protectiveness toward them. *Lord, please let Annie make a commitment to You. I love her so much. I want to marry her and raise these tiny little girls as my own. I feel that she is the mate You've chosen for me, but I know You don't want me to be unequally yoked to an unbeliever. I trust You to work this out, Lord, so I'll leave it in Your hands. Thank You for a safe delivery and for watching over us. In Jesus' name I pray, amen.*

Katie gently placed the baby she was holding at one end of the cradle Gabe had brought downstairs. "I think I'll lie down in the recliner. I'm tired. Is there anything else you need before I do?"

"No, you go ahead. If I need you, I'll wake you. Thank you for your help and support tonight."

"You're welcome. I wouldn't have wanted to be anywhere else. I love Annie. I'm just so glad everything went well and she and the babies are okay."

"I am, too, honey. Go lie down, and I'll see you in the morning."

Gabe laid the baby he was holding in the cradle close to her sister and went into the kitchen to make some coffee. When he came back into the living room, Annie was awake. He sat beside her as she gazed at her little girls.

"They're so tiny, Gabe. Are they all right?" Annie looked up at him with trust in her eyes.

"They're just fine and as perfect as two babies can be." He smiled. "I've delivered several babies, but I still never fail to be amazed at the miracle of birth."

"They are a miracle." Annie looked at her daughters for just another minute. "Gabe, I've been thinking about what the pastor said this morning and what you said last night. I've decided I want to be saved. Can you pray with me? I don't know what to say."

Gabe smiled, elated at her words. "Yes, I can, sweetheart; just repeat these words after me." He bowed his head. "Lord, I love You and I come before You to confess all of my sins. I believe You are the Son of God and that You died for me. Please forgive me, come into my heart, and be Lord and Savior of my life. In Jesus' name I ask and thank You, amen."

Annie smiled at him, and he could see the excitement in her eyes. "I can't explain the overwhelming happiness I feel, Gabe."

"It's hard to explain, but I certainly know how you feel, sweetheart." He leaned over and kissed her. "Annie, I love you and I want you to be my wife. Will you marry me? I want to help you raise these two little girls as my very own, and I'd love for them to carry my last name if that's okay with you."

"Oh, Gabe. I've been fighting my feelings because I was scared, but I know now you're the reason the Lord brought me here. I love you, too, and I'd be honored to marry you. I couldn't ask for a better husband or a better father for the girls."

Gabe kissed her again. "How about getting married on Christmas Eve? It'll be small—just family. Or if you want a big formal wedding, we can wait and plan one. I want you to be happy."

"Christmas Eve is fine. I'd prefer it to be small, with just your family."

"They'll soon be your family, too."

"I like the sound of that. I love all of your family." She smiled.

"They love you, too, Annie." Gabe cupped her chin gently and rubbed his thumb over her soft cheek. He glanced over at the babies sleeping peacefully in their cradle. "What are you going to name them?"

"I've decided to name them Morgan Alexis after my mother and Alex; Molly Katherine, after my aunt and Katie, and they'll carry your last name. I think that Alex would agree it will be best for their last names to be the same as yours and mine—and that you'll be an excellent father." She smiled.

"Pretty names. I think Alex would be pleased, and I'm honored the girls will carry my last name. I'll try my very best to be a good husband and father."

❄

The following week was hectic with the wedding preparations. Annie wasn't able to do too much, so Katie, her mother, and grandmother did most of the work. Grandma Larraine had insisted on making Annie a wedding dress. She had spent the last week finishing it. Annie had tried it on the evening before, and it fit perfectly. It was a beautiful gown, with a lace empire-style bodice in ecru and a satin floor-length skirt.

Christmas Eve dawned cold but beautiful. Snow covered the ground, but the sun was shining. Annie and Katie, as her maid of honor, were in the back of the church getting dressed.

Katie had on a red velvet dress with a white satin sash that tied in a large bow at the back of her waist.

Katie had just finished helping Annie button her gown and fasten her veil in her hair when they heard music start to play. "Who's playing the piano, Katie?"

"I don't know; we don't have anyone who can play but you. I can't imagine who that could be." She handed Annie her bouquet of red roses with white peppermint carnations set on a white Bible, and then picked up her own bouquet made of red and white carnations.

❄

"Katie, it's time," Shane, Gabe's best friend, said from the door. Gabe stood waiting as Shane walked Katie up the aisle and then took his place beside him as his best man. Gabe couldn't wait to see Annie's face when she saw Miss Caroline at the piano. He couldn't let Annie get married without this special person in her life here to enjoy it with her, so he had sent Miss Caroline a plane ticket to fly here for the wedding.

When the wedding march started, Annie appeared at the back of the church on his father's arm. As she walked up the aisle and realized Miss Caroline was at the piano, a brilliant smile appeared on her face and tears filled her eyes. His dad kissed Annie's cheek and then placed her hand in Gabe's before he took a seat next to Gabe's mother and the twins on the front pew.

Annie whispered, "Thank you," as she stepped up onto the podium with him. Her happiness melting his heart, this was undoubtedly the happiest day of his life.

Brother Chris opened the Bible and started their wedding vows. They repeated them, exchanged rings, and were pronounced husband and wife. Gabe lifted Annie's veil and kissed her for the first time as his wife.

"I would like to present to you Dr. and Mrs. Gabriel St. Nick." Brother Chris smiled.

Miss Caroline played the wedding march for them to walk back down the aisle together. She met them in the reception hall and hugged Annie.

"I can't believe you're here! It's so good to see you." Annie smiled and looked up at Gabe. "Thank you for bringing her here."

"You're welcome. I didn't want your day to go by without her; I know how special you are to each other."

"Oh, Annie, the babies are so cute," Miss Caroline said. "I'm so happy for you."

Annie and Gabe cut their cake and opened gifts. She was so tired they didn't spend too much time at the reception. They had taken Miss Caroline to the airport on their way home so she could be with her family for Christmas, and then Gabe had insisted Annie go home and rest.

Christmas morning, Gabe, Annie, and the twins all went to Gabe's parents' house to celebrate. The babies were passed around so everyone could hold them while others opened gifts. Gabe loved his scarf and slippers, to Annie's delight. She had opened snow boots from her new parents; a scarf from Katie, her new sister-in-law; a beautiful sweater from her new grandparents; a new coat and gloves from Gabe; and clothes for the twins from each one. She had just thanked them all when Gabe handed her a card that said, "This gift certificate is good for one piano of your choice at Pianos Are Our Business. Love, Gabe."

Annie gasped, and her eyes lit with delight as she looked up at him. "Oh, Gabe, you already gave me the coat and gloves. This is too expensive."

"No, it isn't. I want you to have a piano of your own, and you needed a heavy coat and gloves. As soon as you're up to it, we'll go shopping, and you can choose the piano you want."

❄

"I don't know what to say." Annie looked up at him. He was so special. What could she have done to deserve him? "Thank you doesn't seem near enough."

"You don't have to say anything. I'll enjoy hearing you play, so we'll both benefit by this gift." He grinned. "When the girls get old enough, you can teach them to play as beautifully as you do."

Annie realized the Lord had given her more than her fondest wish through Gabe, her beautiful twin daughters, her first Christmas spent with a family of her own, and soon a piano to play, as well. Gabe was aptly named. In her eyes, he was an angel, and he had the true giving nature of Old St. Nick.

JEANIE SMITH CASH

Jeanie lives in rural southwest Missouri, the heart of the Ozarks, with her husband, Andy. They were high school sweethearts and have been blessed with two children, a son-in-law, and four grandchildren. She feels very fortunate to have her children, grandchildren, father, sister, and two sisters-in-law living close by. Jeanie and her family are members of New Site Baptist Church and attend services there regularly. When she's not writing, she loves to spend time with her family, spoil her grandchildren, read, collect dolls, crochet, and travel. Jeanie is a member of American Christian Fiction Writers, Monett Christian Writers Guild, and Mid South Writers Group. Her novella *A Christmas Wish* is included in the anthology *Christmas in the Country*, and she has also had two short stories published in local magazines. She loves to read Christian romance and believes a good story that promotes a message of salvation can be a powerful way to touch the lives of many.

Jeanie loves to hear from her readers. Visit her Web site www.jeaniesmithcash.com or e-mail her at jeaniesmithcash@ yahoo.com.

Rescuing Christmas

by Linda Lyle

Chapter 1

"Chris, do you want to keep going, or do you want to get some hot chocolate?" Vanessa yelled over the hum of the idling snowmobile.

"What do you guys want to do?" Chris asked.

"It's your birthday; you choose," Jessica said.

"Not until Friday. It's only Wednesday," Chris said.

"In that case," Deidre said, "I say we find the hot chocolate."

"I second the motion," Jessica said with a shiver. "I'm getting cold."

With a nod, Chris revved the engine and aimed her snowmobile back down the trail toward the park entrance. They passed through the Yellowstone gate and followed the road back into West Yellowstone. Slowing down as they entered the town proper, Chris pulled into a space near their favorite restaurant. Not that there were that many restaurants in the small town to choose from. The other girls pulled in alongside and parked, as well.

"Looks like we'll have our choice of tables tonight," said Jessica with a smile as she checked her hair in the window at the restaurant.

"Great! I'm too tired to deal with anything else tonight."

"Come on, Christmas Jennings. Get in the spirit of the season," Deidre teased.

"Don't call me that," Chris said, punching her friend lightly on the arm.

"I'll make you a deal. You stop wallowing, and I'll stop calling you Christmas."

"I'm not wallowing," Chris said, straightening to her full five feet seven inches.

"Give it up, Deidre. She's still in denial," said Vanessa. "Besides, I'm hungry and cold. Let's go inside where it's warm."

"Yes, before I turn into ice," said Jessica.

The four entered the rustic diner and made for their favorite booth in the corner. It was out of the general flow of the restaurant but had views of the room and out the picture window. Chris took her usual seat facing the door and the picture window with its fairy-tale landscape of snow. After getting their menus, the girls settled into a comfortable silence as they looked over their choices. Although, by now Chris had already memorized the menu since they had been there for two days and ate every meal here.

As a matter of fact, they didn't even have to order the hot chocolate. Ben, the owner, was already pouring them cups as they sat down. She was determined to have a wonderful Christmas and birthday despite *him*. She had no more than finished the thought when the bell on the door announced the entrance of a new customer.

Jessica looked up to see who had come in. She was always on the lookout for Mr. Right. Chris kept scanning the menu then glanced up at Jessica, who looked like she had just seen a ghost.

"What's wrong?" Vanessa asked. She turned around to see what Jessica was looking at and gasped. "It can't be."

"Can't be what?" Deidre asked, a frown marring her smooth brow.

"Oh, no!" Deidre said, the words barely more than a whisper.

At that, Chris looked at the door, but somehow she already knew what she would see: him. Paul Rogers stood in the doorway—his broad shoulders dusted with snow. He stomped the excess off his boots and brushed the snow away with a flick of his hands. A gesture Chris knew all too well. He scanned the room until he caught her staring. She felt the warmth move to her cheeks, but she couldn't break eye contact.

"What's he doing here?" Vanessa whispered.

"I thought he was visiting his father in Denver," Jessica said.

"Me, too," Chris said, the last word nothing more than a squeak.

"He's coming over," Deidre squealed. "The nerve of him."

Chris listened to the conversation going on around her, but she couldn't stop staring at Paul as he crossed the floor in a few long strides. He didn't seem any happier to see her than she was to see him.

"Chris, what are you doing here?" he asked in a gruff voice usually reserved for disobedient children.

"I was about to ask you the same question." In an instant, the warmth turned to red-hot anger. How dare he take that tone with her—especially after what he had done!

"I work here." He opened his jacket to show his park ranger uniform. Chris stared in disbelief. "What are you doing here on Christmas?"

"We're on vacation, if it's any business of yours."

Paul glanced around the table as if seeing the other girls for the first time. Then, his gaze returned to her, but it wasn't the warm look he used to give her; it was as cold as the weather outside.

"Besides, I don't answer to you anymore. I can do as I please."

"Like you ever did anything else," he said under his breath. "Look, let's just agree to keep our distance."

"Fine by me," Chris said, each word clipped and punctuated.

With a nod at each of the women at the table, he put his hat firmly back on his head and walked out the way he had come. Chris stared at his retreating figure until he turned the corner. Before she could let out the pressure rising inside her, the waitress brought out the hot chocolate.

"Are you ready to order?" she asked brightly, totally unaware of the tension around the table.

"I think we'll need a minute," Vanessa said with a smile.

"Sure. I will be back in a few minutes. Enjoy your hot chocolate."

Chris stared at the cup in front of her. What seemed like the perfect ending to a great day now turned her stomach. She pushed the cup away from her along with any desire for dinner.

"You can't let him ruin your birthday!" Deidre said. She always was the first to jump into a situation.

"It's not my birthday," Chris said quietly.

"You know what I mean," said Deidre.

"She's right," said Vanessa. When everyone turned to stare at her, she said, "I know. I'm as surprised as anyone." Those two had been fighting about everything since grade school. "You can't let him get to you. He's the one who walked away from a great thing. Show him what he lost."

"Exactly," chimed in Jessica.

Chris looked around at her circle of friends, never more grateful that she had asked them to come along on this trip. She had known this would be a difficult enough week, even without Paul showing up.

"I'm so glad I have you guys," Chris said. Picking up her mug, she raised it up. "To us."

The other girls raised their mugs in salute and clanked them together with enthusiasm. "To us," they said as one.

"Does this mean you girls are ready to order?" their waitress asked with a grin.

"Definitely," said Chris. If nothing else, she was going to pretend her way out of this nightmare. She refused to wallow in self-pity. It was a show of weakness. With a dazzling smile of sheer determination, she ordered a steak with all the trimmings, even though her stomach was tied in knots.

Three hours later, Chris sat quietly in the window seat and watched the snow fall silently in the moonlight, regretting every ounce of the steak raging like a bull in her stomach. Stress always went straight to her stomach. While she waited for the medicine to kick in, she held her favorite pillow to her chest and stared at the wonder of God's beauty before her. Somehow it didn't hold the same wonder it had the year before when she had looked at a very similar scene with Paul. They had stayed up late at her parents' house, watching the snow, drinking hot chocolate, and making plans for the future. Why had it gone so wrong?

"What are you doing?" asked Vanessa between yawns. She tiptoed across the cold wood floor and sat down on the window seat, grabbing a nearby throw for warmth.

"Regretting."

"Anything in particular?"

"The steak I had for dinner, placing my trust in the wrong man, choice of vacation spot. You pick."

"You couldn't have known that Paul would be here. Wasn't he supposed to be in Denver visiting his father?"

"That's the last I heard," Chris said quietly, looking out at nothing in particular. "He seemed just as surprised to see me as I was him. That's some small comfort."

"That's a bonus," Vanessa said, stifling another yawn.

"You don't have to stay up with me. I'm a big girl. I'll be just fine."

"You keep saying it, but I just don't believe it yet." Vanessa had always been able to read her thoughts just a little too well.

"Well, I'll keep saying it until it's true. Now go back to bed."

Vanessa looked her over for several seconds before standing up. She took off the throw and wrapped it around Chris's shoulders, giving her that look of pity Chris had come to hate with a passion.

"Have it your way. Try to get some sleep. I don't want you falling off the snowmobile tomorrow. I don't want to spend Christmas sitting by your hospital bedside, like in the fifth grade."

"I'll be fine as soon as the medicine kicks in."

"Whatever you say," Vanessa said over her shoulder as she tiptoed back to their room.

Chris leaned her head against the window; the cool of the glass felt good against her hot cheeks. She snuggled into the throw and prayed that the medicine would start working soon.

❄

"Good morning, sunshine!"

Chris jerked awake, her surroundings unfamiliar. She looked around at the sitting room, a fire crackling in the fireplace, and remembered where she was. She straightened up slowly, her aching muscles witnesses to the fact that she had fallen asleep in the window seat. Leaning back against the wall, with a groan she took the steaming cup of coffee that Vanessa was waving under her nose.

"I can't believe I slept here all night." Her reflection in the mirror carried the telltale design of the seat cushion across her cheek. She moaned and closed her eyes.

"I can't believe it, either, but there it is." Vanessa returned to the kitchenette where the smell of coffee vied with the scent of bacon for dominance in the small area.

Chris's stomach rebelled as the smell of breakfast assaulted her senses. She sipped the coffee gingerly, hoping to keep down at least the reviving warmth and caffeine rush of the rich liquid.

"You felt inclined to cook this morning, of all mornings?"

"Sorry. I had a sudden craving for a hot breakfast, and we won't have time to lounge around at the diner this morning if we're going to take the long loop and be back before dark."

Chris had almost forgotten about their plans for the day. There was no way she was going to back out now since she had been the one to insist that they take the Upper Loop.

"You can't wimp out now, you know," said Vanessa.

"Yes, I know. Get off my brain wave. It's too weak to carry two people," Chris said, mustering a small grin that she knew would never fool Vanessa.

"You're going to have to work on your enthusiasm if you're going to fool the other two."

Vanessa grinned and turned back to the hot stove just as Jessica and Deidre emerged from their bedroom.

"You'd better get a move on if we're going to hit the Upper Loop today," Deidre said.

"I'm going, I'm going," Chris said, taking bigger gulps of coffee as she headed for the shower.

Forty minutes later, they were suited up and headed for the park. The heavy clouds looked menacing, but she wasn't about to let a little precipitation keep her from her plans. Keeping busy kept her from thinking, and she needed that more than she had needed that cup of coffee this morning. As they pulled up to the gate to show their passes, a familiar figure stepped out of the gate shack. Chris stifled a moan, glad that the scarf and goggles covered up the effects of last night.

"You girls should head back to your hotel," Paul said firmly, his lips a thin line of disapproval.

"Excuse me?"

"There's a storm front heading in sometime today or tomorrow. It might get dangerous out there." He stood there before her, hands on hips, just like the last night she had seen him. The night he had broken their engagement without any reason whatsoever, telling her he knew best. The surge of anger that rose up inside her threw common sense right out the window.

"How dare you stand there and tell me what to do!" Chris's voice had risen to a pitch often referred to by her friends as "howler monkey." "What I do is none of your business. Now, if you'll excuse me, I have things to do."

She waved her pass at the park attendant and motioned for the girls to follow her as she revved the engine and headed toward anywhere that was away from Paul Rogers.

Chapter 2

Chris's anger kept her warm for the better part of the morning. Every time she thought about Paul, it was resurrected. She would try to focus on the trail and the beauty around her, but it still took several hours before she could calmly look at the situation. She had allowed his bossy attitude to get under her skin and was once again reacting without any common sense. They were already too far to turn back now, as they had passed the halfway mark on the trail. They might as well finish the loop, but from the looks of the clouds rolling in and the feel of the drop in temperature, they had better make a dash for the hotel.

"Girls," she shouted over the engine, "I think we need to drive straight through to the park entrance. No more rest stops."

"I agree," Vanessa said, her voice barely audible over the noise of the wind and the engines.

The other two girls nodded in agreement. Chris pulled her goggles back down and waited for the other three to go in front of her. Thirty minutes later, the snow began to fall, and within an hour Chris could barely see Deidre's taillights right in front of her. She could no longer see the other two girls at all. She willed herself to relax her grip as her shoulders and arms ached from the tension. She knew a moment of fear when a sheet of snow engulfed Deidre. When the gust calmed, she searched the horizon and aimed toward a beacon of light in the distance. A few moments later, the light disappeared completely, so Chris decided to stop for a moment and get her bearings.

As she came to a stop, she realized her mistake. The snowmobile immediately sank several inches. She tried to move, but it refused to budge in the fresh powder. She cut the engine and stepped off. That was her second mistake. She dropped down up to her waist. Obviously, she had gotten off the trail, and now she was stuck. The snowstorm had brought early dusk, making it even more difficult to see. She pulled out her cell phone, but of course there was no service. Looking around, she tried not to panic. Surely the girls would notice she was gone and come back for her or send help. She couldn't have gone too far off the trail. She was praying for help and wisdom when she remembered the emergency kit with the locater beacon.

By the time she pulled herself out of the snow and back onto the snowmobile, a good twenty minutes had passed, but it seemed like an eternity. Chris had just pulled the emergency kit out when she heard the blessed sound of an engine in the distance. Quickly, she stood up on the seat, waving frantically and praying that someone saw her. She breathed a sigh of relief when moments later the sound grew louder. She waved wildly at the driver, who waved back that he had seen her. He killed the engine several yards away and put on snowshoes before crossing to her.

"Good. Someone with more sense than me," she said aloud.

As the figure came closer, there was something familiar about her rescuer that she couldn't quite identify. When the truth hit her, she closed her eyes and looked up to the heavens.

"That's not funny, Lord," she whispered. "Not that I'm ungrateful, mind You, but couldn't You have picked someone else?"

"You all right?" Paul asked, his voice gruff.

"I'm fine. I'm just stuck."

"You're off the trail," he said, looking at the snowmobile.

"I'm well aware of that. Thanks for stating the obvious."

He grunted but didn't reply. He looked from her to his snowmobile as if calculating. She waited, trying to remain patient. She remembered how he liked to think through things, and she knew that it was useless to try to rush him. Just as she was about to lose the last of her patience, he spoke.

"Do you think you can make it to my snowmobile, or do you need the snowshoes?"

"Well, considering that I have never walked in snowshoes, I think I'm better off walking on my own."

"You're probably right. The snow is not as deep over here. I'll walk beside you."

He held out his arm to her, but she pulled away at his touch. Even through the snowsuit, she felt a familiar warmth. He dropped his hand to his side and sighed but didn't speak. She trudged through knee-deep drifts that were getting deeper by the moment. The light of dusk was fading quickly by the time they reached his snowmobile. She hoped he knew his way out of here.

"I don't think we'll make it to the entrance."

Those were not the words she wanted to hear. She swallowed the panic that threatened to spill out in a fit of hysterics. Now was not the time or the place—or the person—for a meltdown.

"What do you mean?" She enunciated every syllable with a calm control she did not feel.

"We're going to have to take shelter."

"What shelter? We're out in the middle of a national park." Despite her best efforts, the howler monkey peeped out on the last note.

"There is a ranger cabin not far from here. I passed it on the way in. It should be fully stocked with firewood and lanterns as well as some foodstuffs, but we've got to hurry before we lose all the light."

It didn't take much convincing for Chris to climb quickly behind Paul on the snowmobile. For the moment, knowing he was there was a comfort. She peered around his shoulder once they were under way and saw the glimmer of light that she had noticed earlier. A few minutes later, Paul pulled the snowmobile onto a narrow trail in a patch of woods and came to a stop in front of a rustic cabin.

"Let's get inside and check things out. We need to make sure the woodpile inside is stocked before the storm gets any worse."

She followed him into the cabin, waiting by the door as he looked for the lanterns by flashlight. Darkness had almost descended outside, and the cabin seemed dark and eerie. Chris shuddered.

"Cold?" he asked. "Let me get a lantern so that I can see, and I'll get a fire going."

His concern made her feel more vulnerable than she had out in the storm alone. Immediately, her defenses went up.

"I'm fine. I'll check for firewood."

Before he could say anything else, she grabbed a second flashlight and headed out onto the porch. The storm was getting worse, and the wind whipped around her, chilling her to the bone. She found the firewood pile with no problem, but hauling wood while holding the flashlight was difficult. Paul had gotten the lanterns lit, so she turned off the flashlight and put it in her pocket so that she could grab a few more pieces. She made it three steps up to the porch when the tip of her boot caught on the upper stair. She felt herself falling, that helpless, sick feeling of being suspended in air and waiting for the thud.

"Chris!"

Strong arms reached and steadied her before she hit the porch, but a twinge of pain radiated from her ankle. It took a few moments to get her breathing steady. In the meantime, Paul pried the firewood from her arms and stacked it in his while holding her steady with the other arm. She hobbled into the cabin, thankful that a chair sat mere steps inside the door.

"Will you just sit still for a moment?" Paul asked, his gruff voice back with a vengeance.

"Fine."

She watched as he piled the stack of wood onto an already full box and started laying a fire. In just a few minutes, a warm glow was spreading across the room. Now that she had sat still for a moment, she felt all the strength ebb from her body. She had been tense for so long that her muscles ached to remain immobile.

"Why do you always have to rush into things?"

"I'm assuming that's a rhetorical question."

"Might as well be. You never listened to me."

"I'm too tired to fight right now," she said quietly.

"That's a first," he said.

He pulled the rustic couch closer to the fire then crossed to her chair. Before she could protest, he picked her up and moved her to the couch. He pulled off her gloves and unbuckled her boots. When he pulled on the left foot, she cried out in pain.

"What's wrong?"

"I think I twisted my ankle when I fell." Chris rubbed the offending spot, but Paul brushed her hand aside to run his hands over her foot and ankle.

"I think you're right. It's a little swollen and bruised. Let's get you out of your snow gear and get it elevated."

She started to protest but was too weary to even argue with Paul Rogers. She had skipped breakfast and only picked at the snack she had brought for the trip. Between hunger and nerves, she was exhausted. He helped her pull off her gear and then disappeared for a moment. He returned with blankets and pillows. He put one pillow behind her head and put the other one under her ankle before covering her with two blankets. He tucked them in tight around her.

"I'm not that cold anymore, and I'm not five."

"I know, but I don't want you going into shock. Just humor me for now."

"Fine."

"What is that? Your new word for the day?"

She ignored him and looked toward the fire. He shrugged

and walked away. She could hear him digging around in the cabinets behind her but was too tired to turn to see what he was doing. A few moments later, she had almost dozed off when the smell of coffee and a beefy aroma filled the air. With an effort, she shifted positions to see what Paul was up to.

"Did I wake you?" Paul asked, a wrinkle of concern creasing his brow. It was a look that had often made her swoon. She fought the urge just now. Anger at his previous attitude fueled her resolve to keep her guard up. He had broken her heart without warning before; he would do it again.

"I wasn't really sleeping. What are you doing?"

"These cabins are always stocked with staples and a kerosene stove. Nothing fancy, but it's hot." She moved to get up, but he motioned her back. "I'll bring it to you."

She watched him prepare two cups of coffee and two bowls of whatever smelled so good right now. Grabbing a tray from the little kitchenette, he made short work of loading it with dishes and silverware. Chris slid higher up on the cushion behind her and accepted the tray with a grateful nod. There was no sense being rude since they were going to be stuck together for a little while. She couldn't walk out and slam a door right now, so she held her feelings in check.

They ate in relative silence, the wind whistling through the trees the only sound in the cabin. When they had finished, he took the trays back to the kitchen. Pretty soon he was going to run out of things to do to keep busy. Then what would they do? Her stomach knotted at the prospect. She watched him take his time with each utensil, scraping and washing, rinsing and drying as if his life depended on whether or not one crumb was left. By the time he had put the last dish away, her emotions had made it back to the surface again.

"Why?"

Chapter 3

The one word hung between them, heavier than the blanket of snow falling outside. He stopped in midmotion, a cup still in his hand. He refused to meet her eyes, but she could see by the cup shaking in his hand that she had hit a nerve. With a deliberateness reserved for neurosurgery, he put the cup in the cabinet and closed the door. She waited, but when he refused to respond, she repeated the question.

"Why, Paul?"

"Let's not get into that right now."

"Then when, Paul? I can't think of a better time than right now." She motioned toward the storm outside that mirrored the turmoil inside her. "How could you just throw it all away, and without a word?"

She hated the pleading sound in her voice, hated that the hurt was so obvious in the very tone of her voice. It was so much easier being angry with him. Anger was rising to the surface as his silence continued. She was about to question him again when a noise, not unlike the squawk of an annoyed chicken, came from the other side of the cabin. Chris looked around to find the source as Paul jumped to his feet and grabbed his backpack from the chair by the door. He ripped into the bag and pulled out a radio. The squawking became more intelligible.

"Base to Rogers. Base to Rogers. Do you read me?"

"Base, this is Rogers."

"Good to hear your voice, Rogers. What's your location?"

"I'm at the ranger cabin near Madison Junction."

"Is Ms. Jennings with you?"

"Yes."

"Good work, Rogers."

"Thanks. Did the other girls make it out okay?"

"Yes. Johnson is taking them back to their hotel as we speak." There was a pause. "How are the supplies in the cabin?"

"Fine. Why?"

"Well, I'm afraid you two are stuck for the time being. It looks like this blizzard will last sometime into tomorrow night, so it will be the day after before we can get in or you can get out." There was a pause. "I hate it for you, kid, but I guess you'll be spending Christmas out there."

"Understood, sir." Paul's features were frozen in a mask of professionalism, but Chris could tell by his tone of resignation and the slump of his shoulders that he was less than pleased by the turn of events.

"Call if you need us. Otherwise, we'll send out a team to help you day after tomorrow."

"Yes, sir. See you then."

Paul set the radio down carefully on the table. He stared at it with such intensity that she was amazed it didn't burst into flames. Instead of screaming or throwing something, he calmly walked over to the fireplace and stoked the fire, putting on another log. He stood with his back to her, staring into the fire as he had stared at the radio. He looked everywhere but toward her. This had been the story of the last six months of their relationship.

"So, that's it. You're just going to ignore me for the next thirty-six hours or so."

"I'm going to check out the cabin and make sure everything is secure."

She watched his back as it disappeared into one of the only two other rooms in the small cabin. Typical. This was so typical of Paul, run and hide instead of talking about what was bothering him. Why couldn't he just stand still and fight like a man?

Chris threw back the blanket, suddenly hot. She needed to move, do something. She stepped carefully, avoiding putting her full weight on the one ankle. It only took a few steps for her to realize that she neither had the strength nor the energy to walk off her anger. She couldn't even pace the floor. She hobbled back to the couch and fell onto the other end. At the very least, she could get a different view. However, Chris was not ready for the view that greeted her. As she looked out the window, a pair of eyes was staring back at her. She did what any normal person would do in her position. She screamed.

Paul was by her side in a nanosecond, looking around like a cop in one of those action movies, brandishing the end of a large flashlight like a weapon. His eyes were narrowed and focused as he searched the room. For a moment, her heart skipped a beat, but not because of whatever wild animal was outside.

"What is it?"

"Outside. On the porch."

What was wrong with her? She couldn't even manage complete sentences. She just pointed mutely to the window. He was at the window in two steps, putting his hands to the window so that he could see out. Suddenly, a muzzle pressed against the window. Paul jumped back and raised the flashlight in defense. The shadow disappeared into the snow again. Paul moved from window to window, trying to catch a better look. If she hadn't been so afraid, Chris would have laughed at the sight of Paul sneaking around the cabin. Instead, she pulled the blanket to her neck and watched in silence.

After several minutes, he came back and perched on the edge of the couch. He patted her shoulder, much like he would have comforted a child. She shrugged it off, and he recoiled as if she had hit him.

"What was it?" she asked.

"I think it was a wolf."

"A wolf? In this storm?"

"Must have gotten separated from its pack. I don't see signs of any more."

"Are you sure?"

"It's hard to tell with the storm, but if there were more, we'd have probably heard them by now."

Chris pulled the blanket tighter around her neck, digging deeper into the corner of the couch. She looked out the window, but no strange eyes appeared again.

"Can it get in?" She hated feeling so weak.

"No. I checked out the cabin. Everything is secure. There's nothing to worry about. He was probably looking for warmth or scavenging for scraps. He's probably more scared of us than we are of him."

"Do you really think so?"

"Yeah. I think I scared him off."

Paul turned around for another look out the window to make his point when a pair of paws scratched at the window. He jumped back again, flashlight in hand. Chris began to laugh, softly at first and then louder.

"What are you laughing at?" Paul demanded. He looked from her to the window and back again.

"You."

"What do you mean?"

"I think you'd better to take a closer look at your wolf."

Paul turned back to the window and stepped closer. The "wolf" was pawing in the air, tongue lolling out, in traditional begging mode. Chris was sure a closer inspection would find that their wolf was actually a stray dog. Granted, it was a large stray dog, a husky/shepherd mix that gave it a wolflike appearance.

"I think we have another victim of the storm," Chris said between rounds of giggles. "Why don't you let him in out of the cold?"

"I don't think so. He could be dangerous," Paul said in his most official tone.

As if he could hear through the storm, the dog cocked his head to the side and whined, turning his big sad eyes toward Paul and pressing his nose against the window. Chris erupted in a fresh fit of laughter. With a resigned sigh, Paul walked over to the door and unlatched it. He didn't have to invite their fellow traveler in. With one bound he was across the room and had thrown himself into Chris's lap, at least what of him would fit, and began licking her face in earnest.

"Okay, okay," she said between giggles and licks. "That's enough. You're very welcome."

The dog promptly stopped and dropped his head into her lap with a sigh. She looked at the big brown eyes that looked at her so adoringly and wondered why she could engender such affection from an animal while his human counterpart seemed so bent on ignoring her.

"Yes, I think he is just as ferocious as they come," Chris said, her lips curving into a smirk.

Paul rolled his eyes and went back into the kitchen. After a few moments of digging, he brought a bowl of water and the leftovers from their makeshift dinner to the fireside. The dog regretfully left her side as if only the pangs of near-death hunger could tear him away. Paul shook his head, a smile slipping from him. She was beginning to think God had sent this dog to save them from themselves, or at least as a referee. As soon as he had licked the bowls clean, the dog reclaimed his spot on Chris's lap, totally ignoring Paul.

"Well, I guess we can see who his favorite is."

"He knows an animal lover when he sees one. What should we call him?"

"He's a stray. Look, no collar, no nothing."

"So?"

"So, when they pick us up, I'll take him to the pound. There's no need to name him or get attached."

"Maybe I want to be attached," Chris said hotly. She cuddled the dog's head close to her own. "I'm going to call him Silver since his fur is that color."

"Oh, brother, here we go again."

"What are you talking about?"

"You get too attached to things. You're always trying to rescue something."

"What's wrong with that? I feel sorry for them. All they want is to be loved."

"You can't save them all."

"No, but I can save this one."

"I give up. Have it your way, but how are you going to get that thing home?" he said pointing to the dog who had now climbed completely on the couch and was hogging the blanket.

"I'll think of something."

"Whatever. I'm going to make some coffee. It's going to be a long night."

"Just ignore him," Chris whispered to the dog. "He's an old grouch."

The dog whined in response.

"I heard that," Paul said from the kitchen.

"Good."

Chapter 4

C hris must have dozed off because when she opened her eyes, the darkness was almost complete. Paul must have put out some of the lamps to conserve fuel because the only light in the room came from the fire and a small lamp on the table in the kitchen. Silver was snoozing hard, having stolen more than his share of the covers. At first, she couldn't find Paul, but then she saw his outline leaned against the window, looking out at the storm.

"Why don't you get some sleep?" she whispered.

She had no idea why she felt compelled to speak so softly. Maybe it was the storm or the hour or the dog asleep on her leg—the dog that was cutting off her blood supply.

"Need to keep the fire going."

"I can take a turn now."

"Not with that ankle."

"It's not that far to the fire," she said, exasperation edging her voice. "The firewood is right there."

"I'm fine. I'm not sleepy anyway."

The last statement was probably true. In the last few months of their relationship, he had only slept a few hours a night. Chris had never been able to get him to tell her what was wrong. He would just shrug his shoulders and sulk in silence. That was the one thing she didn't miss about their relationship.

"Have it your way. You always do anyway."

The last part she muttered under her breath, but from the way his shoulders tightened, he must have heard her. She didn't know how to get through to him, and she had just about lost the will to care if she ever did. She stroked Silver's fur and tried to find a comfortable spot so that she could sleep away this nightmare. Just as she was about to doze off, a loud thump from the back room brought her wide-awake. Silver jumped up, a growl coming from low in his throat. He took a protective position between her and the sound and was soon joined by Paul, armed once again with his trusty flashlight.

"Don't they give you guys real weapons?" she whispered.

"Hush!"

Paul turned the flashlight around and turned it on, pointing the beam in the general direction of the sound. Right now Chris wished he hadn't been so quick to turn the lamps off. She pulled herself up to a crouched position on the couch and followed the motion of the flashlight. She squealed when the light reflected off another set of eyes, but then she laughed when she realized their visitor was only a raccoon.

"How did he get in here?"

"How do you know it's a he?"

"I don't. It's just an expression. Nobody cares."

"I'm sure it's very important to the raccoon."

As if to prove her point, the raccoon stood on its hind feet and proceeded to cast aspersions in the form of high-pitched squawks in Paul's direction. He held up his hands in surrender.

"Sorry."

The raccoon dropped to all fours and waddled over to the mudroom door. It looked from Paul to the room and back again. In the meantime, Silver stood still with his head cocked as if assessing the situation.

"Come here, Silver. Leave the poor raccoon alone. He's stuck out here just like us."

Silver cocked his head to the other side for a moment before returning to a spot near the fire. He lay down with his head resting on his front paws. The raccoon continued to look at Paul like he was the intruder. When Paul didn't immediately leave, the animal stood up on its hind legs and once again began a series of squawks and whistles that almost sounded human.

"Paul, give him something to eat! Maybe he'll go away."

"We're not supposed to feed the animals. It makes them dependent on humans."

"Well, Ranger Smith, I think these are extenuating circumstances."

After a few moments of looking from Chris to the raccoon and back, Paul sighed and opened the cabinet. He pulled out a can of something and poured it into a bowl, placing it an arm's length away from the animal.

"I don't think he's going to bite you," Chris said, slightly amused at Paul's defensive posture.

"He might. Besides, raccoons often carry rabies."

"He's not rabid, for goodness' sake."

"How do you know?"

"He doesn't look rabid. He was just cold, like the rest of us, and looking for a little shelter from the storm."

Paul folded his arms across his chest and watched the raccoon wolf down the bowl of food, even to the point of licking the bowl. Then, he proceeded to give himself a bath, totally ignoring Paul. When he finished, he shuffled back to the mudroom at the back and curled up in an old blanket lying near the door. It had obviously been used before.

"It looks as if we are the ones intruding instead of him," Chris said.

"Well, it's certainly not his first time around humans. It looks like one of the guys has been feeding him on a regular basis."

"I told you he didn't have rabies."

"Whatever."

He added a log to the fire and then returned to his post by the window. Crossed arms and a rigid back were an all too familiar sight. She decided that the raccoon and Silver had the right idea. Maybe a little sleep would put everything into perspective, or at the very least make the moments pass by a little faster. With a sigh, she curled up in the corner of the couch again, leaving the end free.

"You should straighten out and put that ankle up."

"It's not hurting. Besides, you have to rest sometime."

"I'm fine."

"No, you're not. I know when you're tired, and right now you are nearly exhausted." She pushed the blanket aside and took a closer look at the couch. "Look, this is a futon."

She struggled with a rusty latch with no luck. Just as she

raised up to ask Paul for help, she felt and heard the crack of bone against bone. Paul grunted and staggered back.

"Nice shot," he muttered.

"I wasn't aiming at you." She rubbed the back of her head while he did the same to his jaw.

"Why don't you just stand over there," he said, pointing to the fireplace, "and I'll see what I can do."

With a few swift moves, Paul had the futon fully extended. It opened into a full-size bed, although it was by no means expansive. She pointed toward the side nearest the fire.

"You can have that side. I'll take the other side. That way you can get up and see to the fire. The bar in the middle can be the dividing line."

"You are not going to shut up about this until I lie down, are you?" he asked in a resigned tone. He already knew the answer.

"Of course not."

"Fine." He lay down, curling his long frame onto his half. "Happy now?"

"Yes."

She took her blanket and curled up on the other side, facing the kitchen. She wrapped the blanket snuggly under her chin and settled in.

"Chris?"

"Yeah?"

"Thanks. And happy birthday."

Moments later, she heard his steady breathing and knew that he had fallen asleep. All thoughts of sleep had fled with that one phrase. Today she should have been waking up at her parents' house and getting ready for the happiest day of her life.

Today she should have been getting married. Instead, she was lying here, snowbound with the man who had broken her heart on what had become the worst day of her life. She lay there in the silence as the storm subsided outside, but the turmoil in her heart rose to the surface. The tears flowed down her cheeks in silent waves. For what seemed like hours, she grieved for something that she had never had, until exhaustion took its toll and she drifted off to sleep.

Chapter 5

She awoke cold and aching. The futon left something to be desired in more ways than she could count. As her eyes adjusted to the room, she wondered what time it was. With the cloud cover and snow, it was impossible to tell the time of day. The smell of coffee beckoned from the other side of the room, but there was another more pressing matter that concerned Chris at the moment. Last night she really hadn't looked around at all. Her ankle had hurt too much, and she had been too cold and tired to explore the small cabin, but there was no time like the present.

"Coffee?" Paul offered.

"Maybe later."

Chris stood up slowly and gingerly put her weight on the offending ankle. It was still sore, but it felt strong enough to make a tour of the cabin. The mudroom in the back was missing its resident. She felt relieved. Despite her staunch support of the little critter, she had no wish to get too close. Making her way to the only door she hadn't seen into, she prayed it was a bathroom. She had no desire to see what "roughing it" was really like.

"Where are you going?" Paul asked, the frown wrinkling his forehead again.

"Where do you think?"

Now that the immediate danger was past and she had gotten some sleep, his concern was starting to annoy her. She was more than capable of getting across the room without any help or commentary from him.

"Let me help you."

"I don't need any help."

When he reached for her arm, she pushed him away, nearly falling backward. She grabbed one of the wood beams to steady herself. A flutter of wings from above made her hop back to the relative safety of Paul's arms.

"It's just an owl," Paul said quietly. "You probably woke him up."

She looked up to retort, which was a serious error in judgment. For the first time in a long time, the smile on his face made it all the way to his eyes, and she was reminded of the man she fell in love with. He must have read her thoughts because the smile faded and he stepped away. Chris took that moment to beat a hasty retreat to the bathroom before any other natural disasters took place, the greatest of which would be falling in love with Paul Rogers all over again.

Chris doused her face in the cold water, hoping to erase both the traces of her ordeal and the memories that threatened to overwhelm her. She steeled herself, trying to come up with some possible topics of conversation that would leave them in neutral territory. She ran her fingers through her hair and smoothed her clothes while trying to prepare for the day ahead. Taking a deep breath, she opened the door and hobbled to the kitchen for a much-needed cup of coffee. It was already poured and fixed just like she liked it, a little coffee to go with her cream and sugar. He remembered. Quick, think of something else.

"So, do you think we have any more company?"

"I don't think so, but you never know."

"One more critter and I'm going to start looking for an ark," Chris said.

"I don't think we have to worry about a flood. Maybe an ice age," Paul said.

He was looking out at the blanket of snow covering the snowmobile. Only the top half was visible. They would definitely have to wait a little longer. The snow was still falling heavily, although the winds had died down and the clouds seemed a little lighter. Chris moved to his side and looked into the distance. Just then, a break in the clouds made the snow glisten like crystal.

"Look, Paul."

"That's a good sign."

"Just like the rainbow after the flood. God is sending us a little sign of hope."

Paul's snort landed just this side of derisive. Chris looked at his profile, a cold sneer transforming his face into someone she didn't even recognize. What had happened to the warm, loving man of God she had grown to love so dearly?

"What? You don't believe in God anymore?"

"Let's just say I don't have the same naive opinions I once had."

"Paul, I just don't understand what happened. Why won't

you talk about it?"

"Leave it alone, Chris. It's Christmas and your birthday. Let's not dredge up the past. It's over and done with it."

He walked over to the door and grabbed his coat. He bundled up without saying a word. She watched him grab a shovel from the porch and begin to plow a path toward the firewood. It was a futile effort with the snow still falling, but then again, she knew he wasn't out there to be productive. He just wanted to be away from her. The knowledge cut deeper than a knife. She had thought she was over him, but she knew she would never be able to move on until she got some answers. God had put them out here together for a reason. He had gone to a lot of trouble to arrange this reunion, and she intended to get to the answers she needed if she had to hold him hostage here until she did. She was not leaving this cabin until they settled this for once and for all.

Paul stayed outside for over half an hour, but Chris bided her time by checking out the supplies. She was just finishing breakfast when he stomped back inside and slammed the door. Silver raised his head then lay back down when Paul took off his hat and scarf. Paul refused to meet her eyes; instead, he walked over the fireplace and warmed his hands.

"Hungry?"

"A little," he said.

By the tone of his voice, she knew that he was suspicious of her motives. The still small voice told her to wait. She was not patient by nature, and everything in her cried out to know why he had thrown it all away. Why he had thrown her away.

Wait. Now is not the time.

"It's just about ready. I made more coffee. Why don't you have a cup and warm up?"

"Thanks."

As he poured a cup, she put the smorgasbord of canned meat, vegetables, and fruit on the table. It was not the Christmas she had planned, nor the birthday, but she sensed God was trying to do something here that she had been unable to do herself. Her way of doing things hadn't gotten her far, so she was willing to try it His way this time.

"It's ready. It's not much, but under the circumstances I think it's pretty good."

"Smells good," Paul said. After he had filled his plate, he reached for a fork, but she put out a restraining hand. He looked up.

"Shouldn't we pray over the meal? It is Christmas."

He nodded, his face a study in awkwardness. She saved him by giving a short prayer of thanksgiving for the food and the reason for Christmas. He seemed grateful as he ducked his head and ate in silence. This was going to be a very long process for both of them.

When they had finished, Paul surprised her by helping clean up the kitchen. They gave Silver the scraps as a Christmas present, which he greedily wolfed down in short order. He gave the bowl one last lick and then returned to his guard post between the fireplace and the door. Two quick rounds and he was down for the count.

Chris wished that she could lay down her troubles so easily. She racked her brain for something to keep her mind occupied, something to break the tension. She offered up a little prayer for help. Looking around the room, her gaze landed on a stack of boxes on a shelf in the corner.

"Want to put together a puzzle?"

"What?"

"A puzzle. A way to pass the time."

She walked over to the shelf and pulled out a box of puzzle pieces. There was no picture, which could make it more interesting. She took it back to the table. Paul looked confused and relieved at the same time. He quickly cleared the table, and they started separating the frame pieces and sorting the rest into groups by colors. It was something they used to do on rainy, cold days back home. They fell into their old routine without a word. They started at opposing corners and worked their way inward. For once, the silence that fell was not an awkward silence, and she felt no need to fill it with mindless chatter or accusations. There was a peace that transcended the situation. It truly was peace on earth and goodwill to man.

She was surprised at how fast the time flew until she felt her stomach grumbling and looked at the clock. They had been working on the puzzle for hours. Her stomach must have been more vocal than she realized because Paul looked up from the piece he was working on and looked at his watch.

"Hungry?"

"A little." Her stomach growled again, this time louder.

"I'll whip us up something. Why don't you warm up by the fire? After all, it is your birthday."

"Thanks."

This time she really meant it. She hadn't realized how chilled she had gotten sitting near the door. She reassembled the futon into a couch and pulled it back to its place in front of the fire. She stoked the fire and put on another log or two until the blaze regained strength.

"I could have done that," Paul said quietly.

She hadn't heard him approach. He looked disappointed somehow. She took the plate and cup of coffee and sat down on the couch.

"You were busy, so I just took care of it."

He shrugged and she let it drop, but somehow she knew that this moment was important to understanding what was going on in his mind. For the life of her she just couldn't figure out why.

"Why don't I move the table a little closer to the fire?"

"Okay." She moved to get up, but he motioned for her to remain seated.

"I'll get it."

With a shrug, she watched as he carefully pulled the table across the floor so that they didn't lose any pieces. She rejoined him at the table, and they fell back into a comfortable silence. As Chris pondered the significance of his statement, the picture began to take shape.

Chapter 6

At first, Chris didn't recognize the picture, but as more of the pieces were added, she remembered where she had seen this picture before. It was the same puzzle they had been working on six months ago when Paul had abruptly ended their engagement. They had been working on it together, and he had become increasingly silent and uncommunicative. They had fought earlier because she had assembled a wall unit by herself. It seemed like a small thing at the time, a result of tension over the upcoming wedding. Everyone had assured her he was just experiencing nerves and frustration because of the constant tiffs over wedding plans. Now, she wasn't so sure.

Chris had been so proud of the way the wall unit looked and had been making plans to do some other fix-it jobs around the house before the wedding. She had bought the house just a few months before she met Paul. Her father had been in construction, so she knew a lot about repair jobs, especially painting and tile. That was how they had met. She helped her father do a project where Paul was working at the time, and he had been impressed with her skills, especially since she was an instructor at a local college. He thought academic types wouldn't know their way around power tools. That night he had been admiring her work again, but there was a different tone in his voice, something she hadn't heard before.

"I see you went ahead and finished the wall unit," Paul said. His arms were crossed as he looked it over.

"Yeah. I think it turned out well." Chris smiled as she turned on the lamp next to the card table where they had kept the puzzle.

"I thought you and I were going to do that this weekend. Together."

"I know, but I had some free time, so I just did it myself."

"Fine." Paul sat down at the table and picked up a piece. "I guess we can work on the master bedroom this weekend instead."

"I guess."

"What's wrong?"

"What do you mean?"

"Don't get coy with me. Spill it."

"Well." She had hesitated because she had sensed his mood. "I've already hung the pictures."

"What?"

He had gotten up and stalked into the bedroom. He returned a few minutes later and took his seat again. He picked the piece back up without looking at her.

"I thought we were going to keep the bed opposite the window."

"It just didn't look right. Don't you like the way it looks?"

"It looks fine."

They had continued in silence for almost thirty minutes, in which time he had held the same piece in his hand, staring at the puzzle. Suddenly he had thrown the piece down and leaned back in the chair.

"I don't think this is going to work."

"Why, is there a piece missing?"

"No. Yeah! I don't know."

"We're not talking about the puzzle, are we?"

"No."

"You want to rearrange the bedroom?"

"No."

"Then what are you talking about?" Chris could remember the feeling of absolute fear that had taken her breath at that moment.

"I'm talking about us. This." He motioned around the room. "It's not working."

"I don't understand."

"I don't want to get married anymore."

She had stared at him in disbelief as he pushed away from the table, stood up, and walked out the door. She had tried to call him, left sobbing messages on his answering machine until the phone was disconnected. His brother came by and told her that he had moved to Wyoming to work as a park ranger, something he had always talked about doing. Now here they were, doing the same puzzle, yet things were ever so much clearer now. Not 100 percent clearer, but not nearly as black. He had been trying to tell her something that she had refused to hear.

"You've been holding that piece in your hand for the last

five minutes. Do you need a little help?" he asked.

"Hmm?"

"Do you need help with that piece?"

"Yes. I think I do."

She handed him the piece, and he quickly found its home without any trouble at all. The answer had been right in front of her the whole time. She needed to find a way to get him to tell her how he felt that night, to get it out in the open so they could work through it, because she knew that despite everything she had said, she was still in love with Paul Rogers. When he left that night, he had taken her heart with him, and she had never gotten it back. The question was how. How was she going to get him to open up? She lifted up a little prayer and went back to the puzzle before her.

By nightfall, the puzzle was finished. One thing was sure; it had helped her pass the day and then some. She was running out of time. The snow had stopped sometime late in the afternoon, which meant they could probably leave first thing in the morning. She needed more time. If she didn't get him to open up before they left this cabin, she was afraid she would never get the chance again.

A high-pitched series of squawks emanated from the radio sitting on the kitchen counter. Paul came out of the bathroom in three long strides, drying his hands on a towel as he went. He snatched up the radio and turned up the volume.

"Base to Rogers. Base to Rogers."

"This is Rogers."

"What's your status?"

"We're fine. The snow has stopped, but we'll have to dig out the snowmobile before we can get out of here tomorrow. I'm sure Chris's snowmobile is completely buried in the snow. Plus, mine's almost out of fuel."

"How's your food and fuel supply?"

"It's fine. There's enough firewood and kerosene for several more days. Why?"

"Well, the temperature is taking a nosedive overnight. It's going to be frigid tomorrow. You'd be better off staying put another day instead of risking getting stuck out in the weather and getting frostbite."

"I see." Paul seemed to be weighing the situation.

"I think he's right, Paul. Another day won't hurt," Chris said quietly.

He looked up at her, surprise evident in his features. She had never been one to sit still and be quiet for anything. Once upon a time, another day trapped in a cabin with nothing to do would have sent her into fits. He nodded and gave her a wan smile.

"We'll stay put, sir. I'll check in again tomorrow for an update."

"Roger that. Talk to you tomorrow. Out."

The radio squawked once more then was silent. Paul returned it to the counter and looked at her, shrugging his shoulders.

"Well, I guess we're stuck here for another day and night."

"Could be worse."

"Yeah." He looked at the setting sun. "I better go get some more wood now before the temperature drops any more."

"I'll start dinner."

"Great."

He looked as if he might say more, but then he grabbed his coat and bundled up. The blast of cold air as he opened the door was much cooler than it had been during the storm. Silver took the opportunity to go out, but he soon returned to his place by the fire. It was too cold for even the dog. She shivered and then turned to the kitchen to see what was left. Paul made a couple of trips, loading the woodbin until it was above his waist. By then, she had disassembled the puzzle and set the table with another gourmet meal.

Dinner was a much more amiable affair than the previous meals, with a comfortable silence instead of the usual tension. Paul even managed some small talk about the status of the snowmobile. While Paul cleaned up the dishes and fed Silver, Chris did some more digging in the mudroom. Now that their little friend had moved on, she felt more secure. She pulled back a tarp and found a folded cot and a couple of sleeping bags in plastic bags.

"Hey, Paul. Look."

"Hey, this is great. If this cot works, then maybe both of us can get a good night's sleep tonight."

He took the cot and assembled it near the futon. He gingerly sat down on it, testing it with his weight. When he sat down, the frame held, but the center sagged a little. She giggled.

"What?"

"You look like you're sitting at a kiddie desk." He laughed then. The first laugh she had heard from him in a long time. "I think I'd better take the cot."

"You may be right."

They soon had the sleeping bags opened up near the fire to

air out and warm up. They fixed the futon again, and then they both looked around. It was only seven o'clock. Even with the early darkness, it was still way too early to go to bed.

"Now what?" Paul asked.

"I don't know. Let's see what else is on the shelf."

A little digging unearthed a pack of playing cards, a couple of board games, and another puzzle. She looked at Paul.

"I think it's a little dark in here to do the puzzle. We can save that for tomorrow. How about a game of Scrabble?" Paul said.

"Sounds good to me."

They pulled the table closer to the fire. Silver sat down next to her chair and leaned against her with a low bark that was more like a howl. She stroked his silky fur, but he pushed her hand away and let out another low bark.

"I think he needs to go out," Chris said.

"Of course he does. I'll take him."

While Paul was gone, Chris set up the board and put on a pot of coffee. It didn't matter if they stayed up late tonight or not. They had no plans for tomorrow, so they might as well enjoy the moment. She watched him roughhouse with Silver as they came in, and she realized yet again how much she truly loved this man. Now, if she could only figure out how to reach him. Today had been a step in the right direction, but she had to get him talking if they were ever going to make peace with their past.

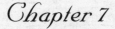

Chapter 7

They were well into their second pot of coffee when they finished their first round of Scrabble. For the first time ever, Paul had beaten her, but not because she hadn't tried. However, she had been a little distracted trying to think of some way to get him talking.

Patience.

Chris hated that word with a passion, mainly because she didn't have any. Paul, on the other hand, had the patience of a saint. He once waited over an hour to talk a scared kitten out of a storm drain when it was beyond his reach. He had taken the kitten home with him, but she had never heard any more about it.

"Paul, whatever happened to that kitten you rescued?"

"What?"

"The kitten you rescued from the drain. What happened to it?"

He quickly tried to cover the shock by finishing his turn. When he looked back up, he shrugged.

"I took him home. His name is Rocky."

"Do you still have him?"

"Yeah. He's almost a year old, but he's still quite the kitten. I hope he didn't tear up my apartment while I was gone."

"Why didn't I know you kept him?"

"Because I didn't tell you."

"Why?"

"I don't know." He shrugged and looked into the fire. "You got all bent out of shape when I suggested you keep it at the house, so I decided to take it home with me until I could find it a good home. When we split up, I decided to keep him."

"I'm sorry."

"For what?"

"For a lot of things, but I'm sorry I just dismissed the idea of keeping the kitten without thinking about what you wanted."

He shrugged, but she could tell it meant something to him that she had apologized. She wondered how many other things she had failed to see because she hadn't taken the time to listen. Even though Paul didn't say a lot out loud, he said a lot with his body language.

"Where are you living now?"

"I have an apartment in town. Really, it's just a room over a garage, but it'll do for now. I want to save up and buy some land and build a house."

"Here?"

"Not necessarily."

"Why not?"

"I don't want to be a park ranger forever. It was just something I wanted to try."

"Oh."

The conversation waned as the game ended, and Paul got up for another cup of coffee. She stared into the fire, another memory starting to surface. They had been talking about their dreams for the future when he had brought up the subject of working in Wyoming or Montana for a season or two. She had quickly dismissed it as a silly idea and then asked what he really planned to do with his life. What else had she missed?

"Want another cup?"

"Yes, but I'll get it."

"I got it."

She smiled and accepted his offer with what she hoped was more grace than she had previously showed. She had spent the last six months angry with Paul, thinking he had dumped her for another woman or something just as bad, only to realize that she was the reason he had left. The wall unit and bedroom had just been the last brick in a wall she had been building between them. She wanted to crawl into bed and cry into her pillow, but she didn't have that luxury right now.

"Penny for your thoughts," Paul said quietly as he handed her the cup.

"Just thinking about the past."

"Oh. Good or bad?"

"A little of both."

"That's the way, isn't it? Good and bad mixed together. We just pray that the good outweighs the bad."

He took a sip of the coffee, and she followed suit, but not because she wanted more coffee. She just needed something to do. Maybe she needed to take up knitting or needlepoint, something to do with her hands. Maybe then she could calm down and see what was going on around her.

"What do you think about knitting?"

"Knitting?" He stopped with the mug halfway to his mouth, one eyebrow raised.

"I was just thinking of taking it up. Right now would be a great time because I would have something to do, and it would help keep me warm."

"Are you cold?"

The concern in his eyes was almost her undoing. He had done nothing but try to take care of her. Even that warning yesterday morning had been out of concern. How could she have been so blind?

"A little."

"I'll stoke up the fire, add some logs. Maybe you should curl up in the sleeping bag. It's almost midnight."

"Maybe you're right." She put her mug down on the table and headed toward the bathroom. "I'll just be a minute."

She closed the door behind her and willed the tears that were forming at the back of her throat to go away. She would have to keep it together until she could get out of this cabin. Suddenly, another day with Paul sounded like sheer torture. After getting ready for bed as best she could under the circumstances, she splashed cold water on her face to cover up the telltale signs of tears before going back to lie in the bed she had made for herself—a very lonely one.

"I've got the sleeping bags ready. They're nice and toasty."

"Thanks."

"It was nothing," he said with a shrug.

"No, I mean thanks for everything. For coming to get me

and taking care of my ankle. I know I didn't act like it, but I am grateful."

"That's okay."

"No, it's not. I just wanted to say I'm sorry."

He nodded but didn't respond. He was embarrassed by her apology. It was evident in the way he ducked his head and looked into the fire, anything to avoid looking her in the eye. She wanted to fill the awkward silence, but nothing came to mind. The only option left was to go to bed and feign sleep, because heaven knew that she was beyond sleep right now.

"Well, good night," Chris said.

"Good night."

She took off her boots again and climbed into the warmth of the flannel-lined sleeping bag. Thankfully, the beds were turned so that both faced the fire without facing each other. Relief washed over her as Paul put out all the lamps except one and went into the bathroom. It was a short-lived feeling as he soon returned, taking his place on the futon. She willed herself not to move until she heard his breathing change, and then she relaxed slightly. She wanted to toss and turn, but the cot was too squeaky for such an enterprise. It was going to be a long night.

Lord, what do I do now?

"Let go."

That was not what she wanted to hear right now. She wanted to hang on with every ounce of her strength. Losing him was bad enough, but actually knowing that she was the reason he had left was almost worse than not knowing why. It was plain and simple. She didn't deserve him. She had one more day with Paul, and she would make it one to remember. If nothing else, she wanted to make it up to him for the way she had treated him.

Lord, show me what to do. Show me how to make it up to him.

God was silent. Maybe the answer was that there was no answer. Maybe she had just gone too far to ever get back. There were some things that you could never take back. She turned toward the wall, away from Paul's cot, and stifled the sound of her breaking heart.

Chapter 8

The sun shone brightly through the window and warmed her face. Chris turned over to get away from the glare, but could find no relief. Prying open one eye, she looked out the window. It was late. She had lain in bed for hours, trying to hold back the tears, to stop thinking about what she had lost. This was her last day with Paul, and she was wasting it here in bed. That is if you could call this thing a bed.

"About time you woke up, sleepyhead," Paul said from the kitchen. He picked up a cup of coffee and fanned the steam in her direction. "Want some? Then you're going to have to come and get it."

That was the Paul she remembered. He gave her one of his devastating grins before putting the coffee cup down on the counter. With a groan, she pulled herself up and pushed away the covers. She didn't feel as bereft of the covers as she thought she would.

"Is it warmer in here, or is it just me?"

"It must be you because the temperature certainly hasn't gone up."

"Maybe it was just wishful thinking."

"Or the fact that I had just stoked up the fire and added a log."

The farther away from the fire she got, the colder it got. It had been wishful thinking. The howl of the wind around the cabin sounded like something from a haunted house. She shivered and then picked up the cup of coffee. Just as Chris was about to take a sip, Silver nudged her from behind. Coffee splashed down the front of her fleece sweater.

"Great! Like I didn't already look bad."

"You don't smell so good, either," said Paul, wrinkling his nose.

"Thanks."

"I'm just kidding." He put down his cup and rummaged through his backpack. "Maybe one of these will fit," he said.

He held up a sweatshirt and another fleece-style sweater. She sized them up while she wiped off as much of the coffee as she could. She took the sweatshirt and held it up to her shoulders. It could almost double as a dress, but she liked her sweatshirts that way.

"I guess we have a winner," she said. "Does that shower work?"

"I think so, if the pipes didn't freeze up last night. I'll check."

Paul disappeared into the bathroom, and she heard the wonderful sound of running water. She hadn't even thought about a shower yesterday because she'd hoped to be back at the hotel by now. A shower was bound to help her spirits, and a fresh shirt would feel nice.

"The shower's all yours, but there's not much water pressure, and the hot water is not so hot."

"I'll make do. What about you?"

"Try to save a little of the warm water, and I'll take a turn and wear this one."

"Okay."

Chris took a shorter-than-usual shower, mostly because warm water was an exaggeration. She freshened up as best she could, given the circumstances, and had to admit she did feel much better. She grabbed her sweater and tried to rinse out some of the coffee, but it was probably useless without some stain remover. With a sigh, she wrung out the wet spot and went back to the living room.

"Feel better?" Paul asked.

"Yeah, I do, but don't get attached to the term 'warm.'"

"That good, huh?"

"Yep." As he headed toward the bathroom, she said, "Don't scald yourself."

She heard him chuckle as he closed the door. Smiling to herself, she draped the sweater over a chair near the fire then went for more coffee. She stood by the fire, drinking the coffee to warm up again. The moaning wind reminded Chris of what tomorrow would bring, and the smile faded from her face.

"What's the look for?" Paul asked.

Chris jumped. She had been so lost in thought that she hadn't heard him come out of the bathroom. Thankfully, the coffee cup was empty.

"You scared me. We almost had another incident."

She held up the mug for emphasis. He smiled, but it didn't quite reach his eyes. He knew something was up. He always knew when there was something wrong. Too bad she hadn't returned the favor. He grabbed the empty mug as it dangled from her hand and took it to the kitchen for a refill.

"You didn't answer my question. What were you thinking about?"

"Nothing. The wind just sounded lonesome."

"Liar." It was more a statement of fact than accusation. When she didn't respond, he said, "Want to talk about it?"

"Not really. Besides, why would you want to talk to me about anything, especially my problems?"

She hadn't meant to be so bold, but it seemed to make Paul all the more interested. He put down the coffeepot without even filling the cup. He crossed the floor until they were mere inches apart.

"I never said I didn't love you anymore, Chris. I just said I didn't think we should get married," he whispered. The words were almost a caress.

She stepped away from him and faced the fire. If he said one more kind word, she was going to break. It was time to change the subject.

"Why don't we put the other puzzle together?"

"No."

Chris jerked around to face him. She had never heard him use that tone of voice before, or assert himself in a discussion. Usually he was the one to run away from conflict. Right now, she wished she had someplace to run to. Spending a day and night in the bathroom didn't seem very practical. She surveyed the room for another exit, but she kept coming back to the same conclusion. She had nowhere left to go.

"Paul, let's just get through this day," she pleaded.

"No. We have spent too many days just getting through. Let's get this out in the open once and for all or neither one of us will be able to get any peace."

"You don't need to explain why you broke it off. I understand now. So can we just drop it?"

"Okay, if you understand, then you tell me why I broke off the engagement."

"Paul, I'd rather not discuss it."

"Why?"

"Because it hurts too much."

The last words came out in a sob. The tears she had been holding back for days, actually months, rose to the surface. In an instant, he was across the room, holding her close to his chest. She fought feebly to get away, but he held her firmly in place.

"Let it out," he said quietly. "For once, just let it out."

The tenderness in his voice was her undoing. The pain and misery she had been pushing down inside her for months came out in a torrent, sliding down her cheeks. She hated this. Hated being vulnerable. Hated feeling so out of control. Sobs shook her body, and still he held her, quietly whispering soothing words and stroking her hair. He held her even after the worst had passed, only releasing his hold slightly to reach for some tissues. She took them and tried to do some damage control, but she knew she looked a mess. It was what people referred to as ugly crying, when your face gets red and puffy. She needed a moment to collect herself, a temporary escape to the bathroom.

"I'll be right back," Chris said.

"Not this time."

"What are you talking about?" Chris said, looking up to face him. He turned her squarely toward him and leaned down to look into her eyes, his grip firm and warm and unbending.

"You can't run this time."

"Me? I'm not the one who always runs away from conflict." She felt the flush of anger sliding up her neck.

"I don't run. I just choose my fights," Paul said.

"Choose your fights?" Chris was almost yelling now. "You never fought with me. You either gave in or walked away. You never even discussed things with me, much less fought. How many times did I try to get you to talk to me when things were bothering you, and you absolutely refused to talk?"

She could tell she had hit a nerve. His grip loosened and she pulled away. She crossed to the bathroom in record time and slammed the door. Something in the slam sounded all too familiar. How many times had they followed this pattern? One or both of them had walked away at a crucial moment in their relationship, even if it was only for a little while. In a moment of clear revelation, she knew that if they didn't do something to change their pattern right now, any hope of reconciliation that she had held on to in the depths of her heart was dead. She splashed cold water on her face, dried it, and then went back into the living room to do battle.

Chapter 9

"Y ou don't get off this easy," she said as she rounded the couch, meeting him at the fireplace once again.

"Get off easy?" Paul looked up from staring into the flames. "Since when I have I ever gotten off easy?"

"Whenever things got difficult, you would crawl into yourself and just walk away. And I let you. I let you get away with it because I thought you needed your space."

"You never wanted to talk, Chris. You just wanted me to agree with you about everything."

"I didn't want you to agree with me all the time, but how was I supposed to know that you didn't when you kept shutting me out?"

Paul ran his hands through his hair and stared into the fire. She was about to speak when he turned back to look at her. It was the same look she had seen many times before. His mouth formed a thin straight line, and his eyes were dark and moody. His body language screamed that he just wanted to be left alone.

"You're doing it again," she said quietly.

"Doing what?"

"Shutting me out. Going into some dark little corner to sulk."

"I don't like yelling."

"I'm not yelling." She forced her voice to stay calm. She prayed to stay calm and keep her patience, because everything in her wanted to scream in frustration.

"You know what I mean."

"No, I don't. I am trying to work out the problem. We can't do that if we don't talk about it."

He leaned on the mantel and continued to run his fingers through his hair. She held her peace a moment. Whenever he was thinking something through, he would play with his hair as if it stimulated brain cells. She missed that.

"How about I go first? I'm sorry. I'm sorry that I didn't pay more attention to what you wanted and needed, but sometimes it's hard for me to know what that is because you don't talk to me."

"We talked all the time."

"Not about things that mattered. We talked about church, sports, and what we were going to do on Saturday. We didn't talk about our future, where we were going to live, if we were going to have kids."

When he didn't respond, she threw up her hands in frustration and crossed to the window, but she didn't see the snow or the blue sky. She just saw a minimovie of their life together going by, headed toward the credits. How could she get through to him?

It hit her like a sudden burst of sunlight after a storm. She couldn't get through to him. The only way that things were going to change was if God got through to him. If He had gotten through to her, surely He could do the same for Paul. But she felt so helpless. There was so little time left.

"Fine. If you don't want to talk, then I can't make you. I'm going to get out the other puzzle."

After she got the box off the shelf, she poured herself another cup of coffee and set up on the table. The air was heavy with tension, so she took a deep breath, a sip of coffee, and prayed that they could find peace. Silver took that moment to come over and lay his head on her knee. He looked at her as if he knew exactly how she felt. She scratched his head and then reached down to hug his warm body.

"What are you going to do with him?" Chris asked quietly.

"With who?" Paul asked, finally looking up from the fire.

"Silver."

"I guess I'll have to take him to the pound."

When she stroked the silky fur of his head and looked into those big brown eyes, she knew that she couldn't let Paul take him to the pound. She had a big backyard. The trouble would be getting him home.

"I'll take him."

"What?" Paul asked, clearly confused.

"I said I'll take him."

"You hate owning pets."

"No, I don't," she said with a frown.

"Anytime I brought it up, you shot it down."

"I didn't like it in theory, but this is different."

"How?"

"I'm already attached. He's got a name and everything."

Silver watched the exchange like fans at a tennis match. He finally stopped and looked at her, head tilted to one side as if he too were questioning her. She leaned down closer to Silver.

"Do you want to come home with me?"

One short yelp that was not quite a bark confirmed what she already knew. Silver was her dog now. He had been since the first night. If she couldn't have Paul, at least she could have company.

"That settles it. He's coming home with me, so I'd better not hear you say anything else about the pound."

"All right, all right," he said, holding up his hands in surrender. "He's your dog, but I still don't see how you're going to get all four of you, your luggage, and the dog in your four-door sedan."

"I'll figure something out."

"Whatever."

He shook his head as if to free himself from any further thought or obligation and turned to stare into the fire again. Chris turned back to the puzzle and began pulling all the pieces out, sorting out the frame as she went. By the time she had it all set out, Paul had taken his place across from her.

"Now you come over here, after I've already done the boring part."

"Yeah, well, this beats staring at the fire or fighting. We might as well make the best of it."

"Fine," she said, sighing in resignation.

There was no sense holding a grudge about him not being willing to fight when the whole point was to settle their differences so that she could move forward, one way or another.

Chris pushed a stack of pieces that went on his side of the puzzle and concentrated on the piece of blue sky in front of her. She whispered a silent prayer as she worked on the frame that God would show her what she needed to do.

"Nothing."

She hated when He answered like that. "Nothing" was her least favorite answer of all time. She wanted to be able to do something, take action, be in control.

"Take it a piece at a time."

Chris looked at the piece of sky in her hand, glancing over to Paul. One piece at a time. She found a home for the bit of sky and picked up another one. The rest of the morning passed in a gentle silence as each new piece found its place in the picture. She wished her life could be put back together so easily. After a while, she lost herself in the process and was surprised when her stomach growled.

"Hungry?" Paul asked.

"What was your first clue?"

He smiled, and she wondered at how they could go from fighting to such light teasing in a matter of hours. Still, the problem lay just below the surface, waiting for an opportunity to rise to the top.

"Let's break for lunch."

"Sounds like a plan."

They fell into their routine. She put on the coffee while he dug something out of the cupboards to heat up on the kerosene stove. As the coffee began its slow but steady drip, she went to the fireplace and stoked the fire, adding a few pieces to keep it going. She hoped tomorrow's temperatures were much higher than today. She didn't look forward to a ride on the snowmobile in this weather.

"How's it coming?" Chris asked when she joined Paul in the kitchenette.

"Slow but sure, just like the coffee."

"Nothing gets done in a hurry around here."

"Nope. That's why I like it here."

"Are you planning on staying here forever?" Chris asked.

"No. It was just something I wanted to do for a while before I had any responsibilities." He stopped suddenly and turned back to the stove as if the fate of the world rested on stirring the soup.

"How long are you thinking of staying?"

"I don't know," he said with a shrug. "Probably just until summer, when the interns come."

"What are you going to do after that?"

"I'm not sure. Maybe go to work for search and rescue."

"You seem to be pretty good at that. You rescued me even when I didn't listen to you."

"Well, you always did like to jump in first and ask questions later," Paul said with a smile that took the sting away. "I admire your sense of adventure."

"Even when it lands you in a remote cabin in a snowstorm?"

"Not so much, but I'll let it slide this time."

"Rogers, this is base. Do you copy?"

Chapter 10

They both stared at the radio as if it were an alien invading their world. Chris suddenly lost her appetite. She had a sinking feeling that said this was not going to be good news. Paul picked up the radio just as it keyed up again.

"Rogers, this is base. Do you copy?"

"Yes, sir."

"I've got good news. It looks like the weather is improving. You can get out today."

"I'll have to dig out my snowmobile."

"Don't worry about it right now. We'll come back for it later. There's a rescue team in the vicinity that's no longer needed. They'll swing by and pick you up within the hour."

"That is good news, sir."

Somehow, Paul's voice lacked the conviction she expected. He seemed almost as reluctant as she did to leave. They were just starting to make progress. Chris walked over to the fire, no longer interested in lunch. She only half heard the rest of the conversation. She wrapped her arms around herself, unable to fend off the cold chill of disappointment.

"Well, that's that. We'd better eat a quick bite and clean up so that we'll be ready to go as soon as they get here."

"Okay."

She forced the food down her throat, answering Paul's small talk with one-syllable responses or a shrug. They cleaned up the cabin and gathered their belongings by the door. Paul took care of the fire, unwilling to put it out completely until their rides arrived. The sound of the patrol pulling up brought a surge of emotions that threatened to overwhelm her, but she swallowed them down.

"How are we going to get Silver back?" she asked, suddenly aware that they hadn't considered the issue.

"Not a problem. They brought a snowcat. We can ride on the inside instead of out in the weather."

"Oh."

She didn't want to sound ungrateful, but she had looked forward to riding back with Paul. Now there was no time to say anything, as the driver of the snowcat stomped into the cabin. Suddenly, the building seemed too small. Her spirits plummeted as she realized her chance was gone.

"You guys ready to go?"

"Yeah," Paul said, a little too quickly for Chris's liking.

"Sure."

"Miss Jennings and the dog can ride with me. I'm headed back to the gate." The driver, Hal, motioned toward another rider getting off of a snowmobile. "Dan's going to help you get your machine out, so you can take it back in."

"What about my rental?" Chris asked.

"We'll take care of it," Hal said with a broad smile. "No

need to worry your pretty little head about it."

Chris tried not to bristle at his attitude since she was grateful not to have to go out in this weather again. Hal headed out the door and motioned for her to follow. She turned toward Paul, looking for any sign that he might want to continue rebuilding their relationship, but he busied himself talking to the other ranger who had come inside.

"Bye, Paul," she said.

He turned and looked at her, and for a moment she thought he would say something, but he gave her a little wave and weak smile.

"Are we going or not?" Hal said from the doorway.

"I guess we're going," Chris said. "Come on, Silver. Let's go home."

The ride back to the park entrance was much smoother but not any quieter. Hal talked a blue streak, but she was grateful since he didn't require any response. She stared at the magical snow world outside, but she didn't take it in. She would say her heart was breaking, but it had never healed to start with. The girls were waiting for her at the main gate. They squealed in delight as she climbed out of the contraption and then in shock as Silver followed quickly on her heels.

"Oh, Chris, we were so worried. Was it horrible being stuck in the cabin with him?" Deidre asked.

"Let's not get into this here," Vanessa said, pulling Chris toward her rental. "Let's get you home to a hot shower, some fresh clothes, and some good food. We'll order in tonight."

"Fine," Deidre said, "but then you have to tell us every detail."

"She'll tell us when she's ready," Jessica said, wrapping her arm around Chris's free side. She leaned in to whisper in her ear. "You don't have to talk about anything."

"Thanks."

Chris crawled on behind Vanessa, suddenly bone weary. The trip back to the hotel was mercifully short, and Chris went immediately to the shower if for nothing else than to get away from prying eyes. She would have gladly fallen into bed in exhaustion, but she knew Deidre would never let her rest until she at least gave the highlights. At least this way she got a reprieve, she got warm, and she got clean. As the hot water warmed her aching bones, she was also grateful that the hotel manager had agreed to let Silver stay with them even though they had a policy against pets. He had felt sorry for her because of her misadventure. She was pretty sure that Deidre had made it sound much worse than it really was. With a weak smile, she turned off the water and got ready.

"Well?" Deidre said.

"Not right now, Dee," Vanessa said.

Vanessa pulled her into the kitchenette where a steak and baked potato with all the fixings were waiting. Next to it was Chris's favorite: chocolate cheesecake with Happy Birthday written in caramel.

"You guys didn't have to do this."

"We already had the cheesecake, so we just waited until you got back."

"Although we almost had to lock Deidre in the closet to keep her away from it," Jessica said, glaring at Deidre.

"I wasn't that bad," Deidre said. "But it wasn't nice leaving me so long with the temptation."

The girls settled down to eat, and Chris was grateful for the distracting banter. It kept her from thinking of other things. Eventually, she would share the details with Vanessa, but for now she gave them a funny version of what happened, including the bossy raccoon and the talkative Hal. Vanessa gave her a look over her cup of coffee that clearly said she would be looking for more accurate details soon, but she remained silent, ever the best friend.

"I'm exhausted," Chris said between yawns.

"It's only seven thirty," Deidre complained.

"She's hardly slept in three days," Jessica reprimanded. "Give her a break."

"Yeah, Deidre, have a heart," Vanessa chimed in. "Besides, if she goes to bed, you can have another piece of cheesecake."

"Well, I guess that'll do." Deidre slid another slice onto her plate, grabbed her fork, and poured another cup of coffee. "I'll leave you alone and enjoy the spoils in our room. Come on, Jessica."

"Night, Chris," Jessica said, grabbing a fallen chunk of cheesecake as she went by.

"Night, girls," Chris called. When the door shut, Chris slumped into her chair. "Nice save, Vanessa."

"You owe me one."

"Yes, I do. Let me help you with this mess."

"Oh, no you don't. You're the birthday girl." Vanessa gave her hand a playful swat as she tried to pick up a dish.

"My birthday has been long over."

"Maybe chronologically, but time stood still until we knew

you were all right, so really today is your birthday as far as we're concerned. Just sit and enjoy the moment."

"I don't know if I'll ever be able to enjoy the moment again," Chris said as tears dripped down her face.

"Oh, honey. What happened out there?"

"I blew it, Vanessa. It was me, not him."

"What are you talking about?"

For the next hour, Chris poured her heart out to her best friend, including all the horrible realizations she had made about herself. A true friend as always, Vanessa listened without comment and handed her tissues. After an hour of confession, Vanessa only had one thing to say.

"You have to leave it in God's hands now, Chris. If it's in His will, it will be, and if it's not, then He'll help you through it to something better."

It wasn't what she wanted to hear, but it was what she needed to hear. She wiped her eyes, blew her nose, and resigned herself to the way things were. She would wait and see what God would do, even if it meant giving up Paul. They turned out the lights and went to bed. Chris figured it would take hours to go to sleep, but the exhaustion of the last few days hit her as soon as she lay down. She woke to the sun streaming through the window.

"What time is it?" she asked, her voice sounding like she'd swallowed marbles.

"It's almost noon, sleepyhead," said Vanessa. She was standing over her bed, holding a cup of coffee.

"Noon?"

"Well, ten o'clock."

"Where are Deidre and Jessica?"

"Shopping for souvenirs and arguing, I'm sure."

"Oh no. I forgot all about Silver." Chris looked frantically around the room and into the common area.

"Jessica and Deidre took him with them."

She pulled a pillow behind her back, slid into position against the headboard, and relaxed. Taking a sip of the coffee, she tried to reconcile the past few days. It all seemed surreal. In an hour, they had to check out and head for home. She shook her head to clear the cobwebs, but she decided it required a hot shower.

An hour later, the girls had packed the car and checked out of the hotel. They were headed for the diner for one last meal before hitting the road. The hotel manager's daughter had gleefully agreed to dog-sit while they were gone.

"I can't believe our vacation is already over," Deidre complained.

"Yeah, back to the grind," Jessica said.

They each ordered their favorite meal of the week, taking their time over coffee, but Chris was ready to leave so that she could try to get back some normalcy in her life. Maybe a routine would help her gain her footing. Chris chose to drive back since she was wide-awake after her long nap. Besides, driving gave her something to do besides think about Paul. She and Vanessa rode in a comfortable silence while the other two crashed in the back with Silver right in the middle.

The trip was uneventful, almost anticlimactic. Chris dropped the girls off one at a time around five, after stopping in town for dinner. Vanessa had offered to go home with her, but she was ready for some silence. Besides, she had Silver, who was happily curled up in the front seat and wagging his tail to the music. As she pulled into the drive, she noticed an unfamiliar car parked on the street. Winter nightfall had already brought darkness, so she couldn't identify the driver. For one moment, she knew fear. Then, a familiar shape stepped out of the truck.

"Hey, it's me," he said.

"You scared me," Chris said, trying to cover her trembling hands, which had absolutely nothing to do with fear or the cold.

"Hey, boy," Paul said, ruffling Silver's fur. Her companion seemed just as happy to see Paul as she was. "Can I come in?"

"Sure."

"Let me get those for you."

He reached into the car and grabbed her luggage, so she pulled out her keys and unlocked the door. She led the way inside, holding the door for Paul. Without asking, he took them straight to the master bedroom but soon stepped back into the hall with them.

"I'm using the other room."

"Oh." He disappeared into another room down the hall and returned empty-handed. "You're not using the master bedroom?"

"No."

"Why?"

"That was going to be our room." She shrugged. "I just never felt like moving in there."

"Let me take a look around and make sure everything's secure."

"Paul, I know you didn't just drive five hours to check the locks."

"No, I didn't," he said, raking his fingers through his hair. "I didn't like the way things ended in the cabin. We didn't finish our conversation."

"You mean our fight?"

"Whatever you want to call it."

"Look at me," Chris said. "Talk to me."

When he did look at her, she wasn't ready for what she saw there. It took her breath away. It was the same look she used to see when they were first dating, before all the wedding plans and renovations had taken precedence.

"I want another chance for us," he said simply. "If that means we have to fight, then so be it." Several moments lapsed as she tried to take in that he had spoken the words her heart had longed to hear. "So what do you think? Will you give me another chance?"

He stood there with his hands in his pockets, looking like a little boy. He was asking for a second chance when she was the one who didn't deserve one. She took a calming breath and crossed to where he stood in the middle of the living room.

"Give you another chance? Paul, I'm the one who needs a second chance." He looked up, and hope filled his eyes. Yes, and something else.

"Maybe we need a second chance," Paul said, pulling her slowly into the circle of his arms. Time seemed to have reversed, and they were standing at her door on their first date. She felt that same giddy feeling as he lowered his lips to hers and sighed the same sigh as they parted.

"I never really got to say thank you," Chris said.

"For what?"

"Rescuing me."

"Same to you, Christmas Jennings. Same to you."

Epilogue

Christmas Jennings watched from the window as her friends and family gathered in the yard. It wasn't the wedding she had originally planned, but it was the one she and Paul had planned together. The warmth of the sun and a spring breeze blew through the open window and made her veil flutter.

"Are you ready?" Vanessa asked.

"I'm way past ready."

"Well, then let's get this party started," Deidre called from the hallway. "Your dad is waiting downstairs."

All the flowers were blooming in their garden. There was no need for more decorations. She met Paul under a bower he had built just for them. It was a simple, heartfelt ceremony with just their friends and family present. The girls had worn dresses of their own choosing in spring colors, and the groomsmen looked sharp in black suits with ties to match the girls they escorted. It was a compromise from the lavish affair that she had planned for Christmas, but this would be a day to remember.

"So, Paul," her father asked as they sat eating chocolate

cheesecake under a billowing tent, "how do you like your new job?"

"It's great. I get to help with more search and rescue and less answering questions about Old Faithful."

Everyone laughed. Paul looked at her, and she couldn't help but smile. After several months of talking and premarital counseling, they had finally realized that they were only just beginning to understand one another. Marriage was a commitment to grow together and required communication on both sides. She knew it wouldn't be easy, but nothing worthwhile ever was. He leaned in and kissed her sweetly on the lips.

"What are you thinking about?"

"I'm just happy."

"Happy to be married to the best-looking man in town," he said with smile, tugging at his tie and striking a pose.

"I'm just glad for that cabin in the woods. I'd like to go back and visit it sometime."

"The cabin?" he asked, his mouth open in surprise. "Why would you ever want to go back to that cabin?"

"Because," she said with a smile, "that was where God rescued Christmas."

Paul's mouth transformed into a grin. He reached out and pulled her chair close to his and kissed her again until the crowd began to cheer. Rosy-cheeked, she reluctantly pulled away.

"I guess I could take you back there on our anniversary."

"This time next year," she said with a smile.

"No, this Christmas. The anniversary of the day God saved both of us from ourselves."

"Amen."

LINDA LYLE

Linda is a training writer from northeastern Alabama where she resides with her roommate, a Maine Coon mix named Goldie. She is currently working on a PhD in Instructional Design while continuing to write freelance. She recently reached the rank of second degree black belt in tae kwon do as well. This is her fifth published work, and she hopes it's not her last. She is single, waiting for that special man sent from God. In the meantime, she tries to make the most of every day by living each moment to its fullest and writing inspirational stories that she prays will touch others.

Jolly Holiday

by Jeri Odell

"Come to me, all you who are weary and burdened, and I will give you rest."
MATTHEW 11:28 NIV

Chapter 1

L uke Jolly slid into the booth next to his partner, Robert. Adam and Matt took their seats across from them. The metal table between them looked well used and a little beat-up, but at least it fit with the rustic appearance of the place.

"Welcome to Bubba's Bar-B-Que, boys." The waitress breezed by, stopping just long enough to drop off four waters.

Not one of the men picked up a menu. The four firefighters ate together here at least once a week and had for the past several years. They'd all long since figured out their favorites.

"I'll take the full rack of baby back ribs with corn on the cob and Bubba's famous beans." Luke quoted their advertisement.

"Kloie!" A scream pierced the air somewhere behind him. "Help! Someone, please help!"

Luke jumped to his feet. Two booths from his, a woman was pulling a young girl to her feet. The child's face was bluish, and her large brown eyes were bulging slightly and filled with fear.

Luke assessed the situation as he strode toward them. His EMT training kicked into gear. Grabbing the panicked woman by the upper arms, he lifted her up and deposited her a few feet away from the choking girl.

"She's choking!" the woman screamed at him.

Matt grabbed the woman around the waist, her arms flailing. "He knows that, ma'am. We're firefighters. Let him do his job."

Luke stood behind the girl, tipping her forward slightly. Without thinking twice, he balled his right hand into a fist and put his arms around the little girl. He grasped his fist with his other hand, placing it near the top of her stomach, just below the center of her rib cage.

The restaurant had grown quiet, except the woman Matt restrained. She was crying and kept repeating, "Please, help her."

Every eye was on Luke as he moved his fist in a quick, hard jerk, going inward and upward into the child's sternum.

A chunk of meat flew from her mouth, landing near the distressed woman's shoe. The little girl began coughing and wiped her mouth with the back of her hand. Her first few gasps of air were loud and deep. Luke held on to her until he was sure her airway was completely unobstructed and she was breathing unlabored on her own.

Luke moved in front of the little girl, squatting to be on her level. Man was she cute.

"Hi, I'm Luke." He smiled.

"I'm Kloie." She held out her right hand in an adultlike manor. He accepted her shake.

"Kloie." He repeated her name, looking into the biggest, roundest chocolate eyes he'd ever seen. "You feel okay now that you're rid of that foreign-body airway obstruction?"

She nodded. "I do." Perfectly arched brows emphasized her words.

Luke chuckled. "I'm glad." He glanced behind him to the woman who'd been nearly hysterical. "Who's the lady with you?"

"My mom, Holly." Kloie lifted those perfect brows. "She doesn't handle emergencies all that well—especially if I'm involved."

Luke smiled and rose, facing Kloie's mom. Matt released her, and she took the few steps to her daughter. An embarrassed red hue darkened her complexion.

She swept the child into her arms both laughing and crying. "Kloie, how many times—"

"I know. *Take smaller bites.*" Kloie shook her head. "I always forget."

Holly held Kloie tightly against her in a death grip. "Maybe after today you'll remember." She kissed the top of her daughter's shiny brunette head. "I can't bear anything happening to you." She said the words softly and more to herself than to Kloie. Then she loosened her hold on the child and faced him. "Thank you. I'm Holly Olson, by the way." She extended her hand, just as Kloie had done. Their eyes were the same shade, but Holly's weren't nearly as big. A sadness resided in them instead of Kloie's sparkle.

"You're welcome." He reached for her extended hand. "Luke Jolly. And I was just doing my job."

"Boys." The older waitress spoke from behind them. "Your meals are up." She pointed to the empty booth all four fire-fighters had vacated. "Best get to it while it's hot."

Matt, Adam, and Robert nodded and headed back to the

table. Luke's gaze returned to Kloie and her mom. "Guess I'd better get to my ribs before they get cold." He winked at Kloie. "And you, young lady, make sure to take small bites and chew your food well."

Kloie nodded, studying Luke. She drew her brows together. "Are you married?"

"Kloie, that is none of your business." Holly's cheeks were back to red. "I'm sorry. The only question Kloie fears is the unasked one."

Luke laughed. "No problem." He turned his gaze to Kloie. "I'm not married. Are you looking for a husband?"

Kloie nodded. "Not for me, of course." She tilted her head to one side. "I'm only nine." Then she gazed pointedly in her mother's direction.

Now, along with the glowing red, horror filled Holly's face. "Please ignore her. I—I am so sorry." She turned to her daughter and pointed. "Kloie, get into the booth now."

Kloie gave Luke one last pleading glance before she slid back into her seat. Her mother sent an apologetic and embarrassed smile in Luke's direction. Then she slid into her side of the booth.

Luke felt his presence was no longer welcome, so he returned to his friends. They were discussing college basketball, but he didn't join in the conversation. He found himself wondering about the Olson girls. Something about Holly's sad eyes left him intrigued.

Holly's cold dinner held no appeal, so she shoved the plate away.

"I'm sorry, Mom, but he is cute."

Holly sighed. In all honesty, she hadn't even noticed his looks, but he could be the most handsome man on earth and it wouldn't tempt her. She'd made up her mind long ago.

"Kloie, I don't need a husband, and I certainly don't want one. Please do not ever, ever do that again."

"I won't." Remorse filled her precocious daughter's voice.

Holly's thoughts returned to her almost rude dismissal of Luke. Guilt heaped itself upon her. He'd saved Kloie's life, and because of embarrassment, she'd behaved badly.

"Kloie, I'm going to offer to buy Luke some coffee and dessert."

A smile lit the little girl's face.

"Don't get any ideas. It's only a way to say thanks. I do not want to get married again, and I do not want you to read anything into a social nicety. Do you understand?"

Kloie nodded, a sheepish expression on her face.

Holly forced herself to get up and walk to Luke's table. He was just finishing his ribs. "Excuse me. I didn't mean to be rude or ungrateful. May I buy you a cup of coffee and some dessert?"

Luke's grayish blue eyes twinkled as she spoke, so she decided she'd better let him know up front she wasn't flirting. "You can enjoy it here with your friends, but I'd like to treat. Order whatever you like and have the waitress put it on my tab."

Suddenly all three men were scrambling to finish their last few bites.

"I've got to get home to the missus," the one with the curly hair next to Luke said. "No time to wait for you to eat dessert."

"Me, either." The guy with the blue eyes across from him

glanced at his watch. "I'm late."

The last guy left at the table—the one who'd held her in place—shook his head. "He'll have to eat alone." He shrugged. "Or maybe he could join you for dessert."

Luke looked down and shook his head. The other three made their way to the cash register.

"They're subtle as bulls in a china shop." Luke rose. "You don't owe me anything." He pulled his wallet from the hip pocket of his jeans and threw a few bucks down on the table.

Kloie was right. He was cute and tall—at least next to her five feet three frame. Holly fought an inner battle—should she ask him to join them or let him leave? Kloie had turned in the booth and was watching them over the top of her seat. Her eyes pleaded with Holly to ask again.

"Really, it's the least I can do." Holly tipped her head toward Kloie. "Please join us."

Luke and Holly glanced at Kloie. Her brown eyes shimmered, and a huge grin split her face. She nodded ferociously.

Luke's gaze returned to Holly. "How can I refuse?" He followed Holly back to her table and slid in next to Kloie. She glowed with excitement. They perused the menu together and each picked a dessert. Holly opted to take a few bites of Kloie's rather than order her own.

When the waitress left with their pie order, Kloie jumped into a conversation with Luke. "Do you have kids?"

Luke grinned. "No, I'm not married, remember?"

"Some people who aren't married have kids," Kloie informed Luke. "You could be divorced."

Holly was trying to think of something to say to get the

subject off poor Luke and his personal life. Sadly, her daughter was the extrovert of the family.

"When I get married, it will be forever. That's the way God intended it." Luke gazed at Holly. "I'm sorry. I didn't mean to sound condemning. I know no matter how hard some couples try, divorce is inevitable."

"I'm not—"

"My mom is a widow," Kloie said informatively, arching her brow as she spoke. "She believes just like you, and we believe in God, too. When I get married, I'll never divorce. Right, Mom?"

Holly nodded.

"I'm sorry to hear about your husband. Do you mind if I ask what happened?" Luke now focused his smoky eyes fully on her.

"He died in a motorcycle accident during my pregnancy with Kloie."

"I never met my dad."

The waitress handed Kloie her chocolate pie and then set a slice of pecan pie in front of Luke. She handed Holly an extra fork.

"My mom tells me stories about him all the time. She wants me to know him really well, even though I never met him."

Luke smiled at Holly. Two dimplelike lines accentuated his chiseled cheeks. Holly saw admiration etched in his expression.

"He was the best man in the world, huh, Mom?"

"He was."

Chapter 2

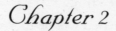

Luke studied Holly. He could tell that his scrutiny made her want to squirm, but she held his gaze. "I'm sure it wasn't easy raising a child alone. Have you been in Jackson long?"

"Almost a dozen years—since right after college. How about you?"

"Just about the same. I worked in Yellowstone every summer and fell in love with Wyoming. I made it my home in my early twenties." Luke took another bite of his pie, savoring the sweetness. He didn't indulge himself often, but he didn't want to refuse Holly's gracious offer.

"Where are you from?"

"California, and I'm guessing you're from somewhere in the South?"

She smiled. "The accent?"

He nodded.

"Sometimes I forget that I'm branded for life by my Alabama roots."

"Alabama? You're a long way from home."

"By choice, I assure you." She glanced at Kloie, and he figured she didn't want to expound.

"Where do you work?" Luke sipped his coffee.

"We sell Christmas trees," Kloie piped up.

He glanced at Holly. She nodded. "It's a temporary gig."

"My grandpa grows them." Kloie licked her fork after her last bite.

"He has a Christmas tree farm in Oregon. This is the first year we've helped him out in this way, but he's had a hard time the past few years finding reliable, honest help."

"Do you have a tree?" Kloie asked, pushing her empty pie plate toward the center of the table.

"Nope." Luke followed her lead, sliding his plate away as well. Only a few crumbs remained.

"Good. You can come and buy one tomorrow." Kloie seemed satisfied with her decision.

"Maybe he doesn't want a tree, Kloie. Most bachelors don't bother with that sort of thing." Holly fixed her gaze on him, daring him to deny the obvious truth.

"Your mom is right. I don't usually decorate."

"But don't you want to this year?" Luke knew her real question: *Don't you want to see us again?* He studied her a moment and then focused on her mom. Yeah, the truth was he did want to see them again. He'd somehow like to be the one to erase the deep sorrow residing in Holly's eyes and replace it with joy.

Wow. That thought caught him off guard, but the truth was since Matt and Robert had both gotten married, Luke had started yearning for that, as well.

"Luke, did you hear me?" Kloie shook his arm.

His eyes remained locked on Holly's. "Yeah, I think I'd like a tree this year."

A red hue crept up from Holly's neck, darkening her whole face. She broke the intense gaze they shared, digging in her purse and pulling out a wallet. "Don't be silly. You don't need to waste your money on a tree."

"Yes he does, Mom." Kloie's eyes accused Holly of treason.

"Here's the thing. . ." Luke focused on Kloie. "I promise to come and buy a Christmas tree, if you and your mom promise to help me decorate it."

Glee danced across Kloie's face. "Can we, Mom? Can we?" Her eyes grew rounder as she appealed to her mother's authority.

Luke saw the inner battle Holly fought. For whatever reason, she'd be happy never to see him again. He and Kloie, however, had other aspirations.

"Yeah, please, Mom." Luke joined his request to Kloie's. "It might even be fun." He raised a brow in challenge.

"Why would you even want a tree?" Holly searched his face for a clue.

Because there is chemistry between us, lady, and I want to see where it goes. He felt it when their gazes connected and certainly when their hands collided over the cream pitcher. "Why not?" was all he voiced aloud.

Holly sighed, obviously frustrated that he'd sided with Kloie instead of her. She removed some cash from her wallet and handed it and the check to Kloie. "Why don't you run up and pay this for me?"

Brown eyes danced as she accepted the responsibility. Luke

slid out so Kloie could take the check to the cashier.

"And don't forget your math skills. Check the change," Holly reminded.

As soon as Kloie was out of earshot, Holly began in a low tone, "You don't have to come and buy a tree just because Kloie wants you to."

"I'm not," Luke assured her.

"If you don't normally, then why this year?" Holly's tone had grown exasperated.

"I'd like to see you again." Luke met her gaze head-on. "Both of you."

Holly shook her head. "I don't date."

"Good, because I don't either." And he didn't. "Haven't for a long, long time. Seems dating leads to expectations. Expectations lead to disappointment. From there it's all downhill."

Holly's mouth dropped open. "You're as cynical as I am. Now I really don't get it."

Luke shrugged. "I'd been thinking about getting a tree this year. I won't be going home for Christmas, so thought I might take the plunge."

Kloie returned, her hand wrapped tightly around a few bills and some change. She counted it back to Holly in a most proficient way. "Did you decide yet?" Her round eyes centered on Holly.

Holly glanced from Luke to her daughter and back again. "Let me get this straight. You will come and buy a tree if we agree to help you decorate it?"

Luke nodded.

"We don't deliver, let alone decorate," Holly informed him.

"But, Mom, it'll be fun."

Luke smiled at Kloie—a faithful ally, if ever there was one. "I'll stop by around closing tomorrow and Kloie can help me find just the right tree. Then I'll take you two to dinner—"

"Wait," Holly started to protest.

Luke held up his hand as if to silence her and continued. "You bought me dessert and coffee tonight as a thank-you, so I will buy you and Kloie dinner tomorrow—also as a thank-you for helping me spiff up a tree with lights, decorations, and tinsel."

Kloie was so excited that she bounced up and down in a silent display of solidarity. Then she told him which tree lot was theirs.

Holly shook her head. "I feel I'm at an unfair disadvantage."

Luke smiled and scooted out of the booth, standing at the end of the table next to Kloie. "You are. And last I heard, majority rules." He grinned at Holly and tugged on one of Kloie's braids. "I'll see you tomorrow at the tree lot." With that, Luke was gone, not giving Holly a chance to change her mind.

What are the odds that in Jackson Hole, Wyoming, population eight thousand or so, Luke would accidentally stumble across a Christian woman whose daughter needed his help? Absolutely zero. Luke Jolly didn't believe in luck, karma, or happenstance. He believed in a sovereign Lord who had heard his recent prayer for a soul mate. Yep, there wasn't a doubt in his mind that the Lord Himself put Holly and Kloie Olson in his path.

Holly grabbed the ringing cell phone from her purse. "Hey,

Mel. I'm just getting home. Can I call you back after my Kloie routine?"

"Kloie routine?"

"Bath, book, bed."

"Got it. I was actually wanting to come by. I finally found a gown for the Christmas gala and needed somebody else to agree that it's perfect for me."

"Sure." Holly would love to run this whole Luke thing by her best friend anyway. "Say an hour and a half?"

"Great. I'll see you at eight thirty. And thanks."

Shortly after Kloie was tucked in for the night, Holly heard a soft rap at the door.

"Hey, Holls." Tiny Mel bounded through the open doorway, holding one arm high in the air, keeping her long garment bag from dragging on the floor. She draped it over the couch and unzipped the bag. Inside lay a beautiful red silk evening gown. She carefully lifted it out, raising the padded hanger high about her head.

"Mel, it's beautiful. If it looks as good on, you've got a keeper."

"Are all your blinds closed?"

Holly double-checked. "Yep."

As Mel pulled her green turtleneck sweater over her head, Holly shared with her the events that unfolded earlier that evening.

Mel wore her no-nonsense expression. "A good-looking fireman—and frankly have you ever seen an ugly one? Anyway, let me recap." She slipped the dress over her head. "A great-looking, single—no ex-wife, no kids—guy saves Kloie's life and wants to take you to dinner?" Mel drew her lips together and raised her brows. "And your objection is?"

"You know my stance on dating."

Mel turned around, and Holly zipped her up. "Until Kloie is grown, I have one focus—her."

Mel turned around and held her arms out.

Holly sucked in a deep breath. "It's gorgeous." She smiled. "Definitely a keeper."

Mel twirled around once. "I've asked you from the beginning—is your rule self-imposed or God-directed?"

"At this point, does it even matter? We are moving to Oregon in one month."

"Have you told Kloie yet?" Mel asked in a quiet voice.

Guilt wrapped itself around Holly like a blanket on a cold day. "No."

"Holly, you've known for months. When do you plan to tell her? It affects her life, as well." Mel always got exasperated with Holly because she avoided hard issues rather than just facing things head-on.

"I thought I'd tell her once school lets out. That way she won't have a dark cloud hanging over her these last couple of weeks."

Mel grabbed her hand and dragged her to the plump armchair that matched her red sofa. "Sit here and think about this. When will she tell her class good-bye? What if the teacher wants to have a party in her honor? You can't do that to her."

Holly laid her head back against the chair, closing her eyes against the tears, but one slipped through anyway. The warm liquid rolled down her cheek.

"I'll talk to her teacher this week and ask the best way to handle it." When Holly opened her eyes, relief had washed over her friend's expression.

Mel grabbed Holly's hand and squeezed. "You don't have to go, Holly. I know you could find a job in another gallery. Why won't you try?"

"I promised Kenton's dad that if he'd loan me the money to make my house payment until it sold, I'd move to Oregon. If I don't keep my promises, how can I expect Kloie to? Besides, doesn't God say—"

"I know. I know. Let your yes be yes and your no be no."

Both women laughed.

"I'm going to miss you so much." Mel bent over and hugged Holly.

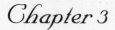

Chapter 3

Holly spent the day both anticipating and dreading Luke's visit to the tree lot. When the bus dropped Kloie off after school, the first words out of her mouth were whether or not Luke had been by yet.

"Not yet. I imagine he'll be by about the time we close since he asked us to dinner."

The afternoon got busy, so neither had time to think about Luke. Sure enough, about half an hour before sundown, a loud, tall, souped-up four-wheel-drive parked in front of the tree lot, and Holly knew instinctively that Luke was the driver.

As he climbed down, Holly's heart thudded against her rib cage. Kloie was right. He was cute. And muscular. And tall. And everything appealing.

Their eyes met. He smiled. She returned it. More thudding. She wiped sweaty palms on the thighs of her jeans. He walked closer. His dark hair styled with the front spiked up a little. . . And blue eyes twinkling, flirting, beckoning.

"Hi." He stopped a couple of feet from her, shoving his gloved hands into the pockets of his down jacket.

"Hi." Her brief greeting sounded throaty.

"Luke! You're here!" Kloie ran to meet their guest. She didn't stop until she was hugging him tight around the waist. Then she loosened her hold and reached for his hand.

"I think I've found the perfect tree for you." She tugged on his arm.

Luke glanced at Holly and shrugged as Kloie led him to the other end of the lot.

Holly watched them go, and a pang of longing twisted her heart. *That's how it should have been, Kloie and Kenton sharing moments. Her dragging her dad around by his hand. But for a reason only God knows, that wasn't to be.*

Holly focused on her end-of-the-day responsibilities, not wanting to think about Kenton and the giant hole he left in both her and Kloie's lives. Holly totaled the day's receipts and counted her cash drawer. She could hear Kloie and Luke shuffling through trees, discussing the merits of each one. Holly tidied up and swept needles from under the tent area. Apparently, Luke wasn't willing to settle for any old tree. He told Kloie that he wanted to make sure he got the perfect tree for him. Kloie giggled a lot as she escorted Luke from one tree to the next. The sound filled Holly with pleasure.

At five thirty, she closed and locked the gate then joined Luke and Kloie. "So, which one will it be?"

"Are you rushing me, lady? Because if so, I can go to a different lot." He folded his arms across his chest—eyes filled with merriment.

"I guess you'll have to do just that because Kloie and I have an important dinner date with a handsome fellow." *I'm flirting and I don't flirt. I barely even talk to men!*

Surprise filled his eyes. "You do, do you? I thought you and Kloie had a date with me."

Kloie giggled.

"Precisely."

"So you think I'm a handsome fellow?" He raised a brow.

"Not me so much, but Kloie definitely does."

Kloie nodded her head. "Very handsome."

It occurred to Holly that both mother and daughter had a crush on this very eligible bachelor.

"Okay. This tree it is." Luke traced his steps back to a tall Noble fir—full and regal.

"Good choice." Holly admired the evergreen.

"It was the first tree Kloie led me to, but I had to be certain there wasn't a better one hiding around here somewhere."

"I told you"—Kloie placed her hand on her hip—"that was the best one."

"You did." Luke tweaked her nose. "But now I know for certain. And you were right all along."

"Why is it girls like to be right?" he asked, paying Holly for the tree.

"We just always are." Holly smiled and took care of Luke's money and paperwork then unlocked the gate. He tossed the tree in the back of his truck and opened his passenger door. Once he lifted Kloie inside, he stood aside for Holly to climb in. She had to stretch to reach the running board.

"We're so tall." Kloie buckled the middle seat belt, and Holly checked to make sure it was snug.

"So, where to, ladies?" Luke asked once he was inside the

truck cab and buckling his seat belt.

"You pick—"

"Sweetwater Café," Kloie injected. "It's my mom's favorite."

"Kloie, Luke asked us out, so he gets to choose where he takes us."

"Hey, I asked." He glanced at Kloie. "Sweetwater it is."

The truck was loud, so they didn't attempt conversation on the ride over.

Once they parked and went inside the cozy log cabin that housed the restaurant, Kloie asked, "Is this your favorite, too?"

Luke chuckled. "Nope. I'm more a Bubba's or Mangy Moose kind of guy, but I have a mom who likes this place when she comes for visits."

"Bubba's is my favorite, too." Kloie followed the hostess to their table. Luke and Holly were on her heels.

Luke pulled out Holly's chair while Kloie claimed the one next to her. Luke sat next to Holly and across from Kloie.

"I especially love eating here in the spring and summer when you can sit out on the deck under the big umbrellas." Holly sipped her water.

"My mom, too. So what do you girls do for fun?" Luke looked over the top of his open menu from one to the other.

"We hike a lot. My mom likes to take pictures of animals."

"Wildlife," Holly corrected, laying her menu aside.

"Are you an artist?" Luke closed his menu.

"Not exactly. I dabble, but don't have the time or money to be great."

"So what do you do—when you're not running the Christmas tree lot? For a living, I mean."

"I worked in an art gallery until I was recently laid off." She straightened her silverware. "I'll look for another job after the first of the year." Not a lie. She would be seeking employment. Just not here.

"Which gallery? I mean there are only what—thirty or forty in our little valley."

"Last count, thirty-two." Holly smiled. "I worked for Rosemary Woods at Desert Wind Gallery. Her main medium is photography, though she has done some oils and watercolors."

Luke nodded. "I think I'm familiar with her. Isn't most of her subject matter the southwestern desert?"

Holly nodded. His knowledge of art pleased her. Another point in his favor. *What am I thinking? I'm moving in thirty short days. And besides, I don't do the guy thing.*

❄

The waitress brought their food. Luke offered to bless it before they ate. The gesture seemed to touch Holly.

"My mom and I pray, too, before we eat." Kloie squirted some ketchup on her fries. "Are you a Christian?"

"Kloie. Why don't you let the man eat in peace?" Holly tried to keep Kloie's inquisitive nature reined in.

"It's all right, really," he assured Holly before focusing on Kloie. "I am. Are you?"

Kloie nodded several times. "If you're a Christian, how come you don't believe in Christmas trees?"

"What do you mean, *believe* in Christmas trees?"

"Some kids at my school don't celebrate Christmas because of their religion. They don't believe in Jesus or Christmas or having trees. So I thought you might be a different religion."

Luke smiled at Holly. "No. Christmas is actually my favorite time of the year. I guess because it's just me and I usually go home to California, I just never bother with the things that make Christmas special—like trees. But you, Miss Kloie, have remedied that. However, the sad truth is, I don't have any lights or decorations to put on my tree."

"We can go buy some," Kloie assured him.

"Can I put you in charge?"

Kloie eyes lit up. "Of picking the decorations?"

He nodded and grinned.

"Yes. I would love that!" She got a faraway look in her eye. "Should we have a theme?"

"A theme? For a Christmas tree?"

"Some people do," Kloie stated matter-of-factly.

Luke knew he was out of his league. "Whatever you think, Kloie. You can decide when we get to the store."

"A theme?" He mouthed the words to Holly while Kloie searched in her pint-sized pink purse for who knew what.

Holly nodded and laughed.

"Mom, may I borrow a pen? I seem to have misplaced mine."

Holly handed Kloie a pen. "Lights, ornaments, popcorn, icicles, an angel." Kloie began to write the items Luke would need to hang from his tree. For the rest of dinner, Kloie discussed in detail her thinking on how his tree should look and offered him a variety of theme ideas—everything from Pooh to sports. Luke hoped he didn't end up dreading his decision to put Kloie in charge of his tree committee.

At the end of the meal, Kloie excused herself to use the restroom.

"What have I gotten myself into? I'm overwhelmed by all this tree talk."

"You have created a monster." Holly giggled, a sweet sound that warmed him.

"I just hope I don't end up with a Barbie tree."

"You can set boundaries and draw lines with her. You don't have to give her carte blanche."

"But when I look in those exuberant brown eyes, I forget the word no is even in my vocabulary."

They both laughed, and Holly, who'd seemed very plain to him at their first meeting, was growing prettier all the time.

Kloie returned. "You ready?" She glanced pointedly at her watch.

"We're ready."

Upon arriving at the store, Kloie grabbed a cart.

"Not a good sign," Luke leaned over and whispered to Holly. He caught the scent of her perfume—light, soft, feminine—and he knew he'd remember that fragrance forever. "Do you think she plans to fill the thing?"

"Not if you say no."

"Do you have a dog, Luke?" Kloie held up some reindeer antlers designed to humiliate dogs.

"Nope, no dog."

"Do you like dogs?" Kloie's expression conveyed that this could be a serious character flaw if he answered the wrong way.

"I do like dogs—cats not so much, except as dog food."

"Luke!"

He'd horrified Holly. "Just kidding—about the cat, but not about liking dogs. However, when you work twenty-four-hour shifts, owning a pet isn't feasible."

"Unless you have a family to take care of them while you're gone." Kloie appeared wide-eyed and innocent, but Luke had a feeling she knew exactly what she was saying.

"See any tree decorations yet?" Holly quickly changed the subject.

They walked up and down every Christmas aisle. Kloie looked, touched, and pondered. She'd decided he should have a "boy" tree, so everything was chosen to reflect manliness.

While Kloie perused, he and Holly got to know each other better. She, too, was a sports fan, making conversation easy and impersonal.

"Kloie, it's been forty-five minutes. If we don't get to Luke's soon, you'll have to forgo the decorating altogether because it will be too late."

Kloie stuck out her lip but didn't argue with her mother. That impressed him.

"Good thing tomorrow is Saturday," he whispered, enjoying another whiff of her perfume.

Luke drove Holly and Kloie back to their car, and then they followed him to his place. Knowing Holly liked art, Luke looked forward to her seeing his cabin.

Chapter 4

"I was better off not knowing." Holly ran on the treadmill next to Mel at the local gym. "I mean suddenly, I have this gaping hole in my life. A hole I didn't even know existed until last night."

"I tried to tell you, but you insisted ignorance was bliss." Mel's gaze met Holly's in the mirror.

"It was. I was happy, content—and now I want more. I want a man for Kloie to look up to and for me to laugh with. And I meet him four weeks before I leave town—for good."

"Don't leave, Holly." Mel wiped her brow with a towel. "Stick around and see where this thing might go."

Mel's words exasperated Holly. "You know I can't. I made a deal and have to stand by it."

Mel rolled her eyes. "Yeah, a deal with the devil."

"Mel!"

"Your father-in-law has been trying to control you since the day Kenton died, and you know it."

"Kenton was their only child and Kloie their only grandchild. They want her nearby. I can understand that. Besides, we'll have a nice place to live—a little two-bedroom bungalow on their grounds. Kloie will have access to the pool, the horses, and the tennis court. He even said I could stay at home with Kloie until she's older—if I want to."

Mel turned off her machine and faced Holly, placing her hands on her hips. "I cannot believe what I'm hearing. Listen to yourself. You've been brainwashed. None of those things matter and you know it. You're trying awfully hard to sell yourself on the move, but I know your heart, Holls."

"Maybe they don't matter, but I'm trying to make the best of this. I promised that if he'd loan me the money to make my house payment after the layoff, I'd move. He did and I will. End of story."

Mel shook her head and restarted her machine. "So tell me about last night." Her words were spoken in a resigned tone.

Thinking of Luke made Holly grin. "Well, it was great from beginning to end. He's funny and kind and oh so patient with Kloie. I haven't laughed so much in a long, long time."

Mel smiled.

"You wouldn't believe his cabin." Holly took a sip of water. "It's this darling little A-frame with a loft bedroom. The whole downstairs is open, and though not terribly big, the openness and high ceiling make it feel large."

Holly went on to describe Luke's place down to the tongue-and-groove ceiling and rock fireplace. "And you won't even believe this—he collects art. He's got pieces by Jim Wilcox, Henry Holdsworth, and G. Harvey. Do you remember the cowboy riding with the Tetons in the background? I showed it to you a couple of weeks ago when we walked past Trailside Galleries. Anyway, he owns it!"

"So you guys have a lot in common?"

"I guess we do." Sweat beaded up on Holly's brow, so she took the towel from around her neck and dabbed it. "Which is one more reason to refuse any future invitations. As far as I'm concerned, Luke Jolly is off-limits."

Holly saw Mel's disapproval in the mirror's reflection but, thankfully, Mel had ceased trying to talk Holly out of—or into—anything.

Holly glanced at the large clock on the wall. She slowed the speed on her treadmill to start her five-minute cool down. "I've got to get to the tree lot. I'm supposed to open at ten."

"Is Kloie here in child care?"

"Nope. I dropped her off at Hayden's for a playdate. They will bring her by the lot later this afternoon."

Mel stopped her machine. "Are we okay?"

"Yeah." Holly smiled at her closest friend. "I know you only nag me because you love me." She gave Mel a quick hug. "I gotta run. I'm late."

She rushed home for a quick shower and change of clothes. Then she rushed out the door and made her way to the lot.

❄

"So you like this Holly chick, huh?" Matt asked at the fire station the next day. They were all sitting around polishing their boots and shooting the breeze.

Luke's grin returned. He'd been fighting a terminal smile since last night. "A lot."

"Are the feelings mutual?" Robert buffed the black leather until it shone.

"I think they are. We had a remarkable first date yesterday. We just clicked. Know what I mean?"

Matt nodded. "I might not have a couple of years ago, but I do since I met Karey. So when are you going to see her again?"

"This afternoon." Luke grinned.

"You're on duty," Adam reminded him.

"Exactly. But we need to gas up."

"And she just happens to be at the shopping center across the street." Robert and he thought alike.

"Precisely." Luke closed the wooden box containing his shoe-shining kit.

"What about the rules governing that sort of thing?" their captain asked.

"What rules?" the four guys asked in unison.

"You know—like how long you should wait before calling a girl back. That sort of thing."

"I'm not into games." Luke said the words with conviction. "I'd like to see Holly again, so I'll drop by and let her know just that."

The captain shook his head. "It's not that simple, man. You're putting a noose around the relationship. After today, you and Holly will be a thing of the past. You'll come across as too eager."

Luke really hated that sort of thinking. "What makes you the expert?"

"Years of dating." The captain offered his credentials.

"That's just it." Luke rose. "I don't want to date—I'm ready for more. I look at Robert and Matt and I want what they have. There is a hole in my life, and I'm hoping Holly's the one who can fill it." With that, Luke left the room.

He'd go see Holly today and give her an honest glimpse of his intentions. He wanted to know her better and see if they had a future.

"Hey, Walt." Luke went into the garage where the engineer polished the red fire engine. He loved the old girl, tenderly caring for her and keeping her in top shape. "You ready to make that fuel run?"

While Walt filled both tanks on the fire engine, Luke crossed the street. Holly waited on a customer, and Kloie was nowhere in sight. Luke settled on a bench near the checkout area. When Holly spotted him, she didn't send the smile of welcome Luke expected.

When the family finished their business with Holly, she finally looked his direction. "What brings you by? Surely you're not in the market for two trees." Her tone was polite but cool. She seemed stiff and reserved.

"I just wanted to drop by and thank you and Kloie for the help last night. The tree adds a nice touch to my place."

"As I already said last night, you're welcome. I've thanked you for saving Kloie, you've thanked us for the decorating expertise, I think we're all thanked out and about even." She wouldn't meet his gaze and kept her eyes focused somewhere near his Adam's apple.

Luke rose. "I see." He started to leave, but after a couple of steps faced Holly again. "I had a nice time, Holly."

"Yeah, we did, too. Especially Kloie." She drew her lips

together in a firm line.

Luke nodded his head and looked around. "Where is Kloie?"

"She had a playdate today, but I'll be sure to let her know you stopped by." Holly picked up a broom and walked past him.

He grabbed her wrist. "Holly, wait." This cool, distant stranger had him perplexed.

She spun around to face him, yanking her arm from his grasp. "What?" The word was so curt and so cold, a man could get freezer burn.

"Did I do something to offend you?"

"No, Luke, you were the perfect gentleman." She said it like it was a crime.

Luke hesitated, but then he just decided to blurt out the question on his mind. "What happened to the warm, funny woman I spent yesterday evening with? When I walked you to your car late last night, you kissed my cheek—"

"I was thanking you for a nice evening—that's all. Being from California, I figured you'd be a bit more savvy picking up verbal and nonverbal clues. I kiss my brother on the cheek, for goodness' sake."

He hadn't seen that coming. "I'm really sorry to have bothered you, Holly. It won't happen again." Luke spun around to leave and nearly mowed over Kloie and another little girl. Just then, the fire engine pulled up and Walt honked the deep, loud horn.

"Hi, Luke. This is my BFF, Hayden."

Luke knew by Kloie's wide-eyed look and her subdued welcome that she'd just heard at least part of her mother's tirade. "Hi, Kloie. I've got to get back to work. See ya."

"Wait, Luke. Can we come with you and see the fire engine?"

He smiled at his little buddy. "You'll have to ask your mom." He refused to even look back at Holly. Boy, the captain had been right. Holly had somehow gotten a bad vibe by his showing up here today. Women. No wonder he steered clear.

Chapter 5

Luke kept moving toward the fire truck, not waiting to see if Kloie gained permission to follow. As he climbed aboard, he heard her call out to him. She and her friend were right on his heels.

Walt let the kids climb all over the engine while Luke tried to process what had transpired with Holly. She didn't remind him of a psycho, but maybe she was.

After fifteen minutes or so, Walt explained to the girls that they had to get back to the station.

Kloie gave Luke a hug good-bye. "Do you have a cell phone?"

At his nod, she held out her hand. She entered her mom's number into his phone book. "Just in case." She sounded certain that he'd one day need it. He was just as certain he'd not ever dial that number.

Holly felt horrible. She'd never been deliberately mean to anyone before. Talk about passive-aggressive. She wished she'd handled the situation better. Luckily, a customer showed up and she didn't have time to dwell. Otherwise, she'd have cried her eyes out.

After work that evening, Holly and Kloie drove to Mel's for dinner. Then Mel was having Kloie spend the night so Holly could do her Christmas shopping and get things home and wrapped without a snoopy Kloie around. She'd store the wrapped gifts in the trunk of her car to prevent a recurrence of last year's nosiness. Kloie had unwrapped her gifts, checked them out, and rewrapped them again. Her curiosity knew no bounds.

"Mom, Luke is the perfect man for us." Kloie's wide eyes were confident.

"No, he's not," Holly snapped. Sometimes her daughter was as tenacious as a bulldog. "I don't like him—not one bit."

"How could you be so mean to him?" Kloie questioned while they waited for a traffic light to change from red to green.

Holly hung her head. Her little tirade was bad enough without Kloie witnessing it. "I was wrong, Kloie."

"Then you need to call and tell him you're sorry. That's what you'd make me do."

And a child shall lead them.

"And you told me," Kloie continued her lecture, "even if I don't like someone, I have to be nice."

Holly's conscience pricked. "You're right, Kloie. I do need to apologize, and I'm sorry you and Hayden had to witness me behaving so ugly. Please don't ever act like Mommy did today."

"I won't." Kloie's words carried force and conviction.

When they arrived at Mel's, the neighborhood kids were gathered next door, building a snowman. "Can I stay out here?"

"For a short while, but not too long. It's cold." Holly relished the chance to fill Mel in on the latest without little ears taking it all in. She pulled Kloie's hood up, tied it tight, and made sure her jacket was zipped up all the way. She had on gloves and snow boots, so she should stay warm—at least for half an hour or so.

Holly kissed Kloie's nose and headed up the sidewalk to Mel's front door.

"Where's your shorter half?" Mel asked as she answered Holly's knock.

Holly pointed and entered, removing her coat. She followed Mel to the kitchen. "You won't believe what I did today." Holly gave Mel a play-by-play of her encounter with Luke.

"Wow." Mel's one word carried much astonishment. "You're always so kind to everyone."

"I felt like a caged animal, and all I knew to do was lash out, because truth be told, I like this guy way too much. He's all I've thought about for the last two days."

"Then why are you shutting him out?"

Holly sighed. "We've been over this."

"Holly, maybe your vow not to date is more about you than it is about Kloie." Mel put the lid on her pan and faced Holly. "Maybe you're not willing to risk loving and possibly losing another man. Maybe it's *your* heart you're guarding, not Kloie's." Mel joined Holly at the table, her knowing eyes probing.

Holly's eyes stung, and she blinked to keep the tears at bay. "Maybe you're right." The words had a ring of truth to them.

Holly pondered Mel's words all the way through dinner. One good thing about having Kloie around was Holly didn't have to work at conversation. Kloie kept things rolling.

After dinner, Holly left to get her shopping done. Driving to the mall, she kept wrestling with God over a much-needed apology to Luke. Kloie's lecture kept haunting her. She knew she must practice what she taught. Kloie would ask again.

❄

Luke's cell phone rang while he and the guys watched a game at the fire station. He didn't recognize the name or the number. He walked into the kitchen and flipped his phone open. "Hello."

"Hi, Luke, it's Kloie."

He pulled the phone away from his ear. The caller ID said Melissa Miller. "Kloie, is everything okay? How did you get my number?"

"I got your number today. Remember? When I took your phone?"

"So you not only added your mom's number to my contact list, but you got my number out?" The kid was determined.

"Yeah." Kloie sounded guilty. "I just called to say sorry. My mom feels bad about the way she acted. Will you forgive her?"

Something about this seemed suspicious. "Does your mom know you're calling me?"

"Not exactly. But she's at the mall tonight. Maybe if you could run into her, she could tell you herself."

"Kloie, I'm at work." The buzzer to the front door rang. "I appreciate the apology," *though I'm sure it comes from you and not your mom.* "But I have to go now. See ya." He shut his phone and went to the door. His jaw dropped when he found Holly standing there.

"I know you probably want to slam the door in my face, but can you give me sixty seconds first?"

Luke nodded and let her into the small office area. Holly took a deep breath and made eye contact. She licked her lips and swallowed. "I'm sorry. I know you must have me pegged for some nutcase, and maybe I am, but that ugly woman you ran into earlier this afternoon wasn't me. I mean, it was me, but I don't usually act like that." Her gaze searched his face.

Luke wasn't sure what to say, so he said nothing.

Holly loosened her scarf. "Here's the thing; I'm horrible with conflict—have been my whole life. It's a character flaw. One of many, actually." She paused for a breath. "You are a really nice man. And most of the time, I'm a nice person, too, though I'm sure you struggle to believe that after today. I have never treated anyone with such disregard or disrespect, and God will not let me live with myself until I apologize."

"Okay." Luke shrugged. "I accept your apology." He opened the door, but she failed to move toward it.

Instead, she held up her gloved index finger. "Just one more minute? Please."

He sighed and closed the door, not sure what to think. He knew he wasn't interested in pursuing "psycho woman" any longer.

"I had a wonderful time with you, and if I were interested in finding a man, you'd be at the top of my list."

Luke nodded, really wishing she'd just leave.

"I can't risk falling in love with you."

Maybe it was the way she said it more than the words themselves, but they touched him and his heart opened itself up—just the tiniest bit. And suddenly things were clear. Holly was afraid to love again. She'd closed her heart off like a vacant house and boarded up the windows and doors. But apparently, she'd sensed the same chemistry between them that he had. And it scared her to death.

"Look, Holly, let's chalk the past few days up to a bad idea all the way around. We've covered all our bases—gratitude, regret, mutual attraction. I think we can part ways without hard feelings."

She nodded and smiled, shoving her hands into the pockets of her wool peacoat.

He studied her face—the clear and flawless skin, the full lips, the perfectly arched brows—so similar to Kloie's.

"Everything I said today was not only horrible, but untrue." Luke grinned. "So I don't lack savvy?"

She shook her head. The moment grew awkward. Luke reached for the door handle. "I appreciate your candor. Thanks for stopping by. We're good." He shrugged his right shoulder.

"Thanks for letting me in." She headed through the door.

Impulsively, he pecked her cheek as she had his the night before. Their gazes met one last time before he closed the door. In her eyes, fear and loneliness had joined the sadness. He leaned against the door, opened his cell phone, and erased Holly Olson from his contact list. Keeping her number might lead to temptation.

Holly met Mel and Kloie at church the next morning. Boy was she shocked when the three of them walked in and she spotted

Luke in a pew about halfway up on the left side. Before she had a chance to react, Kloie hightailed it up the aisle and straight to him.

"Luke Jolly?" Mel asked.

Holly nodded and rushed to save him from Kloie, who had settled herself in the same pew, right next to him.

"Holly." Luke stood, his expression suspicious.

Now he probably wonders if nutcase and her kid are stalking him. Holly cleared her throat. "Do you go to this church?"

Luke nodded. "Have for years."

"Us, too." Kloie's voice was jubilant.

"You do?" Luke looked doubtful.

"Since I moved here." Defensiveness laced Holly's sentence.

Mel tugged on the sleeve of Holly's coat and smiled.

"Oh, I'm sorry. Melissa Miller this is Luke Jolly. Luke, this is Mel."

"She's Mom's BFF," Kloie informed him. Then she turned to Holly. "I saved you seats."

Holly felt mortified. She had no desire to sit in the same building with Luke, let alone the same pew, but Mel slipped past him and Kloie, so Holly had no choice but to do the same or cause a scene. She settled on the other side of Mel, putting as much distance between her and Luke as the situation would allow.

After church, Kloie invited Luke to lunch, but one glance at Holly must have prompted him to refuse. Surely he spotted the horror on her face.

While they waited in line for a table at The Bunnery, Kloie played tag with a group of kids from her school. Mel commented,

"Kloie's right. He is cute."

Holly gave her a don't-you-dare-go-there look.

"I've seen him at church before. I think maybe at a singles event."

Holly never joined Mel at those things. She stuck to the ladies' class and their events.

"His job and roots are here. Mine will soon be many miles away." An idea occurred to Holly. "Why don't you hook up with him?" As soon as the words left her lips, she realized that although she didn't want him, she wanted no one else to have him, either.

"He's into you, not me." They followed the line forward a few steps.

"He's not *into* me. We barely know each other."

"Keep telling yourself that." Mel rolled her eyes.

"Even if that were true, which it's not, I can't let this go any further or someone might get hurt. Probably both me and Kloie."

When they'd finally settled at a table and ordered, Kloie turned to Mel. "What did you think of Luke? Wouldn't he and my mom make a great couple?"

Mel nodded. "Great."

Holly sighed. "Will I never get a break from this again?"

"I just think you've been alone long enough." Kloie stated her opinion matter-of-factly.

"Kloie, I want to be alone. I choose to be alone. What part of that don't you get?"

"Well, I want a dad, and every little girl deserves a dad. And I've *never* had one."

So that's what this is about. Holly's heart ached for her daughter. Maybe when they moved, her grandpa could fill part of the gap.

Chapter 6

"Hi, Luke. It's Kloie."

"Hi, Kloie. What's up?"

"I just wanted to thank you for letting us sit with you the other day in church."

"Sure. Anytime." He wondered what this call was really about.

"My mom and I are going ice-skating tonight."

Ah, now he knew. "You are? Well, have fun."

"Do you ever ice-skate?" Luke could picture her round, inquisitive eyes.

"Not in a long time."

"Maybe you should try it sometime soon. You might really like it."

Luke smiled and shook his head. "Maybe I will—try it sometime."

"Maybe you could come tonight. Then you'll know people and won't have to skate all alone." Her voice dropped to a whisper. "I've got to go now." The line went dead.

Luke closed his cell. Was he nuts to even be thinking about

this? Holly had let him know, in no uncertain terms, she wasn't interested in a relationship. But then again, she was letting fear dictate her life, and that was no way to live.

Luke went to his contact list and punched in M. Then he scrolled to Matt and hit SEND.

"Hey, you and Tristyn up for a night of ice-skating?"

"Karey and I are supposed to go to dinner, but that would work out perfect because we'd have a sitter. Do you mind?"

"Not at all." Yep, showing up with a kid would seem normal enough. Holly would never know that Kloie tipped him off.

❄

Holly and Kloie were tying the laces on their skates when in came Luke with a little boy. Unable to run to him, which was Kloie's normal operating procedure, she yelled to him instead. Not only did Luke look their direction, but so did most of the other people at the rink.

"Hello."

"Hi," Kloie and Holly echoed.

"Who is your friend?" Holly smiled at the dark-haired boy with mischievous brown eyes.

"This is Tristyn. T for short. Remember Matt, the guy who held you in place when Kloie was choking?"

Holly nodded, feeling heat rise up her neck and highlight her face. "Not one of my finer moments. Seems you've seen me at my worst more than once."

Luke chuckled. "Bygones. Anyway, this is his stepson. He and Karey were going to dinner, so here we are."

Kloie was glowing. "Hurry and get your skates, and you can

skate with us. Right, Mom?"

Luke waited for Holly's invitation. Six expectant eyes focused on her. "Sure. That would be nice." The surprising thing to her was that she meant it. She'd probably thought about Luke a million times in the past week. Maybe they could end up being friends.

Holly and Kloie waited on the bench while the guys rented their skates. "Thanks, Mom." Kloie hugged her.

Luke and Tristyn returned with black ice skates in hand. While Luke got his on, Holly helped the little boy with his. She learned T was in kindergarten and had the same teacher Kloie did four years ago. Since he'd only skated once, Kloie, the pro, offered to teach him. That left Holly and Luke gliding around the ice together. Both were proficient. They kept a slow pace conducive to talking.

"Do you skate much?" Holly broke the awkward silence.

"Not for the last decade. As a kid, growing up in northern California, I did. How about you?"

"Just the opposite. Never as a kid and often now. Kloie loves it, so it's a good winter activity when we can't hike and bike."

"So what kept you here after your husband died? I would have thought you'd have wanted to go home to your family."

Holly unbuttoned her jacket. The exercise had warmed her up. "Quite the opposite, actually. I come from a family of left-brained type As. I never fit—still don't."

Another loss—her family's approval. Luke listened closely as Holly shared.

"My older sister, Noel, is a doctor, and my little brother, Clinton, is a lawyer with his eye on politics. And then there's me—the photography major." Holly laughed, remembering. "My dad about fell over when he discovered people actually get a degree with a camera. In his opinion, it's nothing more than a glorified hobby." She shrugged.

"Now if I'd made it big, and become the next Ansel Adams, my degree might've counted for something, but I didn't. So my family considers it a worthless piece of paper. And I am nothing more than a retail clerk selling someone else's art." Holly stopped and sat down on a bench at the edge of the ice, slipping out of her jacket. "I cannot believe I just told you all that."

Luke smiled. "I asked."

"That you did. Now tell me about your family."

Luke watched Kloie showing T how to stop and start. "My family runs a natural grocery store in the bay area. My parents are so not into degrees, they were disappointed when I opted to go to college."

Holly laughed and Luke joined her. "And if I had to get a degree, they'd have much rather had me get one in the arts than in Fire Science."

"Maybe we should trade families," Holly suggested.

"My mom always wanted a daughter and would be thrilled with a right-brained one, but I'm afraid I wouldn't measure up in yours."

"Welcome to my world. I don't measure up, either. But God settled it for me a long time ago. He knit me together, and nothing about me is a surprise to Him."

"Well said. Hey, you want some hot chocolate?"

At Holly's nod, he skated over and bought four.

"Do you ever go home for Christmas?" Luke asked when he returned.

"No. Kloie and I go back every summer for a couple of weeks. My mother—the socialite—turns Christmas into the party season of the year. Formal dinners and Christmas balls are not a fun way for a little girl to spend her holidays."

"No, I guess they wouldn't be."

Kloie and T skated up. He'd gotten the hang of it. Luke handed them each a hot chocolate.

"Guess what, Luke?"

"What, Kloie?"

"We're going to Oregon." After a sip of the warm drink, Kloie wore a chocolate mustache above her upper lip.

"You are? For Christmas?"

Kloie shook her head. "Right after. My granddad has horses and everything." Her eyes grew larger, and she leaned in. "I think he might be rich," she stated in a low tone.

"Sounds like he might be."

The announcer informed everyone the skating session would be ending in fifteen minutes.

Holly rose. "I think we'll call it a night and beat the crowd out the door." She smiled, and a warmth spread through him.

"Yeah, we might do the same." Luke collected the empty Styrofoam cups. "It was nice seeing you two. Maybe we can hang out again before you guys leave."

"Sure—maybe." Holly shrugged.

What kind of answer is that? Do you want me to call or not? Sure. Maybe!

The four of them walked out together and said quick good-byes in the icy, cold parking lot.

❄

"Aren't you glad we ran into someone we knew?" Kloie asked. "It was way better than just you and me."

"You think so, huh? I always kind of like you and me." Holly realized, as Kloie had gotten older, she longed to be part of a real family—with more than two people. Maybe living near her dad's relatives would help satisfy that need.

After Holly got Kloie tucked in, she called Mel. "Guess who we ran into tonight?"

"Luke." Mel didn't even hesitate.

"How'd you know?"

"The glee in your tone."

"There is not glee in my—"

"Holly, face the facts. You enjoy spending time with Luke. Thus the glee."

Holly rolled her eyes, hating that Mel knew her so well—sometimes better than she knew herself. "Okay. Maybe a little," she begrudgingly admitted. "Kloie told him we're moving."

"And?"

"Didn't seem to be a big deal. He said something about hanging out before we go, so now that he knows we're moving in three weeks, hanging out might not be that big of a deal. Right?"

"Hey, you might as well," Mel encouraged.

"Maybe a few weeks of living will make it worth giving him up in the end."

"What do you mean?"

"He makes me feel alive. Do you know how long it's been since a man looked at me with a twinkle in his eye?"

"I'd guess about a decade."

"Yep. Not since Kenton. Can you believe he's been gone that long?" Her voice cracked with emotion.

"I can't, Holls. Maybe a decade is long enough to be alone." Mel spoke the words softly, yet firmly.

"My daughter sure thinks so. What should I do about a little girl who wants a dad and her mother who doesn't?"

"Maybe her mother does and is afraid to take a chance."

Holly chose to gloss over Mel's last comment and return the discussion to Kloie. "She told me every little girl deserves a dad, and yet she hasn't had one her entire life."

"Yeah, she said that at The Bunnery last Sunday, too. I'm sorry, Holly. Kenton would have been a great dad."

A tear rolled down Holly's cheek. "He wanted a baby so much, and he talked to her every night before we went to sleep." Holly's line beeped. "Hey, Mel, I'm getting another call." She pulled the phone away from her ear to see who it was. "It's Luke." Her heart pounded.

"Holls, be nice." With that warning, Mel hung up.

"Hello." Holly tried to sound nonchalant, but her voice betrayed her.

"Holly, Luke."

"Oh, hi."

"Hey, I was sitting here having my quiet time with the Lord, and conviction fell on me like a heavy rain."

"What do you mean?" Dread had fallen over her like a dark cloud.

"I knew you were going skating tonight."

"Kloie?"

"Does it matter how I knew? I'm not confessing for anyone but myself."

Holly laughed at his attempt to keep her daughter out of trouble.

"Anyway, crazy as it sounds with our short, yet bizarre history, something about you intrigues me, and I jumped at the chance to see you again."

Her heart soared at his proclamation. And Holly took the plunge into the pool of honesty. "Luke, I'm intrigued, as well."

Chapter 7

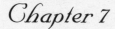

eally?" Luke was shocked by her blatant answer. He hadn't expected it. "Well, as one intrigued person to another, what do you say we get together again?"

"Does this invitation include Kloie?"

Luke laughed. "I think we'd better make any and all plans to include Kloie. Otherwise, we'd break her heart."

"Thank you, Luke, for understanding." Holly's grateful tone shot tenderness through him.

"Hey, if I drop by the tree lot tomorrow, your evil twin won't be around will she?"

"No. I buried her out in the backyard. You won't be running into her again. She is dead and gone."

"Whew. That's a relief."

Holly laughed, and he relished the pure joy of it. His heart skipped to the same tune. "So, if Kloie calls with future possibilities, you don't mind if I show up?"

"No. At least not until we leave for Oregon."

"Oh, I get it. Absence won't make the heart grow fonder."

"Out of sight, out of mind," Holly reminded.

"We'll see about that," Luke said with more confidence than he felt. "Well then, until our next happenstance meeting, I bid you good night."

"Good night, Luke." Her words were soft with a hint of the South, like sweet tea.

Luke held the phone for another minute or two after she'd hung up. Something was happening inside of him. He was on an uncharted trail with feelings and emotions swirling around inside him like a bubbling cauldron. Things he couldn't put names to, but one thing he knew for certain: the thought of seeing Holly again was a much-anticipated event.

And he was going to make sure they didn't forget him while they were away on vacation in Oregon. Maybe he'd even take time off for the last couple of weeks in December, and they could spend the days preceding her trip together. He had some accrued time he needed to burn anyway. That way he could solidify himself in their lives, and when they got back—well, who knew where life might take them, except the Lord?

Luke felt pretty satisfied with himself when he showed up at the tree lot the following morning. He had a plan to woo and win Holly. He'd returned to his earlier way of thinking. Meeting her was no accident, and he wasn't about to waste the God-given opportunity.

When she glanced up from her paperwork and spotted him, her face lit up. Yep, by jolly, unbeknownst to Holly, she was ready for a relationship.

"Hi."

"Luke! Hello." She rose from the card table that had become

a makeshift desk. "Can I offer you some coffee?" She pointed to a thermos.

"Actually, I came by to see if you wanted a latte or anything, but a cup of good old home brew sounds nice."

While Holly poured him some of the hot beverage into a Styrofoam cup, he settled onto an old milk crate.

She handed him the coffee. "I hope you're okay with a little cream and sugar. I mixed it in at home. And sorry about the accommodations; I only have the one folding chair. Kloie rarely sits, and when she does, she prefers that to a real chair." Holly returned to her spot behind the table.

Two little lines appeared between her brows. "How did Kloie get your phone number?"

He told her the cell phone story, and Holly's cheeks grew red. He also confessed to erasing her number, but since Kloie called him, he was able to access it on his incoming call list, which was how he called her tonight.

"She typed my number into your phone?" Holly shook her head, wearing an appalled expression. "Wow. I don't know what to say. Except I'm sorry."

"You're apparently not one of those women who uses your child to snag a date."

"No. Absolutely not. And I hope Kloie isn't this forward with men when she's interested for herself." Concern drew Holly's brows together. "She's never done this before. I don't get it. I've never dated. She's never cared. Why now? Why you?"

"Gee, thanks." Luke acted hurt.

"I didn't mean that quite the way it sounded, but why this sudden need for us to have a man?"

"Hero worship." Luke offered his explanation. "I saved her life. It's a hazard of the job." He grinned at her.

She chuckled. "Do you get hazard pay?"

Luke shook his head.

"I'm in a quandary about Kloie. I'm not sure how to deal with her manipulation. On the one hand, she's suddenly developed this deep desire for a dad, and I need to respect that. But on the other, I can't let this behavior go unchecked." Holly sighed.

Luke shrugged. "I don't envy your position. This parenting stuff isn't easy, is it?"

"Nope. And my guess is that the older she is, the harder it will be. Anyway." Holly smiled at him. "Please don't let Kloie manipulate you into doing anything you don't want to do."

He winked. "I won't. I promise."

"I'm down to only a couple dozen trees. My guess is the lot will sell out days before Christmas."

"Hey, that's good news because I have a couple of weeks off at the end of the year. Maybe we can spend a few fun-filled days on the slopes, snowmobile through Yellowstone, and do some real ice-skating on the pond."

"Kloie's never skied."

"You're kidding. A Wyoming native who's never hit the slopes? Don't worry, I'll teach her."

"I don't want her to get hurt." The same panic from Kloie's choking incident filled Holly's words.

"We'll be careful."

Some customers arrived. Luke rose. "Thanks for the coffee. I'll see you soon. Serendipity."

Holly hoped so. And she hated that she did. Mel dropped by later that day with lunch for the two of them to share—soup from The Bunnery. She settled on the crate Luke recently vacated. "I'm dying to hear about your phone call from Luke."

While they ate, Holly filled Mel in regarding their conversation last night and on his visit this morning.

"Sooo?" Mel probed. "You rattled off a bunch of facts, but what are you thinking? What are you feeling? A good-looking guy is in pursuit, and you sound like an encyclopedia—all facts and figures, but zero emotion."

Mel's appraisal made it impossible for Holly to remain nonchalant. "He's great. He's. . ." She searched for the right words.

"Everything a girl could dream of?" Mel's gaze probed hers. "Say it, Holls. Say it."

"To quote from *Bambi*, I'm twitterpated."

Mel jumped up and pumped her fist in the air. "Finally, you're being honest with yourself. Now admit, having a man around isn't a bad thing for you or for Kloie."

"Maybe if we weren't leaving in less than three weeks." Holly rose and paced in the small space between her office area and the remaining trees. "Common sense tells me I should put a stop to this, but I can't bring myself to actually end things. Yet I know I should. This can go nowhere. I'm moving."

"Just have fun, Holly. For once in your life, forget tomorrow and enjoy today. You know that's a scriptural principle."

Holly chuckled but continued to pace—something she often did when processing. "I guess you're right. I mean, Kloie told

Luke about Oregon, and he never even batted an eye. He knows there is no future in this."

"So he is probably not thinking long-term, either. He probably knows how to live in the moment, unlike some people I know."

Holly rolled her eyes. "By nature, I'm a planner. I can't help it. That's the way God wired me. It's hard for me to adopt your carefree attitude. I keep asking if a few weeks of living will be worth the cost of giving him up when I move. You know I hate pain."

Mel laughed. "Everyone hates pain. How attached can you get in such a short amount of time?"

"Very."

Mel grinned—her wide ear-to-ear grin. "You already are. You're falling for him, aren't you?" Excitement filled her eyes.

"He makes me feel things I haven't felt in a very long time," Holly confessed. "When I'm around him, I feel alive, attractive, vibrant. Very unencyclopedia-like."

Mel hugged her. "Holly, that's wonderful. You're finally waking up from your grief and moving on."

"I hope you're right. I hope I'm not setting myself up for a major heartbreak."

❄

Kloie continued to call Luke several times a day, keeping him posted on her mother's whereabouts. He never mentioned to her that her mom had figured out what she was doing.

So Luke and Holly met at the grocery store and went for pizza afterward. The next night he ran into her at the drugstore and the three of them went to a movie. Wednesday night they saw each other in the church parking lot and took Kloie for ice cream after Awana. No one seemed to care that it was way too cold for ice cream.

Thursday, Luke invited them to a dinner of grilled steaks. Holly enjoyed perusing his art collection again while he cooked. He loved that they had that in common.

When they gathered around his table, they held hands and prayed. He'd intentionally kept all physical aspects out of the relationship, even hand holding, not wanting Holly to feel rushed. However, he grew more certain every day that he was crazy about the both of them. When they got back from Oregon, he planned on taking this to the next level. Sort of officially becoming a couple.

"Tomorrow is Kloie's last day of school, right?" Luke wondered aloud.

"Yep, and we're having a big party." Her eyes sparkled with the excitement of the season.

"And tomorrow is my last day of work until after the New Year. Holly, how many trees are left?"

"Three. I'm sure I'll sell out tomorrow."

"Will your father-in-law be shipping more?"

Holly shook her head. "He's out. Because of the wildfires last summer, the crop was smaller this year."

"That means that we are all three free next week. My buddy Adam invited us up to his family's cabin for some skiing. You could bring Mel. What do you think? We'll be back before Christmas." He wanted the three of them to milk every hour out of every day, so they'd really miss him on their trip.

Kloie's eyes grew as round as a full moon. "Please, Mom.

Please. I've always wanted to learn to ski."

❄

A few days away with her daughter, her best friend, and her. . .
Luke sounded like heaven. "I'll check with Mel." Since school
was out, she should be free. She'd decided to stick around
Jackson this year for Christmas, rather than fly home, so they
could have extra girl time before the move. This would be a
perfect way to spend it. Mel loved a crowd.

"Matt and Robert may show up with their wives, too. I'm
not sure, but it's a pretty large cabin. You, Kloie, and Mel may
have to share a room, if that's okay."

"Sounds great." She hoped it would work out—sort of her
and Kloie's last hurrah in Wyoming.

Chapter 8

I'll take Kloie up and come back and get you," Luke yelled above the noise of the snowmobiles. "Or you can take Kloie up and come back and get me."

"Mel said she knows how to run one of these," Adam yelled over the roar. "She can take Kloie, you take Holly, and I'll wait here at the bottom."

Luke nodded. Adam helped Kloie on behind Mel and had her wrap her arms tight around Mel's waist. He gave her some last-minute instructions then Holly climbed aboard and hugged herself against Luke's back. Her heart pounded. Since Kenton's death, she'd avoided any and all adventure. Fear gripped her midsection, and she prayed all the way up the mountain, burying her head in Luke's back. She couldn't even bring herself to look at Mel and Kloie. She just begged God to keep them safe.

About ten minutes later, they arrived at a sprawling log cabin. Lights were ablaze, welcoming them with a warm glow from the windows. Adam said he'd come up earlier and gotten things ready.

As soon as they stopped, Kloie jumped off the back and

hopped around in excitement. She'd inherited her dad's love of adventure.

Luke unloaded their stuff from the little wagons that were hitched behind the machines. He piled everything just inside the front door. "I'm going to run down the hill for Adam. You guys make yourselves at home. Pick which room you want, and I'll carry your things up when I get back."

He kissed Holly's cheek and left without waiting for a response.

Mel raised her brows but said nothing.

Kloie raced through the cabin to check out every nook and cranny.

There was a fire blazing in the fireplace, and Holly planted herself in front of it, warming her hands.

Mel joined her. "You both *seem* pretty serious."

Holly opted to ignore the observation.

After a few quiet moments, Mel started laughing.

"What's so funny?"

"Holly Jolly." Mel laughed harder.

Holly joined her. "The name would be absurd, for sure, but since I'm leaving, we don't have to worry."

"In case you haven't noticed, we live in the twenty-first century—IM, e-mail, Web cams, faxes, texts, cells, not to mention airplanes, make a long-distance relationship not only possible, but feasible."

Holly had never thought past the move. She'd planned on ending it all on January first. Surely, Luke did, too. He'd never mentioned anything else as a possibility.

Mel laughed again. That time Holly didn't ask but went in

search of Kloie. It was just as well this thing with Luke would be short and sweet. Holly giggled. Holly Jolly *would* be awful.

"Did you find us the perfect room?" Holly hollered from the bottom of the steps.

"Yep." Kloie appeared on the landing. "Come on up and I'll show you."

"Let me grab some of our stuff. Why don't you run down and help?"

Mel, Kloie, and Holly made their way up the stairs, loaded with bags. Kloie led them to the second door on the right—a large room with two double beds.

"Seems perfect." Holly admired the feminine room with floral down comforters draped across the beds. It was inviting. Kloie claimed the bed closest to the window for them, so Mel took the other one. By the time Luke returned with Adam, they'd unpacked and were back downstairs enjoying the fire.

Luke and Adam carried large ice chests into the kitchen. The girls followed. They worked together as a foursome, getting things put away. Holly and Mel had cooked a pan of lasagna and a pan of enchiladas ahead of time and frozen them. The guys planned on grilling for both of their turns.

Mel glanced at Holly and cracked up. Holly knew exactly what she was thinking, and she gave her a stern, you'd-better-not-say-it look. Both guys glanced from one to the other, but thankfully, neither asked questions.

The next morning, bright and early, after Luke stuffed them with his famous blueberry pancakes, everyone hit the slopes.

They used cross-country skis to get over to the ski resort. Once there, Adam's family had a locker filled with all the downhill gear they'd need.

Luke and Holly took Kloie over to the bunny slopes where a ski instructor would work with her. There was a whole group of kids and about four teachers at the "ski school."

"If she spends the day with us, she'll be a pro by tomorrow," the girl at the registration booth promised.

"What do you think?" Luke knew Holly fought an inner fear to even allow Kloie on the slopes. He wasn't sure she'd leave her.

"I can give you a beeper," the perky woman offered. "That way if your daughter needs you, we'll page."

"Mom, I'm nine." Kloie looked at her with puppy-dog eyes that Luke knew he'd be unable to resist.

"You guys can hit the black diamonds today, because tomorrow you may have to stick to the easier trails." The woman gave Holly an encouraging smile and handed her a beeper.

Holly's gaze bounced between the woman, Kloie, and Luke. After what seemed like forever, she agreed. She gave Kloie an extra tight hug before Luke led her away with a firm hand on her elbow.

"I didn't used to be like this," Holly admitted once they were both in the chairlift.

The snow-blanketed earth below them was beautiful and serene. Luke wrapped his arm around her shoulder and pulled her against his side. "I know." Somehow, Kenton's death had trapped her into a life of fear. "Did I ever tell you that after college I fought wildfires?"

Holly shook her head, keeping her eyes straight ahead.

"Robert and I traveled all over the country for several years. It was exciting, until I almost died."

Holly turned and looked at him. "You almost died?"

He nodded. "I had to come to grips with some fear issues myself."

"What did you do?"

"Look down," Luke commanded.

"I don't want to."

"It's beautiful, Holly, and you'll miss it if you keep your eyes straight ahead." He held her tighter.

She leaned forward a few inches and peered over the edge of the lift, her hand clutching his.

"Repeat after me, 'I can do all things through him who gives me strength.'"

She did, but she didn't loosen her death grip on his hand.

"Then you know what I did? I started thanking God and praising Him. Pretty soon my fear was replaced by confidence in a mighty and sovereign Lord."

"Thank God for snow." Holly's words sounded weak and pathetic.

"Yes, Lord," Luke agreed, "we praise You as the Creator. Your creation is beautiful."

"And thank You, Lord, for the view. Your works are marvelous." Her voice was stronger.

He fought the urge to kiss her. Instead, he focused on God. "You tell us be not afraid for You are with us."

"And You're with Kloie, even when I can't be. I can trust her future with You." A tear trickled down her cheek. "That's the real problem, Luke. I trusted God with Kenton, and he's dead. How can I trust God with Kloie? How can I trust God for anything?" A quiet, torrential downpour of tears followed.

Luke let out a long, slow breath. *Lord, what do I say? Give me the words to help her, to comfort her.*

"Holly, all I know for sure is God is good and God is God. His ways are not our ways, so who can understand them? But He promises to use *everything* for our good and His glory—if we let Him."

"I know what you say is true, but there is this fine line between knowing them and believing them. Really believing them." She sniffed.

"What you don't know is that a good friend died in that fire I told you about. And I don't know why that happened, but what I do know is everything I told you is the truth. I'd bank my life on it. But that first year, I just kept asking God to heal my unbelief and restore my faith. I kept reciting those verses over and over until the truth permeated every cell of my body."

Holly nodded. "For most things in life, I do know and believe, but when it comes to Kloie, I'm terrified."

"And I understand."

"I'm going to take your advice, though, and find scriptures on fear, trust in God's goodness, and start praying and memorizing every day."

"For me, that made all the difference. And hearing myself say them out loud built my faith."

Holly dried her cheeks on the sleeve of her coat, dabbing under her eyes with the end of her scarf. "Am I all smeared and raccoon-looking?"

"Just a tiny bit." Luke took his thumb and traced under her eye, removing the remaining smudge. His gaze met Holly's, and deep protective emotions washed over him. His heart pounded. They both leaned in, slowly, until their lips met. Luke kept the kiss short, but there was a tidal wave of emotion in it.

When he pulled back, Holly wore a tender, yet surprised expression. He traced her cheekbone with his thumb. Her lips curved into a slight smile.

The lift came to a halt, startling both of them. "You need to get off." The attendant was annoyed that he had to stop the progress because they'd been caught up in a sweet moment.

They both scrambled to get out of the chair and out of the way. They walked over to the lookout and cracked up.

"How embarrassing!" Holly covered warm cheeks with her gloved hands.

❄

Holly sat by the fire on their last night at the cabin, reminiscing about how quickly the past four days had flown by. Kloie was tucked into bed, exhausted from her fourth day on the slopes.

Luke joined Holly on the love seat, taking her hand and lacing his fingers through hers. She rested her head on his shoulder. These past days he'd often held her hand or placed an arm around her shoulders. He was affectionate, but never inappropriate. They'd become quite comfortable together, and neither mentioned the final separation looming ahead of them in just over a week. Sometimes, for Holly, it felt like the proverbial elephant in the room.

"Thanks for inviting us on this trip. It's been wonderful."

Holly's words were lazy and quiet. "I'm sorry Matt and Robert couldn't make it up."

"Too last-minute for them, I guess." Luke added another log to the fire.

"Adam and Mel seemed to hit it off well."

He returned to the couch and slipped an arm around her. They could hear the other couple laughing in the kitchen. "I think they could have a future."

Unlike us. Holly could hardly bear the thought of leaving Luke behind.

"Kloie is quite the little skier." Adam placed a tray with three mugs of hot chocolate on the coffee table in front of them. Mel followed, carrying a plate loaded with all the fixings for s'mores and a hot tea for herself.

"Yeah. A couple more trips and she'll be flying right on by me." Mel set her tea on the edge of the table and settled onto the couch, tucking her legs under her. "Adam, thank you so much for allowing us to join you and Luke on this wonderful adventure."

"Glad you came." The words were said to all, but his gaze was for Mel alone.

The heat from the fire was making Holly feel groggy. After a few sips of hot chocolate, she decided to turn in.

"I'll walk you up." Luke followed her up the stairs.

At her door, she turned to face him. He took her hand.

"Thanks for another wonderful day," Holly whispered.

Luke placed a hand on each side of her face and gave her a good night kiss she'd not soon forget.

"Let's make this trip the first of many." He placed another

quick kiss on her forehead. "Sleep well." He turned and headed back downstairs.

A stunned Holly stood there watching him go. *First of many? Hello. I'm moving. What part of that don't you get?* She wanted to scream the words. Had he forgotten? Was he thinking they'd have a long-distance relationship? Or was he not thinking at all to make such a comment?

Chapter 9

Christmas Day, Luke knocked on Holly's door at five in the morning. He didn't want to miss a minute with Kloie. He couldn't wait for her to see the three-speed bike he'd purchased for her. And he couldn't wait for Holly to open her little velvet box, either. Boy, would she be surprised.

Holly came to the door a few minutes later in a pair of jeans and a sweatshirt. She looked cute in a disheveled sort of way.

"Hi." She moved aside so he could enter. "I planned on being ready when you got here, but I think I hit SNOOZE. Do you mind brewing some coffee, and I'll finish getting ready? If Kloie gets up, make her come get me before she starts ripping things open."

"Promise." Luke pulled Holly into his arms. "But you don't have to get ready. You're adorable just the way you are." Holly's cheeks turned that familiar shade of red. "I'm crazy about you. You know that don't you?"

She nodded. "Luke—"

He didn't want to hear her protests or objections, so he silenced her with a kiss. Their first kiss since they came back from the cabin. A kiss—slow, tender, undemanding.

"We shouldn't—"

"Don't worry, I have a lifetime supply of those. That well is never running dry."

Holly looked almost panicked. Then he spotted Kloie and understood. The huge grin on her face told Luke she'd seen the sweet moment he'd just shared with her mom.

Holly squirmed out of his embrace, but he didn't care who saw their magic moment. He was ready for the world to know that he and Holly were a couple headed toward a lifetime together.

"Kloie!" Holly sounded like a kid caught with her hand in the candy bin.

"Hi, Mom. Hi, Luke." Kloie still wore the silly grin and a look of expectation.

"Let's open gifts." Holly picked up her camera off the bar separating the kitchen from the living room. "Kloie, do you want to pass them out?"

Kloie cocked her head to the side and gazed at Luke. "I think you should. At Hayden's house, her dad does that."

Luke appreciated Kloie's seal of approval. He accepted the honor with pride. Luke gathered the gifts and stacked a pile in front of Holly, a pile in front of Kloie, and his own he stacked by the leather armchair.

"So, how does this work around here? Do I go first since I did all the work of passing the gifts out?"

"Nope. We take turns, right, Mom? But can we let Luke go first?"

Holly nodded her agreement.

The first gift he chose had homemade paper designed by Kloie. He untaped the seams, so he didn't damage her artwork. When he laid the paper out flat, he saw she'd drawn a Christmas scene with the manger depicted.

"I love the paper, Kloie. I'll save it and use it to hang on my wall next year at Christmas." He removed the box lid and lifted out a framed drawing Kloie made.

"It's us." Kloie confirmed what he thought. "Me, you, and Mom."

Sure enough, she'd drawn and painted three people—a man, a woman, and a little girl. They were all holding hands on a grassy hill with a big yellow sun above them. Luke's heart leaped when he noticed her caption: *My family.*

Thanks, Lord, that Kloie and I are on the same page. It will make life so much easier. Luke hugged Kloie. "I love it. There isn't a better gift on Earth that you could have given me."

He glanced at Holly. She looked concerned or maybe uncomfortable as she studied the artwork.

❄

Holly cleared her throat. "Hey, Kloie, Luke bought you a very special gift. I think he hid it outside."

"I was going to give her that last." His expression was crestfallen.

Kloie jumped up and ran to the sliding glass door that led out to the patio. "This way?"

Luke followed her outside, and Holly heard Kloie's excitement, but she couldn't bring herself to join them. *Lord, what have I done?* With the tip of her index finger, she traced the happy family Kloie had drawn. Then she picked up the tiny, wrapped, ring-sized box off the top of her stack of presents. Her first impulse was to hide it somewhere and not to deal with it at all.

It could be earrings. Surely, Luke wouldn't buy her an engagement ring this soon. They'd only known each other a month. Panic bubbled in Holly. She and Luke needed to talk as soon as possible. Until then, she'd have to wear a happy smile and pretend all was well.

Kloie and Luke brought the new bike through the house. They invited her to join them. Holly laid aside the tiny gift and followed them outside. Kloie rode her new bike around the cul-de-sac a few times.

Luke pulled Holly into his arms. He stood behind her and rested his head on top of hers.

"You seemed less than thrilled by the picture Kloie drew of us."

"I chose never to date because of Kloie. I didn't want her to have various men in and out of her life. We've barely known you four weeks, and she already thinks of the three of us as family. It's way too soon. If things go awry, her heart will be broken."

"How about your heart?"

Broken, for sure. "As our leaving for Oregon draws near, I do feel sad."

"Holly, a trip doesn't have to be the end of us. How long will you be gone—a couple of weeks?"

A trip!

Kloie rode up. "Let's go open the rest of the presents."

Holly was still trying to process how this communication mix-up had happened. Where in the world had Luke gotten the idea they were simply taking a vacation? Holly mindlessly followed Luke and Kloie through the garage, where Kloie left the bike, and back into the house to finish opening the gifts.

Holly knew she and Luke desperately needed to talk, but in the middle of the gift exchange didn't seem like the best time.

They went back to the task at hand, each one oohing and aahing over each item. Holly left the little box until last, praying it would vanish. Finally, she was the last person and that little box was the last gift.

Her heart pounded as she picked up the foil-wrapped gift. Her hand quivered, ever so slightly. She took the tiny red velvet bow off and laid it aside. Moving painstakingly slow, she removed each piece of tape until the red foil wrap fell away.

Holly lifted the lid off the black box. Inside was a jeweler's box with a hinged lid. Slowly, with a ball of dread in her stomach, she opened the lid. There on a bed of black velvet lay a gold band, but not a small one.

She lifted the band from its nest inside the box. *This is a man's ring.* She glanced at Luke, feeling completely puzzled by the gift.

Luke had gone down on one knee. Her heart pounded so hard the noise echoed in her ears.

"Holly, are you familiar with the Jewish wedding traditions?"

Holly shook her head. Her mouth went dry, and her tongue stuck to the roof of her mouth.

Luke's eyes sparked with excitement, much like a Fourth of July night sky. "In Jewish custom, the betrothal is separated from the wedding by one year. During that year of preparation, the bride wears a wedding ring, reminding her of the promise and commitment her future groom has made to her."

Luke took the gold band from her, slipping it on the index finger of her right hand. Holly swallowed and was certain the entire neighborhood heard the sound. Kloie stood quietly behind Luke, a grin splitting her face from ear to ear.

"This ring signifies that you've been chosen, by me, and in one year, I'd like you to become my wife. With this ring, I'm telling you and the world that I'm making a commitment to you—a covenant, if you will—to spend the next twelve months planning and preparing to make a lifetime vow. This gold band will remind you that I'm committed to knowing you better, loving you more, and spending my life with you."

Holly stared at the ring on her finger. Her emotions were jumbled, like someone had stuck them in a blender. She felt happy. She felt sad. She felt confused.

"I want this to be our first Christmas with decades more to follow."

The doorbell rang. Kloie ran for it. "Hi, Hayden. My mom's getting married."

"Really? Hey, I saw your new bike out my window. I got one, too. Do you want to ride?"

Thank heaven some nine-year-olds couldn't care less about Holly's personal life.

Kloie looked to Holly for permission. She nodded her head, thanking God for this opportunity to speak to Luke alone. "Stay in our cul-de-sac."

The door slammed, and both girls were gone.

Boy did Luke feel stupid. Holly was obviously not overjoyed by his gift or his speech. What should he do now? Stay on his knee on the floor until she answered?

"Luke."

By her tone, he knew bad news was on its way. He took a seat at the opposite end of the couch. This truly wasn't what he'd expected.

Holly rose and paced between the couch and the kitchen, apparently taking her time formulating her thoughts and words.

After what felt like forever, she started again. "Luke, you are a really nice guy."

No, not the "let's be friends" speech.

"But. . ."

The dreaded "but". . .

"Somehow, we've severely miscommunicated." Luke's heart dropped, and he felt his hopes and dreams crumbling. How had he misread her by a mile?

"Kloie and I are moving to Oregon in one week. Not vacationing, *moving.*"

Luke didn't understand. "Why?"

"I'm jobless, and as of next Thursday, Kloie and I will be homeless."

Luke shook his head. "There are thirty-two galleries. You told me that yourself. Surely one of them might need you."

"It's more complicated than that. Rosemary's business manager, who runs the gallery, laid me off last September. I had a mortgage, a daughter to feed, and no income. My father-in-law loaned me money to get through the fall with the stipulation that Kloie and I would move when she got through the first semester of this school year."

"You didn't even try to get another job here?" The thought seemed incredulous to him.

Holly stopped, rubbing the back of her neck. "They lost their only child when Kenton died. She's their only grandchild. They've been pressuring me for years. I just finally agreed." Holly sighed.

"Why didn't you tell me you were moving?" he demanded.

"Kloie told you. I heard her." Defensiveness was woven through her words.

Luke stood. "Kloie said you were going to Oregon. Going, not moving."

"I just assumed—"

"Assumed I could read minds?" Luke raked a hand through his hair.

"I'm sorry, Luke. I thought you knew. Until this morning, I had no idea."

"So where does that leave us?"

Holly shrugged. "I have to go. I made a promise."

Luke was angry and felt duped. Surely, if she'd only thought about it, she'd have figured out that he had no idea. None.

Holly removed the ring and handed it back to him. He stared at it a moment before taking it. "I guess I should go."

"I'm really sorry." Holly sniffed, and a tear trickled down her cheek. "I really thought you knew."

"I didn't. I'll tell Kloie good-bye on my way out."

The door slammed behind him.

Chapter 10

Luke waved Kloie down. She and Hayden rode over to him on their brand-new bikes. He wasn't quite sure how to handle this good-bye. Kloie was a smart kid. He'd have to tread carefully. He'd begun to have fatherly feelings toward her, which would only compound the breakup or whatever this was called.

Kloie glanced at the car keys he carried. "Luke, where are you going?" Her brow furrowed.

"Hey, kiddo." He decided this wasn't the time or day for final good-byes. "I'm taking off, but I'll see you later." *Hopefully, a last good-bye will be all right with your mom.*

Kloie wore a knowing expression. "My mom didn't keep the ring, did she?"

Luke's throat constricted. "Nope." *Holly should be the one out here explaining this, not me.* "With you guys moving and everything, we decided this might not work so well after all."

Kloie's bottom lip quivered. "You're never coming back, are you?" Kloie laid her bike down and wrapped her arms around Luke's waist. "I wanted you to be my dad." She let out a sob.

Luke knelt in front of her, wiping her tears away with his thumbs. "I know." His voice cracked. "I wanted the same thing." He wrapped her in a tight hug, and her tears soaked the shoulder of his jacket.

He held her while she cried. He caught a glimpse of Holly watching the scene play out, and he felt angrier with her for not coming out here and facing her own consequences instead of letting him deal with the fallout.

Finally, he peeled Kloie from around his neck. "I need to go, and it's pretty cold out. Maybe you and Hayden should both get inside before you turn into Popsicles."

Hayden laughed. "Bye, Kloie."

Kloie waved. Luke helped her get her bike inside the garage and gave her another quick hug. "Do you still remember my cell phone number?"

Kloie nodded.

"Call me before you leave, and I'll come by to give you one last hug."

Kloie nodded again. Her lips were puckered into a pout.

As Luke drove away, a very dismal Kloie stood on the front porch watching him go.

"I'm really, really mad at you," Kloie informed Holly when she entered the house.

"Honey—" Holly attempted to comfort her daughter, but she went straight to her room. Holly laid on the couch and let her own tears run free.

At noon, Mel arrived as planned. When Holly opened the

door to let her in, her expression changed from holiday glee to panic. "Holly, what's wrong? What's happened?"

Holly took her through the morning's events, and both women were in tears by the end of the narrative.

"Is that what you really want—to give Luke up and leave?"

"No." Holly's eyes burned from all the crying. "He's the best thing that's happened to me and Kloie in a very long time."

"Then don't go. Don't leave him."

Holly cried harder. "We don't even have a place to live."

"Live with me. It would only be temporary. One short year. We could make it work. Fight for him, Holly. He's worth it."

Holly nodded, feeling a sense of purpose.

"Call Mr. Olson and explain what's happened. Surely, he wants you to be happy."

Holly wasn't so sure about the happy part. He wanted them in Oregon. She didn't think he cared if happy was part of the deal. Just thinking about his reaction caused a ball of anxiety to knot in her stomach.

She sucked in a deep breath and paced into the kitchen. "I need to call him, even though I don't want to. With God's help, I'm learning to face my fears. I'm going to do it! For once, I'm going to do the hard thing."

"Atta girl." Mel went and got the cordless phone from its cradle in the kitchen and handed it to Holly.

She dialed and relayed the facts to both of her in-laws. "So, Kloie and I won't be moving after all."

She heard her mother-in-law sniff.

"Dear, why don't you go ahead and hang up? Holly and I have some business to take care of."

Holly heard a click and knew it was only she and her father-in-law on the line. And, of course, Mel, but he didn't know that.

"Holly, you and I made an agreement based on your word and good faith. Surely, you don't plan to rescind?"

Holly glanced at Mel, who'd been listening on another phone. Mel nodded.

"I had no intention of breaking our agreement, but after meeting Luke, I must." *I hope he'll still want me.* "The house closes next week, so I will send you everything I owe you. If you'd like, I'll even include three months' interest."

"Holly, dear, it's not about the money. It's about your word of honor. This deal cost me a lot of time and money, and you need to stand on your word."

Red flags rose. "What deal?"

"Getting the money together to loan to you, of course."

Holly got a nagging feeling in the pit of her stomach. She needed to end this call and place another one to Walter.

"I really must go now, but I'll have Kloie call you later this evening to thank you for all the nice gifts you sent. As always, you overdid."

"Holly, I will not permit you to back out on our agreement."

"You don't have a choice. We aren't coming." The more she stood up for herself, the stronger she felt. "Merry Christmas." And with that, she hung up the phone.

Mel jumped around. "You were great! Way to put the man in his place. And how dare he threaten you." Mel stared at Holly for a minute. "What? What are you thinking?"

"I think he had something to do with my layoff, and I'm

calling Walter to find out."

At first, Walter denied everything, but Holly pushed.

"I'm sorry, Holly." The words carried shame. "I'd accrued a large gambling debt, and he offered to help me out. The one stipulation—your layoff."

Anger shot through Holly. "I can't believe he'd do that!" On the other hand, why should she be surprised?

"Please don't tell Rosemary. She thinks you quit."

"I can't promise, but thank you for telling me the truth. Merry Christmas, Walter."

Holly hung up the phone and immediately dialed her father-in-law. "How dare you speak of honor and the value of a person's word!" Holly laid out what he'd done, and he made no denial.

"Kloie and I will not be coming. She needs an honest man like Luke in her life more than she needs to live near her deceitful and conniving grandfather."

Mel let out a little gasp.

"I will have Kloie call you later, but if you don't give your blessing for us to stay in Wyoming, I might have to tell her the whole story—beginning to end."

Holly didn't like being mean or manipulative, but it seemed to be the language he spoke best.

After Holly hung up, she and Mel hugged and did a little jig. "Who knew being forthright was so freeing?"

"I did." Mel laughed. She had tried a million times to get Holly to be more honest and open.

"Well, it feels good, so thanks for nagging me this past decade. And now, will you go check on my daughter while I drive over to Luke's?"

A smile lit Mel's face. "I will."

Holly drove to Luke's, praying all the way.

❄

Luke had spent the afternoon praying. He realized he'd way overreacted. Holly moving to Oregon didn't have to be the end of them. Sure, it would make it a little harder, but not impossible.

He grabbed his coat and keys, no longer ready to so easily accept her no.

Luke went through the laundry room and into the garage. He opened the door and climbed up into his truck. He started the engine and glanced in the rearview mirror. Holly pulled into his driveway. Surely, that was a good sign.

He hopped out of his truck just as she climbed out of her car. They met somewhere in the middle.

"Were you going somewhere?" she asked.

"To your house."

She smiled. "To my house?" Her voice had a hopeful catch to it.

"To apologize. I don't care if you move to Timbuktu. I still want to get to know *us* better."

Holly took a step toward him. "I'm not going."

He closed the gap. Their breath mingled into visible white clouds. "You're not?"

"Nope." Holly took the initiative. She wrapped her arms around his neck and standing on tiptoe planted her lips against his. "Yes," she whispered when the kiss ended.

"Yes?" Luke asked, though he thought he knew what she meant. However, he wasn't about to take chances. As they'd established earlier today, their communication skills needed work.

"Yes to the ring. Yes to you, and even yes to Holly Jolly."

Luke laughed hard. The name thing had never occurred to him. Then he grew serious. "I love you, Holly. I'm sure of that already."

"I'm sure, too." And they sealed their knowledge with a kiss.

Luke grabbed her hand. "Let's go tell Kloie that it's a jolly holiday after all."

JERI ODELL

Jeri writes from her home in Tucson, Arizona where she is a native. Since the onset of her writing ministry in 1998, she's penned seven Heartsong novels, seven novellas and one nonfiction book. One of her novels, *Hidden Treasures*, was awarded the Romance Writer's of America's Faith, Hope, and Love Inspirational Reader's Choice Award. She currently has a novella in *The Spinster Brides of Cactus Corner* that is one of the top three finalists for the same award. She gives all praise and glory to God. Without Him, she'd have nothing to write because He is the ultimate Author of romance.

Jeri has a deep love for family and friends, holding them near to her heart. Married for thirty-five years, she and her husband, Dean, were high school sweethearts. They are the proud parents of three adult children and are enjoying their newest role as grandparents. Her favorite activity is playing games with family and spending time together.

Dean and Jeri attend a large church in the Tucson area, where she also works part time in the finance office. She is also involved in the women's ministry area, teaching Bible studies on marriage and parenting. For more information, you may visit her Web site at www.jeriodell.com or e-mail her at jeri@jeriodell.com.

Jack Santa

by Tammy Shuttlesworth

To everyone in my family,
no matter where you live, may you remember
and appreciate the true spirit of Christmas.
To my husband and daughters, Caryn and Taryn,
I hope the Christmas traditions we created
as you grew stay with you no matter where you are.
Also, special thanks to my uncle, Ray Johnston,
for allowing me to include his poem in this book.

The LORD *will open the heavens,*
the storehouse of his bounty,
to send rain on your land in season
and to bless all the work of your hands.
DEUTERONOMY 28:12 NIV

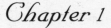

Chapter 1

Hurry, Mommy. Don't wanna miss Santa!"

"I'm sure there's time." Stacy smiled at her six-year-old son. All he needed was a pair of pointy ears and—with his brown eyes and dark, curly hair—Daniel would pass for one of Santa's elves himself.

"I hear the fire trucks, Mommy."

"So do I." Stacy turned and listened as the wobbling wails of sirens grew closer.

Whip Wilson, her closest neighbor, had told her the fire department's parade would travel their small-town streets today—the Saturday after Thanksgiving—to spread their Christmas greetings. Thanksgiving Day had been hard enough to get through as a single parent in a new town. Christmas would be next. *Alone. Without Timothy.*

Without Timothy. The phrase pierced her heart, shattering her composure.

"Mommy!"

"Stand here and watch for them," she managed, pointing to a low window. "Let me know when you see them on our street."

255

Daniel obeyed, and Stacy headed to change out of her pajamas.

"We should have gotten up earlier today," she said. No matter how she tried, she always remembered the old Saturdays. "Timothy and I had so many plans for the future. Now they're gone. Just like him." Familiar tears filled her eyes.

Separating the miniblind fins, she peered out at the persistent low clouds that hung over Antler, Wyoming. They'd produced a light snow yesterday, and more was forecast for tonight. She shivered, still not used to the northern climate.

"Did I make the right decision to separate from the military and move here to Timothy's hometown to run his parents' mobile home park?" There it was again. Another decision she'd made. . .alone. Well, not all alone.

God was with her. Eternally. Always. Forever. With her.

"Mommy!"

"Yes, Daniel." Looking in a mirror, she ran her fingers through auburn curls that touched her shoulders. Her eyes were the same shade as today's sky, but she couldn't change them. She patted powder on the numerous freckles on her cheeks, a result of the Louisiana sun she'd left a month ago, then threw on jeans and a green sweatshirt. Stacy wrinkled her nose. She should have more pride in her appearance, but what did it matter? It wasn't like she was going to meet anyone special anyway.

Chapter 2

Mommy!"

"Things will work out," she told herself, heading to the kitchen.

"They is coming," Daniel said.

"They *are* coming," Stacy corrected as they made their way to the front porch, properly bundled against the chilly temperature.

"Whip says Santa throws candy," Daniel went on as the English lesson went over his head. "Can I stand by the road so I gets lots of candy?" He jumped up and down as he pointed to the strobing red and white lights bouncing off the park's entrance signs.

"Standing by Rudolph would be better." Stacy indicated a painted cutout she and Timothy had purchased their first Christmas together. It stood halfway between the porch and the road.

Daniel roared away, imitating his favorite NASCAR driver. He screeched to a halt, waving both arms at the caravan headed their way.

As she waited, Stacy studied two churches across the road. Built of the same red brick, one's steeple stretched to the gunmetal sky while the other's had no outward ornamentation but a marquee. Tall pines clustered around both as if assigned as guardians of the faith.

The structures brought back warm memories of her childhood, of a time when her life was simple, when Stacy trusted her parents to make everything all right. Now she was the parent—a lonely, single parent. She checked to ensure Daniel was fine then closed her eyes.

Father, I try hard to teach Daniel about You, but how do I know I'm doing things right? Shouldn't a boy have a father to grow up properly? How do I know I'm making the right decisions?

"Merry Christmas!" A public address system broadcast Santa's warm, mellow voice around her neighborhood.

Stacy's eyes flew open, and she found a fire truck stopped in front of their mobile home. Sitting on top, a smiling Santa waved.

"You, too," she replied.

"You have to speak up or your Christmas wish won't come true."

"Come on, Mommy," Daniel shouted from the lawn. "Talk louder to Santa."

With his gloved hands clasped full of candy, Daniel looked as if he were opening every Christmas gift a six-year-old could gather. And, Stacy noticed, Daniel smiled that smile that melted her heart. *How could she tell him no?*

Stacy glanced back toward Santa. His modern-day sleigh—a sleek, red, shiny fire truck with silver bells tied to the front grille—seemed larger than life.

"Happy holidays," Stacy called, trying to sound as if she meant it.

"That's more like it." Santa's voice echoed again around the mobile home park.

A few cars continued to roll slowly ahead of the fire truck. Stacy expected Santa's newfangled carriage to do likewise now that she'd replied.

"Come on, son. Time to go back in before we freeze."

"Mommy?" Daniel appeared at her side so suddenly that Stacy wondered if he'd flown through the yard.

"Yes?"

Daniel frowned. "I think you made Santa mad 'cause he climbed off the fire truck."

A glance confirmed his comment; Santa was walking toward them.

"Cool," Daniel whispered.

Stacy wouldn't call it cool, but she had no choice but to watch Santa draw near. Between a fur-trimmed hat and phony white beard, frosty dark eyes peered at her. Feisty red cheeks, a floppy pillow belly, and the largest pair of black rubber boots she'd ever seen completed his outfit.

"Ho, ho, ho," Santa chortled as he reached her bottom step.

She noticed his padded stomach shook like the proverbial bowl full of jelly.

"Ho, ho, ho, yourself." Stacy was unsure where this conversation was headed. As a child, she hadn't been allowed to believe in Santa, let alone talk with him.

What were the rules in a situation like this?

Santa's phony white beard slipped out of place. She caught a gleaming smile before he tugged it back. "Have you been good?"

"Aren't we all?" Stacy said, feeling strangely at ease with the character in the red suit.

"Not really. Some are far from it." Santa leaned down and winked at Daniel. "Unlike little boys who top my 'good boy list.'"

Daniel grinned. "Me?"

"Daniel," Stacy said, "Santa needs to get back to his sleigh ...er, fire truck. It's cold out here, and he has other children to visit."

"But I wanna know if my name's on his 'good list,'" Daniel said. "Whip didn't say nuttin''bout a list."

Santa stood up and poked a finger under his chin. At least he tried to, but Stacy thought he looked as if he might be trying to shave instead. "Let's see. Whip is Whip Wilson, your neighbor, right?"

Daniel's eyes widened. "You know Mr. Whip?"

"Yes. You're Daniel Waters, right?" Santa asked.

Daniel's grin showed a missing front tooth. "Santa knows me, Mommy!"

"So I see, Daniel." Stacy wondered how much Whip Wilson had to do with Santa...or whomever he was...knowing her son's name. She stared at Santa, trying to see beyond the somewhat skewed beard and padding. Something about his eyes made her want to forget his costume and anything else that went along with her disbelief in Santa.

"So, Daniel, what do you want for Christmas?" Santa asked. "A bike?"

Daniel shook his head.

"A drum set?"

Daniel shook his head again.

Santa scratched his beard without dislodging it. "A train?"

Daniel shook his head for the third time. "I wanna big, big race car I can ride in, but Mommy says they costs-sa too much. Don't you, Mommy?"

Embarrassed that Daniel knew enough to hint at money problems, Stacy thought about climbing under her deck. Maybe she could run inside. Had an adult ever run away from Santa? The thought made her chuckle, and she quickly covered her mouth with her hands. Santa didn't appear bothered by Daniel's candor, or her short laugh.

"Hmm. A magic set?" Santa tried again.

"Nah." Daniel glanced up at his mother before giving Santa his toothless grin. "But I really need a daddy. Do you have one to bring me?"

Chapter 3

Jack Trenton cleared his throat then put his hands on his hips. Before he'd left the fire station, several people had offered hints on how to handle the parade route. "Smile a lot." "Be yourself." "Wave big." "Mean it when you say ho, ho, ho."

No one had mentioned something like this. Of course, no one had planned on him leaving the fire engine. Jack gazed at Daniel's mother. She didn't look happy.

"To be honest, Santa doesn't usually bring daddies," Jack said.

His heart gave a weird bump Jack hadn't felt before. Maybe everyone who dressed as Santa experienced the same thing at one time or another. He knew it was a weak excuse.

He'd seen the boy's mother in church the last month or so. All dressed up and sitting near the back while he sang in the choir. But, he'd never *noticed* Stacy Waters. Not like today. Now, thick reddish brown hair peeked out of a ski cap and radiated sunshine against the dark sky. Expressive gray eyes let him know how unhappy she was with the turn the conversation had taken.

"If you don't have a daddy, that makes you the man of the

house, Daniel," Jack said.

Daniel latched onto his mother's legs. "Does having no daddy make me a house-man thing, Mommy?"

Jack gazed down at the boy. His heart did another weird skip-thing. He knew what it was like to grow up fatherless. Why had he gotten off the truck? The deal was for him to ride around, wave, smile, and shout "Ho, ho, ho" and "Merry Christmas." He wasn't supposed to stop and talk with anyone. Jack doubted he'd get in trouble.

What were the rules in a situation like this?

"Yes, you're my man of the house, Daniel. It's time we got you back inside," he heard Stacy say.

"He's pretty well bundled up," Jack pointed out. "He looks pretty excited. I don't get off that fire truck for just anyone. Will it hurt to let him stay out a few more minutes?"

"It might. Daniel gets sick easily," she informed him.

"I didn't know that."

That wasn't the only thing he didn't know, Jack realized. He knew their names because Whip had told him when Jack asked a few weeks ago. He hadn't expected to see them living here in this mobile home park, though.

"Whip says Santa knows everything," Daniel inserted. "How come you don't?" The little boy brought Jack back to the present.

Jack squatted to Daniel's level. "Santa's a busy man this time of year. I'm helping him out by standing in for him today. My name is really Jack Trenton. I go to the same church you do, and I sing in the choir."

Jack thought Stacy relaxed somewhat as he shared that bit of information.

"What-za a stanning-in?" Daniel probed.

"*Who* is a *stand-in*?" Stacy amended. "A stand-in takes the place of someone else whenever that person can't do what they're supposed to."

Jack thought the explanation somewhat long, but since he hadn't been around a lot of children before, he figured Stacy knew what she was doing.

"Do you feed reindeer?" Daniel quizzed. "What do they eat? Do you make 'em go fast? How do you know which deer goes where?"

"Daniel, remember, there are other children waiting to see Santa," Stacy said. "You go on inside, and I'll be right there. We'll play with your cars."

"Aw, Mommy." Daniel gave Santa a long, sad look.

"Now, Daniel," Stacy answered.

Jack stood up and stared at Stacy. Couldn't she tell how much Daniel wanted to stand there and talk to Santa. . .er, him?

Daniel turned and headed across the porch. Jack's heartbeat matched the *thwump thwump* of Daniel's boots until the little boy disappeared through the front door.

"Why did you send him in so fast?" Jack asked when the door closed. "Don't forget, you can't lie to Santa."

"Right. Well, you told him you weren't Santa, anyway. Plus, Daniel already knows Santa isn't real."

"You're not kidding, are you?"

"No. It's uncommon, but that's how I was raised."

Jack leaned on the stair railing. "I learned Santa wasn't real the Christmas after I lost my dad. I was eight."

"I had lots of friends who believed in Santa," Stacy reflected, stamping her feet and rubbing her gloved hands together. "Most of them were about that old when they found out the truth."

"I can't believe you knew there wasn't a Santa the whole time you grew up."

"It's true. My parents put up a huge tree and there were presents, but my brother and I knew as soon as we could understand that Santa didn't bring them."

"Hurry up, Trenton!" a voice called from atop the fire truck. "We're freezing up here!"

Jack waved in acknowledgment. He gave Stacy what he hoped was one of his best Santa smiles. "I don't think we've been properly introduced. I'm Jack Trenton."

He stuck out a hand, realized he wore obnoxious black rubber gloves, yanked one off, and extended his right hand again. "I'm only doing this Santa thing as a favor. I'm usually one of the ones up there on the truck."

Stacy took the proffered hand tentatively. "It's nice of you to volunteer."

Jack grinned. "If that's a compliment, I'll take it. I'd like to know more about you since we go to the same church, but I seem to have overlooked you in our large congregation. Do you. . .work?"

"Not right now," Stacy said. "I just separated from the Air Force and moved here a month ago."

"I can honestly say I've never known a military woman before."

He thought a gleam of humor resided in Stacy's answer. "I doubt Santa travels much in military circles. Too many missiles ready to pounce on strange, flying objects I would think.

I was in for eight years."

"Really?" He sounded like an electronic toy in need of new batteries.

Stacy nodded. "It's not that rare. Females make up at least twenty percent of the enlisted force."

"I didn't know that."

"I suppose that statistic wouldn't interest most people." She glanced toward the street. "Thanks for stopping by, but your friends are starting to look like icicles. It's supposed to be pretty chilly tonight." She turned toward her door. "I guess you know to dress warmly for your ride back to the North Pole?"

Jack liked Stacy's banter, and her son didn't have a daddy. How sad to be alone at this time of year, or at any time of year. The pain of remembrance rang in his heart. He ignored it.

"Chilly," Jack echoed. "Right. I will. Do you know much about geography?"

"Afraid not. It wasn't my favorite subject."

"Australia is in the southern hemisphere, so it's summer there when it's winter here."

"So you're headed to Australia and not the North Pole?"

Jack laughed. "No. But if I dressed as Santa Down Under, I could wear red shorts and a T-shirt instead of this woolly suit. Maybe I'd ride a Jet Ski instead of a fire truck."

"Sounds like it would be a lot warmer."

"Can you imagine picnicking on the beach at Christmas while you're singing carols?"

"Too chilly to picnic here today," Stacy concurred. "And, it doesn't look like your frozen friends are spreading out any red and white tablecloths on top of that truck."

"Probably not," Jack said. "I'd better go then."

Stacy turned the doorknob. "See you around. At church."

"Stacy?"

"Yes?"

"Could I come back later? After the parade, I mean?"

"I thought Santa only visited on Christmas Eve," she challenged. Jack was positive her eyes twinkled.

"You said you didn't believe in him. So I'll visit as Jack Trenton and not Santa."

"I don't think that would be—"

"I can explain real reindeer to Daniel," Jack interrupted.

"Well..."

Jack didn't blame Stacy for her hesitancy. The only thing she knew about him was he dressed as Santa and rode around on top of a fire truck. They weren't the best credentials in the world.

"Call Whip and have him vouch for me," Jack added. "You can ask him to join us if you'd like."

"I'll do that. You're only coming to talk to Daniel about reindeer?"

Jack nodded.

"I suppose that will be okay." Jack got the idea Stacy didn't think it was.

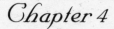

Chapter 4

"Wowsers, Mommy! You asked Santa to visit?" Daniel roared through the kitchen, pretending to squeal his brakes every time he rounded the table's corners.

"Mr. Trenton was only dressed as Santa for the parade, remember?" Stacy asked for the hundredth time. She kept the fact she didn't think Jack Trenton would even show up to herself.

"Can I tell Whip?"

Though she'd checked with Whip to verify Jack's background, Stacy called and got permission for Daniel to visit their neighbor. With her son two doors down, Stacy eyed her humble home. She didn't have much in the way of furniture, but she'd just moved here and wasn't sure she would stay, so what did it matter? It wasn't like she would entertain a herd of elves. The idea was preposterous, wasn't it?

Whip soon escorted Daniel home and took a seat across the worn aluminum kitchen table from Stacy. His neatly combed white hair and ever-present brown tweed sweater always reminded Stacy of her grandfather. Daniel sat with them eating his favorite snack—a peanut butter sandwich.

"Daniel says Santa's coming to visit," Whip began, winking as he spoke. "I've known Jack for twenty years or more. He's a good Christian, but what if he weren't? You know there are some loony-gooney people out there nowadays."

Stacy patted Whip's wrinkled hand. "Besides the fact he's a Christian, I didn't figure the fire department would have someone as Santa if he didn't have a good heart. I appreciate your concern, but I'm relieved you think highly of Jack."

Whip snorted. "I promised your in-laws when you moved here I'd look out for you. A woman alone has to be careful."

"I worry about every decision I make," Stacy said. "But I think Jack will take one look at the worn carpet, tattered sofa, and thirteen-inch TV and forget Santa represents peace and goodwill. I predict he'll run faster than his sleigh can fly."

"Jack Trenton doesn't run from much," Whip said bluntly.

"Well, I have you to protect me if I need it. Come on, Whip. It's not like Jack will be here every day. I haven't met a man yet who wants a woman and a rambunctious boy."

"You looking?" Whip's gaze met Stacy's.

"Not right now."

"Jack may be the one who'll change your mind."

Stacy shrugged. "Maybe, but I don't need anyone else to pick up after. Daniel is enough. As for today, Jack will show up, spend a few minutes in chitchat, then disappear back to his world."

The afternoon revolved around Christmas specials and football games on the few TV channels Stacy got without cable. She enjoyed listening to Whip and Daniel laugh at animated clay reindeer throwing snowballs. Noise was preferable to the silence she faced after Daniel went to sleep at night.

Wandering through the living room, she paused to adjust silver strands on a three-foot tree she'd bought at a local flea market. A kiosk had prewritten letters from Santa to send to children. Stacy had decided not to send one to Daniel since she didn't want to encourage his belief in the mythical character.

Was this morning's parade the wrong decision, then? What about letting Jack Trenton visit?

Stacy studied the tree. White lights threaded the branches, and miniature boxes wrapped in silver dangled from the needle ends. It was by no means the sort of scrape-the-ceiling tree she recalled from her childhood. Without touching Timothy's insurance money, it was what her funds allowed. Another decision she'd made. Like the rest, was it the right one?

Stacy hoped Daniel wasn't disappointed at the small number of presents he got this year. It was hard for a six-year-old to do without a father, or to understand the difference between finances and wishes.

A normal six-year-old shouldn't have to. A normal boy should have two parents, not just one, no matter how much that one loves him.

Tires crunching on gravel sounded in the driveway.

"Santa's here!" Daniel jumped from the couch and skidded to a halt at the front door.

"Wait till he knocks," Whip admonished from the sofa.

"Merry Christmas." Jack's exuberant greeting carried through the metal door.

"Mommy?"

"Ask who it is," Stacy said. "Never open the door unless you know who's on the other side."

"You invited Santa," Daniel reminded her. "Whip's the only one who comes to see us."

Stacy winced. Sometimes Daniel was too wise for his age.

"Who is it?" Daniel called out.

"Jack Trenton."

Relief filled Stacy's heart. As the afternoon waned and Jack hadn't shown, she was sure his gesture to visit had been just courtesy.

"Hi!" Jack entered with a gust of wind that tossed his chestnut hair around.

Stacy took note of his tall, athletic figure clad in well-worn blue jeans, a loose-fitting navy pullover sweater, and not-so-new cowboy boots. He handed her a white plastic sack with the name of a local grocery chain written on the outside.

"Treats for later," he explained, shrugging off a leather khaki-colored coat. "Hope you don't mind."

"Hi, yourself," she managed. "You didn't have to bring anything." Taking his coat and the bag, she silently gave Jack points for not staring at the worn interior.

Jack smiled at Daniel. "I'm glad it's warm in here. It was pretty cold on that truck this morning."

A wide-eyed Daniel tugged at Stacy's shirt. "When will he told me 'bout the reindeer?"

"*Tell* you, and soon, son," Stacy promised.

She heard Jack and Whip trade small talk. "Call me later, Stacy," Whip directed.

"Sure, but I thought you were staying."

Whip nodded at Jack. "No need to now."

With Whip gone, Jack motioned to the TV. "What are we watching?"

"*How the Grinch Stole Christmas*," Daniel answered. "Can you watch it with me?"

Jack chuckled. "It's my favorite show. I'd be honored. When it's over, we'll discuss those reindeer."

Stacy stared at the white bag hanging off one hand and the heavy jacket lying across her other forearm. A woodsy aroma drifted up from it, reminding her of the man in her house. She had to tell herself to put the jacket on the back of a kitchen chair and the bag on the counter. As her fingers lingered on the leather fabric, the rugged scent of a man's cologne wouldn't quit calling out to her. She jerked her hand away.

"That little Cindy Lou Who is the best, isn't she?" Jack stretched his legs beneath the wobbly coffee table and draped his arm over the back of the sofa.

Daniel looked so natural sitting next to him, Stacy's throat tightened. Timothy should be the one sitting there, making small talk and teaching Daniel the words to that "dar-who-yar-lei" song, or whatever it was called. She turned away and busied herself wiping the kitchen sink.

"Need something to drink?" Stacy asked when a commercial came on. "I have water or coffee."

"Coffee's fine, but just one cup or I won't sleep tonight," Jack said.

"Can I have coffee, too?" Daniel asked. "Like Jack Santa?"

"None for you, kiddo. His name is Jack Trenton," Stacy reminded her son. "Santa is just. . ." She looked at Jack helplessly.

"Something I do to make my heart happy," Jack inserted.

While the men—Stacy refused to call Jack a boy—watched the show, she brewed coffee and popped popcorn. She paced between the stove and the counter. At one point she found herself staring out the kitchen window at a nicely customized dark blue truck parked in her driveway. To think this morning when she woke, all she looked forward to was playing with Daniel and figuring out how to get a cherry drink stain out of her carpet.

Stop it. Jack came over here only to talk about reindeer with Daniel.

"You're missing the good parts," Jack called over his shoulder.

Stacy studied the way soft reddish brown curls disappeared beneath Jack's shirt.

No, the view's fine from here.

"I won't be much longer," she replied, reprimanding herself for letting her mind wander in directions it shouldn't. She had to remember what was important. She had to make decisions that affected her and Daniel's lives. It wouldn't do to complicate them with a man, no matter how handsome he was.

❄

Jack didn't know the last time he last enjoyed a Christmas cartoon show as much as this one. With Daniel's small body pressed against him, his body heat warmed Jack more than any pullover. It was an unfamiliar feeling, but Jack didn't mind. It felt good to be needed, even if it was just for tonight.

The show ended, and Daniel pushed himself off the sofa onto the floor as if it was an age-old habit. "Mommy says there's no such thing as Santa."

Jack met Daniel's gaze. He saw adoration in those huge brown eyes, which seemed so much like his own. "Really?"

Daniel nodded. "She says Santa is a made-up guy, like Power Rangers."

Jack ruffled Daniel's hair. "That's one way to look at him."

"You're not made-up, are you?" Daniel asked.

Jack pushed up a shirtsleeve and pinched his arm. "Nope. Feels pretty real to me. Want to try?" He offered Daniel his arm.

Daniel reached out and rubbed his hand across the dark swirls of hair growing above Jack's wrist. "Hey, Mommy! This is neat. Will I have hair on my arm like this when I'm older?"

Stacy's gaze locked with Jack's. Something other than a cute kid question shot between them. "We'll have to wait and see," she managed.

"Okay." Daniel turned to Jack. "Can I call you Jack Santa?"

Jack slid a quick glance at Stacy. *Careful, Trenton,* he warned himself. *She's obviously uncomfortable.*

"If your mommy doesn't mind, it's okay with me," Jack said. "You know, Daniel, while there may not be a real Santa, there is someone known as Kris Kringle, and there are reindeer."

Jack retrieved a book stowed in the plastic grocery bag. He settled back on the sofa and pulled Daniel up beside him. "I checked this out from the Antler Public Library this afternoon."

For thirty minutes, Jack wowed Daniel with facts about the four-legged animals. Daniel seemed to absorb everything. Stacy stayed in the rocking chair and listened, a quilt snuggled around her.

Jack tried to avoid looking at Stacy, but it was hard. She was curled up in that rocking chair with a faded pink and green quilt over her. He didn't think she was cold. More likely, she thought he was invading her space, that a stranger shouldn't lavish so much attention on her child. Did single parents always worry about others interfering? Had his mother worried about that the three times she married after his dad died?

Jack tried to force his mind back to the book, but while he read to Daniel, he kept thinking, *Good thing I'll be leaving soon; a woman like Stacy Waters could easily win my heart.*

Chapter 5

Daniel woke Stacy at the crack of dawn, each shouted word accented by a bounce on her bed. "I. Wanna. See. Jack. Santa. Today."

Stacy pulled him close and kissed him. "I don't know, kiddo. Mr. Trenton didn't say anything about coming back when he left last night."

"Call and ask him."

Stacy ruffled Daniel's head. "I don't have his phone number."

"Jack Santa's neat-o."

Stacy didn't argue with Daniel's assessment of Jack. Six hours and her heart teetered on the verge of falling. . .for Santa. . .er. . . for Jack.

No, the holidays were the reason she was acting this way. They were a lonely time, and she was lonely, and he was. . . handsome.

"How about breakfast so we can get ready for worship?"

"Yippee! I'll see Jack Santa. 'Member, Mommy? He said he sang in the choir."

Stacy didn't correct Daniel's enthusiasm. She didn't want to think about how much she agreed with Daniel's declaration.

❄

Despite praying before going to bed, Jack rose at one in the morning and knelt again, asking God's direction for his life. Sleepless nights were familiar to him, and he dealt with them by prayer or reading his favorite chapters in Isaiah. Before church, he talked with his pastor.

"I don't know what possessed me to get off that fire truck, Herb," Jack confessed. "Can you help me put things in perspective?"

"You said you've seen Stacy here at church. You're a caring man, Jack," Herb Holton replied. "It's not unlike you to share with those who aren't as fortunate as yourself."

"I know, but this seems—is—different. I think Stacy is still hurting from losing her husband, but every once in a while, she'd get this twinkle in her eyes that made me feel special. As if she hadn't laughed much in the last few years and was glad I was there, even though I was dressed as Santa."

Herb laughed. "Santa or not, that sparkle in a woman's eyes will do in the best of men, Jack. Sounds like you already got it bad."

"Oh, no," Jack refuted. "I only went back to visit because of Daniel. You should have seen that kid's smile."

Herb shifted in his chair. "I don't think you're only worried about the boy. I think Stacy matters, too."

"If you're right, Herb, what do I do next?"

"Same as you'd do with any other woman you want to pursue a relationship with."

Easy for Herb to say. He hadn't been passed around while his mother searched for a replacement for love.

❄

Stacy leaned back in the pew and listened to the sermon on love. "The world needs more people willing to love as Christ loved," the minister said at the end. "Are you doing your part to love others?"

Stacy thought she was. Her gaze drifted to the choir in the balcony. Jack's head was barely visible, but soft track lighting highlighted the chestnut color. Upon arriving in Wyoming a month ago, she'd selected a large church. She'd hoped for a while to remain anonymous until she got her bearings, but Jack Trenton had apparently noticed her.

A high-pitched voice drew Stacy's thoughts back to the large fellowship room. Glancing up, she found a petite woman in a mauve mid-length skirt and a soft pink sweater.

"Today the children's choir will present a song they've worked on for several weeks. We planned to present it the Sunday before Christmas, but the children are eager to sing it today."

A group of giggling children wove their way to the front and took their places. Stacy smiled as she watched Daniel in the front row. Though he hadn't been there long, he'd been able to join them. Besides race cars, he loved singing, even if he didn't get all the words right.

"Joy to the world. The Lord has come," the off-key voices caroled; some high, some low, some squeaky. The adult choir sang a barely audible background to the children. At the end, applause greeted the smiling children's faces.

"Was I gooder than the rest?" Daniel asked his mom as he took his seat beside her.

"*Better*, not gooder. You were the best," Stacy agreed, hugging him tightly.

"Miss Tyler said it was a 'prise for our parents, and I kept the 'prise."

"A surprise," Stacy corrected.

"Yeah, that," Daniel agreed, grinning. He was growing up too fast. The gap in his front teeth reminded her of the hole in her heart that had been there since they'd lost Timothy. She turned away to hide her tears.

❄

Jack tried to concentrate on singing the background as they'd practiced with the children. Trouble was, he kept searching for Stacy and missing the choir director's beat.

Frustrated, Jack studied the room instead. On top of a brown carpet, perfectly aligned wooden pews with dark green padded seats marched from front to back like drummer boys. He couldn't see it, but the baptismal sat to the left of the podium.

Jack recalled the night he'd turned his life over to Christ, fifteen years ago, when he was twelve. What a difference knowing his Savior made! He whispered a heartfelt prayer.

Father, how blessed I am You took care of me even before I knew of Your existence. Thank You for giving Your Son so I have hope of eternal life, and for taking care of me. Father, do You think You could keep watch over Stacy and Daniel, too?

With the service over, Jack moved toward the front door, intent on finding Stacy and Daniel before they left. He'd mulled

Herb's wisdom over and decided Herb was right.

"Yoo-hoo, Jack! How'd the Santa thing go?"

Cindy Tyler hurried toward him. She paid no attention to the disapproving looks sent her way by some of the more mature ladies.

"I had fun, Cindy," Jack said as she stopped beside him. "Seeing those kids smile made sitting in that cold seat worthwhile."

"I'm sure a few female hearts fluttered when they saw you, Jack. Mine does every time." Cindy giggled, something she did way too much, in Jack's opinion, for someone in her late-twenties. "Look," she went on, "some from our young-adult group are going to eat lunch. I don't have a partner. Will you come with me?"

Jack had once thought her overtures were Christian friendship. He'd since realized she had him targeted for bigger things, no doubt because of his money.

Stacy's sweet smile came to mind. "Sorry, but I have other plans."

Cindy chewed her lower lip. "What if I pay?"

"It's not a matter of money, Cindy."

"You don't like me, do you? No matter what I do, it's never enough."

"That's not it at all," Jack responded. He didn't want to hurt Cindy's feelings, but every time she approached him with a plan to get together, Jack turned her down. He preferred not to get involved with her. Maybe because he didn't know her well enough?

Yesterday you raced to Stacy's porch then spent the evening with her and her son. You don't know them. At all. Explain that.

Jack couldn't, nor did he want to try.

Cindy tucked a strand of bleached blond hair behind her right ear. "I hope your plans include food."

"I'm sure they will," Jack replied.

"Jack!"

Jack decided he'd do almost anything to keep Stacy's tiny dimple winking at him. "Yep. Just Jack Santa checking in to see how my favorite family in Antler, Wyoming, is doing."

"Mommy? Hey! It's Jack Santa!" Daniel slid to a stop, scrunching up the scatter rug at the door. "Yippee! He came back, Mommy! You said he wouldn't."

Jack wasn't sure, but he thought Stacy looked a little horror-stricken. He didn't blame her after Daniel's comment.

"Well, Daniel sounds glad to see you," Stacy said. "Can you come in?"

"Only if I'm not interrupting anything."

She pushed the rug Daniel had disturbed back into place with one foot. "Daniel was watching another Christmas show, and I was cleaning."

"So I see." Wisps of hair tumbled out of her ponytail, while a dust bunny lodged in her bangs. Jack reached out and flipped the offending bit away.

She jerked back. "What are you—"

"Just a little dirt," Jack clarified. "It didn't go well with your hairstyle."

Stacy stared at Jack. "Did you come back to get the snacks you left here last night?"

Jack shook his head. "I came to see how you and Daniel were. Why don't we get them out and see what's in there?" Jack plopped onto a kitchen chair.

"Candy canes!" Daniel's brown eyes ogled the green and white box Stacy pulled out of the sack.

"You haven't eaten lunch yet," Stacy admonished.

Jack swiped the box from her hand. She grabbed it back. "And neither have you," she said.

"These are more than candy, Daniel. Do you know why we have them?"

Daniel shuffled closer to Jack. "Nope, Jack Santa. Why?"

Jack drew Daniel onto his lap. "Long ago, a man who made good things to eat wanted something to tell the world how great Christ's love is."

"Christ is the Jesus baby. We talked about Him in church."

"Yes, but He didn't stay a baby. He grew up." Jack noticed Stacy join them at the table. It warmed his heart that she loved Christ. She was so unlike his mother in that regard.

"Like I'm growing up?" At Jack's nod, Daniel asked, "Is that it?"

Jack went on to say the hard candy stood for Christ because the Bible refers to Christ as the "Rock of Ages." He held the candy upside down with the hook at the bottom.

"He shaped them into a J because Jesus starts with *j*. Got it?"

"Mommy taught me some letters. I know that one 'cause my middle name is James."

Jack explained how the white showed Jesus' purity, the big red stripe for Jesus dying on the cross, and the three tiny stripes showed how the Roman soldiers treated Jesus.

"Can I have one now?" Daniel asked.

"Not until after you eat some lunch," Stacy inserted.

"Not cool," Daniel said.

"Sure it is," Jack said. "Candy canes are special, just like Jesus." Jack wanted to pound himself on the back for that one.

Daniel tilted his head. "Why's that make it cool?"

"Peppermint makes them sweet. In the Old Testament part of the Bible, they didn't have peppermint, so they used hyssop."

"Hiss-op?" Daniel repeated. "Yuck. Sounds like something you say to a cat."

Stacy's snicker was barely audible.

Jack held back his grin. "Possibly. While candy canes are pretty to look at, they remind us of Jesus and what He did for us."

"Mommy told me Jesus died, Jack Santa."

"I'm glad you know that because it's important. Jesus is a very special person."

"My daddy died," Daniel said. "I don't 'member him, but Mommy does. Sometimes she cries about it."

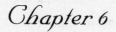

Chapter 6

Stacy pressed her hands on the tabletop and stood up. Despite Daniel's admission about her tears, Stacy's gaze lingered on Jack. No blue jeans for him today. Navy slacks and a beige pullover sweater set off his olive complexion. Jack Trenton would look good in anything he wore, Stacy decided. He'd mentioned red bathing trunks and a white T-shirt when he'd talked about Santa in Australia. It almost made her chuckle, but at least that was better than crying.

"It's lunchtime," she said abruptly. "Do you want to eat with us?"

"Lunch is why I'm here," Jack announced. "I want to take you somewhere special."

Daniel clapped his hands.

"That's not necessary," Stacy rebutted. "It's almost ready."

"What is?" Jack asked.

Stacy didn't think she'd get used to the Wyoming accent compared to the Southern one she'd moved away from.

"Grilled cheese sandwiches and tomato soup," she responded, feeling her cheeks grow hot. Jack was surely used to eating better than that!

Jack leaned toward Daniel. "Is your mommy a good cook?"

"Yes, sir," Daniel answered. "The bestest. 'Cept she puts jelly on my peanut butter sandwiches."

Jack drew back in alarm. "Jelly? Everyone knows you only use bananas or dill pickles with peanut butter."

Daniel giggled. "If I say the nice words, she leaves the jelly off," he admitted.

Jack sent Stacy a warm look. "Then yes, thank you. I'll stay."

❄

Stacy pushed herself away from the table. She knew Daniel was falling in love—if that's what little boys called it. The more she considered it, the more she didn't want Daniel hurt when Jack decided he was done with the Santa routine, for that's what today had to be. Her own feelings were also confused, a fact she should correct. Tomorrow was Monday. Jack would probably relegate her and Daniel to the ranks of a weekend spree designed to make Jack Trenton feel better.

Jack leaned back, linking his fingers behind his head. "So, ready to take a ride?"

"A ride?" Daniel jumped from his chair and roared through the living room, returning to Jack's knee. "In your truck?"

"Yep. My pickup."

"Can we go, Mommy?"

"Don't you want to play with your cars?" Stacy hadn't seen Daniel ignore his little race cars this much in a long time.

"Later, Mommy. Please?"

Jack's gaze met Stacy's, his brown eyes warmer than a mug

of steaming hot chocolate. "I won't keep you out long. I want to show you something. If you don't want to, I'll understand."

Stacy swallowed. What did she expect from Jack Trenton? She knew what her heart had shouted since she first laid eyes on him, even though he'd been dressed as the most absurd Santa she'd ever seen. A Santa she didn't believe in, no less.

What about Daniel? He hadn't had a male figure in his life in over three years. It would be nice to have someone like Jack Trenton around to help her with her son. Jack had done a tremendous job explaining the candy cane's symbolism. How much Daniel absorbed, Stacy didn't know. But he'd listened, gazing at Jack with hero worship in his eyes.

Whip will probably yell at me when he finds out I'm doing this, but it's not a date, Stacy insisted to her heart as she bundled Daniel into his warmest coat. *It's just a truck ride.* Then why did she wish it were more?

"Cool," Daniel said repeatedly as Jack drove down a subdivision street not far from their home. "Look, Mommy!"

Stacy craned her neck and followed Daniel's pointing finger. A pewter sky allowed them to view Christmas displays as if it were twilight and not midafternoon.

"It's beautiful." Stacy's glance roamed around the large, three-story brick home Jack stopped in front of. Different Christmas themes decorated the front and each side of the house.

On the east, elves raised tiny hammers and saws as they rotated through Santa's workshop. On the west were five white wooden reindeer in various poses beside four huge inflatable penguins. On the front lawn, a nativity set complete with camels and donkeys announced the owner's beliefs.

"There must be a zabillion lights, Mommy," Daniel said. "Can we count them?"

"I don't think we need to count; a zabillion comes close." Stacy's eyes followed the prancing white lights chasing plastic candy canes up the driveway. The twinkling stars ended up as streamers around white columns on the front porch.

"Who lives here, Jack?"

❄

Jack knew she'd ask, but Stacy's question settled in the pit of his stomach.

"Someone who works at the fire department," he finally replied. "He does this every year. Usually the street is so crowded you have to wait in line."

"Look, Mommy! Santa's falled off the roof and Rudolph's caughted him!"

Stacy reluctantly dragged her gaze from Jack's to the scene Daniel described. At the realism portrayed by the painted cutouts, she giggled.

"Look on the roof," Jack suggested. "Santa dropped something when he fell."

Jack's voice sounded odd, and it caught Stacy's attention. She turned to study him again. He leaned closer to see out her side of the vehicle. Stacy was uncomfortable, but she couldn't tell if it was the heat from the truck's vents or Jack's nearness.

"Santa lost his toys," Daniel chimed from the backseat.

Stacy looked where a plastic red and yellow car lay on its

side. Not far away, the head of a doll protruded from the end of a huge brown pouch.

"Why would someone put so many things out?" Stacy asked.

"The owner has a history of loss," Jack said. "This is one way he gives back to the community."

Stacy again picked up on something in Jack's voice she couldn't identify. "How do you know?"

"There was an article on the house in the local paper not long ago," Jack explained. "I have a copy if you want to read it."

"Sure." Stacy figured Jack would forget about the offer as soon as he dropped them off. He'd also forget about her and Daniel. The thought made her sad.

Jack revved the engine. "We'd better go. The radio said earlier there's more snow headed our way."

On the way, Jack stopped at a convenience store and left the truck running. "Be right back."

Gaily wrapped cases of soda were stacked halfway up the glass front. A small, shivering junco waited to the left of the entry, his feet tucked beneath fluffy feathers.

"I like Jack Santa," Daniel announced from the backseat. "He's cool."

"He is pretty neat." Stacy trailed a hand over the luxurious leather seat and cringed at the thought of the damage Daniel might do to the expensive interior.

She glanced around the cab. A pine-scented air freshener dangled from the rearview mirror. A compact disk emitted classical Christmas hymns from strategically placed speakers. Jack's driving gloves lay on the seat between them. Stacy wasn't an expert on price or style, but she'd bet you didn't find gloves like that at Wal-Mart.

Money. Jack apparently had lots and she didn't. Oh, she had the insurance fund, but she wouldn't touch it; it was for Daniel's future. Her income came from running the mobile home park for her in-laws while they RV'd across the States for the next few years. It wasn't much, but doing so let her live rent-free. Stacy shook her head. She shouldn't compare their lifestyles. Jack was only being friendly; neither she nor Daniel meant anything to him.

"Here we go." Jack's chipper voice broke into her thoughts. "I got hot chocolate."

Daniel's squeal filled the truck. "I love hot chocky. Does it have white thingies?"

Jack handed three insulated cups in a holder to Stacy, placed a sack on the seat between them, and slid into his seat. "You mean marshmallows? Let me check." Jack pried a lid open and peered inside. "Nope. No white thingies here."

"Mommy likes white thingies, but I don't."

Jack's fingers brushed Stacy's as he handed the cup back to her. The jolt that scurried through him made him think he'd spilled some of the hot liquid on his hand.

"We'll let your Mommy hold it until we get to your place. It can cool off and you won't burn your mouth. Right, Mommy?"

Stacy choked on Jack's use of the intimate word that described her and Daniel's relationship. "Right," she replied. "Let it cool." As she must her rapidly growing affection for Jack Santa...er...Trenton. She'd only met him a few days ago!

As they pulled onto the highway, Jack turned down the

background music. "In Switzerland they ring a bell to herald the arrival of Christkindl, a girl-angel sent from heaven to give gifts."

"Wowsers!" Daniel exclaimed. "A real angel?"

"That's what they say," Jack confirmed. "Some villages even ring as many bells as they have at one time to let folks know there's a midnight service. After the worship is over, families get together and eat huge homemade doughnuts called *ringli* and drink hot chocolate."

"I love doughnuts," Daniel offered. "'Specially the ones that get dust everywhere. Mommy calls them 'dusty doughs.'"

Jack grinned. "Good. Because I got some when I got the hot chocky. I thought we'd ring our own bells and have our own small worship service."

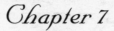

Chapter 7

I like you, Jack Santa. Thanks for the hot chocky and dusty doughs." Daniel's boyish compliment rushed through Jack with the speed of a flying reindeer—even if the animal was mythical.

"I like you, too, scamp." Jack smiled at Daniel and looked across the kitchen table at Stacy.

What about Stacy? Three days wasn't long enough to form a serious opinion let alone dream of something more, especially with his history. He was certainly taken with Stacy Waters. Four days ago, his only worry was who he'd take to the fireman's supper. He didn't wonder any longer. He'd bring Stacy and Daniel.

❅

Jack punched in the digits on the phone that seemed more lifesaving than dialing 9-1-1. He'd waited two days to call Stacy, filling his time by doing odd jobs around his house and throwing more silver icicles on his own Christmas tree. Jack thought perhaps one that didn't scrape his two-story-high cathedral ceiling might have worked, but he couldn't help it. He always went overboard at Christmas; doing so made his empty holidays happier. He also added another toy to the Santa sack on the roof. Jack smiled as he imagined Daniel's reaction when he saw the new addition.

The on-and-off buzzing of an unanswered phone garnered his attention. Six more rings and he'd hang up. It was 5:45 p.m. Why didn't Stacy answer?

Jack thought back to driving Daniel and Stacy home after showing them his lawn. Daniel's chatter had filled the truck. Despite the fact that his own ride home after dropping them off took less than five minutes, Jack couldn't overlook the silence in his pickup. Pulling into his driveway, he'd stared at the lawn decorations that had delighted Daniel. Looking at them without Stacy and Daniel just hadn't been the same.

He wished he'd told Stacy the house and the Christmas sets belonged to him when she asked. But he sensed if he had, Stacy would have refused to have anything more to do with him. Jack could tell by the simple home she lived in that she didn't have much, but money wasn't the important thing in life. Didn't she know that? Praising God, loving others, and enjoying life—that was what mattered, wasn't it?

"Hello?" Stacy's alto sounded breathlessly charming.

"It's Jack Santa." He added a, "Ho ho ho," in case she'd forgotten him.

The silence that filled the phone lines stretched from Wyoming to the North Pole.

"Stace?"

"Sorry, Jack. We just walked in. Daniel's wound up."

"Did you know in Israel at Christmas, pilgrims flock by

the thousands to the spot in Bethlehem where they believe the baby Jesus was born? They call it The Church of the Nativity and mark it with a silver star. I've never seen this, but I hear fifteen silver lamps burn continuously overhead."

"Sounds interesting," Stacy ventured.

"After they worship," Jack went on, "they, the pilgrims, sit out in the fields where they believe the original shepherds heard the message of the Messiah's birth from the angel."

"I'd like to hear more, but Daniel's pulling my leg."

Jack smiled at the thought of Daniel doing just that. "Well, don't let him out of your sight. This might be sudden, but there's a dinner, well, more like a get-together at the fire station where I volunteer. Will you go with me?"

"Daniel, too?"

"Of course Daniel, too."

"When?"

Jack blushed. He'd been so intent on asking Stacy out he'd forgotten to give her the day. "Two Saturdays from now. If it's too short notice, I understand."

His gaze focused on the spiral staircase at one end of his living room. Fancy red and green garland frolicked up the wooden railing. It didn't have the appeal of the simple silver stuff on Stacy's little deck.

"Daniel and I already have plans that night."

"It's okay, Stace. I just thought you might want to go."

"I do, Jack, but it's hard to tell how long we'll be at the other thing."

Where was she going and with whom? He didn't think he was jealous, but the last time he'd felt this way had been the first time his mother remarried after his dad passed away. He was seven, and being pushed away sent him in a downward spiral it took him years to climb out of.

"Got anything planned for Friday evening, then?" He didn't know much about family entertainment available in Antler, but he'd do some quick research.

"Friday's open." Stacy chuckled. "Unless a pack of elves shows up and whisks Daniel off to the North Pole to help with wrapping presents or something."

"You wouldn't trust just any elf who shows up, would you?" Jack asked. "You'd ask for proper ID before you let Daniel go off with him?"

"There have been some pretty strange characters in my neighborhood lately," Stacy admitted. "But like I told Whip last night, all elves undergo thorough psychological testing before I allow them in my home."

"You think I'm strange?" Jack challenged.

Stacy's laugh sounded as if she didn't have a care in the world. "How many other people do you know who recite a reference book on Christmas lore from beginning to end? Hold on, Jack. Daniel won't quit bouncing until he talks to you."

Jack heard a scuffling noise in the background.

"Hey, Jack Santa. It's Daniel Waters. Remember me?"

Jack's heart overflowed with warmth. "I'd never forget a little boy who knows how to take care of his mommy like you do."

Daniel giggled. "Mommy's making samiches for dinner. Mommy? Can Jack Santa eat with us?"

Jack thought Stacy's sharp intake of breath traveled amazingly well through phone lines. "Sorry," she said into the receiver.

"Daniel asked me that as we got home. I explained you were probably busy tonight."

"I told you the other day I'd call you tonight." Jack cleared his throat. "I'm not busy if that's an invitation."

"You're welcome to join us. But it's drizzling again, and if it freezes. . ." Stacy's unspoken concern weighed down the silence.

"I drive a sleigh in my free time, remember? If that fails, my truck has four-wheel drive," Jack assured her.

❄

Stacy watched as the men—Daniel dressed in blue sweatpants and a NASCAR racing shirt her uncle had sent in October on Daniel's birthday, and Jack handsomely attired in blue jeans and a flannel shirt, his sleeves shoved above his elbows—slapped sandwiches together.

Banana peels littered the tabletop, and pickle juice ran along the tiny breaks in the kitchen flooring. The mess didn't matter; watching Daniel enjoy himself was worth it. All right, watching Jack was worth it, too.

"All done, Mommy! Come get it."

Stacy admired Jack's easygoing manner with her son. After she lost Timothy, she didn't think she'd find someone who meshed so easily with Daniel. It wasn't that they were unchristian, but none of the Air Force men she dated gave her son any attention; they weren't interested in building a life for Daniel. She knew Jack Trenton was a Christian, but did that mean she should trust him? There it was. Making a decision. For a few days, worrying about decisions hadn't crossed her mind.

"Yeah, Mommy. All done," Jack parroted.

The joy on Jack's face was comparable to a child opening Christmas presents. He was a natural at having fun, at encouraging Daniel to do things she wouldn't have thought of doing, things a family would do together.

One of the things Stacy liked about Jack was that he seemed eternally optimistic, that he portrayed the idea there was always hope. Maybe when it came to Christianity that was so, but was the same true where family was concerned?

She appreciated Jack's attempt to brighten her and Daniel's holidays. When that time ended. . . Stacy didn't want to think about it. Forcing herself to smile, she took a seat. Daniel handed her a concoction that looked more like a pizza than a sandwich.

"It. . .looks attractive," she commented.

"Jack Santa says these are the best sort of samiches, Mommy." Daniel's face glowed. "But he let me make my own with just peanut butter."

Stacy eyed the plate in front of her. "I guess this is one of those experiences I'll look back and laugh at later on." She pushed at the bread with one finger.

Jack cleared his throat. "Time for grace."

"Why?" Daniel asked. "Is she coming to eat?"

"We call it a blessing, Daniel. Jack calls it grace."

"Okay," Daniel replied. "Grace blessing."

She thought the grin on Jack's face was somewhat silly, but then he sobered. "Shall we?"

Heads bowed, hands clasped, Jack blessed the food and the company. He devoured a sandwich. "It won't bite, you know," he said to Stacy.

"Yeah, Mommy. Nanners don't bite. Eat it." Daniel propped his elbows on the table and took a bite from his own.

"I'm not so sure." Stacy studied her plate. Her stomach rumbled.

Jack grabbed two more slices of bread. "Would you rather have one without bananas?"

"No. I'll try it. I always ask Daniel to take a bite of something before he decides he doesn't want to eat it."

Stacy's first bite consisted of the creamy spread. She chewed it rapidly, afraid a banana or pickle slice might emerge from somewhere.

Jack grinned. "Good, isn't it?"

She dabbed the side of her mouth with a paper napkin. "I didn't get to—"

"I knew you'd like it," Jack cut in.

Before Stacy could dispute him, Jack turned to Daniel. "If Mommy says it is all right, would you like to picnic in front of the TV, scamp?"

"Cool. Can I, Mommy?"

Jack found a black plastic garbage bag under the sink and laid it over the carpeting. He situated Daniel and flipped the channel to a sports broadcast. "Mommy and I will be in the kitchen if you need us."

Stacy watched as Jack got Daniel settled. Seeing him do things with Daniel only made her more aware of the emptiness in her life. What were the chances she'd find someone like Jack to love?

Not too good, Stacy decided. She shouldn't cling too tightly to Jack's brand of craziness. He'd said he only wanted to spread

Christmas cheer then he'd go. A painful ache filled Stacy's heart.

Father, why did You bring Jack Trenton into my life? I've only known him for five days, but it seems like he's always been around. I know I used to say no one would ever take Timothy's place, but with Jack it just seems so. . .natural.

Jack's hand covered hers, interrupting her. "Are you all right?"

"I'm fine," Stacy whispered, but the heartache she and Daniel would suffer when Jack decided it was time to go made her tremble.

Jack squeezed her hand again. "Raising Daniel by yourself can't be easy. Did the military have someplace that helped you before you separated?"

See, he's already pulling away.

"Yes. We had a family support center, and I had plenty of time to go to single-parent support meetings."

Jack narrowed his eyes. "You sound like they weren't much help."

Stacy pushed away the sorrow that often submerged her. "They were. I think it's me. This isn't the best time of year to be alone. It's been over three years. I thought I'd be better adjusted by now."

Stacy reached up to brush away a tear trickling down her cheek.

"It's all right to cry, Stace. Tears won't bother me."

❄

That's a stretch, Trenton. You know very well a woman crying rips a hole in your heart every time. How many times did the same thing happen with your mother?

Several, Jack acknowledged silently. With Stacy, the pain seemed tripled.

"I seem to cry all the time though, Jack. It can't be good for me, or for Daniel when he sees me cry."

What would Stacy do if he put his arms around her and comforted her? Why try? He hadn't been able to help his mother.

"This is the first time I've seen you lose it since I've known you."

"You haven't been with me all the time," Stacy argued.

"Got me there." Jack studied a train-shaped magnet on the refrigerator. "Did you know in Italy children hang their stockings on January sixth, the Feast of the Epiphany? The story is they wait for La Befana, a witchlike person who rides on a broomstick, to deliver toys to Italy's good children."

"I don't think telling me about some old woman in Italy is going to make a difference here." In spite of Stacy's denial, the tension around her eyes seemed to have faded.

Jack propped his elbows on the table and tried to give her what he hoped was a look of disbelief. "What if I told you rumor has it the wise men stopped at La Befana's house to ask for directions to Bethlehem?"

"Now I know you're crazy. Men don't ever ask for directions."

Jack grinned. "They were *wise* men, Stace." He waited, hoping she'd respond, but she didn't.

He summarized the story by telling her that La Befana refused to go with not only the wise men to pay tribute to the Christ child, but a shepherd, too. When she saw a light in the sky, she knew she'd made a mistake. She gathered her children's toys and set off searching for those visitors. Every year she goes out in search of the Christ child but leaves presents for Italy's good children along the way.

"Mommy? Look!"

Jack glanced over Stacy's shoulder and found Daniel staring at the TV. A little girl with blond curls and big blue eyes looked back. A black screen followed with words that explained a drunk driver had killed the child.

Jack cringed. Another life destroyed by people who'd made wrong decisions. It didn't seem fair, especially when he made the emergency runs, picking up the mangled pieces of humanity who had no chance against tons of galvanized steel.

"My daddy got died like that," Daniel announced. "Can we get his picture on TV, too, Mommy?"

Chapter 8

J ack glanced at Stacy as tears flowed down her pale face. The same lips that a moment ago had chuckled at his ramblings about an old Italian woman were now tightly pinched together. Another family destroyed, another woman left to care for a young boy who wouldn't remember his father. . . just like himself.

Jack glimpsed why his mother must have continually sought someone to help her recover from the hurt. Or was it to bury her pain? The difference between his mother and Stacy was that Stacy knew Jesus. Didn't she remember He carried any burden, no matter how heavy? Jack leaned toward her, noticing a subtle flowery perfume.

"Saying it's all right won't help," he murmured. "But I don't know what else to say, Stace. I failed my mother the same way."

Stacy's hands muffled her voice. "People tell me I'll heal in time, but how long will it take before I'm normal again, Jack?"

Jack slid his chair over beside hers. He didn't want her pity because of what happened to him as a child. He hadn't liked feeling helpless where his mother was concerned either. If he were really as good a rescuer as people thought, he'd know how to deal with this.

"I don't know if there is a normal after something like that, but I do have something to tell you that might help, Stace."

"Only if it's not another Christmas story," she mumbled. "I don't think I could take one of those right now."

"I grew up without a father," Jack said softly. "Nineteen years ago. One day he was there, the next he wasn't. It was the same thing. A drunk driver."

"Oh, Jack. I don't know what to say." Stacy reached out and grabbed one of his hands.

Jack didn't care that the tears on her fingers wet his palm. In fact, it seemed significant she hadn't wiped them off. Everything about her seemed to draw him further into her life; her swirling auburn hair, those endless gray eyes, even her fatherless son. He heard the warning bells clanging at his heart, but he turned them off.

He rescued people, didn't he? Wasn't that what he'd dedicated his life to? To save those who needed help. He'd saved others in tougher situations than this. He knew what he was about to do wasn't that kind of help. His heart was beyond that; it had been since the first time he laid eyes on Stacy Waters. He turned her hand over in his and let it lie there without pressure, tracing the lines on her palm tenderly.

"We both know 'I'm sorry' doesn't cover the grief, Stace."

"Everyone says it. . .as if they. . .think that's all that's necessary. It isn't."

Jack drew Stacy gently toward him. "It's all they know how to say. Anything else makes them uncomfortable."

He waited for her to pull away, but she nestled her head against his chest and laid her hand over his forearm. He laid his hand on the back of her head, hoping he provided a measure of solace.

"Someday we'll understand why, Stace. Someday we won't have any more tears."

Stacy's fingers gripped his arm, her strength at odds with the dependence she'd just exhibited. She lurched away, her eyes wide. "We can't do this."

"Do what?"

She motioned toward his chest, the words seemingly caught in her throat.

"We're just helping each other through a rough spot." Jack hoped he didn't sound harsh and uncaring.

Relief filled Stacy's features. "As long as that's all we're doing."

Jack hoped that wasn't true. Impossible as it seemed after less than a week, he wanted more from Stacy. He wanted to hold her when life got rough, to kiss her when he came through the door at the end of the day, to make her laugh when she felt the world was against her. He wanted her not just as a friend but as his lifetime companion.

Was his mind as ready as his heart to throw caution to the wind? No, he'd tried that route before—without success. So had his mother, more than once. Jack frowned.

He hadn't known Stacy long enough to find out her favorite color or what she liked to do on rainy days. Though she was a Christian, did they have anything else in common? She deserved the best of everything, and while he had money, did he have the heart it took to heal another's hurt? Didn't he remember he couldn't help his mother?

"Jack Santa? Did you hurt my mommy?" Daniel's question caught Jack by surprise.

"I don't think so, scamp. Why?"

"'Cause she runned down the hall crying."

"Go away, Jack," Stacy insisted through the bathroom door. "Tell Daniel I'll be out in minute."

Jack leaned his head against the wall, noting a few Christmas cards hanging along the edge of a TV unit. "I won't go till you tell me how I can help."

He'd never talked to a door before, and he felt silly. No, frustrated. He cared about the woman behind it, even if he didn't have a chance to win her heart.

"You can't help. Just go. Tell Daniel to lock the door behind you."

"It's important for me to help you," Jack insisted.

"You can't."

"You won't know that unless you try, Stace. Don't you want to make things better for Daniel?"

Stacy rolled her head against the faded floral wallpaper on the bathroom wall as she listened to Jack's arguments. She crossed and uncrossed her arms. Earlier Jack had run his fingers through her hair and tucked a lock of her hair behind one ear. Stacy pulled the strand back out. Didn't he realize her refusal to allow him to get close to her was to protect Daniel?

Sorrow wedged in her throat. She'd never find someone who measured up to all the things she wanted in a man. What did she want? She wanted someone who would take care of her and Daniel's spiritual, emotional, and physical needs. There, that covered everything.

From the moment Jack Trenton hustled up her driveway in that hilarious, oversize Santa suit, hadn't he attempted to do those very things? Stacy scowled. Yes, he had.

Why? Was there more behind his promise to spread Christmas cheer? No, there couldn't be. So why did her heart feel as if it were one of those race cars Daniel imitated, squealing and roaring around when she saw Jack Trenton?

"I'm not going till you tell me what I can do to help you. Remember, it will help me, too," Jack reminded through the door.

He sounded close to bashing down the flimsy entrance. The idea almost made Stacy laugh. She disguised it by coughing. She didn't have to let Jack know how quickly he'd become entangled in her heart. She'd acted before. She'd done it from the moment Timothy's commander brought her the news about her husband's death.

She was weak, but she couldn't resist Jack Trenton any more than she could tell Daniel no when he smiled at her. She made a decision. If playing with Daniel and making his Christmas a little brighter made Jack Trenton happy, she couldn't fault Jack for *that*.

It was sad, and probably a bad decision she'd live to regret, but she'd talk with Daniel later and hope her son understood that just as Santa was mythical and only visited once a year, Jack Trenton wasn't permanent. She'd keep her heart safely out of the fray so when Christmas was over, she and Daniel could go on with life. Maybe it wasn't the smartest thing to do, but it was the only thing Stacy *wanted* to do at the moment.

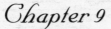

Stacy held a cup of coffee, its warmth soaking through her fingers as she surveyed the snowdrifts outside. Letting Jack talk her out of the bathroom the other night hadn't turned out to be a bad decision after all. It had been one of the better decisions she'd made in a long time. The evening had cleansed her soul and her mind.

Jack had prayed with her for healing, reminding her of God's ability to handle the overwhelming things life sometimes thrusts upon us. She'd shared the worst night of her adult life: when she learned of Timothy's accident. She didn't describe every detail, but she knew he understood her heart's agony.

Jack told her what he recalled of growing up without a dad. The nights he spent sitting in windows wishing on stars, talking to the moon, sure his dad rode in clouds and would walk in the door soon. Before they knew it, it was midnight and Jack left with the promise to call her in a few days.

Stacy sloshed coffee on her hand, and her memory of the time spent talking with Jack the other night abruptly ceased. Today there were other things to deal with. She must weed through papers she should have tossed before she moved to Wyoming. Daniel had spent last night with a friend from church for the first time, but he'd called every hour this morning to see if Jack Santa phoned to ask about him.

Jack.

Though he was comforting, and a good resource in the prayer department, Stacy reconsidered telling him she couldn't have him around, only to hurt Daniel in the end. Hadn't her son already suffered a greater loss than any child should bear? Daniel needed to move forward in life—not get hurt again when Jack left them in a few weeks—which he would surely do.

After a week of below zero, thirty-two degrees warmed up the outdoors. Stacy turned her face toward the window to soak it in. She paused and whispered a prayer of thanks for the clear blue sky. The view wasn't the only blessing. Yesterday's mail held a card, a poem, and small check from her Uncle Ray. She put the poem aside to read later.

The check would help buy something extra for Daniel's Christmas. With little traffic on the main road through Antler, Stacy headed to get Daniel and drove by the bank to deposit the check. She wondered if her meager savings balance would ever grow. She'd invested the insurance money, but her savings was all she had for instant cash. The thought brought Jack and his apparent financial means back to mind. They'd never find common ground to build a life together with such a chasm between their worlds.

With Daniel safely in his car seat, his constant chatter kept her mind off money. He rambled on about the upcoming Santa visit at his friend's party on Saturday. She wasn't sure what he thought about Santa anymore. Maybe she needed to talk with

Whip since she hadn't seen him in a few days.

The phone rang as she opened their front door.

"I get it!" Daniel roared away, stopping amid a squeal of his six-year-old's screechy brake sounds.

"Hello," Stacy heard as she set the groceries on the table. "Yep. It's Jack Santa, Mommy. He wants you."

Stacy's heart hammered as she grabbed the receiver. "Merry Christmas," she answered, hoping she sounded as if talking to Jack didn't bother her at all.

"And to all a good night?"

"That's how the story goes," Stacy replied. "Are there any other kind?"

"Only when I don't get to talk to you," Jack confessed.

Stacy bit her lip. *Jack doesn't mean it. It's part of his Santa act.*

"How was your day?" Stacy put away the canned goods the phone's cord let her reach, frowning at the generic cans she had to purchase.

"Fantastic now that I'm talking to you."

"I'm glad you called, Jack, because we need to talk."

"That's *my* reason. You haven't fixed anything to eat yet, have you?"

"No."

"I'll be right there, and no arguments."

This was the first time in the two weeks she'd known Jack that he'd spoken so forcefully. "I think a better idea is—"

"No phone disagreements. I'm on my way."

Stacy told herself to look disapproving when she opened the

door, but she couldn't help but do otherwise. Jack looked more handsome than ever. He wore a red sweater and navy slacks, and new, expensive tan and bright brown boots peeked out from beneath the slacks. The wavy auburn highlights in his thick hair begged Stacy to reach up and give them a tousle. Jack Trenton looked good. He always did.

"Whoo-ee. Don't we look great tonight?" Jack gazed at the faded camouflaged military uniform she wore that day. "Where's the scampster?"

Stacy stepped back to give Jack plenty of space. "Playing in his room."

"Why isn't he ready to go? We're fixing to get. Places to do and things to see."

"I think that's places to go and people to see."

Jack shrugged. "Whatever. Doesn't matter as long as I have you two with me." He stepped toward her.

Stacy laid a hand on his arm to stop him, but that turned into a mistake. She might as well have plugged into the North Pole's hotline.

"He's. . .uh. . .in his room. I. . .we. . .can't continue this," Stacy said.

Jack arched his eyebrows. "This what?"

"This. . .you calling. . .coming over. . .well, you know." She took a step back, trying to gain some breathing room. "It's not going to last, so we should stop now, before Daniel gets hurt."

Jack frowned. Stacy's eyes clearly said, "before I get hurt, too."

"So *you* decided that me not coming over here would be best?"

Compared to the uniform mixtures worn by firemen and paramedics at the station, Stacy, even in the faded and worn-out military thing she had on, was an improvement. The green and khaki actually made her gray eyes more expressive than normal.

"Yes," Stacy said. "I realized today how. . .immature we've acted since we met."

"I can't believe you think what we did is childish." He held up a finger. "I met you dressed as Santa." He paused to toss his jacket on the sofa. "Okay, that does sound a little ridiculous, but what about the rest? We looked at Christmas lights. We had hot chocolate and made banana and pickle—"

"Stop it, Jack! You don't have to list everything. You only do those things because you feel you have to."

They studied each other. A clocked ticked on the wall. The refrigerator gurgled. The heater purred, filling the rest of the silence.

Jack rubbed his forehead. "I can't believe you think that's the only reason I come over to visit."

"You said so that first day," Stacy countered. "You said playing Santa was something you did to make your heart happy."

He plopped down on the sofa. "What if I told you I did this because I thought it helped you?"

❋

Because that's the problem.

Jack directed his attention toward helping her. She didn't

want help. She wanted. . .his love.

"Did you hear me?" Jack leaned forward and propped his elbows on his knees.

It was a move Daniel now copied with perfection lately. Stacy went to stand behind her rocker and ran her hands across the quilt on the chair back. "That's my point. I. . .you. . .make Daniel think. . .oh, there isn't an easy way to say it."

"Do you know why I'm here tonight, Stace?"

"You came over because—"

"I wanted to see *you*," Jack interrupted. "After we go out to eat, I'm taking you to church."

"You're ignoring the issue."

Jack met Stacy's gaze. "Stace, church *is* the issue. Christians are supposed to take care of each other, to witness Jesus' love to everyone they meet. Did your parents teach you everything you know about the Bible at home?"

"Of course not. We went to worship as a family, but that has nothing to—"

"I know you have your faith, but what have you done lately for your spiritual health?"

"My spiritual—Jack Trenton!" Stacy took a deep breath and tried to lower her voice. "I'll have you know there's nothing wrong with my soul. I read my Bible every chance I get."

Jack grinned. "Me, too. Now, call Daniel out here so you can go change clothes. We'll eat then go worship."

Stacy stared at Jack. He looked as if screaming children and animated characters belting out songs didn't exist. With his long legs stretched out to the side of the table, and his sleeves pushed up above his elbows, only she and Daniel appeared to matter.

"The pizza good?" Jack quizzed Daniel.

Daniel nodded. "The bestest. I like Zappa."

Jack smiled. "I agree. When you're done, we'll play some of those games." He motioned to an area filled with flashing lights and squawking horns. "Don't worry, Stace. I have it on our pastor's good word this is an awesome place for kids."

She nodded but checked her watch. "Won't we be late for church if we don't leave soon?"

"Plenty of time. Besides, Daniel and I need to play."

Stacy returned to picking mushrooms off her pizza before nibbling at it. Daniel downed two pieces before grinning at Jack.

"Okay, Jack Santa. I'm ready."

"Gentlemen, start your engines." Jack motioned to Stacy. "Join us?"

"I'll finish eating. You two go on."

She positioned her chair to keep an eye on them. She told herself it was to keep an eye on Jack in case he let Daniel do something she didn't want him to do. All she saw was Daniel's face light up each time Jack spoke to him. Earlier, Stacy had been determined to tell Jack she wouldn't see him anymore. Yet, here they were in a noisy kids' place, and Daniel was having the time of his life. She couldn't take that away from her son, could she?

"Mommy! Watch me!"

With innate mother's hearing, Stacy picked up Daniel's

shout. He waved before disappearing down an enclosed slide, whooshing out into Jack's arms.

She remembered what it had felt like to lay her head on Jack's chest not long ago. Her cheeks warmed. Stacy instinctively dropped her chin to hide the blush from those around her.

A few seconds later, Daniel pounced onto her lap. "Did you see me, Mommy? Jack Santa let me go down the slide forty-seven-eleven times. It was fun."

"I saw, but I think we're done for the night."

"Aw, Mommy. I wanted you to go down the slide with me," Daniel grumbled.

"No, son," Jack inserted. "Mommy's the boss. Whatever she says, goes."

❄

Jack admitted he was falling for Stacy, and her son, even if he wasn't good enough to merit someone like her. When he hadn't helped his mother, he'd been passed back and forth between relatives who didn't want him. Stacy would never hand Daniel over for someone else to care for. He admired her for the courage she showed in raising Daniel alone.

He wished he could make Stacy see he wasn't spending time with them just to brighten their holidays. His feelings for Stacy were becoming harder to hide. Why couldn't she see how he felt about her?

Stacy cleared her throat as if she could read Jack's thoughts. "We'd better go if we want to get to church on time."

While Daniel shrugged his arms into the jacket Stacy held out for him, Jack grabbed Stacy's coat and waited. She gave him a peculiar glance, but turned and allowed his assistance.

Only a few stoplights and they soon left Antler behind. The ride eastward passed quickly. Daniel sat in the backseat, chatting and singing to himself.

"Now that it isn't snowing, it doesn't seem like Christmas is only a few days away, does it?" Jack asked at one point.

"I heard there's another cold spell on the way," Stacy said.

"Some say the eleventh-century Crusaders brought ginger back from the Middle East with them, which is how gingerbread houses developed."

A quick gaze over at Stacy revealed she'd closed her eyes and laid her head against the headrest.

"Have you ever made a gingerbread house?" she asked. "My brother and I did once. We had graham cracker crumbs and icing everywhere. I think we got more candy in us than on the house."

"You're fortunate to have great memories of your family holidays," Jack replied. "I didn't have any brothers or sisters."

Just me, he thought. *One little boy who couldn't make his mother happy.*

Jack passed a slower vehicle. "Some say the gingerbread house started in Germany and became popular when the Brothers Grimm wrote 'Hansel and Gretel.'"

"Do you stay up at night studying Christmas lore?"

"No. I could tell you about Antler's history if you want, but I've found Christmas legends are more interesting." He gave Stacy a quick smile. "All right. To be honest, I devote my nights and mornings to scripture. Christmas lore is a hobby."

Some hobby, Stacy mused. Jack seemed to know a lot about Christmas. Perhaps the Jack Santa nickname Daniel had given him was appropriate. It was all right for her son to call him Jack Santa, but why was she suddenly starting to think of the man that same way?

"Here we are," Jack announced as they pulled into the church parking lot.

Jack swung her door open and reached for her hand. "You might want to be prepared in case Cindy Tyler approaches us. I'm not sure what she'll do if she sees us together."

Stacy's heart started to pound. "Prepared for what?"

"She thinks I'm the man for her. I've tried to dissuade her, but she doesn't get it," Jack said.

Stacy stared into his dark brown eyes without speaking.

Jack grabbed Stacy's hand. "It'll be fine. Just let me handle things if she says anything."

Before Stacy could exit the vehicle, Jack's hands went around her waist. He picked her up and lowered her until her feet touched the ground. Jack swinging Stacy from the truck was a little frightening, yet comforting in a strange way. Daniel stopped any response she might have made.

"Me, too!" he squealed from the backseat. "Swing me out, Jack Santa!"

Jack did and leaned down to tug Daniel's jacket in place. "There you go. Everyone ready?"

"I am," Daniel said. "Can I hold your hand?"

"You know it," Jack said.

Daniel latched on to Jack's left hand. "Mommy, do this, too."

Stacy did, a little awkward at the outward display of affection. Timothy hadn't done such things, but Stacy liked the way Jack's warm hand felt against her ungloved one.

A woman rushed to greet them as they entered the church. Her fluffy gray hair was pulled back in a bun, and warmth spilled from her eyes. "Well, look who's here."

"Hello, Mrs. Weekly." Jack gave her a quick hug.

Mrs. Weekly looked between Stacy and Daniel. "You're Daniel's mother. I work with him in children's choir. It's nice to meet you." She glanced from Jack to Stacy.

Stacy introduced herself. "Likewise. Daniel just loves singing. Our trips home from worship are usually spent with him repeating what he's learned that day."

Mrs. Weekly smiled. "Daniel's eager to learn and well mannered. You've done a fine job raising him."

"I'm here with Jack Santa," Daniel announced. "He told me about the Jesus-baby story and candy canes."

Mrs. Weekly looked Jack up and down as if picturing him as Santa. She smiled. "Let's head to your classroom, Daniel. I think your teacher put up a new picture of Jesus as a man. You can tell me the Jesus-baby story while we wait for class to start."

Cindy Tyler wasn't in the young adult's class. Stacy wondered if that meant she was in another room or absent. Stacy decided not to worry. After all, nothing serious was happening between Stacy and Jack. Was there?

Stacy was surprised to learn that Jack led the group. The lesson consisted of several readings on wealth. Two Bible verses stuck in Stacy's mind. She marked them down to read later. James 2:5 and 1 Timothy 6:17 and 18. At first, Stacy wondered if Jack purposefully chose those verses because of the differences in his and her financial standings. She put the notion aside as the group broke into discussion. The time flew by rapidly, and too soon, the study ended, and they adjourned to the large auditorium.

Compared to her childhood church where stained-glass windows were the only ornamentation, this room was noticeably different. A high ceiling surrounded by wooden rafters created a feeling of openness and acceptance. The wooden pews were highly polished. Even the smooth blue carpet seemed to beckon her to enter. Jack went to retrieve Daniel, leaving Stacy on her own for a few minutes. She bowed her head and offered a prayer.

Father, thank You for bringing Jack Trenton into my life. I thought I'd never find someone who cared about Daniel more than himself. I don't know where our relationship is headed, but I trust You to work it out.

The minister mesmerized Stacy, and it was time to leave before she knew it. Used to making a quick exit after services, Stacy found that impossible with Jack at her side. Being in the military, often in one place for just a short time, Stacy hadn't made many close friends. Jack seemed to know everyone and paused to say something complimentary to each of them. Most of the women offered Stacy a light kiss on the cheek or a hug before they departed to converse with others.

"If you have a minute, I want to show you something," Jack said when they left the parking lot. "I know it's late and you have to get Daniel up early, so I'll leave it up to you."

"It will only take a minute?"

Jack nodded.

"I guess it's all right."

Stacy enjoyed the Christmas lights on the houses they passed. She barely noticed when Jack braked and slowed the truck. Her eyes feasted upon the scene before her.

"I've seen this before," Stacy commented. The last time had been during the day, but there was no doubt it was the same decorative setup.

"You did, but the owner added something new. I wanted Daniel to see it."

Daniel scooted out of his seat belt and pushed his nose against the window. "What is it, Jack Santa?"

"Up on the roof." Jack leaned across the seat and pointed with one hand.

Jack's breath tickled Stacy's neck, sending shivers down her spine. She was too conscious of his nearness to think of looking at anything else.

"Wowsers, Jack Santa! That's the coolest toy I ever seen."

Stacy mentally corrected Daniel, but she didn't say it. She was too busy breathing a sigh of relief at her son's interruption.

"Do you like it?" Jack asked, moving even closer to Stacy.

"It's the best," Daniel replied.

"You can have it after Christmas," Jack offered.

Stacy's mind whirled. What was *it*, and what did Jack mean Daniel could have *it* after Christmas? She stared out the window, trying to focus on the extravagant display.

"Really?" Daniel's squeal bounced around the interior.

"Scout's honor, scamp."

Elves. Nativity scene. Reindeer. Santa on the roof. Whoa! Stacy found the addition. A shiny, black race car the size of Texas!

"Is it really mine, Jack Santa?" Daniel asked.

Stacy shifted, putting distance between her and Jack. "I think Jack means you can see the car when the owner takes his Christmas decorations down."

"Look at Daniel," Jack whispered. "How long has it been since you saw him smile like that?"

Stacy glanced at Daniel. Jack was right. Daniel's eyes glowed brighter than the floodlights surrounding the house.

Stacy hunched her shoulders. While she hoped her son would grow up to be as generous and caring as Jack Trenton appeared, Daniel didn't need a race car that wouldn't fit on their deck! How could Jack promise such a thing as a gift anyway. . . unless it was his? Was it? That seemed a definite possibility, which meant the mansion under the car was also his.

Which meant Jack must have money.

Plenty of money.

"Our minute is up," Stacy said tartly. "Please take us home."

Chapter 10

Stacy refused to let Jack tuck Daniel in bed. After she ensured her son snuggled beneath his favorite blanket, she stood gazing at him. She always felt closer to God when she watched Daniel sleep. God gave her peace, hope, and love, something she needed just now. She closed her eyes.

Earlier I told You I'd trust You to work things out, but are Jack and his money how You want me to take care of Daniel's needs? Is that the decision You're leading me toward?

Petition complete, Stacy leaned against the doorframe. She watched Daniel move beneath his covers, his thumb slipping toward his mouth.

"I have to be both parents to Daniel," she whispered, her heart filling with emotion. "I have to make the decisions, the sacrifices. I want them to be the right ones, Lord."

While she'd known that fact, she hadn't understood the true measure of love it would take. Since knowing Jack, Stacy was all too aware of the lack in her life, and in Daniel's.

Jack's hand on her shoulder startled her.

"Daniel's a great kid," Jack complimented. "I want you

to know that no matter what happens, he'll be fine. Kids are resilient. They bounce back faster than adults."

A lump filled Stacy's throat. Jack's voice was so concerned, another overpowering feeling stirred in her heart. Stacy knew this wasn't like what she felt for Daniel, or had known with Timothy. Was caring about Jack a problem? Yes, it was. Especially if what she suspected about Jack Trenton and his financial situation was true.

Jack wanted to wrap his arms around Stacy's shaking frame and brush away her doubts. Instead, he rested his hands on her shoulders and whispered a small kiss on the crown of her head.

"Jack," she warned. "I told you earlier this isn't going to work. It's...illogical. Not to mention I'm very upset about the toy car right now."

He'd heard Stacy's arguments before, but Jack Trenton knew what he felt for Stacy Waters was something only God could create.

"Let's not argue in front of Daniel's bedroom," he said.

As he followed Stacy to the kitchen, Jack kept his distance. He felt as clumsy as a high school boy trying to talk to his first crush. He recalled other women he'd dated, how they pressed him into commitments he didn't want. Stacy was different. He cared about her, and he suspected she cared about him.

Jack waited until she seated herself at the kitchen table. "Would you explain why you keep saying that us being together isn't going to work?"

Stacy twisted her fingers in the plastic wrapper of a bread loaf lying on the table. "We're very different, Jack. You go out of your way to do things for people, to make them feel good, to make them smile."

Jack tucked the toes of his shoes on the lower rung of his chair. "So?"

Stacy met his gaze. "I'm not like that. I don't mingle. I prefer to stay out of the limelight. I only want. . .the best for my son."

"You think I don't?"

She shook her head. "You only come here to make Daniel's Christmas brighter."

"You honestly think that?"

She nodded, a solemn gesture that ended with her chin almost resting on her chest.

"Look at me, Stace." Jack paused. "All right, don't. I'm going to say this anyway. I don't just come here to make Daniel smile."

"Then you do it because it makes you feel good," she mumbled into her sweater.

Jack drew a deep breath. He'd never met anyone as stubborn as Stacy. Not even his grandmother, who used to inspect his fingernails before he went to bed to ensure he'd actually cleaned them.

"Did you know hanging a Christmas stocking in North America dates back to the end of the nineteenth century?"

Stacy looked at him from beneath her lashes. "So?"

"Germany gets the credit for starting Christmas trees in the sixteenth century because devout Christians brought the trees into their homes to decorate."

"It's unnecessary to impress me with your knowledge. I already know that you know more about Christmas than any other person I've ever met."

"I haven't told you about evergreens yet," Jack said.

"What about them?"

"Some say they were a part of winter festivals long before Christ was born. They were used as symbols of everlasting life because they stayed green when other plants appeared dead. Romans supposedly gave branches to their friends as a sign of good luck."

"So if I cut down a whole forest of them, my luck will change?" Stacy's eyes were filled with sadness.

"Humor me," Jack said. "I've got one more to tell you."

Stacy motioned for him to continue.

"Holly is a symbol of joy and peace. In England, they placed sprigs of it beneath a young girl's bed to bring sweet dreams. Germans put it in their church decorations to protect the building against lightning."

Stacy shrugged. "Forgive me, but why are you telling me all this?"

"I don't know. It's just that you keep saying 'we can't do this' but you haven't given me a reason why. Don't tell me it's because we don't know each other. I agree that learning about a person takes time, but I can't believe you don't feel something significant for me."

Jack didn't know what else to say. Like all the times he'd failed to help his mother, it appeared he'd also been unable to help Stacy.

Stacy put her hands on the table, staring at the only outward mark she'd been married before. She'd removed her wedding band sometime after the Louisiana summer sun outlined its shape on her finger.

"All right, here's why I can't get involved with you. I lost my husband three years ago, which means I have to raise Daniel alone. I have to make sure he has clothes to wear, toys to play with. Oh, why bother? You won't understand."

"You're right, Stace. I can't fully grasp everything you deal with, but I can tell you this: I didn't have a dad, but having a mom who did those things made my pain a little easier to deal with."

Stacy's eyes were filled with so much hurt, Jack thought he'd said something wrong. "My mother did the best she could," he said. "She wasn't perfect, but before she went off on her marriage sprees, she went out of her way to make up for someone taking my dad away from me. Christmas was her favorite time of year, and she insisted I learn about it. She wanted me to appreciate the different traditions the world uses to celebrate the birth of Christ. It was her way of helping me cope with losing my dad. I wished she'd learned them with me."

Stacy barely met his gaze. "What are you saying?"

"Maybe you need to start a new tradition, something that belongs to you and Daniel, something he'll remember when he thinks back on his childhood."

Stacy finally met his gaze. "I'll. . .consider it."

"Good. And while you do, read this." Jack laid a section of newspaper on the table. "Perhaps it will tell you the things I can't seem to put into words."

The Christmas party at Daniel's friend's church on Saturday consisted of excited children, gallons of punch, hundreds of cookies, and a visit from another Santa.

Stacy found herself comparing the church Santa with the only other one she knew. This one was definitely not as jovial nor as handsome as Jack Santa, she decided.

Jack didn't call or come by to take them to church on Sunday. When Stacy saw that he wasn't at church, she wondered why. The next week also passed without a call from Jack. Whip visited Thursday night.

"Can't stay," he said, without taking off his coat. "I'm headed out to meet someone for dinner. Since I haven't seen you in a while, I wanted to check and see how things are going."

"Things are fine," Stacy responded.

"Doesn't sound like it. Jack called you lately?" Whip asked.

"Not since last week." If there was anyone Stacy could confide in, it was Whip.

"He's been working double shifts at the station. You should have heard the ribbing he took at the station's annual Christmas party last Saturday night."

Stacy couldn't hide the worry in her voice. "You brought the subject up, Whip. Tell me."

"Let's just say the main topic of discussion was the fact no one ever recalled a Santa getting off his truck to talk to someone during the parade."

"Oh," Stacy mouthed. Her throat grew dry. That explained why Jack hadn't been in touch. Not because he was working, but because he'd been kidded about visiting them.

"Why don't you tell me about this person you're going to see tonight," Stacy asked to turn the conversation.

Whip blushed like a young boy caught opening his Christmas gifts ahead of time. "Woman thinks she's going to trap me into marriage."

"You thinking about it?"

Whip chuckled. "Already did. A man can change his mind as well as a woman. Stop giggling! It happens. She whips up a mean sweet potato pie, which is my favorite."

❄

Stacy watched the phone as if it were the only machine left in Wyoming. It didn't do any good to deny that she wanted it to ring so she could hear Jack's voice on the other end.

As Daniel scribbled in a coloring book, Stacy flipped through the phone book and discovered Jack wasn't listed. She thought about calling the fire station but decided that would embarrass not only Jack, but herself, too. She could call Whip for Jack's number, but he probably wasn't back from his dinner date yet.

"I'll just do without hearing from him. I knew this was going to happen. I enjoy being with him, but it's best I don't depend on him to make me smile."

She tried rolling cookie dough to brighten her spirits. The dough stuck to the counter, and the cookies resembled something Daniel's chubby fingers might make instead of the cutter-sharp edges they usually had.

Daniel stuck his finger in the bowl of dough and smacked

his lips. "I'm tired, Mommy."

So was she. Worn-out, frazzled, depressed, worried, and lonely. She was so lonely. She hadn't realized how much she depended on Jack Santa. . .er. . .Trenton to make her happy. Even listening to another round of his Christmas traditions was preferable to hearing her sink drip.

Saturday dawned clear and sunny. Christmas was two days away. Daniel roared through the mobile home while Stacy vacuumed. One of Daniel's tiny race cars ended up inside the vacuum. The dust bag tore as she tried to extract the car, and Stacy burst into tears.

"I'll ask Jack Santa for a new car," Daniel declared, wiping away one of his mom's stubborn tears. Stacy plopped on the floor, staring at the dust and dirt that had fallen out of the cleaner's bag. *If it were only that simple,* she thought.

Daniel fixed peanut butter sandwiches and brought her one. She left it untouched because it reminded her of the one Jack and Daniel fixed for her a week or so ago.

Just after twilight, she heard a car pull up beside their home. Hurrying to the kitchen, Stacy peered out between the miniblinds.

"Oh, my!"

"Who is it, Mommy?"

"Jack Santa!"

Daniel raced to her side. "Why's he dressed so funny?"

Opening the door, Stacy perused Jack's attire. He wore a white beard and black boots, but instead of the Santa suit, red boxer trunks and a similar color muscle shirt were pulled over his regular clothes.

"Australia!" Stacy explained, not quite able to hold back her laughter. Then she watched Jack unload something from the back of his truck.

"He brought my car!" Daniel hurried to the door.

Stacy's smile turned to a frown.

H o, ho, ho!" Jack's greeting boomed through the door. Stacy swung the door open, torn between relief at seeing him and being upset for him bringing the car. "You're going to catch pneumonia dressed like that," she chided.

"Probably," Jack agreed, rubbing his arms. "May I come in?"

Stacy wanted to discuss the monstrosity sitting on her front porch. Jack didn't think she'd allow Daniel to keep that race car, did he? She recalled Jack's promise of that very thing as they drove around looking at lights.

She suddenly remembered the newspaper article she hadn't read and rushed to find it. Scanning it, she listened as Jack and Daniel discussed sports and cartoons. Finally, she joined them in the living room.

Jack laughed and rubbed Daniel's head. Daniel snuggled against his chest. "Did you come to see me, Jack Santa?"

"Yep," Jack admitted. "You and your mommy. Have I told you about Papa Noel?"

Daniel shook his head.

"Sometimes in southern Louisiana people in homes along the Mississippi River light bonfires on Christmas Eve to help guide Papa Noel, or Santa, as he delivers his gifts."

"Can we build a fire in our yard for him?"

"No. We don't do that in Wyoming. Do you know what to do when you see a fire?"

"Stop! Drop! And roll!"

"That's almost right. You do make a good man of the house for your mommy. You should tell an adult about the fire. Got that?"

Daniel nodded. "Could we pretend to build a fire, Jack Santa?"

Stacy cleared her throat. "I don't think so, Daniel."

Jack stared at her. It didn't take much to see that Stacy was annoyed. "I had to go out of town."

"We found plenty of things to keep us busy," Stacy replied.

"Good," Jack answered. "I know I should have called, but. . ."

Stacy turned the television to a holiday special for Daniel to watch. "Can we talk in the kitchen, Jack?"

"Sure." He followed her there.

"I'm not going to mince words," Stacy began. "I will not accept that. . .thing on the front porch."

"Why not?" Jack countered.

"Daniel doesn't need it."

"Of course he does," Jack began. "All little boys ought to have whatever their hearts dream of. The same goes for their mothers," he added.

"So, you think you know what I dream of, Jack? Is that part of your Santa routine, or another angle to Jack Trenton?"

Jack winced. "You read the newspaper clipping. I should have told you to your face about my background, Stace, but I knew you'd use that knowledge as a reason why you couldn't see me any longer."

"Got it in one, Jack."

"I want a woman to accept me for who *I* am, Stacy. The money, the house, the Christmas display, none of them means a thing to me. If they did, do you think I'd work at a volunteer job?"

Stacy paused. Jack had a point.

"Come on, Stace. I want to see you and Daniel smile. That's what I've wanted since I first met you."

"The article about you was. . .touching," Stacy confessed.

"A whole page on a man who fills his yard with Christmas decorations and lights and you call it moving?"

"Because that article helped me understand why you do some of the things you do."

"You're not mad because I didn't tell you it was my house from the beginning?"

Stacy shook her head. "I didn't say I *wasn't*. I'm still trying to sort through all of it, Jack."

"Ask whatever you want, Stacy. I'll answer anything."

She shook her head. "I think the article explained most of it. Despite your money, you look for pleasure in the small things in life, the way a child smiles, for instance."

"Daniel's smile looks a lot like yours."

"He's smiled more in the last three weeks than he has in a couple of years."

Jack trailed a finger down the side of her face. "I suspect you have, too."

"You're right," Stacy admitted.

"My mother searched for years for someone to fill the void created when we lost...Dad," Jack said. "She never found a way, though she married three times."

"She never found another man to love?"

Jack shook his head. "She never *let* herself love someone else. I know now that Mom wouldn't let go of what she had with Dad so she could move on."

"Just like me," Stacy mused.

"I didn't tell you that to compare you to her. My mother wouldn't let go of what she had with Dad because she was afraid she'd forget him. You do realize there's a difference between letting go and forgetting."

Jack picked up Stacy's hands and covered the pale circle on her left ring finger with his thumb. "I don't want to blot out your life before, Stace. If it weren't for those times that led you to me, you wouldn't be who you are today. This might sound sudden, but I want to make new memories, with you, and with Daniel."

Stacy gasped.

Jack pulled Stacy to him. "Well, what do you say?"

"I thought when you didn't call last week, I'd seen the last of you."

"Is that what you really want, Stace?"

Stacy didn't answer. "This year, Christmas isn't about what I want, Jack. It's about Daniel. He's the most important person in my life. I've come to understand he needs something to look forward to."

"Even if it means letting Daniel believe in Santa?"

"If he wants to believe in a red-suited, bearded man, or in this case, a man in red boxer trunks and a muscle shirt, for a few years, who am I to stop him?"

"I hope I'm that man."

"You are, Jack."

"You're doing the right thing, Stace." Jack's voice was filled with admiration as he held her hand. "I don't want to erase what you had with Timothy. I know it's important Daniel remembers that his father loved him. I want to be a dad who helps him live his life for today, and helps you look forward to tomorrow."

"That doesn't mean it's going to be easy."

Chapter 12

S top! Drop! Roll!"

Stacy jerked awake to Daniel's shouts. She grabbed him, raced out the back door, then skirted around the back of their mobile home and ran to the front, wishing she had a cell phone.

"Where's the fire, Daniel?" she asked, her heart beating furiously. She didn't see any smoke billowing from their home's windows.

"Over there." Daniel pointed across the street.

Stacy relaxed a little; a neighbor burned paper trash in his backyard.

"Is that like the bonfire Jack Santa told me about?" Daniel asked.

"Yes." Stacy realized Daniel's shouts echoed the phrase Jack had taught him before Christmas.

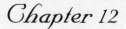

She thought back on that evening, the night her outlook toward Jack Trenton changed as he talked her into letting Daniel keep the large plastic race car, and she realized that loving Jack wouldn't push out Timothy's memories. In fact, Jack encouraged her to keep them in her heart so she could share them with Daniel as he grew. Jack had also promised to do what he could to share her recollections of Timothy and to help teach Daniel about his dad, as well. Jack was more than she'd ever dreamed of as a father for Daniel, and a husband.

Stacy hugged Daniel as they walked back toward their home, stopping to look at the huge, black race car sitting on the deck.

"When I can ride in my race car, Mommy?"

"As soon as the weather warms up." With the battery hidden, the car wouldn't go anywhere; a car that big wouldn't move off their deck anyway. What had Jack been thinking?

He was no doubt trying to make Daniel happy. They'd have to talk about why they couldn't buy Daniel every toy he wanted, no matter how much money he had. She was still coming to terms with his bank balance but had told him, in no uncertain terms, they'd live simply. They'd donated a large sum to a Mother's Against Drunk Drivers chapter in a nearby city and planned on starting a similar chapter in Antler, with their church's help.

Back inside, Daniel played with some new miniaturized race cars he got for Christmas. Stacy remembered her gift exchange with Jack on Christmas Eve, a time that still warmed her heart.

"I hate that I have to work," Jack had said, "but I already told those with families I'd cover tonight." Jack moved closer to her as he spoke, his shoulder just above the top of her head. Emotions rambled around her heart with alarming frequency.

"I think the world forgets to remember *why* we celebrate Christmas," he said. "It's about giving. After all, God gave us the greatest gift of all."

"Giving," Stacy echoed, as she straightened one of the tiny silver packages on her Christmas tree. "That's it. Too many worship the tiny baby and forget to praise the man He grew up to be."

"Sharing at least some of my Christmas Eve with you before I go to work is almost the best present I can ask for." Jack cleared his throat. "Speaking of giving, I have a special delivery for you in my truck."

Stacy grinned. "I wrapped something for you, too." She pulled a bundle out from under the tree. She'd spent a lot of time hand-painting Rudolph's likeness on a dark green sweatshirt.

"I love it. It matches yours, even down to the crooked antlers. It also goes pretty well with that crazy Santa suit I wear, don't you think?"

He'd pulled her close and hugged her. That was all, just hugged her. The tenderness in his hug still lingered today, weeks later. As for his gift, she'd taken it to bed and read throughout the night. She could barely force her eyes open when Daniel bounced on her bed, "Mommy! Santa brought me stuff!"

Bleary-eyed, she'd watched as Daniel tore into the gifts Jack helped her arrange before he left the night before. Daniel's squeals of joy overcame the sounds of shredding paper.

"Look-it, Mommy! Jack Santa gave me a race car!" The small toy replicated the one sitting on their deck that Jack had brought the week before.

"It's Dale Earnhardt Jr.," Daniel had explained. "He's me and Jack Santa's favorite NASCAR driver. See how it's painted all black with a white number, and, oh, Mommy! It's so neat-o!"

Daniel's excitement was no different than the joy Jack's book had brought to her, or the way Jack Santa definitely warmed her heart.

❅

Jack arrived with a store-cooked Easter dinner. Seeing him wear the Rudolph shirt she'd made for him, at Easter no less, gave Stacy a crazy glow inside. He stood in her doorway, looking gorgeous himself.

"Get in here before you catch a cold," Stacy demanded. "Daniel's running a fever. I don't need another one getting sick on me."

"Is he all right? Does he need a doctor?" Jack asked.

"No. I think he's worn-out from all the excitement of hunting eggs at church. He's taking a nap. I just checked on him. I'm sure he'll be fine."

They watched the end of a televised special. While Stacy set the table and put out a relish tray, Jack made a trip to Daniel's bedroom.

"I don't like the way Daniel sounds," Jack said as he returned to the kitchen.

Stacy gave Jack a worried glance but hurried to her son's room. She'd been careful to keep Daniel bundled up every time they went anywhere, including yesterday's egg hunt. Had he caught pneumonia after all? Her heart squeezed in her chest.

"Does he always sound like that when he sleeps?" Jack asked from behind her.

Stacy chuckled. "Only when he snores, Jack."

❄

Daniel soon joined them in the living room, rubbing his eyes but gaining energy as soon as he saw Jack.

"I guess you're right, Stace," Jack admitted after watching Daniel devour three helpings of ham, two of mashed potatoes, and four deviled eggs. "Nothing wrong with him."

Stacy nodded. "I can't believe you've never heard anyone snore before," she teased.

"That's what happens when you grow up as an only child," Jack commented.

The afternoon passed quickly. Daniel wore himself out by continually racing his cars up, down, and across the worn sofa. Stacy gave up trying to stop him.

Eventually, Daniel collapsed on the couch. Stacy and Jack slipped away to the kitchen.

They stared at each other across the table.

"Do you remember when you told me I should start a new Christmas tradition with Daniel so he'd have something special to recall about his childhood?" Stacy asked.

Jack nodded.

"Well, thanks to the book on Christmas lore you gave me, I think I'll do what they do in Italy."

Jack scratched his head. "Would you believe I can't recall what they do there?"

Stacy grinned. "On Christmas Eve, the father sets a big red

candle on the largest windowsill they have in the house. The youngest child lights the candle in honor of the baby Jesus. It burns all night to light the way for travelers or wanderers who need shelter, as they say Mary and Joseph needed a place to stay all those years ago."

"Daniel will like that," Jack said. "Just be sure you use a sturdy holder so the candle doesn't tip over during the night and start a fire. I couldn't bear it if something were to happen to either of you."

"There's one problem, Jack Trenton."

"What's that?"

"Daniel and I...well...this is going to sound rather forward, but...we need a father for him."

"Is that all? I'm still shocked you didn't consider using the one about the children in India riding—"

"Jack Trenton!"

"Yes?"

"Kiss me."

He did, thoroughly. When he finished, Stacy thought her heart would burst from the love she felt for him. "You've made me so happy, Jack...Santa."

"Likewise." He trailed a finger down her jaw. "But we're missing something."

"You mean sealing our promise with a kiss isn't enough?"

Jack shook his head. "Nope."

She thought for a moment. "Daniel?"

"And?"

"A wedding date?"

"And?"

"Prayer?"

Jack nodded. "Yes."

"Amen."

He kissed her again.

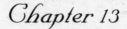

Chapter 13

Daniel screeched to a halt, stopping short of a pile of red-rimmed rocks and sending his voice echoing through the canyon. "Can you hear me, Jack? Hear me, Jack?"

Jack laughed as the seven-year-old scampered back toward him. Stacy clasped his hand, her knuckles white with fear.

"He'll be fine, Stace. He can't fall more than a couple of feet. Let him run out his energy and he'll sleep tonight."

"I'd still rather not watch." She turned her head and looked instead at the South Dakota Black Hills beauty before her. Now in late spring's gentle warmth, shades of green had burst forth and covered the craggy mountains, hiding their quartzy-jagged edges. A calm lake in front of them, where they'd stop later to eat a picnic lunch, waited for Daniel's next stone to skip across. Despite being married for three months, Stacy still couldn't believe her fortune.

She laughed to herself as she recalled Jack's wedding attire. From his sandals and red boating shorts to the white muscle

T-shirt he wore that matched her own red skirt and white blouse, there'd been nothing fancy about their clothing. The only traditional items at the wedding were the vows and the preacher.

She grabbed Jack's hand and snuggled her head on his shoulder. "Remember the poem I showed you from my uncle in Ohio?"

"The one we read at our Christmas Eve wedding to honor how God brought us together?"

"Hmm. I was just thinking about it. The Black Hills remind me of those words because it's so peaceful here."

"I'd say spending our next Christmas in one of those cabins we saw at Custer State Park would be the perfect backdrop for reciting it," Jack said. "Daniel, sit down while your mom reminds us of the opening verse."

Daniel plopped to the ground beside Jack, the bottom edge of his shirt rolled up and filled with rocks he planned to toss into the lake when he had time.

Stacy smiled at the family she thought she'd never have again.

"Let us keep Christmas simple, pure—
As simple as a manger bed,
Or as the shepherds' vision sure,
Or as the bleating flocks they led;
As simple as one shining star,
Or as a mother's newborn love
Or as the hope that came from far
With wise men guided from above," she finished.

"God, bless us," Daniel, Jack, and Stacy asked together, turning their faces to the open sky.

With those words, Stacy knew marrying Jack was the best decision she'd made in a very long time.

Epilogue

Luke Jolly and Jack Trenton filled their plates with fruit slices, a multitude of vegetable bits such as cauliflower and celery, and turkey and ham sandwiches.

"I still can't believe we both traveled twelve hundred miles to attend this conference in St. Louis, only to find we live within eighty miles of each other, can you?" Luke said as he and Jack found seats at a table near the front of the room.

"No," Jack replied, "but, Antler, Wyoming, where I live, is fairly secluded. We don't have our own newspaper or radio station, and TV channels are limited if you don't have cable or a satellite dish."

"I've found lots of places in the West are like that, but that's what I like about living there," Luke said. "You have any family?"

"Yes, I got married two years ago." Jack pulled some pictures out of his wallet. "We took these that fall in the Black Hills of South Dakota when we went on our 'family-moon.' That's what Daniel, my stepson, calls our family trip. It's my favorite photo of us."

"Stepchildren are great. I have one, too. A girl named Kloie. Without her, her mother and I wouldn't have gotten together," Luke admitted. "We have another child on the way in a few months. Can't wait to get home and get the house baby-proofed so we're ready for him."

"Congratulations are in order, then. Stacy and I are expecting our second baby boy in three months! Isn't that a coincidence?"

"Congrats to you, too," Luke said. "We'll have to make sure we keep in touch to see whose son grows fastest."

They turned to eating and within a few minutes an old-fashioned fire-alarm bell clanged throughout the auditorium.

"I heard that bell at my first conference," Jack said. "It means there's a special guest speaker."

The man who strode to the podium glanced around the room. "I'm Dr. Gabriel St. Nick, from Yellowstone City, Wyoming, and I specialize in Obstetrics and Family Practice. Since I'm a surprise speaker, there isn't any biography handy. Let me tell you a little about myself. After many years as a confirmed bachelor, I married a little dynamo named Annie. Our two-year-old twins, Molly Katherine and Morgan Alexis, keep Annie quite busy at home, but we couldn't be happier.

"My wife loves showing our daughters the world outside our Wyoming Victorian home and teaching them not to eat bugs, or how to relandscape the grounds left to her by her aunt. Annie also plays the piano beautifully and plans to teach the girls to play it when they're old enough. By the way, I delivered my own children. Most people call me Gabe, and I'm honored to speak to you today."

A stirring round of applause greeted Gabe as he ended his own introduction.

"I know you've all been trained in the importance of identifying carbon monoxide poisoning. Today I'm going to talk about the heroes who perform the rescues."

"This isn't the normal way we do things," Luke whispered to Jack, his voice blending in with the crowd's murmurs. "It's supposed to be information we can use in our jobs."

"I know," Jack said. "I guess he has a reason. We'll have to wait and see."

Gabe began, "We have various professionals here today. Firemen, doctors, nurses, and paramedics, as well as respiratory and pulmonary technicians. I can't list each specialty here today because I'd probably overlook—"

"Cardiology," someone shouted from the back. A polite laugh from the audience followed.

Gabe acknowledged the laugh with a wave. "You all know carbon monoxide poisoning is life threatening if not properly diagnosed and treated by hospital emergency personnel. Let me remind you of a few of the common symptoms: headache, nausea, dizziness, flu-like symptoms and fatigue, impaired judgment, and shortness of breath."

He sipped water from a glass under the podium and looked around the room as if searching for someone. His gaze landed on Jack and Luke then continued.

"Those symptoms must be correlated with, of course, a cause, such as obstructed motor vehicle exhausts, smoke from fires, nonelectric or kerosene space heaters, for example."

"One reason I'm here to speak today," Gabe began, "is

Paul Rogers, a park ranger at Yellowstone National Park. He thought he was just doing his job one August day as he watched visitors enter the park. A car approached his entrance and a woman jumped out of it screaming. That day could have rapidly turned tragic. Thanks to training Paul received over the years at continuing education meetings such as this, he knew exactly how to respond. Let me read part of the article about the event.

" 'Though the woman had her left arm in a sling and was almost hysterical, Park Ranger Rogers responded professionally. He took the car's steering wheel, and they raced toward a cabin four miles away. There, inside a small cabin room, he found a six-year-old boy unconscious but still breathing. As he'd entered the room, Paul had noticed a charcoal barbecue grill sitting in the middle, with burgers cooking on it. He surmised carbon monoxide fumes had overcome the boy and took the boy for medical treatment. The little boy is healthy today.' "

Gabe stopped reading for a second. "Paul Rogers, I know you're here. Will you please stand?"

The room burst into applause as Paul stood. His tablemates thumped him on the back and forced him toward the front of the auditorium. Gabe shook his hand and motioned for him to stand at the podium.

"Speech! Speech!"

Paul tried to wave them off but it didn't work. They pushed him for remarks. The clamor finally calmed down and Paul cleared his throat. "We all go to work to serve our public. I didn't used to think about what might happen when I responded to a call or a question from someone coming to the park until I got married not long ago. Now, my wife and I have a child on the way. When I helped save that little boy's life, I realized that in our jobs, each of us can become heroes at any time."

Gabe stepped next to him. "Paul, you're right. When you go back to your home state, there will be a ceremony that recognizes you as one of their Citizens of the Year."

The room broke into applause.

Paul blushed. "All I did is what anyone would have done."

"The same thing every rescuer in this room does in each of their jobs—their best," Gabe said. "I'd like everyone to stand now."

Chairs and tables shuffled while the two hundred twenty in attendance rose. "I know I'm honored to be among you," Gabe said. "If just one of you didn't show up for work, a life might be lost. This conference isn't only about gaining the info to help save more lives, but also about recognizing the heroes among us. We have very different jobs in different towns and cities across the United States. I'm going to ask you to remember one thing: Whether it's a parent, your own child, or someone else you rescue, always be a hero in the way you act toward them. God will bless you for it."

Tammy Shuttlesworth

Tammy is a former Ohio resident who now lives in Louisiana. She retired from the USAF after serving our country for twenty years. Besides writing Inspirational Romance, working as a Junior ROTC Instructor at Haughton High School with the LA801st and a group of super teenagers is the best thing she's ever done. She and her husband are blessed with two awesome daughters and a fantastic grandson. In her spare time, she loves walking her miniature dachshund in the woods and watching the varieties of birds that migrate through her yard during the spring and fall. Tammy's military travels inspire most of her stories and this one is no different. She hopes everyone remembers the true meaning of Christmas as they celebrate the season.

A Letter to Our Readers

Dear Readers:

In order that we might better contribute to your reading enjoyment, we would appreciate your taking a few minutes to respond to the following questions. When completed, please return to the following: Fiction Editor, Barbour Publishing, Inc., P.O. Box 719, Uhrichsville, OH 44683.

1. Did you enjoy reading *Wyoming Christmas Heroes*?
   ❏ Very much—I would like to see more books like this.
   ❏ Moderately—I would have enjoyed it more if _____
   _____

   _____

2. What influenced your decision to purchase this book?
   (Check those that apply.)
   ❏ Cover   ❏ Back cover copy   ❏ Title   ❏ Price
   ❏ Friends   ❏ Publicity   ❏ Other

3. Which story was your favorite?
   ❏ *Doctor St. Nick*   ❏ *Jolly Holiday*
   ❏ *Rescuing Christmas*   ❏ *Jack Santa*

4. Please check your age range:
   ❏ Under 18   ❏ 18–24   ❏ 25–34
   ❏ 35–45   ❏ 46–55   ❏ Over 55

5. How many hours per week do you read? _____

Name _____

Occupation _____

Address _____

City _____ State _____ Zip _____

E-mail _____

CONTENTS

This short book is the first in a series to be published by Yale University Press on a variety of legal subjects. The series aims to make available to the nonexpert—whether student, lawyer, or layperson—some prominent and controversial subjects engaging contemporary legal thought.

While the law is central to many aspects of American life, few who have not been to professional school have had an opportunity to study it, and most who have had professional legal training have become specialists, able only vaguely to remember other areas of their calling. It is my hope that this book and those that follow will mitigate, if not remedy, this condition.

The series will not be comprehensive. Its ambition is to explore some controversial subjects in ways that may themselves be controversial. The author of each book in the series will have a point of view and will not be reluctant to express it.

I have tried to do just that, and if I have been persuasive my book should be of interest to students of the Supreme Court—academics and journalists—as well as to its primary audience.

I have tried to write with as little jargon as my skills permit. This book is not a reference work and so I have indulged a liberty: there is a minimum of specific documentation. No law review would be happy with the paucity of footnotes found in these few pages.

The book grew out of a seminar I offered at Yale Law School. I am indebted to the many students there who taught me to see ancient problems from a youthful viewpoint (not that this book is in any way a direct translation of that viewpoint).

I am especially grateful to Lawrence Douglas, Michael O'Neill, and Michael Townsend, who continued the seminar as my research assistants, and to Jody Kraus and Andrew Koppelman, who also did research for me. My thanks too to Amy L. Katz and John Wellington, each of whom read the book in manuscript and made helpful suggestions. I also want to thank my secretary, Isabel Poludnewycz, and my editors at Yale University Press, John Covell and Fred Kameny. All three did their work in ways that showed them to be masters of their respective professions. Finally, my thanks go to Dean Guido Calabresi, who provided environmental support, and to Sheila Wellington, who as secretary of the University gave me a house and as my wife the love that made it into a home.

Some parts of some chapters have appeared in different form in professional journals. But over the years I have changed my mind more than a little. Accordingly, everything has been rethought as well as re-presented in a format that I believe is appropriate for the Contemporary Law Series and the readers we hope it will attract.

INTRODUCTION

The fundamental law governing the United States of America is the Constitution. It is very short. Even with its amendments it has been reproduced in these pages as a slim appendix.

Good constitutions are usually short. Yet they are meant to order the future for unborn generations. Ours is a good constitution and it has endured.

Why? How can a document the bulk of which was drafted more than two hundred years ago retain its central place in our atlas of national values? How can it delineate the structure of government and the basic rights of individuals in today's complex society?

This book, if it is successful, will help in the search for answers to these questions. I maintain that some of the answers can be traced to the courts, especially the Supreme Court, and to the process of adjudication. One thing about the process is clear: it is heavily concerned with the interpretation of our good, but surely not perfect, Constitution.

This book addresses some aspects of that interpretive enterprise. Specifically it asks and examines how public values function in the elaboration of constitutional provisions, especially the due process clause of the Fourteenth Amendment. This means that substantively the book is concerned with constitutional privacy, especially abortion.

But on another level the book is mainly about the process of adjudication and the place of the Supreme Court in interpreting the Constitution. In chapter 1 I give attention to two aspects of adjudication: regulation and the resolution of disputes. One difficult question that emerges is how we in a democracy can tolerate regulation without representation. I believe that this is a problem for all adjudication, common-law and statutory as well as constitutional. It is true, however, that special problems are raised by adjudication involving the constitutionality of legislation—or, as it is called, judicial review. In chapter 2 I examine these problems and try to justify the practice.

To justify judicial review is not necessarily to accept the modalities of its exercise—that is, the approaches to constitutional interpretation taken by the Court and others. In chapters 3 and 4 I inspect certain modalities that I describe as flawed, including the politically popular doctrine of "original intent."

I then describe an approved style of constitutional interpretation: the common-law method, which I discuss in the context of the judicial process. In examining how this process influences interpretation I espouse some commonsense, although academically disputed, notions: that interpreting the Constitution is different from directing *Hamlet* or writing a novel, that being a judge is different from being a critic.

In chapter 6 I apply the common-law method to abortion.

The constitutional regulation of abortion leads me to worry about the public acceptance of the Court's decisions, and in the last part of the book I explore what I have called the politics of the indigestible.

I acknowledge in chapter 7 that the Court makes mistakes, and in chapter 8 I assert what the Court at times seems to deny: not only do other institutions, groups, and individuals interpret the Constitution, but sometimes they have an obligation to contest both the Court's readings and its authoritativeness. While this obligation is being discharged, we have noisy dialogue. I see this as necessary. The consequence of dialogue helps fit the regulation that results from adjudication into the democratic ideology that we profess as a nation.

To the memory of three Yale Law School colleagues: Alexander M. Bickel, Robert M. Cover, and Arthur A. Leff. Each died young. Each, through his writing and teaching, has made a distinctive contribution to the shape of contemporary legal thought.

Designed by Richard Hendel.
Set in Sabon type by
Eastern Typesetting Co., South Windsor, Connecticut.
Printed in the United States of America by
Vail-Ballou Press, Binghamton, New York.

Library of Congress Cataloging-in-Publication Data
Wellington, Harry H.
    Interpreting the Constitution: the Supreme Court and the
process of adjudication / Harry H. Wellington.
        p.   cm.—(Contemporary law series)
    Includes bibliographical references and index.
    ISBN 0-300-04881-5 (cloth)
           0-300-05672-9 (pbk.)
    1. Judicial review—United States.   2. United States—
Constitutional law—Interpretation and construction.   3. Judicial
process—United States.   I. Title.   II. Series.
    KF4575.W45   1991
    342.73'02—dc20
    [347.3022]   90-44755

A catalogue record for this book is available from the British
Library.

The paper in this book meets the guidelines for permanence and
durability of the Committee on Production Guidelines for Book
Longevity of the Council on Library Resources.

10   9   8   7   6   5   4   3   2

HARRY H. WELLINGTON

Interpreting the Constitution

THE SUPREME COURT

AND THE PROCESS OF

ADJUDICATION

Yale University Press   New Haven & London

CONTEMPORARY LAW SERIES

by any other court. For unlike the parties to a dispute, people who find themselves in analogous situations have not had a role in shaping the law. In this sense they have not had their day in court. No Sikh has had Goldman's opportunity to persuade the justices to embrace the perhaps distinctive Sikh point of view. And yet, a Sikh who decided to disregard the guidance offered by *Goldman v. Weinberger* would find that that decision provided a powerful and independent answer to the claim that the right to wear a turban is protected by the First Amendment. To put the point provocatively, the Sikh would find that violence—being kicked out of the air force—was being practiced in the name of the law. This is precisely why *Goldman* can be said to have regulated the future.

Of course we are all bound by a vast amount of law that we had no role in making—old or settled law, as it were. On the whole we accept this. If we do not like the law we think we must work to change it. This accepting attitude suggests that the problem of nonparticipation posed by the regulatory effect of adjudication exists primarily when courts reach results that expand, restrict, or in some other fashion reshape the law by interpreting prior decisions, statutes, or—as in *Goldman v. Weinberger*—the Constitution.

The law would less often be reshaped in adjudication by the interpretation of prior law if the law employed in resolving the dispute were clear to the public and the explanation given in the judicial opinion kept it clear. But such clarity would require the law to be static. For example, a court could not take changing social circumstances into account in reaching its holding without engaging in interpretation that might entail reshaping the law.

If the law were clear and static, a day in court would be important only in sorting out factual matters: what happened, when, to whom, and so on. The parties would have their day in court before a sanction could be imposed for failure to follow the clear, static law. In such a world new adjudication would not result in new regulation; adjudication would deal purely with the resolution of disputes.

It is obvious that in contemporary America such a steady state of legal affairs is impossible. Nor is there much reason to think that one would be desirable. Steady-state adjudication would shift to the legislatures and administrative agencies the entire task of adapting the legal system to new problems. Some societies in the past generated new problems slowly. But because of the rapid social, economic, and technological change that is so much a feature of the late twentieth century, contemporary America is awash in new problems seeking legal solutions. As they are currently organized, legislatures and agencies could not cope with these problems by themselves. Indeed they are now coping badly with a system in which they share with the courts the brunt of an insistent pressure to reshape the law.

In our system the law is much too complex to be very clear even to specialists, and almost surely must remain so. The law must also change over time. One way that it changes is through this process of adjudication, through what Justice Felix Frankfurter once optimistically called "litigating elucidation." This process can be illustrated by returning to *Goldman v. Weinberger*.

The First Amendment to the U.S. Constitution protects religious liberty and free expression. As to religion it provides that "Congress shall make no law respecting an establishment of religion, or prohibiting the free exercise thereof." Goldman's claim was that the air force, acting under congressional authority, prohibited him from engaging in the free exercise of his religion. The facts seemed to place the case squarely within the purview of the amendment. They did, that is, unless the amendment does not mean what it seems to say or is understood as applying only in an anemic fashion to the armed forces.

It is almost always a mistake in the law to read literally and think that that is the end of the matter (although you can get into a lot of trouble if you see a sign that says "Stop" and keep going). It may be that more often than you imagine there is no such thing as a literal reading. Did the headgear rule prohibit the free exercise of religion—"free exercise" is what the language of the First Amendment seems to protect—or did it just restrict Goldman's practices? And is there a meaningful difference between the two? Should the answer turn on how important wearing a yarmulke is to an orthodox Jew, or on whether the restriction imposed by the air force was reasonable, all things considered? Is it important in formulating the answer to understand the purpose of the headgear rule and its relation to discipline in the military? How about the purpose of the First Amendment itself? And how about prior interpretations of the free exercise clause—earlier efforts to order the future—especially in a military setting? And finally, in the context of adjudication, how much deference should the Court pay to the Pentagon on the question of whether the air force needs its rule to maintain discipline?

In its written opinions the Supreme Court addressed some of these issues. Perhaps because of prior decisions it did not pause on the language of the First Amendment. Nor, the Court tells us, was there any question on the basis of prior decisions that review of military rules "is far more deferential than constitutional review of laws or regulations designed for civilian society." But this deference, which has no grounding in the language of the First Amendment, was taken by the Court to new lengths. Justice William H. Rehnquist wrote for the majority: "[T]o accomplish its mission the military must foster instinctive obedience, unity, commitment, and esprit de corps. . . . The essence of military service 'is the subordination of the desires and interests of the individual to the needs of the service.' " The Court, he said, "must give great deference to the professional judgment of military authorities." On issues such as the dress code, the military knows better than the courts.

The Court's opinion is troublesome. For while the military may know more than the Supreme Court about dress codes, does the Court not know more about the Constitution? And, make no mistake about it, *Goldman v. Weinberger* is a case of constitutional interpretation. Yet it is a case where the Court was mute concerning the promise of religious freedom given pride of place in our Bill of Rights. But that regrettable omission is not the point of this discussion. The point is that the law of the First Amendment as it applied to Captain Goldman's right to wear a yarmulke was not clear when Goldman brought suit. Nor was the law static, as the holding in the case made plain. The law of the First Amendment was shaped, fashioned—some would say created—in the process of adjudication.

There is nothing unique about *Goldman v. Weinberger*. It is hardly an extreme example of the unsettled nature of law that is regularly subjected to litigating elucidation in the federal and state courts of the United States. And the clarification, reshaping, or making of law in adjudication regularly takes place whether the law in question is based only on prior judicial decisions (called common law), on a statute, or, as in *Goldman v. Weinberger*, on the Constitution. This means that people are often regulated by courts formulating new rules without an opportunity to be heard on the content of those rules.

People are often regulated by legislatures as well, often without having had an opportunity to be heard. Even as nonparticipation is a problem in adjudication only when the law is being reshaped, so too in the legislature: if the proper procedures have been observed, nonparticipation should not concern us where a statute has already been enacted. Government cannot address issues afresh for each micro-generation. The participation problem requires that the closest attention be paid where there is a proposal to change the law in a way that rearranges the permissible application of sanctions against a person who disobeys the legislative command.

In theory, access to legislators in this situation is available to the alert citizen, the one aware of a pending bill; access to judges is generally not. Moreover, in theory electoral accountability makes legislators into representatives of their constituents (and this means to some extent their agents) in ways that judges are not expected to be, even if the judges are elected (as they are in many states). We require our courts to stand apart, our judges to be disinterested.

Today there is substantial concern with the legislative process because money and interest group politics are believed by many to have corrupted it. The process probably can be repaired, although doing so will require heroic efforts. On the judicial side, however, there is nothing to repair, for nothing is broken: those who are not parties to a litigation are generally not supposed to have a say in the regulation produced by the decision, although sometimes they are permitted or invited to file so called friend-of-court (amicus curiae) briefs.

The question of who is a proper party in litigation is itself complicated and controversial. It is an area of law involving such technical and often critical issues as standing to sue, and the certification of a class of plaintiffs or defendants. Standing may depend among other things on whether a person has sustained sufficient economic injury by the actions of others to seem justified in bringing a law suit. Certification of a class turns on such issues as the legal similarities of otherwise discrete individuals or entities. Liberal rules regarding these matters may sometimes mitigate the problem of participation and regulation, but they do not eliminate it.

This difference between adjudication and legislation—the difference in the theoretical opportunities of affected individuals and groups to be heard—invites us to consider whether anything in the judicial process (in adjudication) might serve as a functional substitute for access to representatives and electoral accountability. There are two types of substitutes, both of which can be illustrated by ringing some changes on *Goldman v. Weinberger*. First, the courts and the lawyers who argue before them are marvelously adept at making nice distinctions between earlier cases and present ones, thus sharply limiting the regulatory consequences of the earlier cases. Suppose that the headgear rule had been applied first to a pilot who was a Sikh wearing a turban. Let us assume that the case had gone to the Supreme Court before Goldman's and that the air force rule as applied to the pilot had been upheld. Goldman's lawyers might have tried to distinguish a turban from a yarmulke and a mental health worker from a pilot. They might have argued along lines suggested (but ultimately rejected) in the actual litigation by Justice John Paul Stevens, who wrote in his concurring opinion: "Captain Goldman presents an especially attractive case for an exception from the uniform regulations that are applicable to all other Air Force personnel. . . . The yarmulke is a familiar and accepted sight. In addition to its religious significance for the wearer, the yarmulke may evoke the deepest respect and admiration—the symbol of a distinguished tradition and an eloquent rebuke to the ugliness of anti-Semitism. Captain Goldman's military duties are performed in a setting in which a modest departure from the uniform regulation creates almost no danger of impairment of the Air Force's military mission."

Justice Stevens rejected this distinction because it would in effect have preferred the orthodox Jew to the Sikh and represented "a fundamental departure from the true principle of uniformity that supports the [Air Force] rule." But I can easily imagine the persuasive force of such a distinction, and particularly the difference—which was not directly addressed by Justice Stevens—between a pilot and a mental health worker. And it may well be that if an argument based on that difference were carefully elaborated, some of the concurring justices making up the majority in *Goldman* would agree with it. Indeed if the posited case of the Sikh had come to the Court before *Goldman*, and if the Court had stressed that the rule was being specifically applied to a pilot, the result in Goldman's case, decided by the narrowest of margins (5 to 4), might have been different.

The second substitute in adjudication for the access to representatives and electoral accountability that characterize the legislative process is the legislature itself, for the regulatory effect of a judicial opinion is usually subject to legislative revision.

Where a judicial decision is based on the common law or on the interpretation of a statute, subsequent legislation can always change the regulatory effect of the adjudication. After all, a legislature has control over such ordinary law—though it may have to speak clearly. Often a legislature can effect change in the constitutional field: two years after *Goldman v. Weinberger*, for example, Congress passed a law that liberalized the headgear rule.[2] The Court had held that the harsh headgear rule was constitutional, but congressional relaxation of the rule was still permissible. This did not alter constitutional law itself: the Court's interpretation of the free exercise clause of the First Amendment stands.

Frequently the regulatory effect of a constitutional decision cannot be changed by statute. The abortion case of *Roe v. Wade* (1973)[3] is an example: the Court recognized the right to an abortion in spite of a Texas statute making abortion a crime. Unless the Court reverses itself—and it may be on its way to doing so, as we shall see—a new statute attempting to reimpose prior law would fare no better.

In cases where there cannot be direct legislative revision because of the constitutional nature of the decision, the Supreme Court has made it clear that it considers itself freer to overrule an "incorrect" prior decision than it does in a case where there can be legislative revision (that is, a case interpreting a statute). This is among the concerns of abortion rights (pro-choice) groups fearing that *Roe v. Wade* (as modified in 1989 by *Webster v. Reproductive Health Services*)[4] may be thought "incorrect" by the Rehnquist Court.

Is it therefore appropriate to conclude that the absence of access and electoral accountability in adjudication is made up for by the capacity of the courts to overrule prior decisions and to see relevant differences between a prior case and a present one? (Recall the distinction I just tried to draw between a Sikh pilot and a Jewish mental health worker.) To answer this question affirmatively, must we be confident that the ability of judges to distinguish a later case from a prior one is the functional equivalent for the parties in the later case of participation in the prior case? I ask this second question because we cannot generally count on the legislatures: they are too busy to review the judiciary regularly, and sometimes the Constitution precludes their doing so.[5] The revision by Congress of the regulation upheld in *Goldman v. Weinberger* may be thought of as the exception rather than the rule.

To answer this second question, we must get a grip on when it is proper to distinguish prior decisions. We might begin by recognizing a deep attachment to a commonplace ideal: like cases should be treated alike. This ideal may be at the heart of our commitment to the rule of law. It certainly is important to any conception we have of formal justice. Yet we expect departures by the legislature from this ideal, or at least we accept them. Like cases are frequently not treated alike. For example, transition rules in tax reform statutes (designed to make it financially easier for a taxpayer to adjust to the new law) treat one regulated group differently from another on the basis of which group has had timely access to important congressmen, not on the basis of relevant differences among the groups. And we commonly give preference through subsidies to one group of citizens over another because its representatives skillfully advocated its cause.

Adjudication, however, is another matter. Our tolerance for departure from the ideal of treating like cases alike is substantially less. One reason may be that judges, unlike legislators, are not easily reached—if they are behaving properly. Another reason is the very fact that judges are not electorally accountable in the same way that legislators are. This is true as a general proposition even where judges are elected. (The fate of Chief Justice Rose Bird in California is unusual: she was voted out of office in 1986 primarily because of her liberal approach in criminal cases.) It seems reasonable to accept greater deviation from the ideal of like treatment where it is appropriate for voters to punish the offending official at the ballot box and hope for redress from a new official.

Finally—and this is a different sort of explanation—the strong ideal in adjudication of treating like cases alike supports the dual purposes of adjudication. We often need regulatory stability for planning, and this is promoted by the knowledge of the planner that the courts can be relied on to try to fulfill the ideal. In resolving disputes treating like cases alike is an ideal that helps to satisfy our conception of fairness and the powerful importance of equal treatment in that conception. Justice Stevens, for example, believed that the headgear rule was constitutional as applied to Goldman at least in part because he thought it would be constitutional if applied to a Sikh in a turban. And he thought this because he believed a Sikh in a turban would be seen by other service personnel as controversial and would present the air force with disciplinary problems. That Goldman had to suffer to protect another's "negative" interest in equal treatment suggests how strong the ideal is. It also suggests that reasonable people may well disagree in particular situations about whether one case is like another. Indeed such disagreement is often a prominent feature of the dissenting opinion, and, more important, makes it difficult to specify what we mean when we insist that courts treat like cases alike.

If we were able to get a firm grip on what it means to treat like cases alike, it would both improve the resolution of disputes and diminish any anxiety over the authority of the courts to regulate—at least this would happen in a society such as ours, where there is a well-developed corpus of decisional law. We would have a system of law capable of adapting predictably to changing circumstances. Put another way, if we had that firm grip we could say that even if the law were not clear and static it was predictable in application, or at least reasonably predictable.

According to an optimistic view of America's legal system this is what we have. While I am not pessimistic I lack that degree of optimism, in part because I know that no one can be very clear about what it means to treat like cases alike. And given the number of potentially relevant factors in even a simple case like *Goldman*, I also know that clarity is not in the cards. Should this then make me pessimistic?

The answer is emphatically no. First, I take comfort in the existence of that strong commitment to the ideal of treating like cases alike. Second, judges strive to achieve that ideal. And third, they are reasonably successful in their efforts because of the nature of the judicial process, some aspects of which it seems profitable to explore.

Consider first the adversarial nature of the judicial process. To advance their desired interpretation of the regulations that em-

power or constrain them, individuals and groups hire lawyers. Part
of the lawyers' task is to distinguish prior cases that may be seen
as contrary to their clients' desired interpretation, and as I have
already observed they are adept at this. The lawyers for the other
side of course emphasize the similarity of the present controversy
to the prior ones. Lawyers on both sides are hedged about in their
adversarial roles by the conventions of the legal profession: each
argues, as law school professors sometime exhort their students to
do, "like a lawyer." And this means that each is talking to the other.
Rarely does it seem to one side that the other is coming totally from
left field. This shared sense of what is relevant in a situation sharply
reduces the number of considerations that might otherwise be
thought germane and makes it much more than merely idealistic to
talk about treating like cases alike.

The conventions of the profession—how a lawyer knows what
counts as a good argument—are a product of many factors, including what is learned in law schools (approaches and substance, social
science, humanistic theory, and "hard" law), at law firms, and in
the practice generally. Nor are these conventions static: they are
constantly being revised under the insistent pressure of social, economic, political, and technological change. To argue in a lawyerly
fashion today is not to argue the way a lawyer would have done
fifty years ago, although both the lawyer of today and the lawyer
of fifty years ago would if competent fit comfortably within what
some might call an interpretive community.[6] The community consists of the advocates, who undertake through the interpretation of
legal materials (texts) to advance their client's cause; the judges,
who pick and choose among arguments and engage in disinterested
interpretation (disinterested at least in the sense that it is not oriented
toward one's client); and the teachers and critics, who evaluate
outcomes and seek to shape tomorrow's results.

Consider second that while the judge at the trial level generally
sits alone, if the case goes on to an appellate court several judges
will address the lawyers' arguments on the meaning of the relevant
law. This is useful. Disinterested discussion helps to clarify distinc-

tions and similarities that may have been blurred by lawyers wanting to win.

But the desirability of a decision agreed to by a majority of judges exposes a difficulty: disinterested decisionmakers themselves may disagree on what is alike and what is unlike. This means that negotiation among the judges of an appellate court seems inevitable. Some thoughtful students of the law however contend that there is a right answer to every question a judge must decide.[7] If this were so and if, as John Milton wrote in 1644, "who ever knew Truth put to the worse in a free and open encounter [with Falsehood],"[8] then negotiation should advance the quest for truth. But the contention that there is always a "right answer" is a strained version of appellate practice in America. For while each judge may have a preferred interpretation, often that judge has an acceptable second-best position as well. Experience at least seems to suggest that this is so. Much scholarly writing and good investigative reporting has been devoted to great cases in the Supreme Court and the hard bargaining that takes place among the justices.[9] This is not surprising: since the Court is regulating the future there is a need for it to express an opinion, and the stakes are high. Conscientious judges may concur or dissent with their colleagues if they do not agree after negotiation. But as a general proposition, negotiation presupposes flexibility, flexibility that is within the conventions of the profession or, again, within the appropriate interpretive community.

The nonpessimistic view of all this is that adjudication has two protections built in for parties who are subject to prior decisional law although they were strangers to the proceeding in which the law was fashioned. These protections, which exist in an uneasy balance and do not function smoothly, may be seen as substitutes for the access to representatives and electoral accountability that characterize the legislative process. The first protection is that where the interpretive conventions of the legal profession determine that precedents are weak, regulation can be changed. The second is that where precedents are strong, because the interpretive conventions of the profession give only narrow leeway for distinguishing prior decisions, disputes will be resolved according to the ideal that like cases should be treated alike.

But trouble remains, and it is part of the reason I am not as optimistic as I should like to be. The "conventions of the profession" may themselves be insufficiently sensitive to the perspectives of some of the many groups that make up the American polity.

Women, who unlike other groups make up a majority of the polity, have had encounters with the law that illuminate this problem of the law's insufficient sensitivity. But these encounters also demonstrate the dynamic nature of law and the ability of adjudication in some situations to respond to new perspectives that are redefining social and political reality. I see this particular story in a relatively optimistic light, although it is far from concluded and there is much to be done. As we shall see, an important part of the story involves the interpretation of the equal protection clause of the Fourteenth Amendment. (Others are federal and state antidiscrimination laws, innovative doctrines of civil liability, and, on the totally pessimistic side, the failure of the Equal Rights Amendment.)

The most famous example of Victorian paternalism toward women in the Supreme Court is the concurring opinion of Justice Joseph P. Bradley in the *Bradwell* case, in which the Court sustained a state law that barred women from practicing law. Bradley had this to say in justification:

> Man is, or should be, woman's protector and defender. The natural and proper timidity and delicacy which belongs to the female sex evidently unfits it for many of the occupations of civil life. The constitution of the family organization, which is founded in the divine ordinance, as well as in the nature of things, indicates the domestic sphere as that which properly belongs to the domain and functions of womanhood. The harmony, not to say identity, of interests and views which belong, or should belong, to the family institution is repugnant to the

idea of a woman adopting a distinct and independent career from that of her husband. . . . [The] paramount destiny and mission of woman are to fulfil the noble and benign offices of wife and mother. This is the law of the Creator.[10]

That was 1873.

In *Goesaert v. Cleary* (1948)[11] the Court upheld a state statute barring any woman who was not the spouse or daughter of a male tavern owner from obtaining a bartender's license. "Beyond question," the Court said, the state could "forbid all women from working behind a bar." Given this conclusion, the Court found the classification—spouse or daughter of a male owner—to be a rational exception to the state's general rule. The premise supporting that general rule does not necessarily rest on the view of women held by Justice Bradley in 1873, but some stereotypical picture of female as a weakling or flower or as something less than a fully autonomous person is required to sustain "beyond question" a law forbidding "all women from working behind a bar." Without that picture would such a law be rational? It would classify all women, because they are women, as never qualified, no matter how well qualified a particular woman might be.

Times change, and in the early 1970s the Court struck down statutes that preferred men to women as administrators of estates, or that automatically gave a serviceman a dependency allowance for his spouse but required a servicewoman to prove that her spouse was a dependent. The argument for sustaining such legislation may be thought to have rested on assumptions of the following sort: it may not be pretty, but wives are more likely than husbands to be dependent, and men are more apt than women to be more experienced in managing money. According to this way of thinking, the interest in convenient administration of the statutes justified the legislative classifications, if the test of constitutionality was whether the classifications were rational. At the time the statutes were passed it was thought that any classification that could be defended as rational was constitutionally permissible. But perhaps because the assumptions could be traced to earlier, discriminatory practices, the Court was moving away from a mere rationality test, though it was moving without saying so. This became clear a few years later. More than rationality was required and administrative convenience would not do. "[P]revious cases establish that classifications by gender must serve important governmental objectives and must be substantially related to achievement of those objectives."[12]

The women's movement was not quite able to marshal the votes needed to pass the Equal Rights Amendment—it needed support from three-quarters of the state legislatures—but its voice was heard in adjudication. To some extent at least, its perspectives became part of the conventions of the profession that argues, decides, and evaluates law for a living.

But unlike women, some groups may not have adequate access to the legal system because they are seen as too deviant or cannot afford lawyers, particularly when free legal services are inadequately supported. This means that the points of view of some parts of society are outside the conventions of the legal profession and are not heard when regulation is produced by adjudication.

Justice Stevens was responding to part of this problem in *Goldman v. Weinberger*: Sikhs in turbans are seen as too deviant. His response was questionable at best, however, for it deprived Goldman of the ability to practice his religion freely. If the Sikh cannot do it, neither can the orthodox Jew.

The legal profession is becoming increasingly open and diverse at the bar, the bench, and the schools. This trend, which has not gone far enough, may improve the situation for Sikhs (and other strangers). Does it not seem logical to infer that my relatively optimistic story about gender discrimination is in part attributable to the increased presence of women in the legal profession?

There is of course a down side, as there always is. A more diverse community is apt to increase the number of perspectives on an issue, to increase the relevance of distinguishing factors in cases, to exacerbate the problem of getting that grip on what is alike in possibly distinguishable cases, and thus to make law more ad hoc. This may solve the problem of lack of access and electoral accountability by reducing the regulatory force of adjudication, but it may be at a substantial cost to efficiency. For if the law is more ad hoc it is harder to use it for planning purposes, or for settling disputes. Moreover, many will worry about the apparent increase in judicial discretion that attends the phenomenon I am describing. They will believe that judges faced with more relevant variables will be less constrained, that theirs is the liberty of choice, that they will choose to make their personal preferences the law. But law made by judges must in the end be politically digestible, and if the judge is disinterested then disciplined discretion in reshaping the law is not an evil. Inefficiency may also be a price worth paying, for professional diversity and the availability of legal services for all are required to justify the regulatory aspects of adjudication. Indeed, the counterpart to these goals on the legislative side is the extension of the franchise.

CHAPTER TWO

Judicial Review

While the regulatory aspects of appellate adjudication in any of its forms may make us uneasy, judicial regulation is generally regarded as most troublesome when the meaning of the Constitution is at stake. This is not simply because constitutional law is often more important than other types of law. It is rather because constitutional adjudication produces regulation that may overturn or veto enacted law, and because this type of judicial regulation is relatively final since it is hard to change.

Consider the standard account of three forms of adjudication: common law, statutory, and constitutional. The common law is made by judges, at least in the sense that the interpretation and application of prior law—so much a part of the process of adjudication—is the interpretation and application of regulation that was itself produced in earlier adjudication. Examples of law that fall at least partly in this category are contracts and torts.

Adjudication involving statutes, such as those regulating security markets or labor unions, implicates other branches of government. These branches are law makers more than the courts are. Here the interpretation and application is predominantly of regulation enacted by a legislature, although prior judicial decisions applying the statute will themselves require interpretation.

Neither common-law nor statutory adjudication generally pits court against legislature; and neither produces regulation that cannot be undone by subsequent legislation. Thus if the majority of a legislature is unhappy about the development of the common law of civil liability (torts), it can change the law by legislation, or at least undertake to do so. Moreover, if one of its statutes is interpreted by the courts in a manner that the legislature takes to be inappropriate, it can revise the statute.

The standard account acknowledges that some observers see in these examples a conflict between court and legislature on the direction law should take and recognizes that some conflict may exist. It recognizes also what I noted in passing in the last chapter: legislatures are too busy and their processes too hedged about to make it realistic to expect systematic legislative oversight of judicial decisionmaking. But the standard account emphasizes that the constraints on courts in the development of law are very different from the constraints that govern the legislative process. I explored some of these differences in the first chapter and shall take up the matter later in the context of constitutional adjudication. These differences tend to defuse conflict. Nor is there any question in a formal sense that the electorally accountable legislature has the final word. Certainly the ideal is not conflict. It is a cooperative relationship between legislature and court, one that reflects the institutional capacities of both in the joint enterprise of ordering the future wisely.

Contrast this with constitutional adjudication, or judicial review. Here one does sometimes find conflict and the potential for judicial finality. The most dramatic situation is one in which Congress has enacted a law, the President has signed it, officials have applied it, and those to whom it has been applied say that all prior governmental action is illegal because it is unconstitutional. In *Goldman v. Weinberger* the Supreme Court of the United States, sitting as an appellate court, had the clear authority to pass on the constitutionality of the governmental action. It had the authority to declare prior governmental action unconstitutional—which in this case it did not exercise.

Marbury v. Madison (1803) is the leading case holding that such authority exists.[1] Marbury, who had been appointed and confirmed as a justice of the peace for the District of Columbia, had not received his judicial commission when the administration of John Adams yielded to that of Thomas Jefferson and his secretary of state, James Madison. Marbury sued Madison in the Supreme Court for delivery of his commission. He claimed that the Supreme Court had "original jurisdiction" to entertain the action under the Judiciary Act, passed by Congress in 1789; that is, jurisdiction as a court of first impression—a trial court—rather than as an appellate court. The Court read the Act as granting it original jurisdiction, but it read the Constitution as denying Congress the authority to make such a grant.

John Marshall wrote for a unanimous Court, and what is most important for our purposes is captured by the language of our greatest chief justice:

> It is, emphatically, the province and duty of the judicial department, to say what the law is. Those who apply the rule to particular cases, must of necessity expound and interpret that rule. If two laws conflict with each other, the court must decide on the operation of each. So, if a law be in opposition to the constitution; if both the law and the constitution apply to a particular case, so that the court must either decide that case, conformable to the law, disregarding the constitution; or conformable to the constitution, disregarding the law; the court must determine which of these conflicting rules governs the case: this is of the very essence of judicial duty. If then, the courts are to regard the constitution, and the constitution is superior to any ordinary act of the legislature, the constitution, and not such ordinary act, must govern the case to which they both apply.

The Constitution did not spell out that the courts were to consider it superior to ordinary law while treating it in the same fashion as ordinary law. Article III establishes the judicial branch and in part provides: "The Judicial Power shall extend to all Cases . . . arising under this Constitution, the Laws of the United States, and Treaties made." And Article VI, the supremacy clause, reads: "This Constitution . . . shall be the supreme Law of the Land; and the Judges in every State shall be bound thereby, any Thing in the Constitution or Laws of any State to the Contrary notwithstanding."

But while this language supported the Chief Justice in his interpretation in *Marbury v. Madison*, it did not require that interpretation. Congress and the President are under an obligation to obey the Constitution. Judicial faithfulness to the separation of powers among the branches of the federal government—an important feature of the Constitution—might well have dictated that the Court respect the understanding that the other branches have of their constitutional authority. This understanding was reflected in the Judiciary Act of 1789 that Marshall and his Court struck down.

But Marshall's view may also be seen as drawing support from the structure of the Constitution and the different functions of the three branches of the central government that result from the separation of powers. Alexander Hamilton addressed structure and function in *The Federalist*, the most famous of the writings explaining and advocating ratification of the 1787 Constitution. He was one of three authors; the others were James Madison and John Jay. Each of the "eighty-five letters to the public" that make up *The Federalist* was signed Publius. Here is some of what Hamilton had to say in No. 78: "The complete independence of the courts of justice is peculiarly essential in a limited Constitution. By a limited Constitution, I understand one which contains certain specified exceptions to the legislative authority; such, for instance, as that it shall pass no bills of attainder, no ex post facto laws, and the like. Limitations of this kind can be preserved in practice no other way than through the medium of courts of justice, whose duty it must be to declare all acts contrary to the manifest tenor of the Constitution void. Without this, all the reservations of particular rights or privileges would amount to nothing."[2]

But in spite of Marshall and Hamilton, the debate has continued. Many scholars, judges, and politicians have participated, and while much of the debate has concerned the scope and modalities of judicial review, some of it has questioned the legitimacy of the practice itself. We shall pick the debate up in the recent past and learn from two scholars.

In 1960 the distinguished constitutional lawyer Charles L. Black, Jr., elaborated in *The People and the Court* on the structural argument supporting judicial review and put a new twist on it. Black wrote: "[T]he prime and most necessary function of the Court has been that of validation, not that of invalidation. What a government of limited powers needs, at the beginning and forever, is some means of satisfying the people that it has taken all steps humanly possible to stay within its powers. That is the condition of its legitimacy, and its legitimacy, in the long run, is the condition of its life. And the Court, through its history, has acted as the legitimator of the government."[3] Moreover, "[t]he power to validate is the power to invalidate. If the Court were deprived, by any means, of its real and practical power to set bounds to governmental action, or even of public confidence that the Court itself regards this as its duty and will discharge it in a proper case, then it must certainly cease to perform its central function of unlocking the energies of government by stamping governmental actions as legitimate."

What a complex system ours is. Because Congress and the President often test the limits of their constitutional power, and—it should be added—because the minority that questions the exercise of that governmental action may be a large part of the total population, our democracy requires a disinterested umpire if it is to enjoy tranquility. Both Hamilton at the beginning and Black a century and three-quarters later insisted that Congress can no more be a fair judge of prohibitions on its power—for example the prohibition of bills of attainder and ex post facto laws, or the First Amendment—than defendants can be fair judges in their own cases. And for the Court to perform the umpire's function, the Constitution must be seen as law and the Court must engage in adjudication. Keep in mind, however, that there are many kinds of umpires and that the Constitution is open-textured: it does not articulate tightly on situations the way the rule book used by baseball umpires does. And remember too that as a general proposition, the primary reason the Supreme Court accepts jurisdiction is to perform its regulatory function. After all, Captain Goldman and Secretary Weinberger had had one trial and one appeal before they arrived at the Supreme Court. A close call at first base is a different matter. Baseball umpires do not regulate the future; they only resolve disputes in today's game.

In 1962 something similar to the differences between baseball and constitutional adjudication troubled Alexander M. Bickel, Black's colleague at Yale and perhaps his generation's best known constitutionalist. In his book *The Least Dangerous Branch*, Bickel was harsh on Marshall. Our greatest chief justice knew "that a statute's repugnancy to the Constitution is in most instances not self-evident; it is, rather, an issue of policy that someone must decide. The problem is who: the courts, the legislature itself, the President, perhaps juries for purposes of criminal trials, or ultimately and finally the people through the electoral process?"[4] Nor were the structural arguments of Hamilton and Black enough. Bickel sought an additional or alternative justification for judicial review. He claimed that the

> point of departure is a truism; perhaps it even rises to the unassailability of a platitude. It is that many actions of government have two aspects: their immediate, necessarily intended, practical effects, and their perhaps unintended or unappreciated bearing on values we hold to have more general and permanent interest. It is a premise we deduce not merely from the fact of a written constitution but from the history of the race, and ultimately as a moral judgment of the good society, that government should serve not only what we conceive from time to time to be our immediate material needs but also certain enduring values. This in part is what is meant by government under law. But such values do not present themselves ready-made. They have a past always, to be sure, but they must be continually derived, enunciated, and seen in relevant application.

And Bickel believed that the Supreme Court was "the institution of our government" best equipped "to be the pronouncer and guardian of such values."

Yet as we move toward the end of the twentieth century, anxiety about judicial review remains. This anxiety is closely related to concern over the ways judicial review is exercised (the modalities), but analytically different from it. The modalities of judicial review are the major concern of this book. Indeed, after this chapter it consists primarily of an inquiry into constitutional interpretation, the sources of law available to decisionmakers (judges and others) as they perform their interpretive functions, and the way process shapes the manner in which they resolve disputes and regulate. The remaining task of this chapter is to clarify the causes for the continuingly stubborn anxiety about the very practice of judicial review itself. But because those causes are related to the stuff of subsequent chapters, the present sketch will be elaborated at various points later on.

The nerve of the problem that generally is thought to create the anxiety was exposed by Bickel: "[N]othing," he wrote, "can alter the essential reality that judicial review is a deviant institution in American democracy."[5] But since access to elected officials is a key aspect of American democracy, this claim slights a feature of adjudication, including judicial review, emphasized in chapter 1; namely, that adjudication contains in its processes the functional equivalent of access. Still, Bickel's contention does rest on two facts; neither one is especially controversial. Nor are the facts really independent; they are in fact closely related.

The first fact is that Supreme Court justices are appointed, not elected, and "hold their offices during good behavior." In our not so short history, none has been removed from office. Put another way, the Court unlike Congress is neither elected nor electorally accountable.

Second, when the Court holds a statute unconstitutional it acts as a countermajoritarian institution. It blocks an outcome achieved by a body that we think of as democratic because its members were chosen by majority rule and reach decision by majority rule.

To get a better perspective on the countermajoritarian practice of judicial review, let's look a little closer at these facts in the context of the American governmental process. My initial purpose is not to justify the practice, but merely to show that many other important governmental practices depart from generally accepted norms of democratic decisionmaking. (This suggests to me that the undemocratic nature of judicial review may not be sufficient to explain the anxiety that surrounds its exercise.) Next, I shall attempt to justify judicial review further and to explain the anxiety that surrounds it.

Consider first majority rule, surely a central feature of democratic decisionmaking. It may seem like a simple concept. Every citizen has one equal vote, and a simple majority wins, in the sense that it gets what it wants. Even if such a system were possible—and there is an elegant body of learning, known as social choice theory, that raises serious questions about it[6]—it is far from clear that in this simple form majority rule is something a people would want to endorse. It is certainly clear that it is not the American way.

Let us remember that while the Supreme Court has announced a constitutional rule of "one person one vote," we live in a country where in the upper house of the federal legislature the half-million or so people who live in Alaska are given a voice equal to that of the twenty-five million or so who live in California, for the Constitution provides that the "Senate of the United States shall be composed of two Senators from each State, elected by the people thereof for six years; and each Senator shall have one vote." Remember too that the Constitution fails to provide for the direct popular election of the President. And it protects the important advantage of wealth in the political process: the First Amendment has been held to forbid significant governmental restraints on people who buy the right to be heard.[7]

Consider now electoral accountability. The Twenty-Second Amendment provides: "No person shall be elected to the office of President more than twice." This means that our Constitution vests the power of the sword in a second-term President who is no more electorally accountable than the Chief Justice of the United States.

If we move from the deep structure of the Constitution to regular and accepted practice within, say, the legislative branches of the federal government, we find further dilution of any simple notion of majority rule or electoral accountability. First, better than 95 percent of the House of Representatives is reelected every two years, and in 1988 the percentage was even higher.[8] It may be that the voters know how their representatives perform and use their knowledge when they vote: if so, the members of the House are surely doing a wonderful job. Second, seniority in both Houses may not count for as much as it once did, but it counts for plenty, and the power of effective committee chairs is substantial. Third, the role—although perhaps not the impact—of the lobbyist is well documented, the influence of the press and the clout exercised by the clients of the legal profession consistently remarked, while congressional staff is ubiquitous, centrally important, and armed with an agenda of its own.[9]

Moreover, the members of the bureaucracy in the independent agencies and the executive branch have substantial job security and often considerable authority over the direction of policy. This is patent with, for example, the chairman of the Board of Governors of the Federal Reserve System, but it is surely true throughout Washington. Anointed though they may be with a mandate from the people, it is hard for the most skillful members of any administration to deal with the numerical weight, civil service protection, and institutional perspectives of the bureaucracy. Policies change at critical times in the life of the nation, sometimes radically, but the direction of these policies is nonetheless influenced by people who are neither elected and subject to subsequent electoral accountability, nor recently appointed by officials who are themselves elected.

Please understand: I am not arguing that this situation is intrinsically good or bad, although in particular cases the results may be awful. The point is not that those organizations able to afford lawyers and lobbyists—large corporations, unions, special interest groups of all sorts—necessarily abuse either the legislative or administrative process, although sometimes they do. The point is simply that they are powerful countermajoritarian forces.

Sometimes it may be desirable for the bureaucracy to deflect the initiatives of the political branches. Elected officials and their political appointees have time perspectives different from those of civil servants. Reelection can powerfully influence a person's point of view—some believe that it alone explains congressional behavior[10]—and short-run political calculations simply are not always in the best interest of the nation. Certainly they are not if the price of reelection is the granting of favors to well-organized groups that are motivated purely by self-interest. But even when the price of reelection is following the will of the majority, the nation is not always well served. A point that Bickel made in justification of judicial review applies to other countermajoritarian institutions as well as to the Supreme Court: "[M]any actions of government have two aspects: their immediate, necessarily intended, practical effects, and their perhaps unintended or unappreciated bearing on values we hold to have more general and permanent interest."

No, the trouble is not so much that the bureaucracy, the special pleaders, and the congressional staffers are countermajoritarian forces; the trouble is that for different reasons each of these participants in the formation of governmental policies must frequently exaggerate the worth of its own position and dismiss others if it is to be effective. These participants are not always motivated by self-interest—though the prospect of subsequent employment has been known to affect present judgment—but they are guilty of having tunnel vision even when they are not so motivated. Nor, on most matters, is the vision of one participant balanced by the vision of others.

One of the justifications for having a federal judiciary, and especially for having the Supreme Court, is that judges as a group are not apt to have tunnel vision. Unlike the bureaucrats, they have the jurisdiction of the generalist. Judges are also unlikely to be short-run political maximizers. Few political actors can be free of self-interest, and Supreme Court justices are a type of political actor.

But Supreme Court justices are far more capable of disinterested perspective—precisely because they are not electorally accountable, or as subject to interest group pressures as elected officials are, or dependent on others, or, as a general proposition, looking to advancement.

What should emerge from these points is a picture of judicial review that is part of the rich fabric of American political life. Majority rule and electoral accountability are very important parts of this life. So are the many other processes and institutions that interact to produce governmental decisions. Judicial review is countermajoritarian; but it is not an oddity on our political landscape. It is a regular feature of that landscape, with structural and functional claims to acceptance as well as textual and historical claims.

The prevalence of nonmajoritarian decisionmaking in America suggests that the anxiety some have about judicial review cannot be fully explained by the fact that it is (as Bickel insisted) a deviant institution in American democracy. And this must be so even for those who believe that any departure from majority rule is suspect because it is inconsistent with pure representative democracy. Perhaps some are anxious because judicial review is often highly visible. But I believe that most are anxious because they believe that judicial review imposes a constitutional constraint on subsequent governmental action. Unlike the decisions of other political actors or bureaucrats, the rulings of Supreme Court justices have the appearance of finality.

If it can be shown, however, that there is often less finality in a constitutional decision than meets the eye, and that judges (unlike bureaucrats) are constrained in the value determinations that they make in constitutional cases by norms applicable generally in adjudication, perhaps those who remain uneasy about judicial review will be able to accept it with more equanimity.

A discussion of finality might profitably begin with an examination of certain types of statutory interpretation, a judicial function that is not technically judicial review. I shall begin with this because I wish to modify the standard account of the judicial function. My claim is that in some situations statutory interpretation forecloses legislative change, that it may have more finality than some imagine, and that it can therefore be more closely related to judicial review than is often supposed.

Statutes sometimes are interpreted by administrative agencies with a zeal that is an example of the tunnel vision I mentioned earlier. Statutes may be read without regard for the surrounding jurisprudence—including its constitutional configurations—into which the statute must fit. Instead of harmonizing the law it administers with the general law, the agency ignores the background entirely. On review, the courts may reinterpret the statute to avoid confronting the constitutional questions presented by the agency's single-minded devotion to its mission.

Consider the National Labor Relations Board (NLRB) back in its springtime. The board had a propensity for reading the Wagner Act of 1935 as if there were no First Amendment to the Constitution. When unions organized, employers were at risk if they spoke in favor of the open shop, as they often did.

Through statutory interpretation the Supreme Court denied the board this power. For the Court to have read the statute as the board did would have raised serious constitutional issues, although the reading might have been constitutional. The Court chose instead to avoid the issue by making an interpretation that was sensitive to the value our law attaches to free expression.[11]

The Court has often been sensitive to free expression when interpreting our labor laws, although it seems to me that there have been some remarkable lapses.[12] It showed sensitivity as recently as in the spring of 1988, when it ruled on a union distributing handbills.[13] Moreover, the Court has restrained the NLRB, seemingly in the teeth of the statute, in cases where the board by exercising its jurisdiction might have trenched on values close to those protected by the religious freedom provisions of the First Amendment. Because the Court did not render a constitutional decision in these cases,

Congress retained formal power to amend the statute and make it conform to the agency's interpretation. But in fact this would not have been easy. It is politically hard to rewrite labor law, and often it is difficult for Congress to be insensitive to values that are of constitutional dimension and that are called to the legislators' attention by the Supreme Court.

Even if the values are not of constitutional dimension—even if they are in the flats, below the foothills of the Constitution—their emphasis by the Court may deter Congress from overturning a decision, even where the decision departs markedly from statutory purpose. *Textile Workers Union v. Darlington Manufacturing Co.* is another example drawn from labor law.[14] In this case the Court thwarted what certainly appeared to be legislative goals in the service of what a majority of the justices took to be an important public value. Among other things the Court held "that so far as the Labor Relations Act is concerned, an employer has the absolute right to terminate his entire business for any reason he pleases" The proposition that had been advanced by the Textile Workers was "that an employer may not go completely out of business without running afoul of the . . . Act if such action is prompted by a desire to avoid unionization." To this the Court replied that the union's position "would represent such a startling innovation that it should not be entertained without the clearest manifestation of legislative intent."

Of course the Act makes it an unfair labor practice for an employer to discharge its employees because they join a union. And of course the union's position was that for an employer to go out of business because its employees joined a union is tantamount to a discharge. This is correct from the employees' point of view, but to the employer going out of business is somewhat different. The employer may find that the cost of staying in a unionized business rather than placing its capital elsewhere is too great, that the best thing to do is to get out, to take the money and run. But the statute is written to protect employees who unionize from being punished by their employer, and to have one's employer go out of business is surely a harsh punishment.

Nor was the question of remedy too troublesome: while reinstatement with back pay is standard in labor disputes, in this case the order of the NLRB was that the employer pay its employees "until they obtain substantially equivalent work . . . ." In short, go out of business if you don't want a union, but pay for breaking the law. It seems that the purpose of the statute supported the union's claim and the board's remedy.

But there is in this case an issue of economic freedom, at least at a symbolic level. The principle is that even a major corporation, generally referred to as an "it," should be free to be or not to be. It is this public value that the Court invoked to deflect the indicated legislative (dare I say majoritarian?) result. And it would not be politically easy after the Court had spoken for Congress to disregard that value and overturn the Court.

Observe that in the context of the case this public value has no constitutional standing: it is indeed in the flats. The constitutional protection afforded business decisions of the type involved in *Darlington*, based on a principle called economic due process, makes it certain that if Congress today made its intent clear the statute would survive judicial review. The foothills of the Constitution would never be reached, let alone the Constitution itself.[15]

In these statutory situations there is more finality than meets the eye but little professional doubt about the appropriateness of the Court's role—however one comes out on the merits of a particular case. Even if the Court did not have the power to declare legislation unconstitutional it would have the power to review administrative actions, and through statutory interpretation it would have the obligation to accommodate particular legislation to the principles and policies, to the public values and morality, that underpin our law.

Let me give a related example, once again from labor law, but not involving an administrative agency. Under the Railway Labor Act, enacted in 1926, the union selected by a majority of employees in a bargaining unit is the exclusive representative of all employees in the unit. The statute is absolutely silent, however, on the question of the union's obligations to the employees it represents. In 1944, ten years before the Court struck down segregation in public schools, the railway brotherhoods discriminated against blacks in the same way that many states did; they did so vigorously, perhaps even with relish. Some employees who suffered sued. Their case made its way through the state judicial system to the Supreme Court, which held that the "fair interpretation of the statutory language is that the organization chosen to represent . . . is to represent all . . . and is to act for and not against those whom it represents." In his opinion for a unanimous Court, Chief Justice Harlan F. Stone reasoned as follows: "It is a principle of general application that the exercise of a granted power to act in behalf of others involves the assumption toward them of a duty to exercise the power in their interest and behalf, and that such a grant of power will not be deemed to dispense with all duty toward those for whom it is exercised unless so expressed."[16]

In short, the common law was a source of law for statutory interpretation. The common-law doctrine that the Chief Justice grafted onto the statute—that an agent must represent a principal fairly—is not a doctrine that a legislature could easily reject by amending the statute over which it theoretically has authority, even under tremendous political pressure from powerful groups.

There is more regulatory finality than we sometimes imagine in the interpretation of statutes, when that interpretation, as in these labor cases, successfully shapes, reflects, and affirms our public values.

———

When we turn from the interpretation of statutes to judicial review, we find that in some situations there is much less regulatory finality than we generally associate with a constitutional decision. *Goldman v. Weinberger* is an example with which we are familiar, and there are many situations where the Court has held that a state possesses the constitutional power to regulate but where Congress retains the authority to remove state power. There are also situations where the Court may hold that a state lacks power because of federal law. In these cases Congress can change the result by changing its law.

Consider additionally some constitutional doctrines that amount to the Court's saying to other governmental entities: "You may be able to achieve the substantive result you desire, but you must proceed toward your objective in a fashion different from the one you have used." There is a whole family of such procedural or structural doctrines. Some impose considerable obstacles to the goals of the governmental entity under review, but I shall begin with three that may not: the doctrines of delegation, vagueness, and overbreadth.

These doctrines are derived from the Constitution. Under Article I Congress has the power to make laws. How much of this power can it delegate? How clear does a criminal statute have to be to give fair warning to a person as a matter of due process? How narrowly must a statute be drawn by a state where the state regulates political expression that is presumptively protected by the First and Fourteenth Amendments?

These doctrines have been much analyzed; some have been described as techniques for introducing flexibility into constitutional adjudication. I am not interested here in that aspect of these doctrines, or in the notion that by invoking them the Court is initiating a dialogue with another branch of government, as it does in many of its decisions. Nor am I now concerned with an idea related to both of these and to statutory interpretation: that the legislature must assume responsibility by speaking clearly and precisely if it wants to achieve a goal that is either in the foothills of the Constitution or that threatens other public values.[17] My interest is merely with the degree of finality that attends constitutional decisions based on these doctrines.

The delegation doctrine (infrequently employed at the federal level) requires that the legislature spell out in more detail the standards a regulatory agency should apply in effectuating the substantive goal of a statute; the vagueness doctrine requires greater specificity in articulating the goal to be achieved by the legislation under review; and the overbreadth doctrine requires that the substantive goal be stated as narrowly as possible. Cases decided under these rubrics are constitutional; they involve judicial review. Yet they lack substantive finality. A legislature can achieve its substantive purpose, but it must proceed in a different way. Each of these constitutional doctrines calls for a closer fit between the ends the legislature wants to achieve and the means it employs. This idea has application elsewhere. The relation of means to ends is important in the application of the equal protection clause of the Fourteenth Amendment to gender classifications (a topic I touched on in chapter 1) and in equal protection analysis generally. I shall return to this later.

———

In his dissent in *Fullilove v. Klutznick* (1980), Justice Stevens applied another variety of structural, or procedural (and therefore nonfinal), review. The case concerned the constitutionality of the minority business enterprise, or "set aside," requirement of the Public Works Employment Act of 1977. Absent an administrative waiver, the provision required that at least 10 percent of federal funds allocated to local public works projects be used to procure services or supplies from businesses owned by citizens "who are Negroes, Spanish-speaking, Orientals, Indians, Eskimos, and Aleuts."

By a vote of six to three, the Court upheld the statute from the predictable equal protection challenge that the statute discriminated on the basis of race. Justice Stevens's dissent rested on procedural grounds: "The very fact that Congress for the first time in the Nation's history has created a broad legislative classification for entitlement to benefits based solely on racial characteristics identifies a dramatic difference between this Act and the thousands of statutes that preceded it. This dramatic point of departure is not even mentioned in the statement of purpose of the Act or in the reports of either the House or the Senate Committee that processed the legislation, and was not the subject of any testimony or inquiry in any legislative hearing on the bill that was enacted."[18]

The Justice went on to describe this as a "malfunction of the legislative process" because of the "perfunctory consideration of an unprecedented policy decision of profound constitutional importance to the Nation." He wrote: "Whenever Congress creates a classification that would be subject to strict scrutiny under the Equal Protection Clause of the Fourteenth Amendment if it had been fashioned by a state legislature, it seems to me that judicial review should include a consideration of the procedural character of the decision-making process. A holding that the classification was not adequately preceded by a consideration of less drastic alternatives or adequately explained by a statement of legislative purpose would be far less intrusive than a final determination that the substance of the decision is not "narrowly tailored to the achievement of that goal."

As Justice Stevens noted, his approach raises questions about the separation of powers: by what right does the Court tell an equal branch of government how to go about its business? This question is also present in at least one of the cases of statutory interpretation discussed earlier (*Darlington*), and similar questions are in any event triggered by the doctrines of delegation, vagueness, and overbreadth. For surely whenever a court tells a legislature that it must speak clearly if it is to accomplish the goal it seems to have in mind—and this happens not infrequently—the court is instructing the legislature on its internal procedures. Thus Justice Stevens's approach, his insistence on structuring the law-making process, may be no more than an extension of an established judicial practice.

The Justice's approach invites us to examine other constitutional interventions by the Court into procedural due process and related areas that may have less finality than we generally associate with judicial review. Consider the regulation by the Supreme Court of police behavior through such continuingly controversial decisions as those that established the *Miranda* requirements and the exclusionary rule. In general terms, and without being more precise than is necessary, *Miranda* requires the police to notify potential defendants of their rights; the exclusionary rule bars the introduction at a trial of illegally obtained evidence.[19]

Neither *Miranda* nor the exclusionary rule calls into question any substantive goal of any governmental entity. Both structure the means of achieving an end; both, perhaps, make the achievement of the end more difficult. So do other things we tolerate and even embrace. For example, police unions may interfere with efficient police work and the efficient administration of criminal justice at least as much and with as much finality as *Miranda* and the exclusionary rule do, and police unions are at least as certain to continue to exist.

Of course there is a difference: police unions came about as the result of majoritarian decisionmaking; *Miranda* and the exclusionary rule did not. And let me make clear that I too share the belief that there is some force in the countermajoritarian objection to judicial review. But I have two points to make: first, the prevalence of other countermajoritarian practices makes this objection to judicial review inadequate to explain the level of anxiety that surrounds it—I believe that some of the anxiety springs from perceptions of finality in constitutional adjudication; second, it is time for me to confess that I am not a true believer in pure representative democracy, if this means that all decisions must be reached by majority vote. As I have suggested, I see some good in countermajoritarianism. By the way, and just to keep it all straight, no one who believes strictly in one person one vote, in pure representative democracy, can believe in judicial review,[20] or, for that matter, in the method for selecting U.S. senators.

The discussion of structural or procedural judicial review that I have just concluded highlights the important role of the Supreme Court as an umpire at the margin of the appropriate processes of other governmental entities. It reveals that judicial review, when the Court fills this role, does not preclude substantive legislative goals, and accordingly that much constitutional adjudication closely

resembles common-law and statutory interpretation in terms of substantive finality: all three may make it harder for legislatures to
reach particular goals; usually none prevents the attainment of these
goals.

The examples I have employed of structural or procedural judicial
review were of course meant to be suggestive; plainly they are not
exhaustive. But I do wish to continue the discussion on one topic
mentioned above, that of equal protection. The place to begin is
with an observation made by Justice Robert H. Jackson in *Railway
Express Agency v. New York* (1949). The case involved a New York
City traffic regulation that barred advertising on delivery vehicles
unless the vehicles were "engaged in the usual business of regular
work of the owner and not used merely or mainly for advertising."
Railway Express had violated the regulation and was fined. It
claimed that its due process and, more emphatically, its equal protection rights had been infringed. If safety on the streets is consistent
with some advertising on delivery vehicles, why the exclusion? The
Court was not sympathetic. But in his concurring opinion Justice
Jackson wrote:

> The burden should rest heavily upon one who would persuade
> us to use the due process clause to strike down a substantive
> law or ordinance. . . . Invalidation of a statute or an ordinance
> on due process grounds leaves ungoverned and ungovernable
> conduct which many people find objectionable.
>
> Invocation of the equal protection clause, on the other hand,
> does not disable any governmental body from dealing with the
> subject at hand. It merely means that the prohibition or regu-
> lation must have a broader [or narrower] impact.[21]

Justice Jackson has a point. He is concerned with the relation of
means to ends, with whether the regulated class is proper given the
legislative purpose. But the point has limited application if the issue
is the relative finality of judicial review, as it is for us. For equal
protection cases vary considerably in the breadth and permanence
of the restraints they impose on legislatures. If the statute in *Railway*

Express Agency had been held unconstitutional on equal protection grounds, it would have been easy enough for the state to achieve its purpose with a new statute that extended the ban on advertising to all delivery vehicles. But the situation is very different when the equal protection clause is used to invalidate statutes that discriminate on the basis of race. Fortunately there can be no easy way around such decisions. They are final in any realistic sense because they conceive a nation profoundly different from one in which the Constitution would permit the discrimination to take place.

Yet even the desegregation cases were initially provisional. The finality we see today reflects our acceptance of an equality principle that has its weight in public values derived and articulated as law by the Supreme Court in 1954. The principle forbids government to discriminate affirmatively on the basis of race (with certain important qualifications). Without public acceptance there would be no finality, but at the time of decision acceptance was in doubt. In the most substantive of constitutional cases there is always doubt about finality at the time of decision, because there is always the possibility of judicial mistake and the possibility that the Court's decision will be politically indigestible. When we talk of mistake and the politics of the indigestible (both of which I discuss in subsequent chapters), we come face to face with questions of constitutional interpretation, the modalities of judicial review, and the sources of law.

PART II

Flawed Modalities

CHAPTER THREE

Original Intent

In 1959, before Charles Black and Alexander Bickel wrote the books discussed in chapter 2, Columbia University's eminent constitutionalist Herbert Wechsler had addressed the justification for judicial review and some of the problems with it. The occasion was the Holmes Lecture at the Harvard Law School; Wechsler's speech, "Toward Neutral Principles of Constitutional Law," remains both influential and controversial.

For Wechsler the text of the Constitution authorized judicial review; no structural or functional arguments of the type employed by Hamilton, Black, and Bickel were necessary. But because the Constitution was law, judicial review had to conform to the method of adjudication. For Wechsler this meant that cases must be decided in a principled fashion. He insisted that "the main constituent of the judicial process is precisely that it must be genuinely principled, resting with respect to every step that is involved in reaching judgment on analysis and reasons quite transcending the immediate result that is achieved. To be sure, courts decide, or should decide, only the case they have before them. But must they not decide on grounds of adequate neutrality and generality, tested not only by the instant application but by others that the principles imply? Is it not the very essence of judicial method to insist upon attending to such other cases, preferably those involving an opposing interest, in evaluating any principle avowed?"[1]

In applying these standards, Wechsler gave the Court low grades in a number of cases, including *Brown v. Board of Education*, the school desegregation decision.[2] While his conception of the judicial process has recently provoked considerable criticism,[3] it was his application of that conception to particular cases and his use of the word "neutral" in elaborating his conception that generated extensive and often harsh contemporary judgments from the academic branch of the legal profession. Some of these judgments are telling, but Wechsler's understanding of the judicial process is similar in content to certain aspects of appellate adjudication discussed in chapter 1. It follows that I have found informative his abstract views on judicial review.

What is missing in Wechsler's argument, and in much of the writing of the time (except for research reports on the history of the Fourteenth Amendment and its bearing on public school segregation), is any sustained attention to the sources of law—that is, the sources on which the decision is based. Wechsler emphasizes a constraint on adjudication: principles—the ground for decision—must be neutral and general. But he tells us little about where the principles come from. Assuming that one agrees with Wechsler, he has stipulated a necessary condition for the use of a principle in constitutional adjudication. But it is not a sufficient condition, unless the Court is free to employ any principle that satisfies the constraint he has articulated.

In a lecture at Indiana University in the early 1970s, Robert H. Bork, then a professor at Yale, took up the source-of-law issue.[4] He argued that Wechsler's approach to the application of a principle in the practice of judicial review also had to be employed in deriving the principle. And the derivation had to be from the Constitution. While it is not clear to me what it means to insist that a principle be neutrally derived, it is clear that one of Bork's dominant concerns was with the Constitution as the source of constitutional law and the proper method to use in its interpretation.

The contemporary debate of which Bork's lecture is an early example can be traced to the Supreme Court decision in *Griswold v. Connecticut* (1965),[5] which addressed the validity of a Connecticut statute making it a crime for a married couple to use a contraceptive device. The Court struck down the statute, holding that Connecticut had violated the constitutional "notions of privacy surrounding the marriage relationship." Later it also invalidated a state statute restricting the sale of contraceptive devices to single persons, and in *Roe v. Wade* it used notions of privacy to grant constitutional protection to abortion.[6]

The text of the Constitution does not talk about privacy, and it might seem strange that the Court would undertake to disassociate itself so dramatically from the text it was interpreting. It could easily have spoken of liberty, which does have its place in the language of the Fifth and Fourteenth amendments.

Probably the reason the Court located the right to privacy at the center of its holding is that from the early 1900s to the mid-1930s, the Court had periodically invalidated state and federal social and economic legislation on the ground that it restricted liberty. In these decisions the Court had held that liberty was protected from undue state interference by the Fourteenth Amendment and from undue federal interference by the Fifth Amendment. These cases are called "substantive due process" cases, or (because they concern the regulation of business and labor) "economic due process" cases. The leading example is *Lochner v. New York* (1905),[7] which invalidated a New York statute prohibiting a work week of more than sixty hours for bakers. The Court held that the law violated the liberty of contract between employer and employee protected by the due process clause; that is, it interfered in an unconstitutional manner with the ability of bakery employees and their employers to fix for themselves, without substantive direction from the state, their conditions of employment.

Lochner and subsequent economic due process decisions were badly received by other branches of government, some of the legal profession, organized labor, and other groups active in the political arena. In the mid-1930s the Court repudiated robust judicial review of economic and social legislation.[8] At the time of *Griswold* the Court felt the need to distance itself from the rejected economic due process approach (as indeed it does today).

The Court's reasoning in *Griswold* was as follows: (1) "[S]pecific guarantees in the Bill of Rights have penumbras, formed by ema-

nations from those guarantees that help give them life and substance." (2) "Various guarantees create zones of privacy. The right
of association contained in the penumbra of the First Amendment
is one. . . . The Third Amendment in its prohibition against the
quartering of soldiers . . . is another. . . . The Fourth Amendment
[which] explicitly affirms the right of the people to be secure in their
persons, houses, papers, and effects against unreasonable searches
and seizures. . . . [and the] Fifth Amendment in its Self-Incrimination
Clause" are still others. (3) According to the Ninth Amendment,
"The enumeration in the Constitution, of certain rights, shall not
be construed to deny or disparage others retained by the people."
(4) "The present case . . . concerns a relationship lying within the
zone of privacy created by [these] several fundamental constitutional
guarantees." And (5) the Connecticut statute sweeps "unnecessarily
broadly . . ." in its regulation of privacy within the marriage
relationship.

In chapter 5 I shall argue that the holding in *Griswold v. Connecticut* is correct. But certainly it is understandable that the character of the Court's opinion—its shotgun approach to the task at
hand and the thinness of a textual basis in the Constitution for a
right to privacy—should have sent Professor Bork and others searching for authoritative sources of law, searching for the proper way
to interpret the Constitution.

This then is the start of the contemporary debate. Before we
examine its content, it is interesting to speculate on what may indirectly have contributed to the texture of that debate. First the
academic side.

Lawyers at universities today are more aware than ever before of
the work of their colleagues on faculties of the arts and sciences.
There is often some lag and sometimes some distortion in the way
the legal academic uses the theories and investigations of other disciplines. But this too has been diminishing, and legal academics
sometimes find themselves—to mix up a metaphor—on the cutting
edge of other people's domain.

Many disciplines—particularly philosophy, literary criticism, politics, and theology—have many theories about interpretation, about the relationship of author, text, and reader. And what could be of greater interest to the lawyer, particularly the lawyer concerned with a text such as the Constitution? I think it is fair to say that exposure to these theories has deepened the law professor's awareness of the complexity and normative implications of reading, of construing a text, of interpreting the Constitution.

The debate involves many other actors, however: practicing lawyers, judges, legislators, concerned individuals, and groups. There are many participants in the debate because of the substantive consequences of constitutional adjudication. To choose the most striking example, what is the origin of the privacy principle that the Court vindicated in *Griswold v. Connecticut* and applied in the abortion cases? Is it a fundamental right, an aspect of constitutionally protected liberty? And how did the justices suddenly "discover" this in the latter part of the twentieth century? And how do we know whether they were right? The answer to these questions has been a matter of no small interest to those seeking to overturn *Roe v. Wade*[9] and to their opponents.

In general terms, what are the sources of law available to participants in constitutional adjudication? What is a good argument? (In chapter 1 I touched on this.) What counts as the justification for a Supreme Court decision interpreting the Constitution? As we shall see, these questions in turn invite consideration of authority: by what right does the Court use a particular interpretive method? And they raise problems concerning control of the judiciary: how are the other branches of government and individuals regulated by the Court to keep the justices in their place?

During the second term of Ronald Reagan (1985–88) all these questions were debated in a remarkably similar vocabulary by politicians, judges, and legal academics. Surprisingly, from all quarters terms like "interpretive review" were set off against "noninterpretive review," or appeals to an unwritten constitution.

This way of speaking, however, is misleading. All the players in this national pastime are engaged in interpretation. The true question is how they go about their task of interpreting the Constitution. The answer—to come back to where we started—is that they search for authoritative sources of law and should do so.

The text of the Constitution is authoritative. It is also vague, opentextured, sometimes ambiguous, and generally in desperate need of elaboration. The search for authoritative sources of law is therefore the search for interpretive tools.

Some might object to this phraseology. To search for authoritative sources implies that if you are skillful or lucky you will find something, as in a treasure hunt. And the critics might claim that the "searcher" creates rather than discovers the treasure. But at this stage such an objection must be rejected: the problem is to identify authoritative sources, not to interpret them. The notion of a search is therefore accurate enough. At the interpretive stage, however—when the tools are used—the claim that there is an act of creation, of making rather than finding, must be confronted. Neither "creation" nor "discovery" is an acceptable account: the interpretive process in adjudication is too complex to be so easily described.

Please do not misunderstand me. There is profound disagreement over what is authoritative. Some may even deny that the text of the Constitution always qualifies. But the disagreement is not an interpretive disagreement. To classify it as such would be to turn all law into interpretation. The disagreement, at the level that interests me, is one about the nature of American constitutional adjudication. It is about the judicial process of regulation and resolving disputes. It is about an institution, not about a text. And this is true even though one's understanding of the institution, the Court, governs the way one interprets the text, the Constitution.

Any attempt to understand constitutional adjudication must come to grips with a familiar problem: how does a people control or check judges who are not electorally accountable—judges who exercise the sovereign prerogative of judicial review? In *The Federalist* Hamilton said the judiciary was the least dangerous branch of government. Today the concern of more than a few Americans is to keep it from becoming the most dangerous.

Some politicians, judges, and legal scholars who see themselves engaged in so-called interpretive review believe that when the text of the Constitution is not clear, the question of authority and the question of control are both answered by reading the text in the light of original intent. To get away from misleading usage let's call them originalists, as others have.[10] By original intent they mean that of the framers, or founders, of the Constitution who drafted the original masterpiece in 1787 (some also emphasize the intent of the delegates to the state ratifying conventions), as well as the intent of those who have amended the document under the provisions of Article V. For many originalists no other source is nearly as weighty or significant in justifying a decision. No other source has the same claim to authority. Nor can any other interpretive method keep the judiciary in check.

As a judge on the U.S. Court of Appeals for the District of Columbia Circuit, the influential originalist Robert H. Bork put his position this way: "[I]f we are to have judicial review, and if the Constitution is to be law, so that the judge does not freely impose his or her own values, then the only way to do that is to root that law in the intentions of the founders. There is no other source of legitimacy. There is no other way that we can say at least in extreme cases that the judge has gone off the reservation."[11]

The originalist position (and there are as many versions of it as there are believers in it) is shaky with respect to both authority and control. Consider first authority. While it may be true, as the distinguished constitutional historian Leonard Levy, has written, that "consensus [about the need for a strong national government], rather than compromise, was the most significant feature of the Convention," it is also true that the founders were deeply divided about most matters that were debated during that hot Philadelphia summer of 1787, and that "various compromises . . . occupied most of the time of the delegates."[12] It should not be surprising, therefore, to learn from recent historical investigation that the founders were also deeply divided over whether it would be appropriate in the future to interpret the Constitution they were drafting by appealing to the history of their private proceedings in Philadelphia. Nor was there any agreement about the relevance to constitutional interpretation of the historical record produced in the subsequent state conventions.

H. Jefferson Powell, of Duke University, has done the seminal work on the subject. This is his conclusion:

> It is commonly assumed that the "interpretive intention" of the Constitution's framers was that the Constitution would be construed in accordance with what future interpreters could gather of the framers' own purposes, expectations, and intentions. Inquiry shows that assumption to be incorrect. Of the numerous hermeneutical options that were available in the framers' day . . . none corresponds to the modern notion of intentionalism [or, the same thing, originalism]. . . . In defending their claim that the "original understanding at Philadelphia" should control constitutional interpretation, modern intentionalists usually argue that other interpretive strategies undermine or even deny the possibility of objectivity and consistency in constitutional law. Critics of this position typically respond with a battery of practical and theoretical objections to the attempt to construe the nation's fundamental law in accord with historical reconstructions of the purposes of the framers. There may well be grounds to support either of these positions. This debate cannot be resolved, however, and should not be affected, by the claim or assumption that modern intentionalism was the original presupposition of American constitutional discourse. Such a claim is historically mistaken.[13]

Powell's conclusion seriously diminishes a basic attraction that originalism (or, as he calls it, intentionalism) would otherwise have. Since the founders did not themselves intend "that the Constitution would be construed in accordance with what future interpreters could gather of the framers' own purposes, expectations, and intentions," the founders' will, or desire, cannot be claimed today as authority for the use of their recorded intentions. To the extent that originalism is authorized, it must either be because, all things considered, it is superior to any other interpretive strategy (I shall shortly argue against this), or because judges and lawyers after ratification employed original intent as their interpretive tool. Contemporary interpreters moved by that past may also employ original intent, but if they do it is only because they respect a tradition of interpretation. No longer can they see themselves as being under an obligation to obey the commands of the founding fathers. They must come to terms with the realization that no such commands were issued.

Yet the belief that the founders mandated originalism has permitted its advocates to equate the founders' intentions with the text of the Constitution. Intentions become a gloss on that text. This is the most powerful basis for the appeal of originalism. It leads to the belief that the people through their state ratifying conventions consented to original intent as well as to the constitutional text, and that they therefore bound the future to respect original intent even as they bound the future to respect constitutional text (and one to the same extent as the other).

The people's consent is of course the weighty basis for the text's authority. But since the evidence demonstrates that original intent was not meant to be a gloss on the text, there was no consent to it. Accordingly the people cannot be invoked, and this deprives originalism of powerful rhetorical support. It leaves the originalists clinging to tradition and leaves open the question of how much we should count on tradition in the quest for authority.

In assessing the weight that the tradition of originalism should have in constitutional adjudication, contemporary interpreters should know what recent historical investigation also demonstrates. James H. Hutson, of the Library of Congress, writes that "[s]ome . . . newly discovered documents raise questions concerning the reliability of the principal printed sources of information

about the drafting and ratification of the Constitution.... "
Hutson's research shows that apart from Madison's notes, the
standard sources for determining the founders' intentions are
highly unreliable evidence of what took place. It seems that
much of the documentary history was subsequently manufac-
tured for political purposes; and Madison's notes themselves are
radically incomplete.

As Hutson puts it: "If Convention records are not faithful accounts of what was said by the delegates in 1787 and 1788, how
can we know what they intended?" And, he tells us, his reason
for writing "is to issue a caveat about Convention records, to
warn that there are problems with most of them and that some
have been compromised—perhaps fatally—by the editorial interventions of hirelings and partisans." Hutson reasons that "[t]o recover original intent from these records may be an impossible
hermeneutic assignment."[14] But even if it were possible today,
through some form of alchemy, to convert the documentary record into a "faithful account of what was said by the delegates in
1787 and 1788," contemporary interpreters would have to keep
in mind that they do not have eighteenth-century minds and that
the founders were of many minds. What we understand about
them as a group, and about what they thought they were up to
when they drafted and ratified the Constitution, is not only fil-
tered through our late twentieth-century consciousness but is necessarily influenced by what we have learned from many students
who have seen different things at different times in different ways.
There is no escaping that all contemporary interpreters are cap-
tives, in one way or another, of prior interpretations.

Today's originalists would therefore have a serious problem even
if the documentary materials had never been cooked. Their problem
is compounded, badly compounded, by Hutson's discoveries: if he
is right, prior interpreters were not reading "faithful accounts of
what was said by the delegates in 1787 and 1788." They were, at
least some of the time, interpreting fiction.

still may rightly be thought to support liberty. The constitutional protection afforded liberty—often under the name of privacy—today is substantially greater than the protections afforded property. Once again contraception and abortion are central examples, even after the weakening of *Roe*.

But if at the beginning liberty and property were united, what does this tell us about the fit between originalism and contemporary legal practice? Originalists simply cannot believe that the relation between property and liberty depicted by Professor Morgan is rooted in the environment that produced it; that the environment is strikingly different today; and that this difference permits liberty to stand free of property, to be regarded on its own, and property to be seen therefore as more accessible to government regulation in the furtherance of the public good.

If one were taken with the authority of originalism, perhaps one might try to reconcile practice with belief by suggesting that an extended conversation with the founders about the late twentieth century would bring the founders to a contemporary point of view. But while such an exercise would surely have promise for a public television series, it would be a profoundly silly approach to reading a text or governing a nation. The point is that there is no congruence between originalism and the judicial practice of constitutional interpretation. And while this does not prove in any scientific sense that originalism is wrong, it does not have to; for a scientific test of right and wrong is not very important to understanding the American way of constitutional adjudication.

My attack on originalism has not yet exposed what I believe to be the underlying conception of adjudication held by its proponents. I shall argue against that conception and at the same time against the contention that originalism is the best strategy, all things considered, for constitutional interpretation.

The originalist conception of adjudication would seem to rest on two broad and interrelated sets of ideas. The first comprises beliefs about the certainty of language and the methods of discovering its meaning. The second is made up of beliefs about the allocation of institutional responsibilities between legislative bodies and courts.

An originalist has to be optimistic about the founders' ability to capture precisely in words some complicated ideas, and about the existence of what we know is missing: a definitive historical record to resolve linguistic ambiguity. This optimism has to persist even though the originalist knows full well that the drafting process involves the skillful use of ambiguity and the purposeful manipulation of what becomes documentary history.[17] The optimism of the originalist must also withstand widespread evidence that the meaning of a text such as the Constitution never remains fixed, that indeed at any time texts are rich with meanings, and that competing accounts of the past are attributable to new information and to fresh perspectives articulated by members of the increasingly diverse historical and legal professions.

An originalist is also apt to embrace a strong version of the standard distinction between making law and applying law: law is made by legislative bodies; it is applied by courts. An originalist perceives the difference between making and applying law as a sharp one at its center. And when it is blurred, an originalist will contend that courts should keep clear of any action that constitutes an assumption by judges of the drafters' prerogative—although it is hard to imagine how they could do so, since judges must act.

Nonoriginalists, who also come in many styles, are likely to see the drafting and ratification of the Constitution and its amendments as a process radically different from the writing of a document by a single author. Because there are many styles of nonoriginalist, I shall speak only for myself in what follows, which explains my perhaps too frequent use of the perpendicular "I."

Whatever I may believe about the utility of searching for intention in my effort to understand single-author texts (what did Shakespeare intend when he wrote *Hamlet*?), I start with great skepticism where the text I am interpreting has been written by a committee. For I am impressed that a constitution is the product of negotiation (as indeed most written law is), that negotiation of complex issues usually leaves major problems unresolved, and that language on which people of divergent views can agree must often be open-textured—to say the least. Let's understand one thing: purposeful ambiguity is to legislative drafting what the fastball is to major league baseball. I doubt that it is even coherent to talk about the intention of a class consisting of the framers at Philadelphia and the ratifiers at the state conventions. How do you obtain the sum of their disagreements?

But if I put my doubts to one side and decide to search for such intent, always mindful of Mr. Hutson's caveat, I know that this perhaps incoherent thing I seek will almost surely not reveal itself with sufficient clarity to be the authoritative source of the meaning of the text—even assuming it were ever appropriate for it so to become. Of course, I also know that the Constitution it-self is what was ratified, not the founders' intention. Yet I know too that I will be greatly benefited in understanding the Constitution if I learn as much as I can about the period of its creation. For to deny the authority of original intent is not to deny the importance of history.

Nor need I accept the sharp distinction between making law and applying law. Although I concede that legislative processes are very different from the judicial process, I see both as part of the common enterprise of governing the future wisely. And because of the diffi-culties inherent in producing a text that controls, over time and in a changing world, the outcome of concrete cases dealing with all aspects of the relation of governments to their constituent parts and of governments to individuals, I see law making as an inevitable and authorized function of adjudication.

So much then for originalism and its authority. The conclusion: not a promising approach to interpreting the Constitution. When we turn to the usefulness of the doctrine in controlling the judici-ary—in keeping it in check—we find that originalism is not effective in the way its advocates seem to believe.

It is hardly surprising that most Americans worry some about controlling the judiciary. Start with the proposition that all aspects of government must be checked if tyranny is to be kept at bay, add to this the federal judiciary's immunity from electoral accountability and its power of judicial review, and you would be foolish ever to let down your guard. This will be so even if you recognize that there are substitutes in the judicial process for representation and electoral accountability, that majority rule is one method among many for reaching important political decisions, and that the regulation produced by constitutional adjudication is often far from final.

Today's originalists seem to worry more than most Americans do about government by the judiciary and the need to check the Court. The ideas behind their concern, which require some investigation, present two sets of problems. The first is closely related to what I have been discussing in the examination of authority I have just concluded.

Originalists believe that if judges are not limited to text and the intention of the founders when interpreting the Constitution, they cannot be effectively checked: they will inescapably convert their personal preferences into constitutional law, and they may bring about dramatic social and political change through constitutional interpretation. These two fears are analytically discrete, for judges may let their personal preferences interfere with their interpretation even if they do not prefer social change but rather prefer the status quo.

I shall undertake to demonstrate that originalism does not itself provide the strong protection from judicial reliance on personal preference that its advocates say it does. And I shall show that judicially mandated change of a dramatic sort is consistent with originalism.

With respect both to the influence of personal preference on constitutional interpretation and to the effecting of dramatic social change through originalism, consider Justice Hugo L. Black, a member of the Supreme Court from 1937 to 1971. However one evaluates historically his vast and important contribution to constitutional law, I think all must agree that he gave the Warren court its substantive direction at least as much as anyone else did. Today's originalists seek to overturn much of the work of the Warren court. Yet Justice Black's approach to constitutional interpretation relied heavily on the language of the document and on the intention of its makers.

Justice Black practiced interpretive review before the term was used (or rather misused) by the profession. He was an originalist. And he was one primarily because he had seen the Court strike down New Deal legislation on grounds that he considered rooted only in the personal preferences of the justices. He sought security in text and original intent from the recurrence of this subjectivity— as originalists do today.

Text and intention were central to Justice Black's view of the First Amendment. Text first. He said: "The beginning of the First Amendment is that 'Congress shall make no law.' I understand that it is rather old-fashioned and shows a slight naivete to say that 'no law' means no law. It is one of the most amazing things about the ingeniousness of the times that strong arguments are made, which almost convince me, that it is very foolish of me to think 'no law' means no law. But what it says is 'Congress shall make no law.' "[18] The Justice went on to say, "I believe [the Amendment] means what it says."

Earlier Black had addressed intention: "It is my belief that there are 'absolutes' in our Bill of Rights, and that they were put there on purpose by men who knew what words meant, and meant their prohibitions to be 'absolutes.' "[19] Maybe; but as with most normative positions based on historical claims, the research of others casts doubt on the Justice's view that protection of speech by the Bill of Rights was intended to be absolute.[20] And the absolutists's position is not made out by appealing to the Amendment's language about expression: "Congress shall make no law . . . abridging the freedom of speech." The contemporary originalist Robert H. Bork is clearly correct when he insists that "[a]ny such reading is, of course, impossible." "Is Congress forbidden," he asks, "to prohibit incitement to mutiny aboard a naval vessel engaged in action against an enemy, to prohibit shouted harangues from the visitors' gallery during its own deliberations or to provide any rules for decorum in federal courtrooms?"[21]

In fact, the language of the Amendment does point to a special status for expression. It creates a stronger presumption against regulation than weaker language would. To say "Congress shall make no unreasonable law . . . abridging the freedom of speech" adds an adjective that weakens a liberty. But the language does not tell a court much. It must look elsewhere to determine the strength of the presumption. And Justice Black knew this. Perhaps it explains his position: "I have to be honest about it. I confess not only that I think the Amendment means what it says but also that I may be slightly influenced by the fact that I do not think Congress should make any law with respect to these subjects. That has become a rather bad confession to make in these days, the confession that one is actually for something because he believes in it."[22]

I do not mean to suggest that Justice Black showed himself to be a willful or dishonest judge by admitting to his personal preference; quite the contrary. But I do mean to suggest that the sources of law to which he restricted himself—text informed by original intent— did not, according to Justice Black's own testimony, preclude his personal preference from influencing his understanding of the Constitution. Originalists believe that limiting judges to text and intent will eliminate personal preference from judicial interpretation. Once again they are wrong.

Justice Black's originalism was also clear with respect to the Fourteenth Amendment, one of the great Civil War amendments imposing constitutional constraints on state action in the racial area and in many other areas as well. Justice Black believed that the draftsmen intended to incorporate the first eight amendments to the Constitution into the first section of the Fourteenth. This would apply to the states the federal Bill of Rights—including those provisions dealing with the rights of the criminally accused.[23]

The Warren Court developed the concept of selective incorporation, which is not quite what Black advocated. But the outcome was much as he had urged.[24] It achieved social change on a very grand scale. It established the Supreme Court as the ultimate arbiter of the substantive content of state criminal procedure. It removed power from state courts and state legislatures. It diminished the importance of state constitutions.

If Justice Black is an example of an originalist, as he certainly is, originalism is a doctrine that cannot be counted on to cabin our least dangerous branch.

Even if originalism were a viable interpretive technique (which it is not), it is not authorized by the Constitution, is based on a misunderstanding of the nature of the judicial process, and fails to control the Supreme Court of the United States. It seems fair to conclude that originalism has little if anything to recommend it. But if not originalism, what?

CHAPTER FOUR

Policing Participation and Restricting Intervention

Early in the last chapter I suggested that contemporary anxiety about the sources of law in constitutional adjudication—of which the interest in original intent is a manifestation—could be traced to the decision in *Griswold v. Connecticut* (1965), in which the Supreme Court held that a state statute making it a crime for married couples to use contraceptive devices violated constitutional "notions of privacy surrounding the marriage relationship." As I remarked, the majority opinion went to extraordinary lengths to avoid the due process methodology that characterized *Lochner*. Because the avoidance of this methodology has also influenced the principal approach to judicial review examined in this chapter, it is useful to look a little more closely at *Lochner* itself.

Lochner v. New York (1905) raised the question of the validity, under the Fourteenth Amendment, of a New York statute fixing maximum working hours for bakery employees. The three opinions are crisp by contemporary standards (one for the Court, holding the statute unconstitutional, and two dissents), which makes them neither gain nor lose persuasiveness. Justice Rufus W. Peckham, who served on the Court from 1895 to 1909, wrote for five Justices. He stated, first, that the "general right to make a contract in relation to his business is part of the liberty of the individual protected by the Fourteenth Amendment. . . . Under that provision no state can deprive any person of life, liberty or property without due process of law. The right to purchase or to sell labor is part of the liberty protected by this amendment, unless there are circumstances which exclude the right." Second, he wrote that such circumstances would seem to include valid state legislation—that is, legislation falling within the rubric of police powers. "Those powers, broadly stated . . . relate to the safety, health, morals and general welfare of the public." Third, "[v]iewed in the light of a purely labor law, with no reference whatever to the question of health . . . [the New York] law . . . involves neither the safety, the morals nor the welfare of the public, and . . . the interest of the public is not in the slightest degree affected by such an act." Fourth, while the law may purport to be a health measure, it is not. "We think that there can be no fair doubt that the trade of a baker, in and of itself, is not an unhealthy one to that degree which would authorize the legislature to interfere with the right to labor, and with the right of free contract on the part of the individual, either as employer or employee." Fifth, other arguments concerning health are frivolous. "Statutes of the nature of that under review, limiting the hours in which grown and intelligent men may labor to earn their living, are mere meddlesome interferences with the rights of the individual."[1] Accordingly, the statute was held unconstitutional.

The first Justice John Marshall Harlan, who served from 1877 to 1911, dissented. He reasoned as follows:

> [I]n determining the question of power to interfere with liberty of contract, the court may inquire whether the means devised by the State are germane to an end which may be lawfully accomplished and have a real or substantial relation to the protection of health, as involved in the daily work of the persons, male and female, engaged in bakery and confectionery establishments. But when this inquiry is entered upon I find it impossible, in view of common experience, to say that there is here no real or substantial relation between the means employed by the State and the end sought to be accomplished by its legislation, ... Nor can I say that the statute has no appropriate or direct connection with that protection to health which each State owes to her citizens, . . . or that the regulation pre-

scribed by the State is utterly unreasonable and extravagant or wholly arbitrary. . . . Still less can I say that the statute is, beyond question, a plain, palpable invasion of rights secured by the fundamental law.[2]

Justice Harlan in effect accepted the majority's concern with contractual liberty, but concluded that the state could interfere with that liberty in the situation at hand.

Justice Oliver Wendell Holmes, Jr. (1902–32), dissented in what has become one of his famous opinions. He saw *Lochner* as "decided upon an economic theory which a large part of the country does not entertain." He made it clear that he did not view the judicial function in constitutional adjudication as having to come to terms with the wisdom or folly of an economic theory reflected in a statute duly enacted by a state legislature. On such questions the Court was to defer to the legislature. A constitution, he said, "is not intended to embody a particular economic theory, whether of paternalism and the organic relation of the citizen to the state or of laissez faire. It is made for people of fundamentally differing views, and the accident of our finding certain opinions natural and familiar or novel and even shocking ought not to conclude our judgment upon the question whether statutes embodying them conflict with the Constitution of the United States."[3]

Holmes's characterization of the Court's opinion as resting on laissez faire economics fits a modern view of the issue raised in *Lochner*. Today most of us would see the New York statute as a protective labor law responsive to a legislative loss of confidence in the private contract regime. We would accordingly be apt to see opposition to the statute as reflecting confidence in the private contract and the underlying economic order with which it is associated; opposition by the Court would thus seem to raise laissez faire economics and the private employment contract to the level of a constitutional requirement.

Yet the majority in *Lochner* purported to see the issue as one of personal liberty. This is not necessarily inconsistent with Holmes's characterization of the Court's approach, or indeed with a present-day analysis if one equates laissez faire economics with personal liberty. Many did and some do. But as Holmes said, the economic theory was widely questioned at the time of *Lochner*. Some believed that employees when dealing individually with their employer had no personal liberty, that the employer had complete control over the terms and conditions of employment. Time changed some to many and ultimately led to the repudiation of *Lochner* and its progeny.

Before the repudiation, however, the programs of the New Deal were placed at risk by *Lochner* and other doctrines (the most important was one that sharply limited congressional power under the interstate commerce clause of the Constitution).[4] President Franklin Roosevelt attacked, most notably with his court-packing plan of 1937 (it encouraged judges over seventy years of age to retire by proposing to add a judge if they did not). This plan failed in Congress, but after it was made the Court did begin to sustain economic regulation. And *Lochner* itself was widely seen as an example of how some powerful old men indulged their personal preferences in the teeth of the people's will, a will manifested through the legislature. The holding and the perceived approach were then explicitly repudiated.[5]

The case of *United States v. Carolene Products Co.* (1938) was an unremarkable example of this repudiation.[6] It stands with others of its time in sustaining economic legislation that probably would have been invalidated less than a decade earlier under the due process clause. Speaking for the Court, Justice Stone made it plain that such legislation was to enjoy a powerful presumption of constitutionality. Judicial review was to be anemic: state law would survive challenge if it had a "rational basis."

The Justice then added a remarkable footnote that is probably the best known of the Supreme Court's marginalia. After suggesting that the presumption of constitutionality might have less force where the Constitution is relatively clear, footnote four of *Carolene Products* goes on as follows:

> It is unnecessary to consider now whether legislation which restricts those political processes which can ordinarily be expected to bring about repeal of undesirable legislation, is to be subjected to more exacting judicial scrutiny under the general prohibitions of the Fourteenth Amendment than are most other types of legislation . . .
>
> Nor need we enquire whether similar considerations enter into the review of statutes directed at particular religious . . . or national . . . or racial minorities . . . ; whether prejudice against discrete and insular minorities may be a special condition, which tends seriously to curtail the operation of those political processes ordinarily to be relied upon to protect minorities, and which may call for a correspondingly more searching judicial inquiry.[7]

If the answers to these questions are yes (they have generally been taken to be rhetorical), the footnote can be seen as "a participation-oriented, representation-reinforcing approach to judicial review."[8] Where the political process fails to function properly, judicial review should be robust; otherwise it should be anemic—that is, no more inquiry of the kind pursued in *Lochner* into the substantive values contained in duly enacted legislation. This is wonderfully attractive. It aims our attention at failures of process rather than of substance in the legislative (or executive) branch. And process is a familiar domain of lawyers and judges. As we saw in chapter 2, some process review permits governmental outcomes, provided only that they are accomplished more scrupulously. In this sense, I argued that judicial review may be less final than is often imagined.

But sometimes process review is troublesome. For example, in Justice Stone's footnote the words "undesirable" and "prejudice" may not reveal themselves easily, indeed perhaps not at all, if a judge is barred from inquiring into the substantive values advanced or curtailed by a statute. Moreover, as Professor Bruce Ackerman of

Yale has persuasively argued, "anonymous and diffuse" minorities may be worse off in the legislative process than the "discrete and insular" ones referred to in the footnote.[9]

In his book *Democracy and Distrust* (1980), however, Professor John Hart Ely effectively discusses the footnote in terms of the malfunctioning of the more majoritarian branches: "Malfunction occurs when the *process* is undeserving of trust, when (1) the ins are choking off the channels of political change to ensure that they still stay in and the outs will stay out, or (2) though no one is actually denied a voice or a vote, representatives beholden to an effective majority are systematically disadvantaging some minority out of simple hostility or a prejudiced refusal to recognize commonalities of interest, and thereby denying that minority the protection afforded other groups by a representative system."[10]

While a malfunction in process may be a good reason for the exercise of judicial review (assuming we can get a grip on what a malfunction means), its absence is not necessarily a good reason for denying review. Are there not substantive malfunctions that require serious judicial review? Is it not the case, for example, that there are areas of individual autonomy and privacy where Government should not intrude without sufficient justification, but sometimes does? Is the capacity of the Court not as great here, and its role not as important, as where the perceived malfunction is one of process?

Do not answer yes too quickly. To paraphrase Alexander Bickel, you may find yourself in bed with voluptuaries of economic due process. Recall that it was in the name of liberty that labor legislation was declared unconstitutional in *Lochner*.

Professor Ely knows this, and he has no trouble giving an emphatically negative "answer" to my questions: "Our government cannot fairly be said to be "malfunctioning" simply because it sometimes generates outcomes with which we disagree, however strongly. . . . In a representative democracy value determinations are to be made by our elected representatives, and if in fact most of us disapprove we can vote them out of office."

While few would suggest that all outcomes with which they disagree strongly are malfunctions, I will suggest that some may be.
More importantly for now, there are several difficulties with Ely's
"answer" to my questions. They are difficulties that undermine the
approach taken in *Carolene Products* insofar as its purpose is to
keep judges from making value judgments. And in the minds of
some students of the Court, especially originalists, making value
judgments means "Lochnerizing," or having judges impose their
personal preferences. Ely sometimes refers to this judicial activity
as "value impositions."

The first problem with Ely's argument is that the judicial diagnosis
of a process malfunction may itself entail a value determination. For
example, given the method for selecting U. S. senators, it is far from
clear to me how a court in many situations can know whether a
legislative apportionment is a malapportionment, unless of course
it develops a theory of political fairness. I challenge anyone to develop such a theory without making value determinations. The repudiation of one person, one vote in the selection of our one hundred
senators reflects a value determination clearly spelled out in the
Constitution. The repudiation by the Supreme Court of similar value
determinations in state law itself reflects a very different value determination about the meaning of fairness in our political processes.
The Court has held that both branches of a bicameral state legislature—its House and its Senate—must be elected in a way that
conforms with the principle of one person, one vote.[11] You won't
find the source of this value determination—the source of law—in
original intent. Needless to say, that does not mean that I think the
Court was wrong; but it is to say that the policing of political
participation has problems within it identical to those that so upset
the originalists.

Second, the judicial cure for a process malfunction may require
judges to make value determinations. Take the First Amendment.
As Ely tells us, "Courts must police inhibitions on expression and
other political activity because we cannot trust elected officials to

do so: ins have a way of wanting to make sure the outs stay out."[12] Agreed. If speech reflects the views of an administration, it does not need judicial protection: no one in authority is apt to stop it. However, it may need judicial protection if the speech attacks those in power.

But when we come to apply the First Amendment to defamation, for example, we find that a court must place a value on reputation if it is to fashion a rule protecting unpopular political expression considered defamatory under state law. The famous case of *New York Times v. Sullivan* (1964), which gives First Amendment protection in many situations to untrue and defamatory statements, may be the correct cure for this process malfunction, but in the line of cases applying and qualifying *Sullivan*, speech sometimes yields to reputation.[13] Where this has occurred, the Court has in effect decided that free expression does not have enough weight to overcome a state's determination that an individual's reputation needs legal protection. Such a decision by the Court requires that the justices come to grips with substantive values and reach judgments about them.

———————

Ely is hardly unmindful that under his elaboration of *Carolene Products* judges make value determinations. Among other things he has this to say:

> Participation itself can obviously be regarded as a value, but that doesn't collapse the two modes of review I am describing into one. As I am using the terms, value imposition refers to the designation of certain goods (rights or whatever) as so important that they must be insulated from whatever inhibition the political process might impose, whereas a participational orientation denotes a form of review that concerns itself with how decisions effecting value choices and distributing the resultant costs and benefits are made . . . I surely don't claim that the words have to be used thus. . . . I claim only that that is

how I am using them, and that so used they are not synonyms.

If the objection is not that I have not distinguished two concepts but rather that one might well "value" certain decision procedures for their own sake, of course it is right: one might. And to one who insisted on that terminology, my point would be that the "values" the Court should pursue are "participational values" of the sort I have mentioned, since those are the "values" (1) with which our Constitution has preeminently and most successfully concerned itself, (2) whose "imposition" is not incompatible with, but on the contrary supports, the American system of representative democracy, and (3) that courts set apart from the political process are uniquely situated to "impose."[14]

Perhaps, then, the raison d'être for a "participational orientation" is not so much that it will control the judiciary, but that it is authorized by the Constitution, properly understood. Judges are empowered to impose participational values, and at least for Ely they should impose them with gusto: *Democracy and Distrust* stands as an elegant defense of the transformation by the Warren Court of American constitutional law through the vindication of participational values.

But problems remain. Yes, the text of the Constitution is concerned with participational values, and it can be understood to authorize judges, in a proper case, to enforce such values. As Ely admits, however, the Constitution is also concerned with other kinds of values, the ones that Ely finds unsuitable for judicial enforcement. Yet if we have judicial review, the First Amendment, for example, must be elaborated. And as I have just demonstrated in discussing *New York Times v. Sullivan*, this requires judges to make substantive value judgments.

I suggest that the desire to limit judges to participational values is influenced by a rather idealized conception of nonjudicial decisionmaking. As I argue in chapter 2, the regular and accepted practices of the legislative branches, congressional staff, and the bureaucracy generally lead to a complex structure of government requiring many individuals and organizations to make "substantive" value determinations. More than a few of these individuals and organizations are not elected. They bring to their tasks qualities different from those of nonelected judges. They are constrained in their decisionmaking in ways different from the ones that constrain judges, and the consequences of their decisions differ too. Expectations ought to be realistic. One who worries about judicial power should ask: judicial power compared to what? In answering that question it is well to remember, after reviewing the work of the House of Representatives, that even there it is difficult to make a strong affirmative case for the discipline of electoral accountability. Money counts, incumbents get it, and they are regularly returned to office.[15]

What this suggests is that not only are distinctions between "participational" and "substantive" values themselves a product of value imputation, but that the judicial imputation of either type of value can be seen as compatible with American democracy.

In an important sense the judicial review of *Carolene Products* imposes an obligation on the justices of the Supreme Court that is further removed from the normal task of judges than other approaches to constitutional adjudication: *Carolene Products* requires justices to be political philosophers and to work at a very high level of abstraction. To police participation in what Ely calls "the American System of representative democracy," each justice has to understand, develop, invent (what is the right word?) that system and then be prepared to impose it. When a group loses in the political branches and appeals for redress to the judicial, the courts must decide whether the loss is consistent or inconsistent with representative democracy. What is the starting point for decision? Is it some form of liberal theory? Republican theory? Conservative theory? Social choice theory?

For a court, such a question imposes a task that is different in kind from the sort that a case like *Goldman v. Weinberger* entails. *Goldman* deals with a vital but narrow issue: the free exercise of a religious practice in the military. If you were to make the mistake of thinking about the judge's task in terms of personal preferences, you might think of the Court's decision (if you think it wrong) as the rough equivalent of a narrow constitutional amendment. To understand, develop, or invent the American system of representative democracy is the rough equivalent of having an openended constitutional convention.

Well, perhaps this is hyperbolic: when interpreting the free exercise clause of the First Amendment the Court should not be clausebound; it should attend to the place of religious liberty in American society. But the push of Justice Stone's footnote—the condition precedent to applying that form of judicial review—is often toward stratospheric philosophizing, as it is in reapportionment. High irony this, given the ambition of participational theorists to restrict the role of the Court.

Participational theorists seem to share Bickel's belief that "nothing . . . can alter the essential reality that judicial review is a deviant institution in American democracy." Accordingly, such review should be contained, limited, or channeled. This is accomplished, so they believe, by policing participation not substance. Review that fits the criteria set out in 1938 in Justice Stone's footnote should be searching; elsewhere great deference is to be paid by the Court to the work of electorally accountable bodies. Moreover, participational theorists believe that their approach to judicial review is authorized by the text and structure of the Constitution and that it controls judges by preventing them from imposing their personal values on the nation.

Other approaches brought to the practice of constitutional judging are based in the virtues of authority and control (claimed as well by the originalists) and in a belief in the undemocratic nature of judicial review. One approach lacks nuance but from time to time has had powerful political support, and often distinguished academic and judicial support. It is the approach grounded in across-the-board judicial restraint, and I shall talk a little about it at the end of this chapter. Other approaches, based on the same foundational beliefs and concerns, attempt to discriminate among constitutional questions (as the participationalists do). There are many conflicting positions: robust review should be limited to individual rights; it should be limited to separation of powers or to federal-state relations. And there is the first paragraph of Justice Stone's footnote: "There may be narrower scope for operation of the presumption of constitutionality when legislation appears on its face to be within a specific prohibition of the Constitution, such as those of the first ten Amendments, which are deemed equally specific when held to be embraced within the 14th."

In my discussion of Justice Black in chapter 3 I have pointed out the trouble with the first paragraph of the footnote as a source of law: adjudication involving the Bill of Rights is not dramatically different from adjudication involving less textually explicit provisions of the Constitution. Even the First Amendment is open-textured. It requires a great deal of interpretation. If there is to be deference to electorally accountable departments of government through a presumption of constitutionality, why not defer here as well? After all, legislators are under an obligation to work within the Constitution. A text with more words can be seen as giving more information to them as well as to judges. So why not the same presumption? The question is, how powerful should that presumption be?

Felix Frankfurter, who served on the Supreme Court from 1939 to 1962 and was an active adviser to President Franklin Roosevelt while a distinguished professor at Harvard, was a justice who believed that the presumption of constitutionality should be powerful indeed. He was more or less committed to across-the-board judicial restraint. Throughout his career, Frankfurter was influenced (although never inordinately) by the work of James Bradley Thayer

There are several additional problems with the authority of originalism. Let me sketch a few. Consider first the following statement of Edmund Morgan, one of our most eminent colonial historians:

> For the colonists, as for other Englishmen, property was not merely a possession to be hoarded and admired; it was rather the source of life and liberty. If a man had property, if he had land, he had his own source of food, he could be independent of all other men, including kings and lords. Where property was concentrated in the hands of a king and aristocracy, only the king and the aristocracy would be free, while the rest of the population would be little better than slaves, victims of the external efforts of rulers to exploit subjects. Without property men could be starved into submission. Hence liberty rested on property, and whatever threatened the security of property threatened liberty.[15]

If we assume that Morgan is correct—and this is an assumption worth indulging—and if we assume that the colonists' attitude toward property still had a grip on the attitude of the founding fathers and the amenders who composed and approved the Bill of Rights, although perhaps a somewhat weakened grip, what are we to say about the constitutionality of contemporary governmental regulation that has so substantially reduced the "security of property"?

Once again an example from labor law will suffice. Under the National Labor Relations Act an employer must permit its workers, who are on its property, to solicit for the union during their free time.[16] Surely using the employer's property for union purposes diminishes the value of the property to its owner. Why is this not a violation of the Fifth Amendment, which, among its many virtues, protects property?

The answer may be that today liberty and property are not joined at the hip. They are discrete concepts, although sometimes property of the Harvard Law School. In 1893 Thayer published an article, "The Origin and Scope of the American Doctrine of Constitutional Law," in which he concluded that the Court should declare an act of Congress unconstitutional only "when those who have the right to make laws have not merely made a mistake, but have made a very clear one,—so clear that it is not open to rational question." Thayer went on: "This rule recognizes that, having regard to the great, complex, ever-unfolding exigencies of government, much which will seem unconstitutional to one man, or body of men, may reasonably not seem so to another; that the Constitution often admits of different interpretations; that there is often a range of choice and judgment; that in such cases the constitution does not impose upon the legislature any one specific opinion, but leaves open this range of choice; and that whatever choice is rational is constitutional."[16]

Thayer rested some of his case on the structure of the Constitution. He seemed to see a strong relation between the scope of judicial review and the judicial nature of the power that the Court exercises. Thayer emphasized that this judicial nature meant that the constitutionality of a statute was generally not considered by the Court for some time. Thayer argued that if the scope of review was meant to be broader, if the Court was to do more than correct "very clear" mistakes, earlier intervention would have been provided for in the Constitution—something in the nature of a judicial council of revision to conform legislation with fundamental law.

I confess that I do not understand this argument. It does not seem to me that there is any relation between the time of review and its purportedly limited scope, let alone a necessary relation. Indeed, the argument seems to run the other way: time and a specific case give the Court an opportunity and a perspective different from those of Congress. Strong deference to the interpretation by Congress of the Constitution mitigates this judicial advantage.

On certain premises, however, a good argument can be made for Thayer's conclusion. The premises are that judicial review is a deviant institution, and that there are no sources of law for interpreting the Constitution except the personal values of the interpreters. Since it is my claim in this book that neither premise is correct, I think Thayer himself has made a very clear mistake. Nevertheless, I do want to insist that the views of the legislature may be of weight in constitutional adjudication, for legislators too are duty-bound to respect constitutional limits. I recognize, of course, that the question of a statute's constitutionality may not be closely attended to by the legislature; indeed that sometimes the approach in the law-making body is to leave a hard constitutional question to the judiciary. These are factors to be taken into account by judges in deciding how strong a presumption of constitutionality (if any) should attach to challenged legislation, and there are many others that I shall address in subsequent chapters. This much seems clear: the answer to the question of how to restrict judicial intervention appropriately will not be found in Justice Frankfurter's across-the-board judicial restraint any more than it will be in the approach to policing participation taken in *Carolene Products*.

PART III

The Common-Law Method

CHAPTER FIVE

Sources of Law and the Process of Adjudication

Questions of where, whether, and how strong a presumption of constitutionality should attach to governmental action are related to questions about both the authority of the Supreme Court when it interprets the Constitution and the control of the least dangerous branch. The relations are of the following sort. Start with the proposition that the Constitution does not easily reveal itself. Often it is open-textured and vague: it is a constitution; it is not a tax code. What then are the appropriate sources of law—the appropriate materials—available in the interpretive enterprise?

In the article he wrote in 1893, James Bradley Thayer sharply distinguished that enterprise from what judges normally do, and thereby placed himself in opposition to John Marshall, who had emphasized the similarity between judicial review and other forms of adjudication. Thayer's strong presumption of constitutionality— his "very clear mistake" rule—can find some support in the countermajoritarian nature of the Court (remarked earlier). It also can find support in doubts about the authority of the Court to employ the normal sources of law used by courts in adjudication. Thayer himself deduced this lack of authority from the nature and structure of the Constitution: its nature is political, and its structure brings the Court into the interpretive process only where there is a case or controversy. The Court is not a council of legislative revision. If it were, perhaps it would be permissible for it to employ standard techniques of interpretation that rely on normal sources of law for elaborating a text. But it acts only after Congress has made its policy choices, and given the Constitution's political nature the Court must be extremely deferential to the congressional decision. That is the limit of its authority.

Doubt about the Court's authority to engage in more robust review, moreover, would surely be fed by a belief in the proposition that the standard judicial methods of interpretation invite judges to impose their own values on the nation.

In this portion of the book, I shall maintain that what might be called a common-law method of judicial review best explains American constitutional law, and that while far from perfect it is normatively superior to rival approaches. My plan is first to review briefly the process of adjudication, with special attention to the Supreme Court. This review draws on chapter 1 and can be thought of as an inquiry into the method of generating the materials to be used in interpretation; that is, the sources of law. Second, I shall look at one aspect of the sources of law question from a substantive perspective, as contrasted to a methodological perspective. But even here I shall not be free from methodology. For my attention will in part be directed toward Alexander Bickel's search for the purpose of judicial review; one that is bound up with the process of adjudication, as I think it must be. In *The Least Dangerous Branch* Bickel writes: "The search must be for a function which differs from the legislative and executive functions; which is peculiarly suited to the capabilities of the courts; which will not likely be performed elsewhere if courts do not assume it."[1] Armed with "a function that differs from the legislative and executive functions," I shall be prepared to say something about substance and presumptions of constitutionality in the troublesome area of privacy and abortion.

We begin with John Marshall. In *Marbury v. Madison* he pointed the way. For in holding that the Constitution is law, law to be applied by "the judicial department," Marshall committed the Constitution to a governmental branch that can take the long view because it is removed from electoral politics (this commitment was not necessarily exclusive, but as it turned out it was irrevocable). And he committed the Constitution to the one department of government that many students of law would say finds its authority in the ideal of a rigorous adherence to principle. But what can that mean, given the nature of adjudication?

Principles in law are contextual, they are constructed through the process of adjudication, and they have many sources. While these sources differ in common-law, statutory, and constitutional adjudication, these three types of adjudication have a strong family resemblance. We can learn a great deal about that resemblance by inspecting adjudication and remembering some of its features. Out of many features I shall again call attention to just a few that I discussed in chapter 1. My object is to place substantive interpretation—the derivation and elaboration of principles—in the context of constitutional adjudication. It is a context different indeed from others where interpretation is practiced. Reading poetry, directing a play, understanding and teaching the Bible are examples of interpretive projects that occur in contrasting environments. There are similarities between constitutional interpretation and interpretation as it is practiced elsewhere, but because the legal environment is so different from other environments, the similarities are dominated by the differences.

Recall first that in adjudication various groups interpret the Constitution in accordance with the understanding of their membership. Their lawyers argue to establish and through governmental power to impose on the nation that understanding, the understanding of their clients. Other lawyers, representing other interests, argue for a different interpretation, one shared by their clients. Constitutional principles and legal sanctions emerge from this dynamic, adversarial process; in this methodological sense, the process itself is a source of law.

This process, resulting as it does in the imposition of sanctions, is different from most interpretive processes. Indeed where else does an interpretive process bestow authority on officials to take away property and even life? And this authority, like the prospect of execution, concentrates the mind wonderfully. The participants in appellate adjudication—the lawyers and the judges—are bound to be fully aware of, and influenced by, the consequences of their activity.

Second, recall that in constitutional adjudication the claims the advocates make are about the text of the Constitution and how that text has been and should be interpreted. This entails client-interested explanations of such matters as prior decisional law, historical context, and present circumstances. It entails an appeal to tradition and aspiration—an appeal to values and morality. All these matters are deeply contested, but the contest is itself constrained by the process of adjudication. The players are members of an interpretive community. They remember their professors exhorting them to argue "like a lawyer," and they know that those before whom they contest will listen only to certain types of arguments.[2]

Often the effort of the advocate is to depict these contested matters in the least challenging, most conventional of ways; that is, normal, common, public ways, ways that are consistent with the aspirations, morality, and general understandings of the population. If you were an advocate, wouldn't you want to present your client's claim in a way that was as close as possible to what you took to be the conventional understanding of relevant materials? Even such an understanding must be explained and applied, extended, and perhaps, at least to some extent, transformed. You want your client to win, and it is apt to help if you can depict the client's values as public values or, to put it the other way round, if you can interpret public values so that they encompass the client's claim.

Your adversary will do the same.. Both of you are trying to persuade disinterested—here in the sense of not client-interested—judges who will render a decision disposing of the dispute and write an opinion regulating the future.

Third, at the appellate level a majority decision requires the assent of other judges to the reasoning of its author. Indeed, before an author is selected to write, the members of a court must vote on the case. There are many reasons why voting itself is an important part of the process that may shape the principle on which a decision turns.

Consider the Supreme Court. In the contest for votes, it would appear that in addition to reasoned arguments justices have used personal flattery and emotional appeals, and have even traded votes.

Evidence also suggests that a justice may vote with the majority even while disagreeing with its treatment of the case, and then bargain to influence the Court's opinion. Justices also may threaten to write dissenting or concurring opinions or try to form voting blocks to influence opinions. In cases of extreme importance, justices may assent to the majority opinion to make it unanimous, even if they have some misgivings about it.

Once a vote is taken, the opinion is assigned. If part of the majority, the Chief Justice assigns the opinion; otherwise the assignment is made by the senior Associate Justice who shares the majority view. The ability to assign the opinion is itself a sometimes powerful opportunity to influence the eventual outcome. For example, the opinion may be assigned to a justice who does not hold firm views, but who has a vote that is needed for a majority. The task of writing often persuades an equivocal author, and the draft majority opinion is the starting point for draft dissents and concurrences.

The opinion writing process is a product of conflict and compromise. Majority positions may turn into minority positions and back again. Opinions are written and changed in an attempt to get votes and in response to the views and arguments of other justices. Justices may circulate draft dissenting and concurring opinions for the purpose of shaping the final results. And these tactics do work, at least some of the time.[3]

What all this means is that in the voting and writing processes, negotiation plays a role in formulating constitutional principles. In this methodological sense, then, negotiation too is a source of law.

Fourth, principles once established through this process have a life of their own. For it is emphatically the nature of the judicial process that principles be applied in as disinterested and consistent a fashion as possible. As I observed in chapter 1, both a commitment to the rule of law and broad-based participation in regulating through adjudication require that like cases be treated alike. This process of applying principles in a consistent and disinterested fashion is an interpretive process itself subject to the other features of adjudication—the inescapably political features—that I have just described.

Some students of adjudication find an intolerable tension between advocacy and negotiation on the one hand and the ideal of a consistent, disinterested application of principles on the other. This is particularly true if one imagines the judicial task—and many students seem to—as performed by a lonely scholar in a quiet corner of a library. The reality is otherwise, and the student who neglects context initially is bound to be disappointed by the degree of uncertainty in the law. Too often cynicism results from this disappointment, the realization that one's expectations are unrealistically high because one's conception of the enterprise is wrong.

Of course there is tension. The ideal of a rigorous adherence to principle is contextual. Judges are not scholars, critics, or priests. While it is not quite true that the process makes the product, neither is it false that it does, that constitutional interpretation is the practice of nonpartisan, principled politics.

In practice law changes, after negotiation within a court, because of the judges' skeptical receptivity and reserved openness to the claims of various groups—claims shaped and presented by lawyers using legal arguments and trying to win cases. This is the way all law develops through adjudication, including constitutional law.

For all its similarity to other forms of law development, however, the development of constitutional law through adjudication is distinctive. One or more agencies of government have acted, and in acting they have explicitly or implicitly interpreted the Constitution as permitting them to do what they have done. It is the correctness of this interpretation that is being challenged. This is why it is so important to get straight the Court's special function, to locate its interpretive strength. And surely it is now clear why this is so. It is not simply because judicial review is undemocratic. It is because judicial review sometimes is more final, more difficult to change, if change is seen as desirable, and because the process of adjudication is hardly a model of pure reason. Like all governmental processes, it has a political dimension. Unless there is an interpretive strength in the politics of appellate adjudication—a special function—judges ought to be modest and respect the product of other political processes.

The task of locating the Court's special function is not easy, but in chapter 2 we made progress. Let's look again, and again begin with Bickel's reminder "that many actions of government have two aspects: their immediate necessarily intended, practical effects, and their perhaps unintended or unappreciated bearing on values we hold to have more general and permanent interest."[4]

At least in individual rights cases, it is just these values that lawyers invoke in behalf of their clients. In *Goldman v. Weinberger*, for example, the arguments were about the value of religious freedom and its free exercise in the armed forces. The constitutional text to be interpreted or reinterpreted by the Supreme Court was the First Amendment—the Air Force had acted on the basis of a congressional authority that was itself based on implicit or explicit constitutional interpretation. To cite another example, the value of equal protection of the law, textually lodged in the Fourteenth Amendment, was at issue in the gender cases surveyed in chapter 1. In each of those cases other branches of government, either state or federal, had explicitly or implicitly interpreted the Constitution and decided that it was permissible to make distinctions turn on gender.

The "values we hold to have more general and permanent interest," some of which the lawyers representing Goldman said had been improperly disregarded by the air force, and which Weinberger's lawyers said had been properly respected, are the source of legal principles. These values must be weighed by the lawyers and judges who take part in the process of adjudication. Their weight changes from one generation to another as they are used in interpreting constitutional text. They are the values that form a public morality, the ethical principles, the ideals and aspirations that are widely shared by Americans—even as their application is deeply contested.

Of course legislators are often professionally concerned with this public morality. They are concerned with interpreting public values, with shaping and contributing to them. One cannot begin to think about statutes dealing with the death penalty, for example, without coming quickly to such issues. But consider the environment in which legislators function. It is often hard for them to resist pressure from their constituents who react to particular events (a brutal murder, for instance) with a passion that conflicts with their more general, permanent, shared values. While we rarely lynch people today, legislators frequently adopt a "lynching" frame of mind that is deeply at odds with our moral ideals. Nor is it an easy matter for legislators to interpret public values when there are well-organized interest groups insisting on their own self-interested positions.

The clients of lawyers are also self-interested. But the lawyers are arguing to judges who are disinterested—meaning here that they are not electorally accountable, are not paid by clients, and if on the Supreme Court are rarely concerned with professional advancement. And the lawyers are arguing specifically about the effect of governmental action on interests claimed to be constitutionally protected. These interests have a textual basis. The constitutional text has been elaborated through the process of "litigating elucidation." The lawyers' arguments are made in terms of that prior elucidation. The adversarial effort is to distinguish or support, undermine or contract, extend or overrule the prior law by reinterpreting its meaning and basis; that is reinterpreting the language, history, and public values that are the sources of law.

The process of constitutional interpretation in the legislature usually takes a different form. Often it is not at all explicit. But even when constitutional issues are addressed, they are generally one small factor considered along with many others in a larger legislative project directed toward promulgating policies or developing a program to regulate an area of life, at wholesale and prospectively. In the situation that brought about *Goldman v. Weinberger,* for example, one can imagine that Congress empowered the Pentagon to develop rules of dress with at most a passing concern having been expressed by either entity about the free exercise of religion; presumably Congress acted at the behest of the Pentagon after listening to its spokespersons and to no one else. Another example is provided by legislation passed in 1988 aimed at reducing America's drug problem: while noting that drug dealers and users had due process interests, Congress failed to give these interests careful consideration. Due process interests were seen as obstacles to an effective policy that were to be overcome as summarily as possible.

Courts also regulate the future, and the Supreme Court in particular must be more concerned with the regulatory aspects of its work than with the dispute resolution aspects. But it is not formulating a drug policy or producing a dress code on the basis of information that is developed in legislative processes, where the public interest contends with many private interests, and where concern for the individual may receive inadequate attention. The Court has before it a well-defined controversy, one that is rich in the details of the particular and that sharpens the constitutional interests that may have suffered as a result of the formulation or implementation of a legislative program. In giving effect to these interests in their present context through the processes we have examined, the Court must articulate the principles used to elaborate text in the past, principles that often acquired their weight in public morality and that must be reinterpreted in terms of a contemporary understanding of that morality.

What do I mean by principles acquiring their weight in public morality? I can answer this by asking you to consider again the gender discrimination cases discussed in chapter 1. There we saw that the distinctions legislatures have been permitted to make between women and men when enacting regulatory statutes have turned on changing national attitudes about the importance of gender equality. These attitudes reflect widely shared public values. They constitute a public morality.

The constitutional principle requiring that equality be considered by the Court is derived from the text of the equal protection clause, its weight from what I have just described as public morality. This way of viewing the issue is reflected in the case law: because the goal of equality between the sexes has a more prominent place in our current national catalogue of public values than it did in the past—because it weighs more in our public morality—states no longer may justify gender distinctions on grounds of mere rationality, as they did before. "[C]lassifications by gender must serve important governmental objectives and must be substantially related to achievement of those objectives."[5]

The weight of public morality as a source of law, along with other sources of law (language, precedent, structure, and history), is determined by the Court through the process of adjudication. As we have seen, this process results in a unique form of interpretation. But like all interpretation, it is creative. It would be wrong to think of it as the equivalent of digging for gold and finding the ore. Among the participants in adjudication—the lawyers and judges—there must be a constructive reworking of the materials that constitute the sources of law used in elaborating the text. Interpretation is interactive. The participants working with the appropriate materials make law; but they are constrained by the methodological and substantive conventions of adjudication.

When the attention of the legislature has been focused primarily in formulating a program, as was the case when Congress passed the act of 1988 concerning drugs, courts should not assume that the legislature has carefully interpreted the Constitution. It follows that a presumption of constitutionality on the part of the courts would be misplaced. Given the comparative disadvantage of the legislature (through inability or unwillingness) to attend to a program's effect on constitutional interests, judicial review should be robust. Legislative advantage is in the general design of the program and not in its constitutional side effects. Sometimes, however, this distinction between the program and its impact on constitutional interests is elusive. Regulation in the privacy area provides an example.

But we must stop and back up before we can go forward to the privacy area and examine some of the applications and difficulties with the position I am developing about presumptions of constitutionality on the one hand and public values or morality on the other.

First, let me make clear that it is only through example, and in context, that we can get a feel for this concept of public morality that I am inviting you to see as a source of constitutional law, and that some commentators have suggested is nothing more than the value imputation of the constitutional interpreter.[6]

Second, public morality, as I have suggested, is one source of law among many used to interpret the Constitution. Its role has been central, for example, to the jurisprudence of the Supreme Court in the area of capital punishment. It has been a source of law for determining when the death penalty constitutes "cruel and unusual punishment," as these words are used in the Eighth Amendment. Other sources of law in constitutional adjudication used to interpret the text are constitutional structure, history and precedent.

Some believe it makes no sense to think of public morality as a source of law for protecting individuals or groups against the will of the majority as that will is manifested in legislation. For while legislation itself may not always represent the will of a present majority, at other times it does; and while public morality and public values, "values we hold to have more general and permanent interest," are often not the same as the action positions of a present majority, sometimes they are.

Consider as an example the recent Supreme Court decision striking down the conviction of a person who violated state law by burning an American flag as an act of political protest. The Court held by a vote of 5 to 4 that the conviction was an abridgment of speech banned by the First and Fourteenth Amendments.[7]

The decision led to lopsided votes of condemnation in the House and Senate, the passage of a federal statute (itself later held unconstitutional) aimed at protecting the flag, and a quick, unsuccessful call by the President for a constitutional amendment—a call that he subsequently renewed without success.

I think the Court's decision was correct for reasons rooted in the purpose and development of the law of free expression. But because of the powerful symbolic significance of the flag, I would be hard put to defend the Court in terms of public values as such. Indeed, in many areas of constitutional law the role of public values or morality is limited. Structure, history, and precedent serve as presumptive vetoes over legislation aimed at restricting speech, interfering with religion, and distinguishing among people on the basis of their race. But—and it is an important but—public morality may have a role even where other sources of law are central. In the first place, it may assist a court in its interpretive task of determining how to deal with the weight of a presumption of unconstitutionality. An example is provided by the defamation cases (discussed briefly in chapter 4) in which free expression conflicts with the protection of a person's reputation.

In the second place, public morality may have a role after the fact. Constitutional decisions must be politically digestible. If they are not they will not survive, and public morality can influence political digestibility. I address this question in part IV.

But in the area of substantive due process (or, if you prefer, constitutional privacy), public morality is the workhorse of interpretation, and *Griswold v. Connecticut* is the beginning of contemporary law.

———

Let us hypothesize that in 1960 a state had enacted a statute very different from the one eventually struck down in *Griswold v.*

Connecticut (1965); one that made plain in its preamble that slower population growth was its goal and that adduced reasons relating to the state's environment and economy for such a policy. There would have been little room for the Court to question the validity of the statute's purpose. If, however, the means deployed in the hypothetical statute to achieve its goal had been to make it a crime for married persons to have sexual intercourse "between the tenth and twentieth day after the onset of the female partner's last menstrual period," this would have raised an easy constitutional question, a question of personal liberty under the due process clause. The Court would have had to ask itself whether such a restriction offended public moral standards, and if it did (as it seems to me it clearly would have done), whether constitutional doctrine, interpreted in light of these standards, sustained or invalidated the legislation.

Notice, however, that in implementing its policy the legislature could not possibly have failed to consider the constitutional questions, for it could not possibly have ignored public moral standards (indeed it must have undertaken to have "read" them), to have interpreted public values, to have shaped and contributed to them. But whatever the standard of deference to the legislature ought to be, if there is judicial review this statute is unconstitutional. My claim is that this is an example of a very clear legislative mistake. Indeed, I constructed the hypothetical statute to require invalidation even if judicial review were as anemic as Thayer would have it when the constitutionality of a federal law is before the Court.

Griswold v. Connecticut is more complicated than the hypothetical statute. On the one hand, the purpose of the Connecticut statute was to regulate morals; on the other, the means established to effectuate that purpose were less clearly offensive to public morality. The statute provided that "[a]ny person who uses any drug, medicinal article or instrument for the purpose of preventing conception shall be fined not less than fifty dollars or imprisoned not less than sixty days nor more than one year or be both fined and imprisoned."[8] Here, as with the hypothetical statute, the legislature must have been fully engaged with the moral aspects of the legal issue that eventually came before the Court. Under these circumstances, and having in mind the differences between the legislative and judicial processes, how robust should judicial review be? Here temporal considerations must be addressed.

My claim is that because *Griswold* was decided in 1965 and the challenged statute was enacted in 1879, judicial review should rightly have been robust. The passage of time should have eliminated any deference that the Court might have paid toward the legislature's interpretation of public morality. In other words, the responsibility of the Court in *Griswold* was similar to the one it would have had in a situation where the legislature had been concerned with developing a program and had given only passing attention to the consequences of the program's implementation on the constitutional interests of individuals. I shall try to support this claim as we try to place ourselves in 1965 and work out the appropriate holding for the Court in *Griswold*.

In an earlier chapter I examined the Court's opinion holding the Connecticut statute in *Griswold* unconstitutional. The majority opinion was written by Justice William O. Douglas, who served on the Court from 1939 to 1975. According to the second Justice John Marshall Harlan (1955–71) the Connecticut statute, which he too believed was unconstitutional, embodied a "moral judgment [of the Connecticut legislature in 1879] that all use of contraceptives [including use by married couples] is improper."[9]

In 1965, the year of *Griswold*, the moral judgment contained in the statute would seem on analysis to be inconsistent with prevailing public values. As I have argued, the task of the Court is to make such an analysis and connect it with constitutional doctrine. If we are to have judicial review (and in chapter 2 I attempted to demonstrate that judicial review is constitutionally authorized), so much is required from the Court. The analysis cannot, however, satisfy people who demand mathematical exactness: they are bound to find all law disappointing.

The place to begin analysis is a statement in Justice Harlan's opinion that "the intimacy of husband and wife is necessarily an essential and accepted feature of the institution of marriage, an institution which the State not only must allow, but which always and in every age it has fostered and protected." This intimacy resists standardization through a detailed official code of behavior and only the most general legal controls may be placed on it. Enormous discretion for working out the particulars of the relationship must belong to each couple. The existence of this discretion—of control by husband and wife over their intimate relations—is a central feature of the general arrangement between the couple and the state at the time of marriage. It is an arrangement that creates a complex of moral as well as legal rights and obligations on the part of the couple and the state, rights and obligations intrinsic to the institution of marriage that change as the institution changes, but that have and retain a logical, internal consistency.

The need for private control establishes the area of liberty (or privacy) granted to individuals in marriage. This liberty imposes two types of moral obligations: one between husband and wife, the other between the couple and the state. Interference by the state with this granted liberty can intrude on the marriage relationship in ways that are profoundly at variance with basic aspects of that institution.

Apart from the personal degradation that would be endured if the Connecticut statute were enforced, we might ask whether the statute did not substantially interfere with a major reason for marriage. While procreation may once have been a sufficient explanation for the institution of marriage and the only officially acceptable justification for sexual relations, this was no longer the case in mid-twentieth century America. Then, as today, an increasingly important part of the reason for marriage—for the establishment of a state-protected institution—was the growth and nurturing of love. And the pursuit of sexual gratification is a vital aspect of love, while the fear of unwanted pregnancy materially reduces the prospects of sexual gratification.

I submit that this description of marriage accurately reflects the public attitudes that prevailed in 1965. But the Connecticut statute was enacted in 1879, and the state legislature must have addressed public attitudes that prevailed then, which surely were different from what they were nearly a century later. Procreation rather than intimate sexual relations then was central to the institution of marriage.[10] In eighty-six years attitudes shifted, public values changed, and the additional weight that public morality attached to intimate relations imposed a greater burden on the state to justify its interference with that aspect of constitutional liberty.

My claim about marriage is of course not a claim that childbearing and childrearing do not remain an important part of marriage. It is rather that other values became increasingly important as well. Nor does my claim fail to recognize that love and sexual gratification exist outside marriage and that they can and do fail to exist within marriage. This is not the point. The point is that the state has undertaken to sponsor one institution that by 1965 had the romantic and sexual relationship at its core (along with other values). This relationship demands liberty in the practice of the sexual act.

As Harlan suggests, the Connecticut statute is therefore an arguably unconstitutional condition on the privileges that flow from a state-supported institution. He writes [remember that this was a generation ago]: "It is one thing when the State exerts its power either to forbid extramarital sexuality altogether, or to say who may marry, but it is quite another when, having acknowledged a marriage and the intimacies inherent in it, it undertakes to regulate by means of the criminal law the details of that intimacy."

To determine whether the ban on the use of contraceptives is indeed an unconstitutional condition in the marriage context requires further rumination and reflection in the project of interpreting public morality. Thus far the argument is that the act of marriage entitles the married couple to a large area of liberty in respect of their love life, and that the Connecticut statute restricts that liberty. The claim is not that there are no limits on liberty.

Let me, then, make some assertions that I submit were clear in 1965: the state would be taken to have broken its moral obligation arising from its relationship to marriage were it to ban sexual in-

tercourse between married couples, regulate the frequency of intercourse, or regulate the day or time of day when intercourse was
permitted. And while such hypothetical regulations are distinguishable from a prohibition on the use of contraceptives, the distinction
with respect to the second hypothetical regulation is more apparent
than real.

A ban on intercourse would be a clear violation of the arrangement
between the state and the couple, and for this reason it is difficult
to imagine the simultaneous existence of such a ban and marriage
in anything resembling its present form. This would not be true of
a statute stipulating the occasions on which a couple's sexual appetite might be indulged. Yet such a statute would be deeply inconsistent and in sharp conflict with the entire concept of the marriage
relationship. It would recall the fine print in a contract for the sale
and purchase of a used car that totally contradicts the general import
of the transaction; it would smack of fraud. And so too does the
Connecticut statute, given its potential effect on the love life of
the married couple: the ban could dramatically diminish pleasure
because of the fear of unwanted pregnancy. There can be no question that this can impose a major strain on the state-protected
relationship.

My claims concerning public attitudes toward intimate relations
in marriage are supported by data about contraceptive practices in
Connecticut circa 1965. Before the Connecticut statute was invalidated, legal sanctions were not imposed on married couples who
used birth control devices; if they had been, the state legislature
might well have changed the law. Moreover, some types of contraceptives could be purchased at any drugstore in the state, for although the statute made it illegal to use contraceptives, it did not
make it illegal to sell them. These facts constituted evidence helpful
to the Court's task of interpreting public values in the context of
the question before it, namely whether the anti-use statute had become unconstitutional in 1965. While various inferences may be
drawn from the evidence, and while some common behavior is
widely regarded as immoral even by those who engage in it, the

evidence of public acceptance of contraceptive practices tended to support the Court's decision. It was better evidence than the existence of a statute that had relevance to prevailing moral views in 1879, but carried little weight so many years later.

If I am correct in my interpretation of public morality, the Connecticut statute was properly struck down. For as Justice Byron R. White wrote in his concurring opinion, there is "nothing in this record justifying the sweeping scope of this statute, with its telling effect on the freedom of married persons, and therefore [I] conclude that it deprives such persons of liberty without due process of law."[11]

Those of you who worry about *Lochner* in my analysis of *Griswold* are of course right. Both are substantive due process cases. But let me quiet your fears. First, while the bulk of decisions from the *Lochner* era were concerned with economic legislation, in two cases a searching review of laws restricting personal liberties was also undertaken. These cases have never been overruled and provided some precedential support for *Griswold*.

In *Meyer v. Nebraska* the Court upset a statute drastically restricting the teaching of "any subject to any person in any language other than the English language." A language instructor "taught [German] in school as part of his occupation." The Court said: "His right thus to teach and the right of parents to engage him so to instruct their children, we think, are within the liberty of the [Fourteenth] Amendment."[12]

In *Pierce v. Society of Sisters*, the Court held unconstitutional under the due process clause an Oregon statute requiring that children could attend only public schools. In defending the right of parents to send their children to private schools, the Court said: "The child is not the mere creature of the State; those who nurture him and direct his destiny have the right, coupled with the high duty, to recognize and prepare him for additional obligations."[13]

My second point is that the problem with *Lochner*, and with many other cases from the same period, was not that the freedom of contract was seen as an aspect of constitutionally protected liberty. Given perceptions about the employer's control over working conditions, the problem with *Lochner* was rather that the Court attached more weight to that liberty than it could justify by an appeal to public values. These values in *Lochner, Meyer, Pierce,* and *Griswold* were a relevant source of law for elaborating constitutional text through the process of adjudication.

CHAPTER SIX

Public Morality

The Tragic Problem of Abortion

Public values are also relevant to the abortion issue. In examining that issue, my plan is initially to put aside questions of judicial deference to the legislature, to assume that the appropriate style of judicial review is robust. Later I shall raise questions concerning the appropriateness of giving very little weight to legislative judgments about a woman's "liberty interest" (to use the descriptive phrase employed by the Chief Justice in his abortion opinion of 1989). We begin not at the beginning but with *Roe v. Wade*,[1] and in particular with the Court's holding. The Texas statute that was declared unconstitutional in *Roe* was of the strict variety: except to save the life of the pregnant woman, it was a crime to "procure an abortion." The Court held that a pregnant woman has a "fundamental" "right of personal privacy," "founded in the Fourteenth Amendment's concept of personal liberty ... [which is] broad enough to encompass the woman's decision whether or not to terminate her pregnancy." The right "is not unqualified and must be considered against important state interests in regulation." These interests, however, must be "compelling" if they are to serve as the justification for limiting a "fundamental" right.

The state of course has "an important and legitimate interest in preserving and protecting the health of the pregnant woman . . . and . . . it has still another important and legitimate interest in protecting the potentiality of human life. These interests are separate and distinct. Each grows in substantiality as the woman approaches term and, at a point during pregnancy, each becomes 'compelling.' " The interest in the health of the woman increases during pregnancy because later abortions are more difficult to perform safely. This state interest becomes compelling "in the light of present medical knowledge . . . at approximately the end of the first trimester." "With respect to the State's important and legitimate interest in potential life, the 'compelling' point is at viability." A fetus becomes viable when it is "potentially able to live outside the mother's womb, albeit with artificial aid. Viability is usually placed at about seven months (28 weeks) but may occur earlier, even at 24 weeks."

From this it follows that:

(a) For the stage prior to approximately the end of the first trimester, the abortion decision and its effectuation must be left to the medical judgment of the pregnant woman's attending physician.

(b) For the stage subsequent to approximately the end of the first trimester, the State, in promoting its interest in the health of the mother, may, if it chooses, regulate the abortion procedure in ways that are reasonably related to maternal health.

(c) For the stage subsequent to viability, the State, in promoting its interest in the potentiality of human life, may, if it chooses, regulate, and even proscribe, abortion except where it is necessary, in appropriate medical judgment, for the preservation of the life or health of the mother.

This trimester framework seemed to command the support of a majority of the justices until July 6, 1989, when the Court decided *Webster v. Reproductive Health Services* (which I discuss below). According to an opinion in this case by Justice Harry A. Blackmun, which strongly supported the approach he had fashioned in *Roe,* *Webster* did not make "a single, even incremental, change in the law of abortion." But if we count noses and assume fixed perspectives, *Webster* did indicate that a majority of the Court was no longer committed to the trimester framework. What this will mean about pregnant women's constitutional rights is unclear. Little light was shed on this question in the two abortion cases decided by the

Court in the summer of 1990. Clear enough, however, is the survival
and potential enhancement of the state's two regulatory interests.[2]

———

While the state's interest in the health of the pregnant
woman is important and has led to legislation and litigation since
Roe, this issue need not be given any detailed consideration here.
The central, tragic problem in *Roe* is the conflict between the state's
interest in the survival of the fetus and a woman's interest in terminating her pregnancy.

It is natural to think of legislation "protecting the potentiality of
human life" as addressing a moral issue directly. While important
instrumental or policy reasons may be adduced for such legislation—
economic growth, for instance—they are plainly secondary. The
state of Texas and many other jurisdictions (some shortly before
Roe v. Wade) had made their moral judgments on fetal life in the
same sense that Connecticut in *Griswold* had pronounced its judgment on the morality of contraception.

In the procedural posture of *Roe,* review of the state's judgment
on fetal life was mandated by the plaintiff's claim that this judgment
had impermissibly abridged her liberty. Putting to one side any
question of judicial deference to the legislature, the issue of first
importance for the Court was how to weigh her interest in that
liberty. This required that an inquiry be made into the nature of the
principle the plaintiff was asserting and that attention be paid to
the interest the state had protected.

The Court itself approached the case more or less along these
lines. It did not, however, get far. Much of Justice Blackmun's opinion is devoted to a history of abortion and is related only remotely
to the task at hand. We are told that the constitutional principle
asserted by the plaintiff is an aspect of the "right of privacy,"
"founded in the Fourteenth Amendment's concept of personal liberty and restrictions upon state action." The Court elaborated: "The
pregnant woman cannot be isolated in her privacy . . . . The situation
therefore is inherently different from marital intimacy, or bedroom

possession of obscene material, or marriage, or procreation or education."

The Court also had this to say:

> The detriment that the State would impose upon the pregnant woman by denying this choice altogether [whether or not to terminate her pregnancy] is apparent. Specific and direct harm medically diagnosable even in early pregnancy may be involved. Maternity, or additional offspring, may force upon the woman a distressful life and future. Psychological harm may be imminent. Mental and physical health may be taxed by child care. There is also the distress, for all concerned, associated with the unwanted child, and there is the problem of bringing a child into a family already unable, psychologically and otherwise, to care for it. In other cases, as in this one, the additional difficulties and continuing stigma of unwed motherhood may be involved.

But this and the citation of a number of cases are all the Court had to say on this branch of the case.

The Court did no better when it undertook to examine the argument the state had advanced to justify its statute prohibiting the plaintiff from terminating her pregnancy. First, a fetus is not a person within the Fourteenth Amendment. Second, the Court does not know "when life begins": it does know that "the unborn have never been recognized in the law as persons in the whole sense." And third, "[i]n view of all this, we do not agree that, by adopting one theory of life [namely, that it "begins at conception and is present throughout pregnancy"], Texas may override the rights of the pregnant woman that are at stake."

With the opinion of the Court as background, let's now see if we can articulate the principle implicated in *Roe*, and then ascertain how powerful it is, how much it weighs, when it conflicts with the state's interest in the potential for human life. My object is not to construct a justification for the holding in *Roe* that proceeds on a theory different from what I take to be the Court's. For example, since abortion law is a restriction on the liberty of women, equal protection is a likely candidate for such an alternative theory. But my ambition here is to understand *Roe* in its own terms.

With this in mind, consider a statute making it a crime for any person to remove another person's gall bladder, except to save that person's life. Assume that the express purpose of the statute is to preserve gall bladders, it being determined that these organs can survive only so long as they are housed within a living person's body.

I think this is an "uncommonly silly law" (as Justice Stewart said of the Connecticut contraception statute). I think also that it is unconstitutional, that it deprives people with diseased gall bladders of their liberty without due process of law.

To be sure, it is bizarre for the survival of sick gall bladders to be of concern to a state legislature, or indeed to anyone (except perhaps for some medical scientists). This means that the liberty interest asserted need not weigh very much to be constitutionally vindicated. All that need be demonstrated is that it is a constitutional interest.

You may have to uphold the gall bladder statute if you deny the existence of substantive due process (that is, deny that the subject matter of state legislation can be tested under the due process clause) and if you contend that the words "due process" in the Fourteenth Amendment require only procedural regularity (that is, if you contend that the phrase "substantive due process" is an oxymoron). If this is your position, you will certainly uphold the statute unless you claim that privacy is not a part of substantive due process and that it has independent constitutional status. But even though most justices and many commentators worry about *Lochner*, they also accept the existence of substantive due process, and the continuing validity of the cases discussed at the end of the last chapter and of *Griswold* and its progeny. Accordingly, it seems a truth generally acknowledged that constitutional law recognizes the existence of a "substantive" liberty interest. This means that my silly and irrational gall bladder statute is unconstitutional.

Now contrast gall bladders to fetuses. It is entirely understandable that a state should be concerned with the survival of the unborn. There is nothing whatever irrational about it. This means that the liberty interest of the pregnant woman who wants an abortion must have sufficient weight—and, as I shall claim, weight in public morality—to overcome a state's rational, if unwise, abortion law.

But before I get to weight, I wish to examine more closely the claim of the person with the diseased gall bladder; the claim is that the statute infringes on the person's liberty. What is the nature of this liberty interest, this principle that is being asserted, and how does it relate to the principle that might support a constitutional right to an abortion?

The person claims the right to be rid of an organ that has caused acute pain and may do so again, and claims further that to be deprived of this right imposes a regimen that is highly uncongenial, and that the mental strain of a potential rupture is psychologically unsettling. The principle to which this claim is being related is one that is commonly recognized, namely that every person has a right (qualified by context) to decide what happens to his or her body.

The point to notice about this principle (and it is of course a principle that can be asserted by a woman claiming a right to an abortion) is that it has nothing to do with the destruction of the diseased gall bladder once it has been removed from the body. In the case of abortion, the principle has nothing to do with the death of a fetus once it has been removed from the womb.

Professor Judith Jarvis Thomson of the Massachusetts Institute of Technology discerned the distinction between the death of the fetus and the right to an abortion before the decision in *Roe v. Wade:*

[W]hile I am arguing for the permissibility of abortion in some cases, I am not arguing for the right to secure the death of the unborn child. It is easy to confuse these two things in

that up to a certain point in the life of the fetus it is not able
to survive outside the mother's body; hence removing it from
her body guarantees its death. But they are importantly different. . . . A woman may be utterly devastated by the
thought of a child, a bit of herself, put out for adoption and
never seen or heard of again. She may therefore want not
merely that the child be detached from her, but more, that it
die. Some opponents of abortion are inclined to regard this
as beneath contempt—thereby showing insensitivity to what
is surely a powerful source of despair. All the same, I agree
that the desire for the child's death is not one which anybody
may gratify, should it turn out to be possible to detach the
child alive.[3]

It should be observed moreover that since the principle we are
considering does not support an independent claim to "secure the
death of the unborn child," there is considerable logic in the decision
by the Court in *Roe* to fix on the onset of viability as the point at
which substantial state regulation is permissible. At that point, and
quite apart from how one counts fetal life, the woman may still
plausibly claim that she wants the fetus removed. She has no claim,
however, to a procedure that entails the destruction of the fetus if
there is a procedure available that does not destroy it. At a minimum, therefore, the state must be able to insist on the use of such
a procedure.

Society's clear interest in the well-being of a fetus that can live
apart from its mother, however, suggests that the state can do more.
Roe undertakes to prescribe what more the state can do in the "stage
subsequent to viability." It tells us that in most cases the well-being
of a viable fetus outweighs the woman's right to decide what happens
in or to her body. I shall return shortly to the significance of viability
in the context of *Webster* and Justice Sandra Day O'Connor's earlier
assault on the trimester framework of *Roe*.

Our task is now to determine whether *Roe* is right about the
weight it assigned to the principle or liberty interest of the mother,

for we have determined that if it is sufficiently weighty it could support a woman's constitutional claim to an abortion.

———

Assume for a short time the validity of the position taken by Texas in *Roe*, namely that "life begins at conception and is present throughout pregnancy." Does the acceptance of this assumption (or its rhetorically more provocative version that the "fetus [embryo, fertilized ovum] is a person from the moment of conception") necessarily conclude the abortion issue? This is the question to which Professor Thomson attends in her short and splendid article from which I have just quoted. She has a good deal to say, all of it is interesting, and some of it is important to a proper understanding of *Roe*.

Given this assumption about fetal life (which Thomson makes for the purpose of the argument even though she does not believe it), Thomson wisely declines to defend an unqualified right to abortion. Her argument, nevertheless, is heroic: some abortions, she says, are justified by resort to the principle that "the mother has a right to decide what shall happen in and to her body." Her major forensic tool is a vivid analogy:

[L]et me ask you to imagine this. You wake up in the morning and find yourself back to back in bed with an unconscious violinist. A famous unconscious violinist. He has been found to have a fatal kidney ailment, and the Society of Music Lovers has canvassed all the available medical records and found that you alone have the right blood type to help. They have therefore kidnapped you, and last night the violinist's circulatory system was plugged into yours, so that your kidneys can be used to extract poisons from his blood as well as your own. The director of the hospital now tells you, "Look, we're sorry the Society of Music Lovers did this to you—we would never have permitted it if we had known. But still, they did it, and the violinist now is plugged into you. To unplug you would be to kill him.

But never mind, it's only for nine months. By then he will have recovered from his ailment, and can safely be unplugged from you." Is it morally incumbent on you to accede to this situation? No doubt it would be very nice of you if you did, a great kindness. But do you have to accede to it?

Thomson's question is meant to be answered no, and it seems to me that no is the only answer that can be defended by an appeal to our attitudes and practices. Nor do I see how her example can be distinguished from abortion where pregnancy results from rape.

Even if one does not grant this much (and I am sure there are those who will not), some features of Thomson's position are worth noticing. First, the example of the violinist would be very different if you had to be hooked up to his circulatory system for nine minutes rather than nine months. The principle, that one is entitled to decide what happens in and to one's body, must not only be accommodated to other principles but must be flexible enough to tolerate relatively minor violations even for relatively minor reasons. Time is important and so is the nature of the violation. A compulsory vaccination is different on both counts from a compulsory pregnancy.[4]

Second, if you agreed to be hooked up to the violinist's circulatory system, your moral position would of course be dramatically changed. This may seem to diminish the claim to abortion of a woman who becomes pregnant after having consented to intercourse. But her situation is different. While observable differences do not mean that she should prevail if the fetus is assumed to be indistinguishable in any relevant way from the violinist, they do suggest—to the extent it is possible to relax the assumption equating fetal life to the life of a person such as the violinist—that consent counts for less than might have been thought.

The woman may have taken all the precautions she could. Contraception is not foolproof, and the principle of "assumption of risk" can be pushed too hard. Sexual intercourse is not voluntary in the same way that going to a baseball game or agreeing to be plugged into another person's circulatory system is voluntary. It makes sense to speak of voluntariness in contrast to rape, but confusion on this issue should be carefully avoided. To say that Betty goes to the opera voluntarily, Betty voluntarily has sexual intercourse, and Betty voluntarily eats food is not to say that in each case Betty has exercised the same degree of volition.

On the other hand, even if sexual intercourse were a matter of life and death, as eating is, the woman who became pregnant (but was not raped) is not in the position of the person who has been kidnaped in Thomson's example, for this person probably received no benefit from having been hooked up to the violinist's circulatory system.

I think not only that it is possible to relax the assumption that a fetus is like the violinist, but that the assumption is impossible to maintain. Let me call attention to an attitudinal difference that I believe is quite generally held. To save the life of the mother, we are prepared to accept the death of the fetus. Even Texas provided for this. However, suppose that the fetus is removed and placed in an incubator because it appears that it can live. Two days later it is determined that the mother will die if she does not receive a small blood transfusion. The only blood available that matches hers is that of the infant in the incubator. The infant will survive if it keeps its blood but will die if it gives its blood to its mother, who will then survive. I do not think we are now prepared to kill the infant to save the mother.

Part of the reason may be related to the fact that the principle supporting some abortions does not give the "right to secure the death of [even] the unborn child." We are prepared to accept the death of the unborn child to save the mother, but we are not prepared to accept the death of the infant in the incubator because most of us perceive that the fetus has less of a right to life than the infant does. The infant has as much of a right to life as anyone; indeed, it would not matter if its mother were the President of the United States.

To take another example, we are not apt to be surprised or to think it madness if a person favors the abortion of a badly deformed fetus and at the same time opposes infanticide. This again may be related to the limiting factor in the principle that supports abortion, but it also reflects a difference in attitude toward fetal and infant life. Surely we would be bewildered by a person who favored infanticide and opposed abortion.

————

The example of the deformed fetus purports to show that its survival counts less than the survival of a deformed infant. It does not purport to say anything about the morality of aborting such a fetus, a question to which I now turn. The claim I wish to make is that if one agrees with the main features of the argument thus far, common sense requires that abortion be permitted here.

Consider the following story: Mary and Jane are identical twins. Mary is married in the summer and goes to Europe on her honeymoon. She becomes pregnant and finds it difficult to sleep. She goes to a physician and is given thalidomide, which helps a great deal. Shortly after, evidence is published of the effects of thalidomide on the development of fetuses.

During the summer when Mary is on her honeymoon in Europe, Jane is at work in New York. While walking alone one afternoon she is assaulted and raped. A month later she discovers that she too is pregnant. The sisters seek moral counsel together.

We can explain to Jane that she would be a very nice person if she carried the fetus to term, but that it is morally permissible for her to have an abortion, even if the fetus is considered "a person from the moment of conception."

Having told this to Jane, what shall we say to Mary? I do not think we can now tell her that it is impermissible for her to have an abortion and at the same time persuade ourselves that we are being fair to her. Nor do I think we have to. We can say to Mary (1) that we do commonly draw an important moral distinction between fetal life and other kinds of human life, (2) that this distinction does not mean that fetal life may be disregarded, but that it does enable us to make other distinctions that in its absence would be morally impermissible, (3) that one such distinction, which has considerable intuitive appeal, counts the survival of a fetus that "would be born with grave physical or mental defect" less than the survival of a normal fetus, and (4) that while the chief appeal of this last distinction rests in a widely held preference for the birth of a healthy child, it also gives weight to the principle that a woman "has a right to decide what shall happen in and to her body." Support for the final point may be found in two observations. First, as a rule it is emotionally more painful for a woman knowingly to carry an unwanted defective fetus than it is for her to carry an unwanted healthy fetus. Second, when she engaged in intercourse, the risk that she would have to carry a gravely defective fetus was knowable, but (if we can argue from a conclusion) it was a risk she did not assume. For in assessing the degree of risk assumed, it is permissible to take into account the degree of volition involved in the act creating the risk in the first place. In this respect, Mary is not Jane; but neither is engaging in sexual intercourse the same as going to an opera.

I have been making arguments by taking note of commonly held attitudes and reasoning from them. This is a way of constructing public morality. It should help judges in their task of deciding how much weight to assign to a pregnant woman's liberty interest in an abortion, the weight, in the abortion context, of the principle that she has a right to decide what happens in or to her body. Put another way, for the Court and the lawyers who argue before it, reasoning from these commonly held attitudes should be an important method for interpreting the values—the public morality—that are a source of law in elaborating the term "liberty" in the Fourteenth Amendment of the Constitution.

Now, observe first that while this approach is concerned with the weight of the principle that supports a woman's claim to an abortion, it is also related to the state's interest in the potential for life. Indeed it is difficult to think about one apart from the other; there is bound to be a tragic conflict between them. The person who wants a diseased gall bladder removed runs into no such tragic conflict, for the

state has no interest in the survival of the gall bladder. The nature
of the conflict will shortly become clearer, when we investigate such
terms as "compelling state interest" and the relation of the word
"compelling" to the nature and weight of the principle that supports
the abortion claim and other claims that might be based on the same
principle.

Second, my arguments do not justify the sweep of *Roe v. Wade*.
Nor am I able to do so, although someone following the approach
I have used may be able to make more progress. I would be pleased
to see that done, for as a legislator I would certainly support the
outcome of *Roe*.

In my discussion of abortion so far, I have assumed that
the Court was not to defer at all to the legislature's decision to limit
a woman's right to an abortion. I now want to ask whether this is
appropriate. My argument has been that deference is inappropriate
in situations where the legislature is concerned with enacting a program of some sort (for example, a war on drugs or a dress code for
the armed forces) and is for whatever reason inattentive to the effect
the program will have on the constitutional interests of individuals—
inattentive, that is, to those values that must always have their
weights reassessed, and that "we hold to have more general and
permanent interest." The Connecticut statute in *Griswold* was not
the work of an inattentive legislature; but it was passed in 1879 and
was too old to be considered a reflection of public morality in 1965
on the question of contraception. While the statute could have been
repealed, that it had not been did not relieve the Court of its responsibilities. Nor is legislative inaction much of a guide to anything.
Inaction can be attributed to innumerable causes; in Connecticut it
seems most likely that the statute was not repealed because it was
not generally enforced.

Roe does not fit well either. As I have been maintaining, the
protection of fetal life is connected too closely with the woman's
rights over her body for distinctions to be drawn as easily as they

are where the legislative program is a dress code or a war on drugs. With respect to the statute under review in *Roe* we must assume that attention was paid to public morality by the legislative branch, and that its view of that morality was entitled to some respect by the Court. There is certainly room for disagreement as to how much. Many factors must be attended to: one is the question of when the legislation was passed (as in *Griswold*). The Texas statute was old— its language can be traced to 1857—but at the time of *Roe* other states had recently enacted abortion legislation, some quite restrictive, others pro-choice. A companion case to *Roe* involved a contemporary Georgia statute that was less strict than that of Texas but more restrictive than the Court's decision in *Roe*.[5] *Roe* was a decision for the nation, and to the extent that public morality can be teased out of state legislation, the legislation of all states counts. This is some evidence that in 1973 public values were more supportive of abortion than the Texas statute was.

In thinking about public morality and legislation, the history of a statute's enactment can also be important. It may show, for example, that a narrow, well-organized interest group was able to an unusual extent to work its will on legislators concerned primarily with reelection. Legislative history is often not readily accessible to a court. One way of reconstructing it, however, is to do what I have done earlier in this chapter: to take note of commonly held attitudes and reason from them. If abortion legislation departs markedly from the insights provided by this judicial analysis, the Court should discount legislative interpretation of public morality. This means that statutes like that of Texas are much too restrictive; it also means that *Roe v. Wade*, when decided in 1973, went too far.

But if one says this, isn't one failing to give weight to the legislative judgment? Doesn't the Court come out the same way it would if the legislative contribution to public morality were ignored? Perhaps, but this is a matter of degree. The Court should defer when it is in doubt, not when it has confidence in its conclusions. Such confidence suggests legislative failure, and legislatures do fail.

But isn't this the process review criticized in chapter 3? Yes and no. What I criticized in chapter 3 was the limitation of judicial review to considerations of process values. I also expressed concern about a court's ability to know what constituted a process failure without attending to substantive values. These problems are not present as such in *Roe v. Wade*.

If one thinks that on balance *Roe* was wrong when it was decided for having gone too far, this does not mean that the decision should be overruled. The Supreme Court's decision is not neutral with regard to the issues of public morality that I have addressed, and later abortion decisions have not been either. The Court has moved massively into a debate, and the terms of the debate are now different from what they were. I shall look some at this debate in the following section and in more detail later.

This much, however, should be said now. The doctrine of adhering to precedent, called stare decisis, is grounded in the principle of treating like cases alike and in important considerations of policy. Stability, in its many different aspects, is often especially important: individuals and institutions use prior decisional law in their efforts to organize the future. And the courts themselves build in related areas on their prior holdings. Thus even when an earlier decision is seen as a mistake, policies may dictate sticking to precedent.

In constitutional adjudication, where nonjudicial change can sometimes be difficult, stare decisis has less of a grip than it does where statutory interpretation or the common law is involved. Nevertheless, prior constitutional decisions are a major source of law.

Assuming that *Roe v. Wade* went too far when it was decided, the justification for modifying little or none of it is complex. The decision in *Webster* in 1989 did weaken the precedential value of *Roe*, but the future of *Roe* remains unclear, and we can expect the Court to be struggling with that future for many years, even as it has in the recent past. I shall try to explain in the next part of this book that the struggle relates to the political digestibility of *Roe*. At this point, however, I want to advance what I take to be a very strong reason why the Court should not depart very much further from *Roe* than it already has.

Before *Roe* the states were free to regulate abortion. There was considerable diversity: state law ranged from the strict Texas statute at issue in *Roe* to strongly pro-choice legislation in New York.[6] Our federal system permits great diversity. Often diversity is good, but sometimes too much of it is very bad, and the abortion area is an example. Before *Roe v. Wade*, a rich woman from Texas could get a legal abortion in New York, but a poor woman from Texas could not afford legality, and illegality too often led to tragedy.

As an original proposition, this consequence of the diversity of federalism is difficult to use as a ground for the decision in *Roe v. Wade*. In many areas of life wealth makes a huge difference, but legislation generally does not have to be especially sensitive to this difference. There are some specific exceptions. For example, an indigent defendant in a criminal case has the right to have a written transcript of the trial available on appeal. This right, which reflects the special concern of the Court with criminal procedure, rests on equal protection: the indigent defendant has the right to a transcript because the wealthy defendant can pay for one.[7] But wealth is not a so-called suspect classification under the equal protection clause of the Fourteenth Amendment; and since it is not, the Constitution offers little protection to the poor.[8]

If *Roe v. Wade* were to be totally discarded, the constitutionally unbounded regulation of abortion would be returned to the states. It is difficult to predict the consequences of such an event: *Webster* galvanized the pro-choice forces, which in turn fomented chaos among pro-life politicians before stiffening the resolve of some of them. But it does seem likely that substantial legal diversity would result if *Roe* were overturned. Indeed, by March 1990 the territory of Guam and the legislature of Idaho had passed extremely restrictive abortion statutes. (The Idaho statute, however, was vetoed by the governor and did not become law. And the Louisiana legislature followed suit that summer.)

If diversity of state abortion laws were constitutionally permitted, it would have a disproportionate adverse impact on poor women, and this alone supports stare decisis. The doctrine of stare decisis rests heavily on policy considerations, on the consequences of departing from precedent and establishing a new regime. Those consequentialist concerns may not have much affirmative force in the fashioning of new rules where previously the Constitution was not thought to apply, but along with the principle of deciding like cases alike, these concerns are the foundation on which stare decisis rests.

Consider this from a related but slightly different perspective. Ideally an institution engaged in regulating—in ordering the future wisely—should look at all the consequences of its actions. When the Court regulates through judicial review it sometimes cannot do this, because it lacks the authority to test legislative action by certain criteria. But when it is examining its own precedents, there is no such lack. Indeed, stare decisis places the Court under an obligation to act as wisely as possible, to consider all the consequences of overruling its own interpretation of the Constitution. This requires that judicial attention be paid to the disproportionate impact that overturning *Roe* would have in some of the nation's fifty states and its several territories on poor women—namely, the probable increase in deaths caused by back-alley abortions.

Since 1973 the Supreme Court has had many occasions to pass on the constitutionality of legislation aimed at regulating abortion. Until *Webster* in 1989 the Court had been protective of a woman's right of choice, apart from the question of public financing (funds may be provided for delivering babies but withheld for terminating pregnancies).[9] I think it is fair to say that *Webster* extended the ability of states to withhold public financing, by sustaining a Missouri law that prohibited public employees from assisting in an abortion and public facilities from being used for an abortion, except where necessary to save the life of a pregnant woman.

After *Roe* and before *Webster*, the Court had generally invalidated regulations purportedly justified by concern for the woman's health or her need to know about abortion procedures and fetal development, as well as regulations requiring the consent of the woman's male partner.[10] *Webster* did not change this. But when one considers together the plurality opinion in *Webster* written by Chief Justice Rehnquist and joined by Justices Byron White and Anthony M. Kennedy, the opinion by Justice Antonin Scalia calling for the flat overruling of *Roe*, and opinions in earlier cases written by Justice O'Connor, it becomes clear that abortion law is unstable.[11] After 1973 state regulation of abortion had to be consistent with the trimester framework established by *Roe*. One way or another Justices Rehnquist, White, Kennedy, Scalia, and O'Connor have rejected that framework. And without it, precedents are at risk.

The risk is especially great if the state's interest in potential human life is considered "compelling" throughout pregnancy. For this is another way of saying that the woman's right is less of a shield against restrictive state regulation than the Court in *Roe* said it was. Recall that in *Roe* the Court held that this state interest became compelling at viability.

The plurality opinion in *Webster*, while specifically rejecting the trimester framework of *Roe*, did not specifically describe the quality of the State's interest. It specifically omitted a statement that the interest in potential human life is compelling throughout pregnancy. But this is probably because the opinion called the woman's right simply a "liberty interest" and declined to describe it as "fundamental." "Fundamental" is the word used by the Court in *Roe*. By definition, a fundamental right has weight; to overcome it, it would seem that a state must show that its interest in regulation is very substantial indeed. It is not clear in the abortion context what a state must show to overcome a woman's "liberty interest." But it is clear that that interest has greater weight in public morality today than it did before *Roe v. Wade*, and that at least part of the reason for this is the *Roe* decision itself.

At any rate, *Webster* itself was no great surprise. First of all, numerous efforts have been made to overturn *Roe* on the nonjudicial front. These have ranged from the proposing of constitutional

amendments to the bombing of abortion clinics. The political process
has been actively engaged. In part IV, I shall explore this engagement
and its relation to the development of constitutional law. If one puts
to one side the flag-burning issue, which is special in that it is isolated
and contained, it seems fair to say that in the latter half of the
twentieth century only the school desegregation case *Brown v. Board
of Education*[12] has had larger public repercussions than *Roe*. Perhaps the school prayer decisions come closest to it in their impact.[13]

In the second place, since 1973 the justices on the Court who
accounted for the majority in *Roe* have diminished in number, and
two of those who dissented—White and Rehnquist—have remained.
Accordingly, well before *Webster* the decision's future was in considerable doubt. The Solicitor General, the chief government advocate before the Court, asked for the reversal of *Roe*, and its
framework was sharply questioned by Justice O'Connor, who was
not a member of the Court in 1973. She wrote a separate, and
carefully restricted, opinion in *Webster* because she thought the
Missouri statute was constitutional under *Roe* and the abortion
funding cases. Here, from a dissenting opinion, is some of what she
said earlier about *Roe* and the state's interest in the survival of the
fetus:

> In *Roe,* the Court held that although the State had an important
> and legitimate interest in protecting potential life, that interest
> could not become compelling until the point at which the fetus
> was viable. The difficulty with this analysis is clear: *potential*
> life is no less potential in the first weeks of pregnancy than it
> is at viability or afterwards. At any stage in pregnancy there is
> the *potential* for human life. Although the Court refused to
> "resolve the difficult question of when life begins," . . . the
> Court chose the point of viability—when the fetus is *capable*
> of life independent of its mother—to permit the complete pro-
> scription of abortion. The choice of viability as the point at
> which the state interest in *potential* life becomes compelling is
> no less arbitrary than choosing any point before viability or

any point afterward. Accordingly, I believe that the State's interest in protecting potential human life exists throughout the
pregnancy.[14]

Justice O'Connor's last sentence may be correct, but it does not
mean that the Court was wrong in *Roe* when it held that the beginning of viability is the point at which the state's interest becomes
compelling. First, do we not generally feel sorrier when a woman
miscarries late in her pregnancy than we do when she miscarries
early on? And does not the woman feel a greater loss? While both
of these feelings are complex—they have to do with the burden of
pregnancy and the shattered expectation of birth—one element is
the increasing value that we attach to the life of the organism in the
womb between conception and delivery. I say "we." I know that
some of us do not have feelings related to time: eight minutes or
eight months is the same. But few if any public values are held by
everyone, and the distinction I am urging does seem widely shared.
That we use different terms to describe the organism in the womb—
zygote, embryo, fetus—tells us something about time and the value
we place on the organism's survival. This relation between time and
value probably will deepen when American women are able to obtain
and use RU-486 (the French abortion pill that induces a miscarriage
early in a pregnancy). Public practices tend to support public values
and vice versa.

   This suggests that because we are concerned with public values,
it is reasonable to see a connection between the duration of a pregnancy and the degree of the state's interest in preserving the life of
the organism in the womb. It does not in itself suggest that the
moment when the fetus becomes viable is the salient point at which
the state should constitutionally be allowed to prohibit abortion.
But there is a second reason for thinking that in *Roe* the Court was
correct in assigning the importance it did to viability.

   The principle that supports a woman's right to an abortion must
itself influence judgment about what constitutes a sufficient state
interest to defeat the woman's right. Put more generally, the concept

of a compelling state interest is related to the nature of the right it trumps. Justice O'Connor, however, seems to think otherwise. It would appear that she sees the state interest and the woman's right as discrete. This might be analytically clean, but it is substantively wrong.

If the woman's right to an abortion included the right to demand the death of the fetus, viability would be irrelevant. It would, as Justice O'Connor insists, be a totally arbitrary point within the nine months of a pregnancy. But the woman has no such right: the death of a fetus from abortion is a consequence of the woman's having exercised a right based on and coextensive with the principle that she may decide what happens in or to her body. Thus, while it is not inescapably true that the state should be prevented from regulating before viability, it is inescapably true that viability is relevant in considering the extent of state power over the abortion decision.

––––––––

The relation of viability to a woman's right to an abortion was not substantially clarified in either the Chief Justice's or Justice O'Connor's opinion in *Webster*. Missouri imposes certain testing requirements before an abortion may be performed past the twentieth week of pregnancy. The object of the tests is to determine whether a fetus is viable. Viability is rarely possible before twenty-four weeks, but it is possible to misjudge the length of a pregnancy's term by four weeks. Justice O'Connor thought that this provision and the other provisions of the Missouri statute properly before the Court were consistent with *Roe*. This meant that the state's interest in potential life was, under *Roe*, "compelling" at the time that viability testing was required.

The Chief Justice agreed, but thought that the testing requirements were inconsistent with some of the language used by the Court to strike down state abortion laws enacted after *Roe*. This led him to reject the trimester framework. But he said little about the nature of the state's interest in potential life before viability. He did say, "[W]e do not see why the State's interest in protecting potential human life should come into existence only at the point of viability [*Roe* did not say it did], and there should therefore be a rigid line allowing state regulation after viability but prohibiting it before viability." He also said that the "Missouri testing requirement . . . is reasonably designed to ensure that abortions are not performed where the fetus is viable—an end which all concede is legitimate— and that is sufficient to sustain its constitutionality." The Chief Justice also cited Justices White and O'Connor, both of whom had said in dissenting opinions in earlier cases that the state has a compelling interest in protecting potential human life throughout pregnancy.[15]

How can a pregnant woman have any right to an abortion if the state has a compelling interest in protecting the fetus throughout pregnancy? Well, perhaps the woman's right is greater. Justice O'Connor, who continues to describe that right as "fundamental," said this: "[J]udicial scrutiny of state regulation of abortion should be limited to whether the state law bears a rational relationship to legitimate purposes such as advance of these compelling interests [health and potential life], with heightened scrutiny [that is, more than a rational or reasonable relationship between regulatory ends and means] reserved for instances in which the State has imposed an 'undue burden' on the abortion decision. . . . An undue burden will generally be found 'in situations involving absolute obstacles or severe limitations on the abortion decision,' not whether a State regulation 'may inhibit abortions to some degree.' And if a state law does interfere with the abortion decision to an extent that is unduly burdensome . . . the possibility remains that the statute will withstand the stricter scrutiny."[16]

Should Justice O'Connor's approach become law and pro-choice political efforts in the states fail to maintain or produce liberal abortion statutes, we can look forward to years of "litigating elucidation." But given the principle that supports a woman's right to an abortion, can it be that the viability of the fetus is unrelated to what constitutes an "undue burden" on the abortion decision? The first quotation that we read from a dissent by O'Connor suggests that that was the Justice's position, and if that is so it was wrong. But perhaps subsequent exposure to the abortion issue through the process of constitutional litigation has changed her mind.

———

Justice White dissented in *Roe v. Wade*. In 1986 he wrote a major dissent in a case invalidating a Pennsylvania law purporting to regulate abortion within the guidelines established by *Roe*. This was the first case in which the Court had been asked to reconsider *Roe* by the Solicitor General.[17]

One provision of the Pennsylvania law that was struck down "was designed to ensure that a woman's choice of an abortion is fully informed . . . ." In the course of disagreeing with the majority, Justice White quoted with approval the decision by a court of appeals to the effect that the "root premise is the concept, fundamental in American jurisprudence, that '[e]very human being of adult years and sound mind has a right to determine what shall be done with his own body.'" This is of course one way to articulate the principle vindicated by *Roe*. Yet in another portion of his dissent Justice White stated: "The governmental interest at issue is in protecting those who will be citizens if their lives are not ended in the womb. The substantiality of this interest is in no way dependent on the probability that the fetus may be capable of surviving outside the womb at any given point in its development, as the possibility of fetal survival is contingent on the state of medical practice and technology, factors that are in essence morally and constitutionally irrelevant."

Justice White is wrong about medical practice and technology. Viability before twenty-three or twenty-four weeks does not seem to be in the medical or technological cards.[18] He also seems, along with Justice O'Connor, to have forgotten the nature of the principle at stake in *Roe v. Wade* and the way in which the principle and the state interest in potential human life are bound together.

This forgetfulness—if that is what it was—was not especially important in the Pennsylvania abortion case. But Justice White clearly was forgetful, either for the first time or again, in the case of *Bowers v. Hardwick,*[19] in which he wrote for the Court. The case involved the constitutionality of Georgia's sodomy statute (Bowers was the state's attorney general); the Court held for the state by a vote of five to four.

The Georgia statute made sodomy a criminal offense, punishable by imprisonment of one to twenty years. And it defined the crime: "A person commits . . . sodomy when he performs or submits to any sexual act involving the sex organs of one person and the mouth or anus of another." To paraphrase and quote the Court, Hardwick was charged with violating this statute by committing sodomy in the bedroom of his home with another adult male. After the state decided not to prosecute, Hardwick brought a suit in federal court challenging the constitutionality of the Georgia statute. "He asserted that he was a practicing homosexual" and that the statute "placed him in imminent danger of arrest."

Over a sharp objection by the dissenting justices, the Court purported to limit the issue before it: "The only claim properly before the Court . . . is Hardwick's challenge to the Georgia statute as applied to consensual homosexual sodomy. . . . We express no opinion on the constitutionality of the Georgia statute as applied to other acts of sodomy."

I shall address the procedural aspects of this case shortly. It is clear, and should be remarked now, that the issue before the Court would have been less sensitive if the constitutionality of the statute as applied to a married couple had been the issue before it. Moreover, the case would almost surely have come out the other way given the language of the opinion in *Griswold v. Connecticut.* Georgia in fact acknowledged that the statute would have been unconstitutional if applied to a married couple.

But is the principle that supports Hardwick's claim, which is an application of the "liberty interest" that supports a woman's claim to an abortion, basically different from the claim of a married couple? Such a couple would have the additional argument drawn from the specific application of the principle in *Griswold*. Did Hardwick need that additional argument?

The Court stated—misstated, I believe—the principle at stake in *Roe v. Wade:* "The Due Process Clause of the Fourteenth Amendment . . . confer[s] a fundamental individual right to decide whether or not to beget or bear a child." This formulation foreclosed Hardwick's claim; indeed it would greatly dim the chances of a married couple. The Court did not take responsibility for this description of the principle set forth in *Roe*. It relied on a prior decision.

In *Carey v. Population Services International* (1976) a New York statute regulating the sale and advertising of contraceptives was held unconstitutional.[20] In the course of the opinion the Court did describe the principle established in *Roe v. Wade* in words similar to those quoted above. But in the context of *Carey* this should be read as a limited formulation of a larger principle, a formulation sufficient to resolve the case then before the Court.

The "right to decide whether or not to beget or bear a child" rests on the more general, qualified right of a woman to decide what happens in or to her body. This more general right, or principle, is the basis of Hardwick's claim. To defeat this claim by describing the principle in terms of a set of applications that have already been decided is not to be true to the process of adjudication. It is to fail to treat like cases alike. And the cases—*Roe v. Wade* and *Bowers v. Hardwick*—are alike to the extent that they rest on the same principle, as they should be seen to do.

But the principle may weigh differently in the two cases. I have argued that public morality is an appropriate source of law for a court in elaborating "liberty" in the due process clause of the Fourteenth Amendment. If *Bowers v. Hardwick* had been before the Court prior to its decision in *Griswold*, Hardwick could not have succeeded. It is indeed far from clear that he could have made out his case when he brought it by an appeal to public morality if he had been forced to limit judicial consideration to the rights of homosexuals. This was the Court's approach. It was the wrong approach, for here too the Court was not true to the process of adjudication.

Start instead with a married couple. *Griswold* controls. The public values that support that decision were strengthened by it. We can find a good deal of evidence for this in the hearings on the confirmation of Robert H. Bork for a seat on the Supreme Court. President Reagan nominated Bork to fill the vacancy created when Justice Lewis F. Powell, Jr., retired in 1987. The Senate turned Bork down, at least in part because he had publicly disagreed with the result in *Griswold*. Indeed the hearings suggest strong political approval of the principle advanced in *Griswold*, if not the weight of the principle.

Griswold involved only a state ban on the use of contraceptive devices by a married couple. Subsequent decisions, including *Carey*, invalidated state regulation of the sale of contraceptives to single persons. This evolving law reflected changing social attitudes toward sexual behavior, and perhaps influenced them. It seems reasonable to think that the evolution from *Griswold* to *Carey* would be repeated if a sodomy statute were held unconstitutional when applied to a married couple. Its application to an unmarried, heterosexual couple would probably be held unconstitutional. I say "probably" because I think the ruling would hinge at least in part on how much weight the Court gave to the many legislative judgments that sodomy is immoral, and, on the other side of the balance, to the lax enforcement of these statutes where the "crime" is performed in private.

This last point needs to be considered against the background of another case, *Stanley v. Georgia* (1969), "where the Court held that the First Amendment prevents conviction for possessing and reading obscene material in the privacy of [the] home."[21] For if liberty of expression has greater protection in one's home, why not other forms of liberty? Surely the answer, if there is one, can not turn on the text of the First Amendment, for it makes no distinction between activities performed in public and those performed in private.

At any rate, I suspect that the Court too was unsure about the constitutionality of the statute as applied to an unmarried heterosexual couple. This suggests that it should never have heard the case.

It did not have to: the case came from a court of appeals to the justices on a petition for certiorari (a formal request, made by the party who lost in the lower court, for review), and the Court did not have to grant the petition. (It generally takes four justices to grant certiorari, and it is done or not without oral argument). Nor did the Court have to explain itself if it denied the petition. Today almost all the Supreme Court's appellate jurisdiction is on petition for certiorari. It is almost all a discretionary jurisdiction. This means that on most occasions the justices decide what to decide, and, so long as there is a case, when to decide it. When the central constitutional issue rests on the interpretation of public values, judicial ambivalence counsels judicial restraint. And judicial restraint is best achieved by deciding not to decide. But the Court took the case, and once it had taken it the process of adjudication required that all the substantive issues I have adumbrated needed to be thought through before the weight of the principle that a person has the right to decide what happens in and to her or his body could properly be determined in the context of homosexual sodomy. This is part of the obligation of treating like cases alike. For if the conclusion were that heterosexual sodomy performed in private between unmarried consenting adults could not be criminalized, it would be difficult to make sodomy a crime for homosexuals. Indeed, it would be possible only if the Court determined that it was permissible under the equal protection clause for a legislature to draw distinctions in a criminal statute that turned on nothing but raw prejudice. For while AIDS is more prevalent among male homosexuals than among heterosexuals, surely there are less drastic ways to prevent its spread than by criminalizing for one group what is (hypothetically) legal for the other group.

Thinking through these issues is the central point of what Professor Wechsler referred to in his Holmes Lecture, perhaps unfortunately, as neutral principles (see chapter 2). As I see it, it is an aspect of the process of adjudication, a process that includes interpreting many sources of law, including public morality, as they come to bear on the meaning of constitutional text.

I have tried to do some interpreting of public morality at a substantive level, first with *Griswold* and then with abortion. And I have tried to undertake this interpretive enterprise while taking account of the unique environment that is the province of appellate adjudication.

CHAPTER SEVEN

Judicial Mistake

The common-law method of constitutional adjudication that we have been examining better explains the Supreme Court's role in American government than either originalism or Justice Stone's footnote in *Carolene Products* does. Normatively it has the advantage of building change into law, change that takes into account contemporary substantive values as well as participational values.

An additional strength of the common-law method is its experiential familiarity: it is how courts generally adjudicate (or, more accurately, it is related to how they adjudicate). And as a method, it has some of the controls that exist in statutory interpretation, where the joint enterprise of ordering the future wisely is a cooperative undertaking between legislature and court. In constitutional adjudication, at least in those areas where public morality is the major source of law, judicial deference to the legislature serves a similar function where deference is due. But the relative finality of the Supreme Court's constitutional holdings, as contrasted with statutory holdings, raises the stakes. What is the constitutional substitute for legislative statutory revision? In thinking about this, recall that statutory revision, where it is possible, is itself problematic because legislatures are too busy to give regular review to decisional law and because it may be difficult to overturn statutory interpretation even when it is contrary to legislative purpose. This is often so where decisional law generates widespread public support.

One substitute for legislative revision is of course formal constitutional amendment. Under Article V of the Constitution (which also provides for the calling of a convention) two-thirds of both Houses of Congress may propose amendments to the Constitution. But the process is extraordinarily difficult: for an amendment to be adopted, three-fourths of the states must give their consent as well.

The Constitution has been amended only four times to overturn a Supreme Court decision. The Eleventh Amendment was adopted in response to the Court's holding in *Chisholm v. Georgia* that a state could be sued in federal court by a plaintiff from a different state.[1]

Constitutional amendments (and the Civil War) reversed the Supreme Court's *Dred Scott* decision, which upset the Missouri Compromise by ruling in effect that blacks were not citizens protected by the Constitution.[2] The Thirteenth Amendment ended slavery as an institution, and subsequent amendments guaranteed particular rights for blacks. But as we all know, the implementation of these rights has been and remains an exceedingly slow process.

The Sixteenth Amendment was adopted to change the results of *Pollock v. Farmer's Loan and Trust Co.*, in which a federal income tax was struck down.[3]

The Twenty-sixth Amendment overturned the Court's ruling in *Oregon v. Mitchell* that a federal law lowering the minimum voting age in state elections to eighteen was unconstitutional.[4]

It should be added that some proposed amendments have been of a structural sort: these have been aimed at affecting Court decisions indirectly by placing curbs on the Court rather than by attempting to overturn specific decisions. They have included unsuccessful efforts to subject the Court's decisions to another governmental tribunal, to require more than a majority of justices to strike down a law, to submit the Court's decisions to popular referenda, and to allow Congress to reenact laws held unconstitutional by the Court.

Given that only four Supreme Court decisions have been reversed by constitutional amendment even though there have been many unpopular decisions, it would seem that Article V is not an effective means of changing unpopular Court decisions. Success in its use requires that an extraordinary combination of social, economic, and political forces combine to achieve super majorities in multiple forums. Indeed, efforts to overturn especially controversial decisions are the least likely to clear the hurdles of Article V. But Professor Bruce Ackerman, in a number of lucid and provocative articles, has urged his readers to think of a political event that transforms the nation—the New Deal, for example—as the equivalent of a constitutional amendment authorized by "We the People," as he puts it.[5] Under this view, which Ackerman constructs from a close reading of American political history, there are additional methods available for amending the Constitution. Accordingly, the "constitutional amendment" plays a more important role in checking judicial power—as well as in explaining the exercise of judicial power—than is normally ascribed to it.

Judicial power is itself lodged in Article III, which after setting forth the Supreme Court's original jurisdiction, authorizes a grant of appellate jurisdiction as to law and fact, "with such Exceptions and under such Regulations as the Congress shall make." Students of Article III disagree about the extent to which this "exceptions clause" permits "jurisdiction stripping." But Congress does have substantial power to take jurisdiction away from the Court. It is however a power that has been exercised sparingly.

Congress had success with the exceptions clause in 1869, when it undertook to limit the Court's application of a reconstruction statute. In *Ex parte McCardle*, a southern newspaper editor held in military custody appealed from a denial of habeas corpus by challenging the constitutionality of the Military Reconstruction Act. Oral argument was heard before the Supreme Court, and Congress, fearing a threat to its reconstruction program, enacted a law repealing an earlier statute that had granted the Court jurisdiction to review circuit court denials of habeas corpus petitions. The Court promptly dismissed the editor's appeal, reasoning that "jurisdiction is the power to declare the law, and when it ceases to exist, the only function remaining to the courts is that of announcing the fact and dismissing the cause."[6]

While proposals to strip the Court of its jurisdiction have recently been introduced as legislation in a number of areas—school prayer cases, reapportionment, and abortion are examples—all have failed in Congress. In any event jurisdiction stripping does not eliminate the constitutional decision deemed offensive by the strippers. Earlier Supreme Court decisions remain authoritative to the extent that Supreme Court decisions are authoritative. Stripping removes the power of the Supreme Court to review decisions of lower courts. This means that the Court is denied the authority to police decisional conformity with its prior holdings.

Congressional restraint means that judicial review of the scope of the exceptions clause has been limited. Historically, congressional control of the Supreme Court's appellate jurisdiction has been little more than a political threat. But it is widely recognized that Congress does have broad control over lower federal courts. While there is disagreement about how extensive its power is, we do know that among other things Congress can restrict the remedies a court may impose, at least in some situations. For example, federal courts have limited authority to issue injunctions in labor disputes, and to some extent Congress can specify the court in which a case may be heard. Sometimes this power can sharply reduce the impact of a constitutional decision. Thus the bar on labor injunctions enacted in 1932 mitigated the effect on organized labor of Court rulings from the time of *Lochner* that protective labor legislation was unconstitutional.[7]

These formal controls, and others, such as control over the judiciary's budget, including control over judges' salary increases, would, if used, affect the development of law in different and perhaps unpredictable ways. According to one's view of adjudication, some of these controls are plainly wrongheaded ways to cabin the judiciary. Here there is room for substantial disagreement. It is clear, however, that in practice the controls are not comparable to the legislative power of statutory revision. Therefore if one is concerned about controlling the judiciary—and at one time or another most organized interest groups are—the search must be elsewhere. Please remember that the issue is not only democracy, at least not as it is practiced in the United States; it is finality.

Let me then make this claim: the substitutes in constitutional adjudication for statutory revision are separation of powers (in a nontechnical sense) and the American people (in perhaps more than a metaphorical sense). To unpack this claim it may be helpful to start with a bicentennial political document.

In a lecture delivered in the fall of 1986 at Tulane University, Edwin Meese III, then the attorney general of the United States, drew a sharp distinction between the Constitution and constitutional law. He quoted the legal historian Charles Warren to the effect that "however the Court may interpret the provisions of the Constitution, it is still the Constitution which is the law, not the decisions of the Court." Meese continued: "By this, of course, Charles Warren did not mean that a constitutional decision by the Supreme Court lacks the character of law. Obviously it does have binding quality: It binds the parties in a case and also the executive branch for whatever enforcement is necessary. But such a decision does not establish a 'supreme law of the land' that is binding on all persons and parts of government, henceforth and forevermore."[8]

"Henceforth and forevermore" is a long time. But how about until the Court overrules itself or there is that extraordinary constitutional amendment overruling the Court? This is not Meese's vision of the role of the judiciary in American government. It is, however, the Court's view—or at least it has so advised the nation. In a dictum in the desegregation case *Cooper v. Aaron* (1958), the Court made it clear to state officials in Arkansas who were resisting the integration of a high school in Little Rock that they were bound by a prior Supreme Court decision, by constitutional law (namely the holding in *Brown v. Board of Education*), and not by the officials' different interpretation of the Constitution. Put another and by now familiar way, *Brown* did not merely resolve a dispute; it regulated the future of those who were not parties in the adjudication.

The Court stated it this way:

> [W]e should answer the premise of the actions of the Governor and Legislature that they are not bound by our holding in the Brown case. It is necessary only to recall some basic constitutional propositions which are settled doctrine. Article VI of the Constitution makes the Constitution the "supreme Law of the Land." In 1803, Chief Justice Marshall, speaking for a unanimous Court, referring to the Constitution as "the fundamental and paramount law of the nation," declared in the notable case of Marbury v. Madison . . . , that "It is emphatically the province and duty of the judicial department to say what the law is." This decision declared the basic principle that the federal judiciary is supreme in the exposition of the law of the Constitution, and that principle has ever since been respected by this Court and the Country as a permanent and indispensable feature of our constitutional system. It follows that the interpretation of the Fourteenth Amendment enunciated by this Court in the Brown case is the supreme law of the land, and Art. VI of the Constitution makes it of binding effect on the States "any Thing in the Constitution or Laws of any State to the Contrary notwithstanding." Every state legislator and executive and judicial officer is solemnly committed by oath taken pursuant to Art. VI, Para. 3, "to support this Constitution."[9]

As Professor Gerald Gunther of Stanford University has pointed out, it is not clear that *Cooper v. Aaron* is merely following *Marbury v. Madison*, as the Court seems to imply. *Cooper* insists on "judicial exclusiveness" in constitutional interpretation, *Marbury* only on "judicial authority to interpret the Constitution."[10] This distinction is of course extraordinarily important. In one way or another, many presidents have accepted judicial authority and rejected judicial exclusiveness. None did it with a clearer understanding of the structure of adjudication and the American system than Abraham Lincoln. He separated the resolution of disputes (once done, surely exclusive) from regulation, a powerful and potentially final method of ordering the future when large constitutional issues are at stake. And with respect to such regulation, he rejected judicial exclusiveness. Here is what Lincoln said on this matter in his First Inaugural Address, on March 4, 1861:

> I do not forget the position assumed by some that constitutional questions are to be decided by the Supreme Court, nor do I deny that such decisions must be binding in any case upon the parties to a suit as to the object of that suit, while they are also entitled to very high respect and consideration in all parallel cases by all other departments of the Government. And while it is obviously possible that such decision may be erroneous in any given case, still the evil effect following it, being limited to that particular case, with the chance that it may be overruled and never become a precedent for other cases, can better be borne than could the evils of a different practice. At the same time, the candid citizen must confess that if the policy of the Government upon vital questions affecting the whole people is to be irrevocably fixed by decisions of the Supreme Court, the instant they are made in ordinary litigation between parties in personal actions, the people will have ceased to be their own rulers, having to that extent practically resigned their Government into the hands of that eminent tribunal.

Meese is no Lincoln, and he doesn't get it quite right when he insists that "the necessary distinction [is] between the Constitution and constitutional law." While this distinction is an acceptable shorthand if it is not taken too seriously, there is every reason to assume that Meese was very serious indeed. The former attorney general is an adherent of originalism, and true belief in the separation between the Constitution and constitutional law is consistent with at least some versions of that flawed doctrine. But separation cannot be rigorously maintained. The Constitution is a two-hundred-year-old text that has been interpreted and reinterpreted by people in numerous roles: critics, advisors, and participants in institutional decisionmaking. Try as one might, one cannot recover the pristine or preinterpreted Constitution. It exists only as parchment.

But what are we to say about the authoritativeness of the Supreme Court's constitutional interpretations? Should we side with the Court's dictum in *Cooper v. Aaron* or with Abraham Lincoln? And should it matter that the Court was defending its antisegregation decision while Lincoln articulated his position as part of an attack on the Court's holding in favor of slavery in *Dred Scott?* These questions raise large issues requiring a framework for discussion. One framework is suggested by the process of constitutional adjudication as we have observed it (lawyers arguing to win, judges negotiating to achieve a majority decision) and from the sources of law used by the participants in that process—for example history, precedent, and public morality. The disagreement that exists over the persuasiveness of the decisions rendered by the Supreme Court, coupled with the impossibility in many situations of effecting legislative revision, makes it appropriate sometimes for the Court itself to change its prior rulings. And as Lincoln seems to have suggested, sometimes it is also appropriate for others to work for judicial revision. A major first question then—a question that I examined glancingly in the last chapter—is when. Put this question a little bit differently: how should the Court get information to decide whether it should overrule its prior decision, and what kind of information does it need? One thing the Court might like to know initially is whether its prior decision was, to use Lincoln's word, "erroneous." So let's begin by trying to develop a conception of judicial mistake.

I am interested in two types of judicial mistake. Each is related to a type of justification that a court might offer for a decision. And it is this relationship that connects the topic of judicial mistake with that of the sources of law. Courts—at least appellate courts—generally believe themselves obligated to justify their holdings. There are many standard modes of justification: an appeal to a legislative command, to a judicial precedent, to history, to an analogous development in another jurisdiction or in a related area of law. Moreover, the consequences that will attend a decision can serve as its justification; so can an appeal to public values.

My interest is with these latter two types of justification. The first, or consequentialist, justification, explicitly looks to the future. The claim is that the holding and others that follow it will change the behavior of individuals or institutions. The line of decision serves a policy, it effectuates a societal goal; the justification is in terms of benefits and costs.

The second type of justification in a sense looks to the past. It is not couched in what will be or in a goal toward which we are moving. The holding has persuasiveness because it vindicates public values by articulating a principle connected to these values; the justification is made in terms of rights and obligations.

I am not saying that a decision justified by an appeal to public values does not have significant consequences. It does. *Roe v. Wade* is clear proof of this. And as I suggested in chapter 6, some of these consequences constitute an important reason for not overruling *Roe* even if a majority of the Court now believes that *Roe* was to at least some extent a mistake (as *Webster* suggests they do believe). Nor am I contradicting my frequently made claim that regulation, as contrasted with the resolution of disputes, is almost always the principal reason for constitutional adjudication in the Supreme Court. But there is more than one way to justify a piece of regulation, and my point is that in this class of cases the Court has not undertaken to justify the initial decision by the consequences that will flow from that decision.

An analogy may help. Assume a statute so clear that for a given set of facts we can get away with saying that there are no questions of interpretation. When a court applies the statute, it will rest its opinion on the plain meaning of the statute and the authority of the legislature to enact it. That authority and the statute's plain meaning are the justification for a decision that has consequences; the consequences, however, are not the justification for the decision. In *Roe* public values are the source of the Court's authority. They are the source of law used to elaborate "liberty" in the due process clause. They serve as the justification for the decision. That decision has had enormous consequences for American society in general and women in particular.

The two types of justification I am interested in are hard to discover in pure form. Courts understandably tend to mix them together. Still, one justification or the other may dominate a decision. And in trying to understand judicial mistake, it behooves us to try to draw the distinction.

Consider the following examples. First policy. The decision in *New York Times v. Sullivan* is justified in consequentialist terms.[11] The case held that absent actual malice, the First Amendment, incorporated into the Fourteenth Amendment and thereby applied to the states, bars them from awarding damages to public officials for false and defamatory statements relating to their official conduct. At its most abstract, the goal to be fostered through this holding is the sound working of American democracy; somewhat less abstractly, the goal is "a commitment . . . that debate on public issues should be uninhibited, robust, and wide-open." The Court's justification took this form: without the holding, "critics of official conduct may be deterred from voicing their criticism, even though it is believed to be true and even though it is in fact true because of doubt whether it can be proved in court or fear of having to do so." The common law of defamation, the Court reasoned, "dampens the vigor and limits the variety of public debate." In short, the decision was justified by predictable consequences that serve a desirable goal.

Contrast this with the dissent in *Olmstead v. United States* (1928) of Justice Louis D. Brandeis, a member of the Court from 1916 to 1939. At issue in that famous case was whether wiretapping by federal officers constituted an unreasonable search and seizure under the Fourth Amendment. Listen to Brandeis:

> The makers of our Constitution undertook to secure conditions favorable to the pursuit of happiness. They recognized the significance of man's spiritual nature, of his feelings and of his intellect. They knew that only a part of the pain, pleasure and satisfactions of life are to be found in material things. They sought to protect Americans in their beliefs, their thoughts, their emotions and their sensations. They conferred, as against the government, the right to be let alone—the most comprehensive of rights and the right most valued by civilized men. To protect that right, every unjustifiable intrusion by the government upon the privacy of the individual, whatever the means employed, must be deemed a violation of the fourth Amendment.[12]

Now of course, if Brandeis is "doing" history he sounds like an originalist. He is attributing a great deal to the "makers of our Constitution," given that he is concerned with a contemporary technology in a strange world. But he is not performing as a historian in any conventional sense. His is a quest for the wellsprings of our public morality.

I know one might argue that the holding urged by Brandeis in *Olmstead* is justified by him in much the same way the *Sullivan* rule is justified: in consequentialist or policy terms. But to follow this line of reasoning would be mistaken. It would show either an insensitivity to linguistic nuance or a determination to conflate concepts that it is useful although difficult to keep separate. In *Sullivan* the justification for a decision protecting expression is the timid behavior of critics of the government who are faced with the common law of defamation. In *Olmstead* Brandeis is not concerned directly or principally with the behavior of government officials who authorize wiretapping; his concern is with the individual's right to be let alone. The decision that he would have had the Court adopt did not depend for its validity on the subsequent conduct of the officials; less wiretapping was desirable, but the justification for the proposed decision was individual privacy. That right was what Brandeis wished the Court to vindicate. In contrast, *Sullivan* rests on a prediction about how potential critics of government will conduct themselves when they are released from the fear of litigation: an increase in "the vigor and variety of public debate" not only is desirable, it is the justification for the rule. The right of the individual to speak—to exercise autonomy—is a welcome side effect.

This distinction between two types of justification for constitutional decisions suggests in turn a distinction between two types of judicial mistake. If it became clear that *New York Times v. Sullivan* did not have the consequences the Court predicted, that the behavior of potential critics of government did not change, and that "the vigor and variety of public debate" had not been altered by the decision, then *New York Times v. Sullivan* would be either a constitutional mistake or at least a decision in quest of a new justification.

The distinguished jurist Benjamin N. Cardozo, who served on the Supreme Court from 1932 to 1938 after a long career on the New York Court of Appeals, spoke in a different context about common-law cases: "Those that cannot prove their worth and strength by the test of experience, are sacrificed mercilessly and thrown into the void."[13]

I would not think this was proper if there were independent reasons for sticking to precedent, and there is good reason to believe that Cardozo did not think so either. But put that to one side for now and assume, in a particular case, that the policies that explain stare decisis are insufficient to support an adherence to precedent. How should we interpret Cardozo's "test of experience"? What does it mean? The answer, I suppose, lies in social science investigation: empirical research based on a statistically valid methodology. In addition to *New York Times v. Sullivan*, consider some other candidates, hypothetical and real, for this "test of experience": a constitutional decision to exclude the introduction in criminal trials of illegally obtained evidence because of the presumed deterrent effect that this exclusion has on police behavior; a constitutional decision rejecting juries of fewer than twelve members because of the presumably decreased protection that the defendant has when the jury is smaller; a determination that the death penalty is unconstitutional in felony murder cases because it fails to deter felony murder.

Without in any way implying criticism of the social sciences, I think we know that even if they were possible, scientific tests of experience would fall short of clear conclusions in at least some of these situations, or in others we could think of.[14] Nor are we apt to get better results from any other "test of experience," such as informed intuition.

This conclusion about the lack of clear conclusions gives me pause about the enthusiastic use of consequentialist or policy justifications in constitutional law. This use seems acceptable enough if the evidence on which the policy is based is clear. This may be the situation some of the time. When it is not, when judges rely on intuition but not knowledge and social scientists or other data collectors cannot tell them very much about the consequences of legal rules, should not policy be the domain of the legislatures? Should it not be subject to the trade-offs of elective politics? And generally, should judicial inquiry into the policy aspects of such decisions not be restrained?

If this problem is viewed through the lens of judicial mistake, with only a weak presumption in favor of stare decisis, a judicial declaration of unconstitutionality should prove difficult to reverse because of the difficulty of disproving its empirical assumptions. And unless the societal goals that the policy serves have changed, this is the only proper reason for overruling the decision. Public or political reaction, for example, is not evidence that the exclusionary rule is wrong if the exclusionary rule deters illegal searches and seizures and if deterrence is the reason for the rule.

This suggests that while forward-looking justifications for constitutional decisions may appear to respond to the regulatory aspects of adjudication, such justifications can sometimes be troublesome:

either they may have more finality than is healthy for a constitutional solution based on problematic assumptions, or they may tend not to endure for reasons that are at best difficult to explain.

Two caveats. First, the exclusionary rule as judicial policy is substantially less troublesome than defamation and the First Amendment, because it redirects governmental activity without changing the government's goal (as I have noted earlier). In this sense it is far less final than *Sullivan*, which substantially restricts the government's protection of reputation. Second, while what I have said should be taken as requiring a justification and not a rationalization for a constitutional rule, it should not be taken as a criticism of the holding in *New York Times v. Sullivan*, or the exclusionary rule cases, or any other substantive constitutional holding. It questions only the Court's justification. Thus the exclusionary rule could perhaps be justified in Brandeisian terms as an aspect of "the privacy of the individual," without regard to its effect on police practices.

Let me turn now to a second type of judicial mistake, one associated with decisions that are justified in terms of public values. As I have suggested, it is not difficult to imagine that public values are sometimes less than scrupulously regarded in the give and take of the legislative process, with its necessary compromises, trade-offs, and essential goal orientation. Nor should it be surprising that mistakes occur in the judicial process. In the interactive process of deciding on grounds of public values, even the most conscientious judge can get these values or their weights wrong.

But what is the criterion here for judicial mistake? What is the meaning of Cardozo's "test of experience" in this context? It cannot be based on an empirical investigation, or at least I do not think it can. Perhaps it can be the community's reaction to a judicial decision. When the Justices get public values wrong in constitutional cases, they hear about it. Of course, it is also true that when they get them right they hear about it. In both situations there may be turmoil, resistance, and threats from other governmental entities, from private groups, institutions, and individuals. There is always discussion and analysis; some of it may even be informed and dispassionate.

Put it all together, and when considered along with what the Court has said it may constitute a rich political dialogue, one that may give the Court the information it needs if it is to know whether it has made a mistake.

CHAPTER EIGHT

The Authoritativeness of the Court's Constitutional Interpretation

The rich political dialogue that sometimes follows a Supreme Court decision takes many forms and invites us to make some distinctions. If accepted, this invitation will take us back to Attorney General Meese and President Lincoln, and into the role of citizens and groups in our political culture.

One broad and probably necessary distinction is between government officials and private citizens. Edwin Meese and the Supreme Court in *Cooper v. Aaron* were disagreeing about the obligation of officials to consider themselves bound by the Supreme Court's interpretation of the Constitution. Like Lincoln, however, Meese should not be understood to have suggested that the Court's holding in a case did not control the outcome of that case: all officials, he agreed, were under an obligation to respect the aspects of the Court's actions that resolved the dispute at hand, and to give effect to these aspects if they were called on to do so. The disagreement is over interpretation as binding regulation in a case where the official disagrees strongly with the Court's constitutional interpretation, where the official believes that the Court has made a mistake.

Government officials—federal and state—are under an obligation to support the Constitution. When they act in their official capacity they are bound by oath to conform that action to the constraints mandated by the Constitution. And so, at a very general level, the question is what an official who interprets the Constitution differently from the Court should do.

Certainly *Cooper v. Aaron* is a plausible gloss on *Marbury v. Madison*: The Constitution is law and the judicial department is peculiarly well suited to say what the law is. Once it has spoken, that's that: other officials are under an obligation to recognize that they must obey.

But this argument begs the question; it assumes that the Supreme Court's interpretation is in effect supreme law. It assumes that we have a rule recognizing this, a bright, clear, or clean "rule of recognition," lodged either in the text of the Constitution or in constitutional practice, making the Court's interpretation final and binding regulation. But the text does not answer the question: "This Constitution," Article VI reads, "shall be the supreme Law of the Land." The text is silent about the authoritativeness of the Court's interpretation of "this Constitution." Nor does practice provide a bright rule of recognition. Most of the time the Court's contested interpretations are accepted as regulation; there may be kicking and screaming by some, but the gauntlet of resistance is not thrown down.

Consider the Court's relatively recent adventures with the constitutionality of federal minimum wage legislation when applied to employees of state and local government. The decision in *National League of Cities v. Usery* (1976) had denied Congress the power to set a minimum wage for city employees.[1] This decision, overruling the case of *Maryland v. Wirtz*,[2] was enthusiastically received by most municipal and state officials, for it gave them more authority and flexibility over local budgets. Nine years later the Court held in *Garcia v. San Antonio Transit Authority* that *Usery* had been a mistake.[3] *Garcia* overruled *Usery*. In it the Court concluded that the earlier Court (or the Court earlier) had misunderstood the reach of congressional power under the commerce clause and the constraint imposed by the Tenth Amendment ("The powers not delegated to the United States by the Constitution, nor prohibited by it to the States, are reserved to the States respectively, or to the people"). Parenthetically, *Garcia* is like *Goldman v. Weinberger* in that Congress can change its regulatory effect by changing the statute that the Court held constitutional.

State and municipal officials were very upset by *Garcia,* thought it wrong, and have tried in a variety of ways to reverse it. But they did not attack the authority of the decision as regulation. And given judicial review, and the justifications for it that we have examined, this must be the standard response of the government official. First, without this response, and since the Constitution is a form of law, it would be difficult or even impossible to achieve the stability needed to make a complex system work, especially a federal system. Second, the Supreme Court adjudicates disputes, but it is the regulatory effect of its adjudication that is the Court's reason for being. Because other courts decide first, the Supreme Court is not needed to resolve a particular dispute, although a particular dispute is necessary to the jurisdiction of the Court under Article III of the Constitution.

But the standard response of accepting the Court's regulation is not the only response. Our practice has another side that shows itself from time to time and has found expression in the strong words of great political figures. In the last chapter we heard from Lincoln. Here is Jefferson, in a letter to Abigail Adams written in 1804:

You seem to think it devolved on the judges to decide on the validity of the sedition law. But nothing in the Constitution has given them a right to decide for the Executive, more than to the Executive to decide for them. Both magistracies are equally independent in the sphere of action assigned to them. The judges, believing the law constitutional, had a right to pass a sentence of fine and imprisonment; because that power was placed in their hands by the Constitution. But the Executive, believing the law to be unconstitutional, was bound to remit the execution of it; because that power has been confided to him by the Constitution. That instrument meant that its co-ordinate branches should be checks on each other. But the opinion which gives to the judges the right to decide what laws are constitutional, and what not, not only for themselves in their own sphere of action, but for the Legislature & Executive also, in their spheres, would make the judiciary a despotic branch.[4]

And here is Lincoln again, this time from the great Senate campaign debates with Stephen Douglas:

> I have expressed heretofore, and I now repeat, my opposition to the Dred Scott Decision but I should be allowed to state the nature of that opposition. . . . . I do not resist it. If I wanted to take Dred Scott from his master, I would be interfering with property. [But] I am doing no such thing as that, but all that I am doing is refusing to obey it as a political rule. If I were in Congress, and a vote should come up on a question whether slavery should be prohibited in a new territory, in spite of that Dred Scott decision, I would vote that it should.
>
> We oppose the Dred Scott decision in a certain way. [We] do not propose that when Dred Scott has been decided to be a slave by the court, we, as a mob, will decide him to be free. We do not propose that, when any other one, or one thousand, shall be decided by that court to be slaves, we will in any violent way disturb the rights of property thus settled; but we nevertheless do oppose that decision as a political rule which shall be binding on the voter, to vote for nobody who thinks it wrong, which shall be binding on the members of Congress or the President to favor no measure that does not actually concur with the principles of that decision. [We] propose so resisting it as to have it reversed if we can, and a new judicial rule established upon this subject.[5]

The practice of official disagreement may take many forms besides letters, addresses, and debates. But in the first place, let's put to one side the situation where an official feels capable in good faith of distinguishing a statute, for example, from the regulation created by a prior Court decision. This may be done by interpreting that decision in a good, lawyerly fashion. Consider the following from Andrew Jackson's veto message, delivered in 1832, of a statute providing for a national bank. An earlier statute establishing such a bank had been held constitutional. In the famous case of *McCulloch v. Maryland* (1819), the Court relied in part on the

nature of the bank as a "necessary and proper" adjunct to the
functioning of federal governmental policy.⁶ Jackson wrote:

> [Under] the decision of the Supreme Court [it] is the exclusive
> province of Congress and the President to decide whether the
> particular features of this act are necessary and proper in order
> to enable the bank to perform conveniently and efficiently the
> public duties assigned to it as a fiscal agent, and therefore con-
> stitutional, or unnecessary and improper, and therefore uncon-
> stitutional. Without commenting on the general principle
> affirmed by the Supreme Court, let us examine the details of
> this act in accordance with the rule of legislative action which
> they have laid down. It will be found that many of the powers
> and privileges conferred on it can not be supposed necessary
> for the purpose for which it is proposed to be created, and are
> not, therefore, means necessary to attain the end in view, and
> consequently not justified by the Constitution.

President Jackson was suggesting that while a national bank might
have been constitutional earlier since Congress and the president
decided it was "necessary and proper" to the functioning of the
federal government, he did not believe that the legislation placed
before him for his constitutional decision was necessary and proper.
He read *McCulloch* as empowering him to make an independent
determination of that question.

But even if a prior Supreme Court decision cannot be read in such
an empowering way, isn't it perfectly proper for a president to
exercise the veto and rest its exercise on constitutional grounds?
The president is operating in the executive realm. There is no judicial
review of the executive action. Is it not appropriate for the president
to join issue with the Court over their disagreement? This was President Jackson's position—indeed he went beyond it—in another
portion of his bank veto message:

> It is maintained by the advocates of the bank that its constitu-
> tionality in all its features ought to be considered as settled by

precedent and by the decision of the Supreme Court. To this conclusion I cannot assent. Mere precedent is a dangerous source of authority, and should not be regarded as deciding questions of constitutional power except where the acquiescence of the people and the States can be considered as well settled. [If] the opinion of the Supreme Court covered the whole ground of this act, it ought not to control the coordinate authorities of this Government. The Congress, the Executive, and the Court must each for itself be guided by its own opinion of the Constitution. Each public officer who takes an oath to support the Constitution swears that he will support it as he understands it, and not as it is understood by others. It is as much the duty of the House of Representatives, of the Senate, and of the President to decide upon the constitutionality of any bill or resolution which may be presented to them for passage or approval as it is of the supreme judges when it may be brought before them for judicial decision. The opinion of the judges has no more authority over Congress than the opinion of Congress has over the judges, and on that point the President is independent of both. The authority of the Supreme Court must not, therefore, be permitted to control the Congress or the Executive when acting in their legislative capacities, but to have only such influence as the force of their reasoning may deserve.

But does this also mean that where the president favors a statute but believes it is unconstitutional even though it raises questions that are indistinguishable from other questions that the Court has held constitutional, the presidential oath of office requires a veto? While the case is not apt to arise—presidents are practical politicians—the answer is no. Presidents are free to recognize that they may be fallible; they too can defer. Their deference may result from the realization that they are not always under an obligation to interpret the Constitution because they have taken an oath to "preserve, protect and defend" it.

Suppose now that there has been no prior Supreme Court decision. The president favors the legislation but believes it is unconstitutional. Is there an obligation to veto it because of the presidential oath to protect the Constitution? The president cannot defer to a prior Court decision, but there is nothing wrong in deciding that it is prudent to leave the constitutional question to the courts. Alexander Bickel once wrote about the passive virtues, those exhibited by the Court when it decides not to decide if a decision on the constitutional merits is unwise for the nation. Some have thought this impermissible where the Court's jurisdiction is mandatory.[7] Whatever the answer to this question, now largely moot (today the Supreme Court's jurisdiction is almost entirely discretionary), the passive virtues must be available to a president, governor, or legislator. Surely then, in assessing constitutional responsibility, we can state the following as the minimum demanded by practical politics: it is permissible when prudent for partisan political actors to leave constitutional interpretation to the judicial department.

Please understand that while I may be disagreeing with some of the implications in President Jackson's veto message, I am not suggesting that practical politics justify violating one's constitutional oath. My claim is an interpretive one: leaving constitutional questions to the judicial branch can be consistent with supporting, preserving, protecting, or defending the Constitution, and therefore with the oath taken by a legislator or executive. While others may disagree, it seems to me that this is an easy case.

It is easy, too, to state the obligation of federal and state judges who disagree with Supreme Court interpretation. Here there is no separation of powers, no argument for horizontal authority or in some situations for equal authority. Here hierarchy is the nature of governance and it demands that the Supreme Court's interpretation of the Constitution be followed as regulation or, to use Lincoln's term, as the "political rule." The judge who thinks the Court is mistaken must try hard to distinguish prior cases, but if it is not possible to do this in good faith the judge must either follow the Court (if conscience permits) or resign.

Lincoln's case is much harder. There a nonjudicial officer knows the scope of the Court's interpretation, believes strongly that it is mistaken, and is prepared openly to disregard it as regulation. While Lincoln's position on *Dred Scott* must be right no matter what (there are some things that are so evil they can neither be accepted nor dodged by resignation), and while there may be other situations where rejection by an official of a Supreme Court decision as a "political rule" is a felt political necessity, I want to suggest that such rejection can most easily be justified where the source of law that supports the decision is public morality and the official is strongly of the opinion that the Court has made a mistake.

This claim applies to state as well as federal officials, to governors and legislators as well as presidents and members of Congress. It must therefore rest on arguments that are different from some of those advanced by the presidents I have quoted. Some of what they said turned on the tripartite nature of the federal government, on the horizontal, equal division of authority, on the separation of federal powers among the executive, legislative, and judicial branches.

The basis for my claim rests at least in part on the nature of public morality. Remember that this is an interactive concept: it is neither found by the decisionmaker who uses it as a source of law nor created by the decisionmaker. Moreover, in adjudication it emerges through the distinctive process that we have been examining. It is a decisionmaking process that is very different from executive and legislative processes; and process shapes substance. How could it be otherwise when the evidence considered and the analysis employed are so powerfully influenced by institutional considerations?

Accordingly, in a sense we can say that the official who disagrees with a judicial interpretation of the Constitution based on public morality is claiming that the Court has made a mistake and is trying actively to persuade the country and the Court of this mistake.

I take it to be the function of all our government officials to try to respond to public values and at the same time necessarily to shape them, to press us to accept their understanding, to "read" public values in a way that accentuates what they in their institutional roles believe to be desirable for the country.

While federal judges are often better positioned than other public officials to perform this interpretive function—their role defines them as disinterested and the constitutional structure shields them from short-run political pressure—Supreme Court justices are fallible. This is why they should give some deference to the legislature and executive when public values have been addressed by these agencies before judicial review, and it is why public officials may claim some authority after such review. But given our general practice of accepting the authority of the Court's interpretation, and the need for stability that such a practice serves, serious challenges must be reserved for issues of profound moment—as they have been.

I shall return to this shortly, but now let's look at another process involving government officials that sometimes may be used either to reinforce or to undermine the Supreme Court's interpretation of the Constitution.

The interpretive battle for the meaning of the Constitution has many participants and takes many forms. One additional form involving government officials is the nomination of a Supreme Court justice and the confirmation process before the Senate.

Surely it is appropriate for the president to nominate a qualified person who shares the administration's perspectives on constitutional issues. Depending on the times, this shared perspective may emphasize reinforcing or undermining existing Court interpretations of the Constitution. But it is often not easy to forecast whether a potential nominee shares the administration's perspectives. Constitutional issues can shift dramatically.

Felix Frankfurter was a political liberal who believed in judicial self-restraint and deference in constitutional interpretation to the legislative branch. He brought to judging a strong presumption that statutes are constitutional. Statutes regulating the economy were the issue of the day when he was appointed in 1939. Did the commerce clause empower Congress to order labor relations? Did the due process clause permit it to set minimum wages? His answer about congressional power was an emphatic yes. It remained so when the issues shifted to whether Congress could substantially curb the political and civil rights of individuals in the name of national security.

The point is of course not whether FDR would have been disappointed with Justice Frankfurter's role in postwar America, but rather—contrary to the views of many—that judicial philosophy and not political ideology may govern constitutional interpretation, and that although the two are related in complex ways, they are not the same.

This conclusion probably means that in spite of all the rhetoric about the long-run impact of judicial appointments, an administration is apt to be preoccupied with forecasting a potential nominee's position on the present constitutional agenda. How successful the forecast will be depends on the transparency of the agenda and knowledge about a nominee's position. In the case of Robert Bork, there was both transparency and knowledge.

What about the Senate's role in this phase of the interpretative battle? The Constitution provides that the President "shall nominate, and by and with the advice and consent of the Senate shall appoint . . . Judges of the Supreme Court." There is disagreement over how the Senate should go about discharging its obligation to consent or not to consent. All would agree that it should do so with dignity. And probably all would agree that it should inquire into a nominee's intellectual and moral qualifications to sit at the top of the federal judiciary. But should the Senate focus on issues similar to those that the president addresses in making the nominating decision? Sometimes in the past it has done so; sometimes not. And although the Senate's approach and decision call for constitutional interpretation, they like many other approaches and situations are not subject to judicial review. In this technical sense and in many other senses as well, the Senate's approach and decision on a Supreme Court nomination are political questions.

What then should one advise the conscientious senator? The answer, I believe, is that each senator should focus on issues similar to those that a president properly addresses when making a nominating decision. The reason for this conclusion is simply that the regulatory aspect of Supreme Court decisions are subject to revision by the Court itself. As we have seen, the process of adjudication entails the refinement, extension or contraction, distinguishing or rejecting of prior constitutional interpretations.

Consider at least some of what this means. First, lawyers representing clients shape cases to achieve interpretations consistent with interests that their clients share with others similarly situated or likeminded. Second, such factions or interest groups press their interpretive position with a variety of other methods, including the lobbying of legislators to do what is possible. And what is possible may include legislation that restricts or eliminates the future effect of the Court's constitutional pronouncements, legislation that removes jurisdiction from the Court, and proposals for constitutional amendments. The failure of these legislative attempts is not unimportant in establishing the climate in which subsequent adjudication takes place. For unless Supreme Court justices were to see themselves as infallible, they would hear at least as background noise the views of other interpreters of the Constitution, including officials who oppose the regulatory aspects of Supreme Court decisions. As we shall see, the public forum is another place for this sort of noise: the learned and popular journals, the newspaper and television screen, and the political platform, parades, and rallies. Given the nature of public values, this noise is of interest where those values are a source of law.

One way of thinking about the art of advocacy, and ultimately of judging, is to recognize that background noise has in it good and bad interpretive arguments that must be distinguished along with reasons and rationalizations. Like the wheat and the chaff, they must be separated.

All this means that constitutional interpretation is a dynamic, complex process. Senate confirmation proceedings are a part of that process. Indeed they are especially vital. If properly conducted, the hearings should produce a lot of wheat and very little chaff. How important the hearings are should depend on what is known about a nominee's judicial philosophy, for how a potential Supreme Court justice views constitutional adjudication, and how that view articulates on the present constitutional agenda, can critically influence the Court. And as we know, the Court is the institution that not only has the authority to interpret the Constitution but that has an interpretive voice which, while not exclusive, is surely more influential than any other.

In sum, the appointment of a Supreme Court justice and the confirmation process before the Senate must take account of the following truth: the nature of constitutional interpretation in the process of adjudication inevitably means that constitutional law is shaped, influenced, indeed made by those authorized to interpret. This is not a dirty little secret. And neither is it an institutional failure demanding systemic reform.

We have seen that Supreme Court justices, while the most important, are not the only government officials authorized to interpret the Constitution. But what about the role of ordinary Americans, nonofficials? What is their role?

Start with the proposition that professionals have an obligation to interpret the Constitution. Professionals include, but are not limited to, lawyers—practicing as well as academic—and other students of the Constitution such as historians, political scientists, philosophers, and journalists. In a sense all are undertaking to shape the law through analysis.

No one would suggest, however, that the law professor (the critic) writing in a professional journal about the unconstitutionality of, let us say, the Georgia sodomy statute is making law in any way similar to that of the Supreme Court when it sustained the constitutionality of that statute in *Bowers v. Hardwick* (see chapter 6). Yet both law professor and Court are interpreting the Constitution, and the law professor's interpretation is not necessarily unimportant to a continuing discussion of the soundness of the Supreme Court's decision and to efforts of advocates to distinguish and undermine the decision in its regulatory aspect.

Moreover, the work of a scholarly critic is not the only or even the most important type of private activity that counts. Action calculated to produce legislation is a powerful method of law reform, of law creation, of law making. So too is action calculated to result in litigation. The first needs no special examination here. (Remember that the Court's constitutional interpretation may not be susceptible to legislative amendment.) The second does.

Recall the civil rights movement that followed *Brown*. One target of the heroic efforts to desegregate the South was discrimination that could plausibly be seen as private activity, although often it was private activity that was consistent with state law. An example of this would be the refusal of the owner of a lunch counter to serve blacks. If truly private, discrimination was not barred by the equal protection clause of the Fourteenth Amendment. And at the time, and before the Civil Rights Act of 1964, it was not thought that federal statutory law reached private discrimination—discrimination, that is, by individuals who are not government officials. Much litigation ensued over what was private and what was state action, over what constituted enough state involvement in an event to make the equal protection clause applicable. The line moved. To reduce discrimination, state action was found in situations where a generation earlier it probably would not have been.[8]

This was accomplished in the end by the process of adjudication. But if we focus on the primary activity that gave rise to the litigation perhaps we can make some interesting observations. First, distinguish between activity that is protected by the free speech provisions of the First and Fourteenth Amendments and other activity. To advocate the desegregation of a lunch counter is permissible. The advocates may claim that desegregation should happen because it is the right thing even if it is not constitutionally required. They may also claim that desegregation is constitutionally required—indeed they are likely to, whether state law requires segregated facilities or is silent about the matter. They would insist that all state law consistent with segregation is unconstitutional.

Second, action that entails more than speech—occupying another's property might be an example—may constitute the primary activity that results in litigation. That activity too may be justified in the two ways that advocacy can be justified (desegregation is the right thing; the constitutionally required thing). But here the activity may not be protected. Even if it is peaceful—and whether an occupation would be so characterized is not itself always so clear—it may be illegal. Whether it is may depend on whether the constitutional claims are ultimately vindicated. An interesting aspect of this is that the answer itself is influenced by the activity: professionally and skillfully advocating an outcome that turns on an interpretation of the Constitution may properly influence the judiciary in interpreting the Constitution. As we have seen from chapter 1 on, this is the way adjudication works.

There is another point to be made about private activity directed at precipitating litigation through action with the hope of shaping constitutional doctrine. As a society we must be tolerant of the competing views of various groups about constitutional meaning, particularly when we are trying to construct a public morality and regulate by adjudication. For a public morality must be as inclusive as possible and adjudication needs its substitutes for the access and accountability that theoretically exist where regulation is by legislation. This means that the political speech we hate must be vigorously defended and that the state must not be harsh in its response to peaceful civil disobedience—although too often it has been.

———

Bombing abortion clinics is another matter. There is no room for condoning violence. But whatever our substantive views (save one to be addressed in a moment), many other forms of activity in the controversy over abortion since *Roe* (and now since *Webster*) must be seen as acceptable behavior. There have been many actors, public and private, and their actions have taken many forms. What follows are some examples.

First, as much as those of us who favor choice may regret the attempt of state legislatures to limit *Roe*, none of us ought to think that this legislative activity or the private political action that supported and promoted it was improper.

Second, we should not find politically improper the activity of those who peacefully picket abortion clinics or peacefully try to persuade pregnant women to find an alternative. While we may see them as insensitive, if their actions are peaceful they are permissible.

Third, we may find it very unwise and wrongheaded, but not politically improper, for groups to punish pro-choice public servants or to pressure officials to apply a litmus test to government appointments.

Finally, we may want to vote against a president who calls for a constitutional amendment returning the regulation of abortion to the states or employs rhetoric calculated to undermine *Roe*, but we should not find these actions politically improper.

If you favor restrictive abortion laws, you should feel the same way about the activity of pro-choice advocates, which has intensified and become increasingly successful since *Webster*. You should feel this way (and this is the imbalance between pro-choice and pro-life positions) unless you believe that abortion is murder, that a fetus should be entitled to constitutional protection throughout pregnancy. If this is your position, you cannot be very happy with *Webster* (it is only incrementally better than *Roe*), you must be very unhappy about the state of public morality, and you will almost surely want to spend as much time as you can in changing the values that support American attitudes about fetal life and women's rights.

Finally, what are we to think of demonstrations that have taken place in Washington by thousands of people, sometimes hundreds of thousands, aimed directly at persuading the Supreme Court justices to uphold or overturn *Roe*? Notice that such a demonstration is not an attempt to start a law suit and change the law through "litigating elucidation." This distinguishes it from the civil rights activity we have just discussed. Nor are the demonstrations aimed at Congress. We understand when a march on Washington is aimed at bringing pressure to bear on our legislative branch. But a massive demonstration aimed at the Court? Well yes, of course. We should see this as entirely proper although we may think it is politically unwise. A public demonstration is another form of rich dialogue and one that connects with the nature of constitutional adjudication. It is a perfectly respectable aspect of the ubiquitous and diverse dialogue among Americans. It serves a function in the construction of public morality. It shows an intensity of commitment to certain values that are widely shared, values that are a source of law that the Court must weigh in its effort to determine whether *Roe* was a mistake or, more precisely, how much of a mistake *Roe* was.

There are two, nontrivial risks with this form of dialogue. If approved, political activity aimed at the Court may undermine belief in the law. In the teeth of all that we know about the process of adjudication and the sources of law, some persist in seeing the Supreme Court as an apolitical institution. It is not; and as I have tried to show, this is not a sign that the Court is malfunctioning. Accordingly, to approve of political activity directed at the Court is a risk we should take once we know the truth about law and politics. Mendacity is at least as great a risk, as Lincoln taught us when he talked about fooling the people, and truth is its own virtue. Truth does not of course mean what some critical legal scholars seem to say, namely that there is no difference between law and partisan politics.[9] This is as far from reality as the vision of an apolitical Court. I have tried to mark out the difference and to show how distinctive the Court is when compared to other political institutions. Surely we can accept this limited retreat from orthodoxy without abandoning ourselves to the long night of nihilism.

Second, peaceful protest of any kind can lead to violence. But we have had a history of protests leading to violence. It is never welcome, but we can stand it; fortunately America is a strong nation.

———

To be sure, there has been some violence surrounding the abortion issue. This is unfortunate; it is also inevitable. The constitutionalization of a woman's qualified right to an abortion was bound to be deeply contested. And that is why abortion is a testing case for the view of adjudication advanced in these pages. According to this view, courts are a special environment for the practice of interpretation, and public values—public morality—are a source of law available to judges when they are called on to interpret the Constitution.

While Supreme Court justices are fallible, there generally is acquiescence, if not approval, of their regulatory decisions. This means that even when the Court's constitutional interpretations are seen as a mistake by the majority of Americans, they are easily digested and become law. But sometimes, as with abortion, there is departure from standard practice; then constitutional interpretation by the Court endures only when it is proved by struggle to be politically digestible. Yet what is proved politically digestible turns in part on the Court's prior interpretation. For what the Court decides is both derived from public values and in turn shapes public values. It is this interaction—this complex and robust dialogue—that ultimately makes final the meaning of our fundamental law.

The Constitution of
the United States

We the People of the United States, in Order to form a more perfect Union, establish Justice, insure domestic Tranquility, provide for the common defence, promote the general Welfare, and secure the Blessings of Liberty to ourselves and our Posterity, do ordain and establish this Constitution for the United States of America.

ARTICLE I

SECTION 1. All legislative Powers herein granted shall be vested in a Congress of the United States, which shall consist of a Senate and House of Representatives.

SECTION 2. [1] The House of Representatives shall be composed of Members chosen every second Year by the People of the several States, and the Electors in each State shall have the Qualifications requisite for Electors of the most numerous Branch of the State Legislature.

[2] No Person shall be a Representative who shall not have attained to the Age of twenty five Years, and been seven Years a Citizen of the United States, and who shall not, when elected, be an Inhabitant of that State in which he shall be chosen.

[3] Representatives and direct [Taxes]¹ shall be apportioned among the several States which may be included within this Union, according to their respective Numbers[, which shall be determined by adding to the whole Number of free Persons, including those bound to Service for a Term of

---

1. See Amendment XVI.

Years, and excluding Indians not taxed, three fifths of all other Persons].[2] The actual Enumeration shall be made within three Years after the first Meeting of the Congress of the United States, and within every subsequent Term of ten Years, in such Manner as they shall by Law direct. The Number of Representatives shall not exceed one for every thirty Thousand, but each State shall have at Least one Representative; and until such enumeration shall be made, the State of New Hampshire shall be entitled to chuse three, Massachusetts eight, Rhode Island and Providence Plantations one, Connecticut five, New York six, New Jersey four, Pennsylvania eight, Delaware one, Maryland six, Virginia ten, North Carolina five, South Carolina five, and Georgia three.

[4] When vacancies happen in the Representation from any State, the Executive Authority thereof shall issue Writs of Election to fill such Vacancies.

[5] The House of Representatives shall chuse their Speaker and other Officers; and shall have the sole Power of Impeachment.

SECTION 3. [1] The Senate of the United States shall be composed of two Senators from each State, [chosen by the Legislature thereof,][3] for six Years; and each Senator shall have one Vote.

[2] Immediately after they shall be assembled in Consequence of the first Election, they shall be divided as equally as may be into three Classes. The Seats of the Senators of the first Class shall be vacated at the Expiration of the second Year, of the second Class at the Expiration of the fourth Year, and of the third Class at the Expiration of the sixth Year, so that one third may be chosen every second Year[; and if Vacancies happen by Resignation, or otherwise, during the Recess of the Legislature of any State, the Executive thereof may make temporary Appointments until the next Meeting of the Legislature, which shall then fill such Vacancies].[4]

[3] No Person shall be a Senator who shall not have attained to the Age of thirty Years, and been nine Years a Citizen of the United States, and who shall not, when elected, be an Inhabitant of that State for which he shall be chosen.

[4] The Vice President of the United States shall be President of the Senate, but shall have no Vote, unless they be equally divided.

2. See Amendment XIV.
3. See Amendment XVII.
4. See Amendment XVII.

[5] The Senate shall chuse their other Officers, and also a President pro tempore, in the absence of the Vice President, or when he shall exercise the Office of President of the United States.

[6] The Senate shall have the sole Power to try all Impeachments. When sitting for that Purpose, they shall be on Oath or Affirmation. When the President of the United States is tried, the Chief Justice shall preside: And no Person shall be convicted without the Concurrence of two thirds of the Members present.

[7] Judgment in Cases of Impeachment shall not extend further than to removal from Office, and disqualification to hold and enjoy any Office of honor, Trust or Profit under the United States: but the Party convicted shall nevertheless be liable and subject to Indictment, Trial, Judgment and Punishment, according to Law.

SECTION 4. [1] The Times, Places and Manner of holding Elections for Senators and Representatives, shall be prescribed in each State by the Legislature thereof; but the Congress may at any time by Law make or alter such Regulations, except as to the Places of chusing Senators.

[[2] The Congress shall assemble at least once in every Year, and such Meeting shall be on the first Monday in December, unless they shall by Law appoint a different Day.]5

SECTION 5. [1] Each House shall be the Judge of the Elections, Returns and Qualifications of its own Members, and a Majority of each shall constitute a Quorum to do Business; but a smaller Number may adjourn from day to day, and may be authorized to compel the Attendance of absent Members, in such Manner, and under such Penalties as each House may provide.

[2] Each House may determine the Rules of its Proceedings, punish its Members for disorderly Behaviour, and, with the Concurrence of two thirds, expel a Member.

[3] Each House shall keep a Journal of its Proceedings, and from time to time publish the same, excepting such Parts as may in their Judgment require Secrecy; and the Yeas and Nays of the Members of either House on any question shall, at the Desire of one fifth of those Present, be entered on the Journal.

[4] Neither House, during the Session of Congress, shall, without the

5. See Amendment XX.

Consent of the other, adjourn for more than three days, nor to any other Place than that in which the two Houses shall be sitting.

SECTION 6. [1] The Senators and Representatives shall receive a Compensation for their Services, to be ascertained by Law, and paid out of the Treasury of the United States. They shall in all Cases, except Treason, Felony and Breach of the Peace, be privileged from Arrest during their Attendance at the Session of their respective Houses, and in going to and returning from the same; and for any Speech or Debate in either House, they shall not be questioned in any other Place.

[2] No Senator or Representative shall, during the Time for which he was elected, be appointed to any civil Office under the Authority of the United States, which shall have been created, or the Emoluments whereof shall have been encreased during such time; and no Person holding any Office under the United States, shall be a Member of either House during his Continuance in Office.

SECTION 7. [1] All Bills for raising Revenue shall originate in the House of Representatives; but the Senate may propose or concur with Amendments as on other Bills.

[2] Every Bill which shall have passed the House of Representatives and the Senate, shall, before it become a Law, be presented to the President of the United States; If he approve he shall sign it, but if not he shall return it, with his Objections to the House in which it shall have originated, who shall enter the Objections at large on their Journal, and proceed to reconsider it. If after such Reconsideration two thirds of that House shall agree to pass the Bill, it shall be sent, together with the Objections, to the other House, by which it shall likewise be reconsidered, and if approved by two thirds of that House, it shall become a Law. But in all such Cases the Votes of both Houses shall be determined by Yeas and Nays, and the Names of the Persons voting for and against the Bill shall be entered on the Journal of each House respectively. If any Bill shall not be returned by the President within ten Days (Sundays excepted) after it shall have been presented to him, the Same shall be a Law, in like Manner as if he had signed it, unless the Congress by their Adjournment prevents its Return, in which Case it shall not be a Law.

[3] Every Order, Resolution, or Vote to which the Concurrence of the Senate and House of Representatives may be necessary (except on a question of Adjournment) shall be presented to the President of the United States; and before the Same shall take Effect, shall be approved by him, or being

disapproved by him, shall be repassed by two thirds of the Senate and House of Representatives, according to the Rules and Limitations prescribed in the Case of a Bill.

SECTION 8. [1] The Congress shall have Power To lay and collect Taxes, Duties, Imposts and Excises, to pay the Debts and provide for the common Defence and general Welfare of the United States; but all Duties, Imposts and Excises shall be uniform throughout the United States;

[2] To borrow money on the credit of the United States;

[3] To regulate Commerce with foreign Nations, and among the several States, and with the Indian Tribes;

[4] To establish an uniform Rule of Naturalization, and uniform Laws on the subject of Bankruptcies throughout the United States;

[5] To coin Money, regulate the Value thereof, and of foreign Coin, and fix the Standard of Weights and Measures;

[6] To provide the Punishment of counterfeiting the Securities and current Coin of the United States;

[7] To establish Post Offices and post Roads;

[8] To promote the Progress of Science and useful Arts, by securing for limited Times to Authors and Inventors the exclusive Right to their respective Writings and Discoveries;

[9] To constitute Tribunals inferior to the supreme Court;

[10] To define and punish Piracies and Felonies committed on the high Seas, and Offenses against the Law of Nations;

[11] To declare War, grant Letters of Marque and Reprisal, and make Rules concerning Captures on Land and Water;

[12] To raise and support Armies, but no Appropriation of Money to that Use shall be for a longer Term than two Years;

[13] To provide and maintain a Navy;

[14] To make Rules for the Government and Regulation of the land and naval Forces;

[15] To provide for calling forth the Militia to execute the Laws of the Union, suppress Insurrections and repel Invasions;

[16] To provide for organizing, arming, and disciplining, the Militia, and for governing such Part of them as may be employed in the Service of the United States, reserving to the States respectively, the Appointment of the Officers, and the Authority of training the Militia according to the discipline prescribed by Congress;

[17] To exercise exclusive Legislation in all Cases whatsoever, over such

District (not exceeding ten Miles square) as may, by Cession of particular States, and the Acceptance of Congress, become the Seat of the Government of the United States, and to exercise like Authority over all Places purchased by the Consent of the Legislature of the State in which the Same shall be, for the Erection of Forts, Magazines, Arsenals, dock-Yards, and other needful Buildings;—And

[18] To make all Laws which shall be necessary and proper for carrying into Execution the foregoing Powers, and all other Powers vested by this Constitution in the Government of the United States, or in any Department or Officer thereof.

SECTION 9. [1] The Migration or Importation of such Persons as any of the States now existing shall think proper to admit, shall not be prohibited by the Congress prior to the Year one thousand eight hundred and eight, but a Tax or duty may be imposed on such Importation, not exceeding ten dollars for each Person.

[2] The privilege of the Writ of Habeas Corpus shall not be suspended, unless when in Cases of Rebellion or Invasion the public Safety may require it.

[3] No Bill of Attainder or ex post facto Law shall be passed.

[[4] No Capitation, or other direct, Tax shall be laid, unless in Proportion to the Census or Enumeration herein before directed to be taken.]⁶

[5] No Tax or Duty shall be laid on Articles exported from any State.

[6] No Preference shall be given by any Regulation of Commerce or Revenue to the Ports of one State over those of another; nor shall Vessels bound to, or from, one State, be obliged to enter, clear, or pay Duties in another.

[7] No Money shall be drawn from the Treasury, but in Consequence of Appropriations made by Law; and a regular Statement and Account of the Receipts and Expenditures of all public Money shall be published from time to time.

[8] No Title of Nobility shall be granted by the United States: And no Person holding any Office of Profit or Trust under them, shall, without the Consent of the Congress, accept of any present, Emolument, Office, or Title, of any kind whatever, from any King, Prince, or foreign State.

SECTION 10. [1] No State shall enter into any Treaty, Alliance, or Confederation; grant Letters of Marque and Reprisal; coin Money; emit Bills

6. See Amendment XVI.

of Credit; make any Thing but gold and silver Coin a Tender in Payment of Debts; pass any Bill of Attainder, ex post facto Law, or Law impairing the Obligation of Contracts, or grant any Title of Nobility.

[2] No State shall, without the Consent of the Congress, lay any Imposts or Duties on Imports or Exports, except what may be absolutely necessary for executing its inspection Laws: and the net Produce of all Duties and Imposts, laid by any State on Imports or Exports, shall be for the Use of the Treasury of the United States; and all such Laws shall be subject to the Revision and Controul of the Congress.

[3] No State shall, without the Consent of Congress, lay any Duty of Tonnage, keep Troops, or Ships of War in time of Peace, enter into any Agreement or Compact with another State, or with a foreign Power, or engage in War, unless actually invaded, or in such imminent Danger as will not admit of delay.

ARTICLE II

SECTION 1. [1] The executive Power shall be vested in a President of the United States of America. He shall hold his Office during the Term of four Years, and, together with the Vice President, chosen for the same Term, be elected, as follows:

[2] Each State shall appoint, in such Manner as the Legislature thereof may direct, a Number of Electors, equal to the whole Number of Senators and Representatives to which the State may be entitled in the Congress: but no Senator or Representative, or Person holding an Office of Trust or Profit under the United States, shall be appointed an Elector.

[[3] The Electors shall meet in their respective States, and vote by Ballot for two Persons, of whom one at least shall not be an Inhabitant of the same State with themselves. And they shall make a List of all the Persons voted for, and of the Number of Votes for each; which List they shall sign and certify, and transmit sealed to the Seat of the Government of the United States, directed to the President of the Senate. The President of the Senate shall, in the Presence of the Senate and House of Representatives, open all the Certificates, and the Votes shall then be counted. The Person having the greatest Number of Votes shall be the President, if such Number be a Majority of the whole Number of Electors appointed; and if there be more than one who have such Majority, and have an equal Number of Votes, then the House of Representatives shall immediately chuse by Ballot one of them for President; and if no Person have a Majority, then from the five highest on the List the said House shall in like Manner chuse the President. But in chusing the President, the Votes shall be taken by States, the Representation from each State having one Vote; a quorum for this Purpose shall consist of a Member or Members from two thirds of the States, and a Majority of all the States shall be necessary to a Choice. In every Case, after the Choice of the President, the Person having the greatest Number of Votes of the Electors shall be the Vice President. But if there should remain two or more who have equal Votes, the Senate shall chuse from them by Ballot the Vice President.][7]

[4] The Congress may determine the Time of chusing the Electors, and the Day on which they shall give their Votes; which Day shall be the same throughout the United States.

[5] No person except a natural born Citizen, or a Citizen of the United States, at the time of the Adoption of this Constitution, shall be eligible to the Office of President; neither shall any Person be eligible to that Office who shall not have attained to the Age of thirty five Years, and been fourteen years a Resident within the United States.

[[6] In Case of the removal of the President from Office, or of his Death, Resignation, or Inability to discharge the Powers and Duties of the said Office, the Same shall devolve on the Vice President, and the Congress may by law provide for the Case of Removal, Death, Resignation or Inability, both of the President and Vice President, declaring what Officer shall then act as President, and such Officer shall act accordingly, until the Disability be removed, or a President shall be elected.][8]

[7] The President shall, at stated Times, receive for his Services, a Compensation, which shall neither be increased nor diminished during the Period for which he shall have been elected, and he shall not receive within that Period any other Emolument from the United States, or any of them.

[8] Before he enter on the Execution of his Office, he shall take the following oath or Affirmation: "I do solemnly swear (or affirm) that I will faithfully execute the Office of President of the United States, and will to the best of my Ability, preserve, protect and defend the Constitution of the United States."

7. See Amendment XII.

8. See Amendment XXV.

SECTION 2. [1] The President shall be Commander in Chief of the Army and Navy of the United States, and of the Militia of the several States, when called into the actual Service of the United States; he may require the Opinion, in writing, of the principal Officer in each of the executive Departments, upon any Subject relating to the Duties of their respective Offices, and he shall have Power to grant Reprieves and Pardons for Offenses against the United States, except in Cases of Impeachment.

[2] He shall have Power, by and with the Advice and Consent of the Senate, to make Treaties, provided two thirds of the Senators present concur; and he shall nominate, and by and with the Advice and Consent of the Senate, shall appoint Ambassadors, other public Ministers and Consuls, Judges of the supreme Court, and all other Officers of the United States, whose Appointments are not herein otherwise provided for, and which shall be established by Law: but the Congress may by Law vest the Appointment of such inferior Officers, as they think proper, in the President alone, in the Courts of Law, or in the Heads of Departments.

[3] The President shall have Power to fill up all Vacancies that may happen during the Recess of the Senate, by granting Commissions which shall expire at the End of their next Session.

SECTION 3. He shall from time to time give to the Congress Information of the State of the Union, and recommend to their Consideration such Measures as he shall judge necessary and expedient; he may, on extraordinary Occasions, convene both Houses, or either of them, and in Case of Disagreement between them, with Respect to the Time of Adjournment, he may adjourn them to such Time as he shall think proper; he shall receive Ambassadors and other public Ministers; he shall take Care that the Laws be faithfully executed, and shall Commission all the Officers of the United States.

SECTION 4. The President, Vice President and all civil Officers of the United States, shall be removed from Office on Impeachment for, and Conviction of, Treason, Bribery, or other high Crimes and Misdemeanors.

ARTICLE III

SECTION 1. The judicial Power of the United States, shall be vested in one supreme Court, and in such inferior Courts as the Congress may from time to time ordain and establish. The Judges, both of the supreme and inferior

Courts, shall hold their Offices during good Behaviour, and shall, at stated Times, receive for their Services, a Compensation, which shall not be diminished during their Continuance in Office.

SECTION 2. [1] The Judicial Power shall extend to all Cases, in Law and Equity, arising under this Constitution, the Laws of the United States, and Treaties made, or which shall be made, under their Authority;—to all Cases affecting Ambassadors, other public Ministers and Consuls;—to all Cases of admiralty and maritime Jurisdiction;—to Controversies to which the United States shall be a Party;—to Controversies between two or more States;[—between a State and Citizens of another State;]⁹—between Citizens of different States;—between Citizens of the same State claiming Lands under Grants of different States[, and between a State, or the Citizens thereof, and foreign States, Citizens or Subjects].¹⁰

[2] In all Cases affecting Ambassadors, other public Ministers and Consuls, and those in which a State shall be a Party, the supreme Court shall have original Jurisdiction. In all the other Cases before mentioned, the supreme Court shall have appellate Jurisdiction, both as to Law and Fact, with such Exceptions, and under such Regulations as the Congress shall make.

[3] The trial of all Crimes, except in Cases of Impeachment, shall be by Jury; and such Trial shall be held in the State where the said Crimes shall have been committed; but when not committed within any State, the Trial shall be at such Place or Places as the Congress may by Law have directed.

SECTION 3. [1] Treason against the United States, shall consist only in levying War against them, or in adhering to their Enemies, giving them Aid and Comfort. No Person shall be convicted of Treason unless on the Testimony of two Witnesses to the same overt Act, or on Confession in open Court.

[2] The Congress shall have Power to declare the Punishment of Treason, but no Attainder of Treason shall work Corruption of Blood, or Forfeiture except during the Life of the Person attainted.

---

9. See Amendment XI.
10. See Amendment XI.

ARTICLE IV

SECTION 1. Full Faith and Credit shall be given in each State to the public Acts, Records, and judicial Proceedings of every other State. And the Congress may by general Laws prescribe the Manner in which such Acts, Records and Proceedings shall be proved, and the Effect thereof.

SECTION 2. [1] The Citizens of each State shall be entitled to all Privileges and Immunities of Citizens in the several States.

[2] A Person charged in any State with Treason, Felony, or other Crime, who shall flee from Justice, and be found in another State, shall on demand of the executive Authority of the State from which he fled, be delivered up, to be removed to the State having Jurisdiction of the Crime.

[[3] No Person held to Service or Labour in one State, under the Laws thereof, escaping into another, shall, in Consequence of any Law or Regulation therein, be discharged from such Service or Labour, but shall be delivered up on Claim of the Party to whom such Service or Labour may be due.]¹¹

SECTION 3. [1] New States may be admitted by the Congress into this Union; but no new State shall be formed or erected within the Jurisdiction of any other State; nor any State be formed by the Junction of two or more States, or Parts of States, without the Consent of the Legislatures of the States concerned as well as of the Congress.

[2] The Congress shall have Power to dispose of and make all needful Rules and Regulations respecting the Territory or other Property belonging to the United States; and nothing in this Constitution shall be so construed as to Prejudice any Claims of the United States, or of any particular State.

SECTION 4. The United States shall guarantee to every State in this Union a Republican Form of Government, and shall protect each of them against Invasion; and on Application of the Legislature, or of the Executive (when the Legislature cannot be convened) against domestic Violence.

ARTICLE V

The Congress, whenever two thirds of both Houses shall deem it necessary, shall propose Amendments to this Constitution, or, on the Application of

11. See Amendment XIII.

the Legislatures of two thirds of the several States, shall call a Convention for proposing Amendments, which, in either Case, shall be valid to all Intents and Purposes, as part of this Constitution, when ratified by the Legislatures of three fourths of the several States, or by Conventions in three fourths thereof, as the one or the other Mode of Ratification may be proposed by the Congress; Provided that no Amendment which may be made prior to the Year One thousand eight hundred and eight shall in any Manner affect the first and fourth Clauses in the Ninth Section of the first Article; and that no State, without its Consent, shall be deprived of its equal Suffrage in the Senate.

ARTICLE VI

[1] All Debts contracted and Engagements entered into, before the Adoption of this Constitution, shall be as valid against the United States under this Constitution, as under the Confederation.

[2] This Constitution, and the Laws of the United States which shall be made in Pursuance thereof; and all Treaties made, or which shall be made, under the Authority of the United States, shall be the supreme Law of the Land; and the Judges in every State shall be bound thereby, any Thing in the Constitution or Laws of any State to the Contrary notwithstanding.

[3] The Senators and Representatives before mentioned, and the Members of the several State Legislatures, and all executive and judicial Officers, both of the United States and of the several States, shall be bound by Oath or Affirmation, to support this Constitution; but no religious Test shall ever be required as a Qualification to any Office or public Trust under the United States.

ARTICLE VII

The Ratification of the Conventions of nine States shall be sufficient for the Establishment of this Constitution between the States so ratifying the Same.

Done in Convention by the Unanimous Consent of the States present the Seventeenth Day of September in the Year of our Lord one thousand seven hundred and Eighty seven and of the Independence of the United States of America the Twelfth.

ARTICLES IN ADDITION TO, AND AMENDMENT OF, THE CONSTITUTION OF THE UNITED STATES OF AMERICA, PROPOSED BY CONGRESS, AND RATIFIED BY THE LEGISLATURES OF THE SEVERAL STATES, PURSUANT TO THE FIFTH ARTICLE OF THE ORIGINAL CONSTITUTION

AMENDMENT I [1791]

Congress shall make no law respecting an establishment of religion, or prohibiting the free exercise thereof; or abridging the freedom of speech, or of the press; or the right of the people peaceably to assemble, and to petition the Government for a redress of grievances.

AMENDMENT II [1791]

A well regulated Militia, being necessary to the security of a free State, the right of the people to keep and bear Arms, shall not be infringed.

AMENDMENT III [1791]

No Soldier shall, in time of peace be quartered in any house, without the consent of the Owner, nor in time of war, but in a manner to be prescribed by law.

AMENDMENT IV [1791]

The right of the people to be secure in their persons, houses, papers, and effects, against unreasonable searches and seizures, shall not be violated, and no Warrants shall issue, but upon probable cause, supported by Oath or affirmation, and particularly describing the place to be searched, and the persons or things to be seized.

AMENDMENT V [1791]

No person shall be held to answer for a capital, or otherwise infamous crime, unless on a presentment or indictment of a Grand Jury, except in cases arising in the land or naval forces, or in the Militia, when in actual service in time of War or public danger; nor shall any person be subject for the same offence to be twice put in jeopardy of life or limb; nor shall be compelled in any criminal case to be a witness against himself, nor be deprived of life, liberty, or property, without due process of law; nor shall private property be taken for public use, without just compensation.

AMENDMENT VI [1791]

In all criminal prosecutions, the accused shall enjoy the right to a speedy and public trial, by an impartial jury of the State and district wherein the crime shall have been committed, which district shall have been previously ascertained by law, and to be informed of the nature and cause of the accusation; to be confronted with the witnesses against him; to have compulsory process for obtaining witnesses in his favor, and to have the Assistance of Counsel for his defence.

AMENDMENT VII [1791]

In Suits at common law, where the value in controversy shall exceed twenty dollars, the right of trial by jury shall be preserved, and no fact tried by a jury, shall be otherwise re-examined in any Court of the United States, than according to the rules of the common law.

AMENDMENT VIII [1791]

Excessive bail shall not be required, nor excessive fines imposed, nor cruel and unusual punishments inflicted.

AMENDMENT IX [1791]

The enumeration in the Constitution, of certain rights, shall not be construed to deny or disparage others retained by the people.

AMENDMENT X [1791]

The powers not delegated to the United States by the Constitution, nor prohibited by it to the States, are reserved to the States respectively, or to the people.

AMENDMENT XI [1798]

The Judicial power of the United States shall not be construed to extend to any suit in law or equity, commenced or prosecuted against one of the United States by Citizens of another State, or by Citizens or Subjects of any Foreign State.

AMENDMENT XII [1804]

The Electors shall meet in their respective states and vote by ballot for President and Vice-President, one of whom, at least, shall not be an inhabitant of the same state with themselves; they shall name in their ballots the person voted for as President, and in distinct ballots the person voted for as Vice-President, and they shall make distinct lists of all persons voted for as President, and of all persons voted for as Vice-President, and of the number of votes for each, which lists they shall sign and certify, and transmit sealed to the seat of the government of the United States, directed to the President of the Senate;—The President of the Senate shall, in the presence of the Senate and House of Representatives, open all the certificates and the votes shall then be counted;—The person having the greatest number of votes for President, shall be the President, if such number be a majority of the whole number of Electors appointed; and if no person have such majority, then from the persons having the highest numbers not exceeding three on the list of those voted for as President, the House of Representatives shall choose immediately, by ballot, the President. But in choosing the President, the votes shall be taken by states, the representation from each state having one vote; a quorum for this purpose shall consist of a member or members from two-thirds of the states, and a majority of all the states shall be necessary to a choice. And if the House of Representatives shall not choose a President whenever the right of choice shall devolve upon them, before the fourth day of March next following, then the Vice-President shall act as President, as in the case of the death or other constitutional disability of the President.—The person having the greatest number of votes as Vice-President, shall be the Vice-President, if such number be a majority of the whole number of Electors appointed, and if no person have a majority, then from the two highest numbers on the list, the Senate shall choose the Vice-President; a quorum for the purpose shall consist of two-thirds of the whole number of Senators, and a majority of the whole number shall be necessary to a choice. But no person constitutionally ineligible to the office of President shall be eligible to that of Vice-President of the United States.

AMENDMENT XIII [1865]

SECTION 1. Neither slavery nor involuntary servitude, except as a punishment for crime whereof the party shall have been duly convicted, shall exist within the United States, or any place subject to their jurisdiction.

SECTION 2. Congress shall have power to enforce this article by appropriate legislation.

AMENDMENT XIV [1868]

SECTION 1. All persons born or naturalized in the United States, and subject to the jurisdiction thereof, are citizens of the United States and of the State wherein they reside. No State shall make or enforce any law which shall abridge the privileges or immunities of citizens of the United States; nor shall any State deprive any person of life, liberty, or property, without due process of law; nor deny to any person within its jurisdiction the equal protection of the laws.

SECTION 2. Representatives shall be apportioned among the several States according to their respective numbers, counting the whole number of persons in each State, excluding Indians not taxed. But when the right to vote at any election for the choice of electors for President and Vice President of the United States, Representatives in Congress, the Executive and Judicial officers of a State, or the members of the Legislature thereof, is denied to any of the male inhabitants of such State, being twenty-one years of age, and citizens of the United States, or in any way abridged, except for participation in rebellion, or other crime, the basis of representation therein shall be reduced in the proportion which the number of such male citizens shall bear to the whole number of male citizens twenty-one years of age in such State.

SECTION 3. No person shall be a Senator or Representative in Congress, or elector of President and Vice President, or hold any office, civil or military, under the United States, or under any State, who, having previously taken an oath, as a member of Congress, or as an officer of the United States, or as a member of any State legislature, or as an executive or judicial officer of any State, to support the Constitution of the United States, shall have engaged in insurrection or rebellion against the same, or given aid or comfort to the enemies thereof. But Congress may by a vote of two-thirds of each House, remove such disability.

SECTION 4. The validity of the public debt of the United States, authorized by law, including debts incurred for payment of pensions and bounties for services in suppressing insurrection or rebellion, shall not be questioned. But neither the United States nor any State shall assume or pay any debt or obligation incurred in aid of insurrection or rebellion against the United States, or any claim for the loss of emancipation of any slave; but all such debts, obligations and claims shall be held illegal and void.

SECTION 5. The Congress shall have power to enforce, by appropriate legislation, the provisions of this article.

AMENDMENT XV [1870]

SECTION 1. The right of citizens of the United States to vote shall not be denied or abridged by the United States or by any State on account of race, color, or previous condition of servitude.

SECTION 2. The Congress shall have power to enforce this article by appropriate legislation.

AMENDMENT XVI [1913]

The Congress shall have power to lay and collect taxes on incomes, from whatever source derived, without apportionment among the several States, and without regard to any census or enumeration.

AMENDMENT XVII [1913]

[1] The Senate of the United States shall be composed of two Senators from each State, elected by the people thereof, for six years; and each Senator shall have one vote. The electors in each State shall have the qualifications requisite for electors of the most numerous branch of the State legislatures.

[2] When vacancies happen in the representation of any State in the Senate, the executive authority of such State shall issue writs of election to fill such vacancies: *Provided,* That the legislature of any State may empower the executive thereof to make temporary appointments until the people fill the vacancies by election as the legislature may direct.

[3] This amendment shall not be so construed as to affect the election or term of any Senator chosen before it becomes valid as part of the Constitution.

AMENDMENT XVIII [1919]

SECTION 1. After one year from the ratification of this article the manufacture, sale, or transportation of intoxicating liquors within, the importation thereof into, or the exportation thereof from the United States and all territory subject to the jurisdiction thereof for beverage purposes is hereby prohibited.

SECTION 2. The Congress and the several States shall have concurrent power to enforce this article by appropriate legislation.

SECTION 3. This article shall be inoperative unless it shall have been ratified as an amendment to the Constitution by the legislatures of the several States, as provided in the Constitution, within seven years from the date of the submission hereof to the States by the Congress.[12]

12. See Amendment XXI.

AMENDMENT XIX [1920]

[1] The right of citizens of the United States to vote shall not be denied or abridged by the United States or by any State on account of sex.

[2] Congress shall have power to enforce this article by appropriate legislation.

AMENDMENT XX [1933]

SECTION 1. The terms of the President and Vice President shall end at noon on the 20th day of January, and the terms of Senators and Representatives at noon on the 3d day of January, of the years in which such terms would have ended if this article had not been ratified; and the terms of their successors shall then begin.

SECTION 2. The Congress shall assemble at least once in every year, and such meeting shall begin at noon on the 3d of January, unless they shall by law appoint a different day.

SECTION 3. If, at the time fixed for the beginning of the term of the President, the President elect shall have died, the Vice President elect shall become President. If a President shall not have been chosen before the time fixed for the beginning of his term, or if the President elect shall have failed to qualify, then the Vice President elect shall act as President until a President shall have qualified; and the Congress may by law provide for the case wherein neither a President elect nor a Vice President elect shall have qualified, declaring who shall then act as President, or the manner in which one who is to act shall be selected, and such person shall act accordingly until a President or Vice President shall have qualified.

SECTION 4. The Congress may by law provide for the case of the death of any of the persons from whom the House of Representatives may choose a President whenever the right of choice shall have devolved upon them, and for the case of the death of any of the persons from whom the Senate may choose a Vice President whenever the right of choice shall have devolved upon them.

SECTION 5. Sections 1 and 2 shall take effect on the 15th day of October following the ratification of this article.

SECTION 6. This article shall be inoperative unless it shall have been ratified as an amendment to the Constitution by the legislatures of three-fourths of the several States within seven years from the date of its submission.

AMENDMENT XXI [1933]

SECTION 1. The eighteenth article of amendment to the Constitution of the United States is hereby repealed.

SECTION 2. The transportation or importation into any State, Territory, or possession of the United States for delivery or use therein of intoxicating liquors, in violation of the laws thereof, is hereby prohibited.

SECTION 3. This article shall be inoperative unless it shall have been ratified as an amendment to the Constitution by conventions in the several States, as provided in the Constitution, within seven years from the date of the submission hereof to the States by the Congress.

AMENDMENT XXII [1951]

SECTION 1. No person shall be elected to the office of the President more than twice, and no person who has held the office of President, or acted as President, for more than two years of a term to which some other person was elected President shall be elected to the office of the President more than once. But this Article shall not apply to any person holding the office of President when this Article was proposed by the Congress, and shall not prevent any person who may be holding the office of President, or acting as President, during the term within which the Article becomes operative from holding the office of President or acting as President during the remainder of such term.

SECTION 2. This article shall be inoperative unless it shall have been ratified as an amendment to the Constitution by the legislatures of three-fourths of the several States within seven years from the date of its submission to the States by the Congress.

AMENDMENT XXIII [1961]

SECTION 1. The District constituting the seat of Government of the United States shall appoint in such manner as the Congress may direct:

A number of electors of President and Vice President equal to the whole number of Senators and Representatives in Congress to which the District would be entitled if it were a State, but in no event more than the least populous State; they shall be in addition to those appointed by the States, but they shall be considered, for the purposes of the election of President and Vice President, to be electors appointed by a State; and they shall meet in the District and perform such duties as provided by the twelfth article of amendment.

SECTION 2. The Congress shall have power to enforce this article by appropriate legislation.

AMENDMENT XXIV [1964]

SECTION 1. The right of citizens of the United States to vote in any primary or other election for President or Vice President, for electors for President or Vice President, or for Senator or Representative in Congress, shall not be denied or abridged by the United States or any State by reason of failure to pay any poll tax or other tax.

SECTION 2. The Congress shall have power to enforce this article by appropriate legislation.

AMENDMENT XXV [1967]

SECTION 1. In case of the removal of the President from office or of his death or resignation, the Vice President shall become President.

SECTION 2. Whenever there is a vacancy in the office of the Vice President, the President shall nominate a Vice President who shall take office upon confirmation by a majority vote of both Houses of Congress.

SECTION 3. Whenever the President transmits to the President pro tempore of the Senate and the Speaker of the House of Representatives his written declaration that he is unable to discharge the powers and duties of his office, and until he transmits to them a written declaration to the contrary, such powers and duties shall be discharged by the Vice President as Acting President.

SECTION 4. Whenever the Vice President and a majority of either the principal officers of the executive departments or of such other body as

Congress may by law provide, transmit to the President pro tempore of the Senate and the Speaker of the House of Representatives their written declaration that the President is unable to discharge the powers and duties of his office, the Vice President shall immediately assume the powers and duties of the office as Acting President.

Thereafter, when the President transmits to the President pro tempore of the Senate and the Speaker of the House of Representatives his written declaration that no inability exists, he shall resume the powers and duties of his office unless the Vice President and a majority of either the principal officers of the executive department or of such other body as Congress may by law provide, transmit within four days to the President pro tempore of the Senate and the Speaker of the House of Representatives their written declaration that the President is unable to discharge the powers and duties of his office. Thereupon Congress shall decide the issue, assembling within forty-eight hours for that purpose if not in session. If the Congress, within twenty-one days after receipt of the latter written declaration, or, if Congress is not in session, within twenty-one days after Congress is required to assemble, determines by two-thirds vote of both Houses that the President is unable to discharge the powers and duties of his office, the Vice President shall continue to discharge the same as Acting President; otherwise, the President shall resume the powers and duties of his office.

AMENDMENT XXVI [1971]

SECTION 1. The right of citizens of the United States, who are eighteen years of age or older, to vote shall not be denied or abridged by the United States or by any State on account of age.

SECTION 2. The Congress shall have power to enforce this article by appropriate legislation.

NOTES

CHAPTER 1 *Regulation and Dispute Resolution*

1. *Goldman v. Weinberger,* 475 U.S. 503 (1986).

2. "[A] member of the armed forces may wear an item of religious apparel while wearing the uniform of the member's armed force [except] (1) [where] the Secretary determines that the wearing of the item would interfere with the performance of the member's military duties; or (2) . . . that item of apparel is not neat and conservative." 10 U.S.C.A. §774 (1989).

3. *Roe v. Wade,* 410 U.S. 113 (1973). Efforts have been made in Congress (but no statute has been passed) to overturn *Roe* by legislation based on section 5 of the Fourteenth Amendment. Such legislation would almost surely be unconstitutional.

4. *Webster v. Reproductive Health Services,* 109 S. Ct. 3040 (1989).

5. An interesting view of the duty that courts should assume because of this legislative work load, among other factors, may be found in G. Calabresi, *A Common Law for the Age of Statutes* (Cambridge: Harvard University Press, 1982).

6. See S. Fish, *Is There a Text in This Class? The Authority of Interpretive Communities* (Cambridge: Harvard University Press, 1980).

7. R. Dworkin, *A Matter of Principle* (Cambridge: Harvard University Press, 1985), 119–45.

8. John Milton, *Areopagitica* (1644).

9. B. Woodward and S. Armstrong, *The Brethren* (New York: Simon and Schuster, 1979), is an example of investigative reporting. D. O'Brien, *Storm Center: The Supreme Court in American Politics* (New York: W. W. Norton, 1986), and B. Schwartz with S. Lesher, *Inside the Warren Court* (Garden City, N.Y.: Doubleday, 1983), are examples of scholarship.

10. *Bradwell v. State of Illinois,* 16 Wall 130, 141 (1873).

11. *Goesaert v. Cleary,* 335 U.S. 464 (1948).

12. *Craig v. Boren,* 429 U.S. 190, 197 (1976).

CHAPTER 2 *Judicial Review*

1. *Marbury v. Madison,* 1 Cranch 137 (1803).

2. *The Federalist* No. 78, at 466 (A. Hamilton) (C. Rossiter ed. 1961).

3. C. Black, *The People and the Court: Judicial Review in a Democracy* (New York: Macmillan, 1960; repr. 1977). The first quotation is at p. 52, the second at p. 53.

4. A. Bickel, *The Least Dangerous Branch* (Indianapolis and New York: Bobbs-Merrill, 1962; repr. 1986). The quotation is at p. 3. The next long quotation is at p. 24.

5. Bickel, *Least Dangerous Branch,* 18.

6. K. Arrow, *Social Choice and Individual Values,* 2d ed. (New York: John Wiley and Sons, 1963). For a good explanation of this literature see Farber and Frickey, "The Jurisprudence of Public Choice," 65 *Tex L. Rev.* 873 (1987).

7. *Buckley v. Valeo,* 424 U.S. 1 (1976).

8. "In 1986, 98 percent of the [House] incumbents won [reelection]." *New York Times,* September 25, 1988, sec. 4, p. 1.

9. On these matters the literature is extensive. I have found the following books most helpful: R. Arnold, *Congress and the Bureaucracy: A Theory of Influence* (New Haven and London: Yale University Press, 1979); J. Choper, *Judicial Review and the National Political Process: A Functional Reconsideration of the Role of the Supreme Court* (Chicago: University of Chicago Press, 1980); R. Fenno, *Congressmen in Committee* (Boston: Little, Brown, 1973); M. Fiorina, *Congress, Keystone of the Washington Establishment* (New Haven and London: Yale University Press, 1977); M. Malbin, *Unelected Representatives: Congressional Staff and the Future of Representative Government* (New York: Basic Books, 1980); K. Schlozman and J. Tierney, *Organized Interests and American Democracy* (New York: Harper and Row, 1986).

10. Stigler, "The Theory of Economic Regulation," 2 *Bell J. Econ & Mgmt. Sci.* 3, 11 (1971).

11. *NLRB v. Virginia Electric & Power* Co., 314 U.S. 469 (1941).

12. One such lapse is *International Longshoremen's Ass'n v. Allied International Inc.*, 456 U.S. 212 (1982). The case held that the First Amendment did not protect the peaceful picketing of ships destined for the Soviet Union by union members protesting the Soviet invasion of Afghanistan.

13. *Edward J. DeBartolo Corp. v. Florida Gulf Coast Bldg. & Constr. Trades Council*, 485 U.S. 568 (1988).

14. *Textile Workers Union v. Darlington Manufacturing Co.*, 380 U.S. 263 (1965).

15. See for example *Ferguson v. Skrupa*, 372 U.S. 726 (1963).

16. *Steele v. Louisville & N.R.R.*, 323 U.S. 192, 202 (1944).

17. Bickel, *Least Dangerous Branch*, 111–98.

18. *Fullilove v. Klutznick*, 448 U.S. 448, 549–50 (1980).

19. *Miranda v. Arizona*, 384 U.S. 436 (1966); *Linkletter v. Walker*, 381 U.S. 616 (1965); *Mapp v. Ohio*, 367 U.S. 643 (1961).

20. R. Dahl, *Democracy and Its Critics* (New Haven and London: Yale University Press, 1989), 188–89.

21. *Railway Express Agency v. New York*, 336 U.S. 106, 112 (1949).

CHAPTER 3 *Original Intent*

1. Wechsler, "Toward Neutral Principles of Constitutional Law," 73 *Harv. L. Rev.* 1, 15 (1959).

2. *Brown v. Board of Education*, 347 U.S. 483 (1954).

3. See generally Tushnet, "Following the Rules Laid Down: A Critique of Interpretivism and Neutral Principles," 96 *Harv. L. Rev.* 781 (1983).

4. Bork, "Neutral Principles and Some First Amendment Problems," 47 *Ind. L.J.* 21 (1971).

5. *Griswold v. Connecticut*, 381 U.S. 479 (1965).

6. *Eisenstadt v. Baird*, 405 U.S. 438 (1972), is the contraception case. *Roe v. Wade*, 410 U.S. 113 (1973), is the abortion decision.

7. *Lochner v. New York*, 198 U.S. 45 (1905).

8. *Nebbia v. New York*, 291 U.S. 502 (1934); *West Coast Hotel Co. v. Parrish*, 300 U.S. 379 (1937).

9. *Roe v. Wade*, 410 U.S. 113 (1973).

10. See Brest, "The Misconceived Quest for Original Understanding," 60 *B.U. L. Rev.* 204 (1980).

11. These remarks were made on May 8, 1987, at the judicial conference of the Court of Appeals for the Federal Circuit. See 119 F.R.D. 45, 68 (1988).

12. L. Levy, "Constitutional History, 1776–1789," *American Constitutional History* (New York: Macmillan, 1989), ed. L. Levy et al., 18–36.

13. Powell, "The Original Understanding of Original Intent," 98 *Harv. L. Rev.* 885, 948 (1985).

14. Hutson, "The Creation of the Constitution: The Integrity of the Documentary Record," 65 *Tex. L. Rev.* 1, 2 (1986).

15. E. Morgan, *The Birth of the Republic, 1763–89* (Chicago: University of Chicago Press, 1956), 16.

16. *Republic Aviation Corp. v. NLRB,* 324 U.S. 793 (1945).

17. "On July 26 [1787] the [Constitutional] Convention adjourned until August 6 to allow a Committee on Detail to frame a 'constitution conformable to the Resolutions passed by the Convention.' Generously construing its charge, the committee acted as a miniature convention and introduced a number of significant changes." Levy, "Constitutional History," 32.

18. "Justice Black and First Amendment 'Absolutes': A Public Interview, 37 *N.Y.U. L. Rev.* 549, 553 (1962) (footnotes omitted).

19. Black, "The Bill of Rights," 35 *N.Y.U. L. Rev.* 865, 867 (1960).

20. See L. Levy, *Legacy of Suppression: Freedom of Speech and Press in Early American History* (Cambridge: Harvard University Press/Belknap, 1960), vii.

21. Bork, "Neutral Principles and Some First Amendment Problems," 47 *Ind. L.J.* 1, 21 (1971).

22. "Justice Black and the First Amendment 'Absolutes,' " 553.

23. See *Adamson v. California,* 332 U.S. 46, 68 (Black, J., dissenting).

24. See for example *Duncan v. Louisiana,* 391 U.S. 145, 162 (1968) (Black, J., concurring).

CHAPTER 4 *Policing Participation*

1. *Lochner v. New York,* 198 U.S. 45 (1905).

2. *Lochner v. New York,* 69–70.

3. *Lochner v. New York,* 75.

4. See for example *Carter v. Carter Coal Co.,* 298 U.S. 238 (1936).

5. See for example *Nebbia v. New York,* 291 U.S. 502 (1934); *West Coast Hotel Co. v. Parrish,* 300 U.S. 379 (1937).

6. *United States v. Carolene Products Co.,* 304 U.S. 144 (1938).

7. *United States v. Carolene Products Co.,* 152n.

8. The phrase is John Hart Ely's. See J. Ely, *Democracy and Distrust: A Theory of Judicial Review* (Cambridge: Harvard University Press, 1980), 87.

9. Ackerman, "Beyond Carolene Products," 98 *Harv. L. Rev.* 713 (1985).

10. Ely, *Democracy and Distrust,* 103 (emphasis in original, footnote omitted).

11. See *Reynolds v. Sims,* 377 U.S. 533 (1964).

12. Ely, *Democracy and Distrust,* 106.

13. *New York Times v. Sullivan,* 376 U.S. 254 (1964). See for example *Gertz v. Robert Welch, Inc.,* 418 U.S. 323 (1974).

14. Ely, *Democracy and Distrust,* 75n.

15. See generally Wertheimer, "Campaign Finance Reform," *Annals of the American Academy,* no. 486 (July 1986): 86.

16. Thayer, "The Origin and Scope of the American Doctrine of Constitutional Law," 7 *Harv. L. Rev.* 129 (1893).

CHAPTER 5 *Sources of Law*

1. A. Bickel, *The Least Dangerous Branch* (Indianapolis and New York: Bobbs-Merrill, 1962; repr. 1986), 24.

2. Compare Fiss, "Objectivity and Interpretation," 34 *Stan. L. Rev.* 739 (1982); Fiss, "Conventionalism," 58 *S. Cal. L. Rev.* 177 (1985).

3. See for example D. O'Brien, *Storm Center: The Supreme Court in American Politics* (New York: W. W. Norton, 1986), 213–75.

4. Bickel, *Least Dangerous Branch,* 24.

5. *Craig v. Boren,* 429 U.S. 190, 197 (1976).

6. J. Ely, *Democracy and Distrust: A Theory of Judicial Review* (Cambridge: Harvard University Press, 1980).

7. *Texas v. Johnson,* 109 S. Ct. 2533 (1989). The statute mentioned in the next paragraph is the Flag Protection Act of 1989, 18 U.S.C.A. §700 (Supp. 1990). The Court declared it unconstitutional in *United States v. Eichman,* 58 L.W. 4744 (1990).

8. *Griswold v. Connecticut,* 381 U.S. 479, 480 (1965).

9. *Poe v. Ullman,* 367 U.S. 497, 546 (1961) (Harlan, J., dissenting). *Poe v. Ullman* was an earlier case involving the Connecticut statute, but the Court did not there reach the constitutional question. Harlan, in dissent, wrote that the statute violated due process. What he said on the merits in Poe, he incorporated by reference into his opinion in *Griswold.*

10. See generally J. D'Emilio and E. Freedman, *Intimate Matters: A History of Sexuality in America* (New York: Harper and Row, 1988).

11. 381 U.S. at 507.

12. *Meyer v. Nebraska,* 262 U.S. 390, 400 (1923).

13. *Pierce v. Society of Sisters,* 268 U.S. 510, 536 (1925).

CHAPTER 6 *Public Morality*

1. *Roe v. Wade,* 410 U.S. 113 (1973).

2. *Webster v. Reproductive Health Services,* 109 S. Ct. 3040 (1989). *Hodgson v. Minnesota,* 58 L.W. 4957 (1990), and *Ohio v. Akron Center for Reproductive Health,* 58 L.W. 4979 (1990), were decided by the Court on June 25. Both involved the constitutionality of requiring parental notification before an abortion could be performed on a minor. See note 16 to chapter 6, below.

3. Thomson, "A Defense of Abortion," 1 *Phil. & Pub. Affairs* 47, 66 (1971). The next quotation in the text from this article is at Thomson, p. 48.

4. Compare *Jacobsen v. Massachusetts,* 187 U.S. 11 (1905), with *Cruzan v. Director, Missouri Department of Health,* 58 L.W. 4916 (1990).

5. *Doe v. Bolton,* 410 U.S. 179 (1973).

6. For a summary of the diversity of state laws on abortion at the time of *Webster, see New York Times, June* 25, 1989, sec. 1, p. 20.

7. *Griffin v. Illinois,* 351 U.S. 12 (1956).

8. See for example *San Antonio Independent School Dist. v. Rodriguez,* 411 U.S. 1 (1973). In the context of financing public education, the Court held that poor is not a suspect classification and education is not a fundamental right. The case came from Texas. Local property taxes financed education within a school district and there were vast differences in per-pupil expenditures among rich and poor districts within the state.

9. The two principal cases on public funding are *Maher v. Roe,* 432 U.S. 464 (1977) and *Harris v. McRae,* 448 U.S. 297 (1980).

10. See generally *Akron v. Akron Center for Reproductive Health,* 462 U.S. 416 (1983); *Missouri v. Danforth,* 428 (1976) (spousal consent).

11. See *Akron v. Akron Center for Reproductive Health,* 462 U.S. 416 (1983).

12. *Brown v. Board of Education,* 347 U.S. 483 (1954).

13. *Engel v. Vitale,* 370 U.S. 421 (1962); *Abington School Dist. v. Schempp,* 374 U.S. 203 (1963). See *Wallace v. Jaffree,* 472 U.S. 38 (1985).

14. See *Akron v. Akron Center for Reproductive Health,* 462 U.S. 416, 460–61 (1983) (emphasis in original).

15. What Justice White actually said was that "the State's interest, if compelling after viability, is equally compelling before viability." *Thornburgh v. American Coll. of Obst. & Gyn.,* 476 U.S. 747, 795 (1986) (footnote omitted).

Justice O'Connor said this: "The State has compelling interests in ensuring maternal health and in protecting potential human life, and the interests exist 'throughout pregnancy.' " *Thornburgh v. American Coll. of Obst. & Gyn.,* 476 U.S. 747, 828 (1986).

16. *Thornburgh v. American Coll. of Obst. & Gyn.,* 476 U.S. 747, 828 (1986). In *Hodgson v. Minnesota,* 58 L.W. 4957, 4968 (1990), Justice O'Connor agreed with the Court about the unconstitutionality of a state law requiring notification of both parents before an abortion could be performed on a woman under eighteen.

17. *Thornburgh v. American Coll. of Obst. & Gyn.,* 476 U.S. 747, 785–814 (1986).

18. The plurality opinion in *Webster* (joined by Justice White) seems to acknowledge that "23½ to 24 weeks gestation is the earliest point in pregnancy where a reasonable possibility of viability exists." *Webster v. Reproductive Health Services,* 109 Sup. Ct. 3040, 3055 (1989) (quoting the finding of the District Court).

19. *Bowers v. Hardwick,* 478 U.S. 186 (1986).

20. *Carey v. Population Services International,* 431 U.S. 876 (1976).

21. *Stanley v. Georgia,* 394 U.S. 557 (1969), quoted in *Bowers v. Hardwick,* 478 U.S. 186, 195 (1986).

CHAPTER 7 *Judicial Mistake*

1. *Chisholm v. Georgia,* 2 Dall. 419 (1793).

2. *Dred Scott v. Sandford,* 19 How. 393 (1857).

3. *Pollock v. Farmer's Loan and Trust Co.,* 157 U.S. 429 (1895).

4. *Oregon v. Mitchell,* 400 U.S. 112 (1970).

5. See for example Ackerman, "The Storrs Lectures: Discovering the Constitution," 93 *Yale L. J.* 1013 (1984); Ackerman, "Constitutional Politics/Constitutional Law," 99 *Yale L. J.* 453 (1989).

6. *Ex Parte McCardle,* 7 Wall. 506 (1869).

7. Norris-LaGuardia Act, 29 U.S.C. §101–15 (1982).

8. Meese, "The Law of the Constitution," 61 *Tulane L. Rev.* 979, 983 (1987).

9. *Cooper v. Aaron,* 358 U.S. 1, 17–18 (1958).

10. Gunther, "The Subtle Vices of the 'Passive Virtues': A Comment on Principle and Expediency in Judicial Review," 64 *Colum. L. Rev.* 1, 25 (1964).

11. *New York Times v. Sullivan,* 376 U.S. 254 (1964).

12. *Olmstead v. United States,* 277 U.S. 438, 471–85 (1928).

13. B. Cardozo, *The Nature of the Judicial Process* (New Haven: Yale University Press, 1921), 22.

14. See for example Klevorick & Rothschild, "A Model of the Jury Decision Process," 8 *J. Legal Stud.* 141 (1979); Levin, "Education, Life Chances, and the Courts: The Role of Social Science Evidence," 39 *Law & Contemp. Probs.* 217 (1975).

CHAPTER 8 *The Court's Constitutional Interpretation*

1. *National League of Cities v. Usery,* 426 U.S. 833 (1976).

2. *Maryland v. Wirtz,* 392 U.S. 183 (1968).

3. *Garcia v. San Antonio Transit Authority,* 469 U.S. 528 (1985).

4. The letter is dated September 11, 1804. It is reproduced in Gunther, *Constitutional Law,* 11th ed. (Mineola, N.Y.: Foundation Press, 1985), 22.

5. The first paragraph is from a speech delivered on July 10, 1858; the second is from a speech delivered on October 13, 1858. Both speeches are excerpted in Gunther, *Constitutional Law,* 23.

6. *McCulloch v. Maryland,* 4 Wheat. 316 (1819).

7. A. Bickel, *The Least Dangerous Branch* (Indianapolis and New York: Bobbs-Merrill, 1962; repr. 1986), 111–98; Gunther, "The Subtle Vices of

the 'Passive Virtues': A Comment on Principle and Expediency in Judicial Review," 64 *Colum. L. Rev.* 1 (1964).

8. The state action issue, however, was not resolved, as such, in the lunch counter sit-in cases. See for example *Peterson v. Greenville,* 373 U.S. 244 (1963); *Bell v. Maryland,* 378 U.S. 226 (1964).

9. For an interesting account of constitutional theory, written by a critical legal scholar, see M. Tushnet, *Red, White and Blue: A Critical Analysis of Constitutional Law* (Cambridge: Harvard University Press, 1988).